WHEN TRUTH SLEEPS

C J Lock

ISBN-13: 978-1973856184

DEDICATION

To all Ricardians who wish the story could end differently, but
nevertheless, know the truth

Table of Contents

1.REDEMORE PLAIN 8

2. THE PALACE OF WESTMINSTER 17

3. BAYNARDS' CASTLE 28

4. THE PALACE OF WESTMINSTER 35

5. WESTMINSTER ABBEY 44

6. THE PALACE OF WESTMINSTER 51

7. WESTMINSTER HALL..59

8. THE WHITE TOWER, LONDON................................72

9. THE PALACE OF WESTMINSTER 84

10. ST GEORGE'S CHAPEL, WINDSOR 97

11. THE PALACE OF WESTMINSTER..............................106

12. THE PALACE OF WESTMINSTER..............................113

13. THE PALACE OF WESTMINSTER..............................120

14. THE TOWER OF LONDON 129

15. GRAFTON MANOR..134

16. THE TOWER OF LONDON 142

17. LEICESTERSHIRE..145

18. THE TOWER OF LONDON 154

19. THE PALACE OF WESTMINSTER..............................161

20. THE PALACE OF WESTMINSTER..............................167

21. THE PALACE OF WESTMINSTER..............................173

22. THE PALACE OF WESTMINSTER..............................180

23. THE PALACE OF WESTMINSTER..............................186

24. THE PALACE OF WESTMINSTER..............................192

25. BURGUNDY 202

26. BLETSOE 209

27. THE PALACE OF WESTMINSTER..............................218

28. THE PALACE OF WESTMINSTER..............................227

29. THE PALACE OF WESTMINSTER..............................233

30. THE PALACE OF WESTMINSTER..............................250

31. THE PALACE OF WESTMINSTER...257

32. THE PALACE OF WESTMINSTER...262

33. THE PALACE OF WESTMINSTER...266

34. THE CITY OF LONDON 276

35. THE PALACE OF WESTMINSTER...285

36. CROSBY PLACE..293

37. THE TOWER OF LONDON 303

38. THE TOWER OF LONDON 319

39. THE TOWER OF LONDON 325

40. BAYNARD'S CASTLE 332

41. GREENWICH 351

42. THE TOWER OF LONDON 365

43. TOWER OF LONDON 374

44. THE PALACE OF WESTMINSTER...384

45. THE PALACE OF WESTMINSTER...395

46. MIDDLEHAM CASTLE 402

47. MIDDLEHAM CASTLE 411

48. MIDDLEHAM CASTLE 415

49. MIDDLEHAM CASTLE 430

50. MIDDLEHAM CASTLE 436

51. MIDDLEHAM CASTLE 439

52. MIDDLEHAM CASTLE 447

53. MIDDLEHAM CASTLE 451

54. MIDDLEHAM CASTLE 454

55. MIDDLEHAM CASTLE 462

56. MIDDLEHAM CASTLE 466

Epilogue I. 473

Tower of London 479

Epilogue II – Alternate Ending 486

Author's Notes...491

ACKNOWLEDGMENTS

This book has languished long in manuscript form, having originally been written some time ago, even before 'The Gloucestre Chronicles' and has suffered many tweaks and amendments. It was written as a foil to watching Richard's death at the Battle of Bosworth as portrayed by the actor Aneurin Barnard in the BBC production of "The White Queen." He was played, for notably the very first time, as a normal man caught up in difficult times. I never cared one way or the other about Shakespeare's Richard. I knew it was a fiction. He was not real, not like the Richard so richly painted by Sharon Penman and Rosemary Hawley-Jarman, who long ago stirred my interest in this fascinating man. It was this Richard, breathed into life on our television screens just as the ongoing debate about his mortal remains really took hold, which propelled me into a whole new world of in-depth discussions on social media and fostered many wonderful new friendships along with it. We have laughed, we have cried, and without those friends, I wouldn't ever have had the courage to put my work out there in print. So, along with the usual suspects, I thank Amanda Geary once more for her willingness to proof my words and for our discussion around how the story should end. Thanks also to Helen Verderber Larsen for prompting me to pick up these words from where they lingered for so long on my hard drive. Finally, I thank Aneurin Barnard for making people see Richard the real man and not some ridiculous monster. It was a long time coming!

Foreword

We all have dreams that our lives could have turned out differently. We wonder what would have happened if we had chosen another path, turned a different corner. Have said no, when we could have said yes.

The same can be said for the lives of others, and in particular when the life concerned is someone like King Richard III.

How many times have we all heard someone say; "If only I had a time machine and could go back to August 1485." What would we have done? What could we have done? And if the 'butterfly effect' had changed the course of Richard's life, would it really have changed history? Are we sure that the change would have had the desired effect? For none of us really know what would have happened if Stanley had remained loyal on that fateful day.

Richard may not have died on the 22nd August, that much is true. If not, would he have been king for a long time? Remarried? Had children? Died peacefully in his bed? We like to think so, but we cannot know for certain. All we know for certain is that it is what we wish for him... what we dream of...

A Dream within a Dream

Take this kiss upon the brow
And, in parting from you now,
Thus much let me avow-
You are not wrong, who deem
That my days have been a dream;
Yet if hope has flown away
In a night, or in a day,
In a vision, or in none,
Is it therefore the less gone?
All that we see or seem
Is but a dream within a dream.

I stand amid the roar
Of a surf-tormented shore,
And I hold within my hand
Grains of the golden sand-
How few! yet how they creep
Through my fingers to the deep,
While I weep- while I weep!
O God! can I not grasp
Them with a tighter clasp?
O God! can I not save
One from the pitiless wave?
Is all that we see or seem
But a dream within a dream?

Edgar Allan Poe

1.REDEMORE PLAIN
Leicestershire August 1485

Alone.

In the middle of the battlefield, the press of the fight slackens. The grinding,
clashing sound of steel against steel diminishes as the battle wears down to an inevitable end. Victory, when it comes, appears to occur suddenly, but in reality is a gradual escalation over time as the field falls increasingly still.   The roaring rush of voices, hoarse, tribal cries. "Tudor!" "A' Plantagenet!" "For England!"
Now only echoes in his ears. Echoes to resound in his consciousness with deafening clarity for days...months...years.

He looks around, the battle decisively won as the sun climbs, blazing a path across the second quarter of the sky. Early morning mists have rolled away under the increasing heat of the August morning, revealing the true breadth of death and destruction wrought on this day. The dead and dying from both armies lay strewn over the Leicestershire plain, a grotesque, vivid tapestry of mangled, dismembered and pulverised human flesh. Verdant green fields have, in the course of a few scant hours, been transformed into a morass of mud, blood and bone. Through the slit of his visor, he stares out as men in his opponent's livery capitulate, at least, those still able bodied enough to realise their cause is lost. They fall on their knees in the mire, begging and pleading for mercy, whilst others, more determined, abandon their cause and flee the field, stumbling over the bodies of their dead comrades in their haste to escape retribution.

Some with more success than others.

On the edges of the plain are a score of his own men, hunting down the final combatants, seeking out the key adversaries to capture, kill or ransom. The elation of victory surging renewed strength into limbs debilitated by the mornings efforts. For the first time in hours, there is the luxury of time and space to breathe, finally free from the threat of the next well aimed sword thrust, the fall of an axe or the reverberating thrum of the stray arrow. Men of his personal household turn their attentions to the final rout as he is left to survey the spoils of their triumph.

Raising a gauntlet clad hand, his vambrace marbled with blood of the vanquished, he lifts off his helm. It seems to feel twice the weight he remembers from when it was first placed upon his head that morning as a long anticipated dawn had crept over the horizon. Dropping it unceremoniously into the quagmire at his feet, he throws back his head and closes his eyes. His face is streaked with blood and sweat, a bitter taste courses down the back of his throat, stripped raw from barking commands and harrying the charge.

His first indrawn breath outside the confines of his helm makes him sick to the pit of his stomach and he is grateful that he ate but sparsely that morning. The familiar charnel house smell of the battlefield invades his body like a ravaging army of its own. The visceral odour of the slaughterhouse, the stench of dis-embowelled corpses mixed with the coppery, metallic tang of fresh blood assails his senses. Shuddering involuntarily, he exhales with effort, ridding himself of the stench of death. He knows he will have wounds somewhere on his body after such a furious fight and they will undoubtedly need attention, but at this moment he feels no pain.

Just a bone weary exhaustion. Limbs leaden and heavy, only his Italian plate armour keeps him standing. Relief and exultation, although the latter much subdued at present, are the only emotions present as he gathers his thoughts and considers what his destiny now holds.

What awaits him in London?

With the uncertainties of the past few months, he is no longer sure who will be anticipating his victory, or who will fear it. He shakes his head vigorously, releasing the dark hair plastered wetly against his face and neck. A commotion to his right flares in his peripheral vision where a small contingent of men gather round a corpse and he watches for a moment, eyes narrowed into the sun.

Items of armour and clothing are being cut away and discarded, a lobstered gauntlet is kicked into a scrubby bush by a booted foot, a chain mail sabaton is trodden into the mud. A broadsword, mired with blood and hair, is raised – it's edge glints dangerously in the morning light - anticipating the plunge.

Inhaling deeply, he ignores the tightness in his chest.

"Cease!".

The men clustered around the body pause and turn at the sheer authority in his voice, the hoarseness rendering it unrecognisable as his own. Driving his sword into the ground next to his fallen helm, he crosses the rutted ground towards the armed men who part in silence to let him through. One by one, they sink to their knees in sudden acknowledgement, heads bow in deference, to a man. A partially clothed body lies in the dirt. Supine, mortally wounded. Eyes half open, staring endlessly into death above a halberd injury which has opened flesh and exposed an expanse of bloody bone and brain.

So close! Not too long ago they had locked eyes in the heat of battle. A reverent hush descends, to be broken by a lone voice.

"Your Grace?"

He stops. His attention distracted from the body of his foe, he turns slowly, armoured heel sinking into the mud, to face Lord Thomas Stanley who is also kneeling in obeisance. For a few seconds he glares at him, unseeing, in the deafening silence, then takes in the outstretched arm that reaches out towards him. There, a gloved hand, remarkably clean he notices absently, offers up a gold circlet. A cinquefoiled crown last seen fixed to a battle helm whose wearer charged, harried and slaughtered his way through the field. A circlet that marked out a king, determined to win the fight for his kingdom, or die in the attempt.

Calmly, he takes the crown without any hesitation and places the circlet onto his tousled, sweat darkened hair. Stanley, brazen or foolish, does not break the gaze but watches with a mixture of defiance and certainty.

"Long live the king!"

The shout from the lips of Stanley himself, remaining on his knees before his sovereign. All the men around regard this tableau carefully, yet echo his words with enthusiasm. The cry takes up, ripples around the field. More men, clad in partial armour, brigandines and salletts alike, flow in from the outer reaches of the plain. Their fighting is done, their enemies dead.

The king looks at the man who kneels before him. He has had good reason to doubt this particular lord's loyalty over the past few months and there are still many questions to answer, but not now. Quiet falls for seconds only as he gathers his thoughts. Palpable tension fills the air, some men exchange knowing glances in anticipation. One soldier, his sleeve badged with a running hound, turns and spits on the ground in disgust, giving the kneeling man a sidelong glance loaded with contempt.

"Stanley...." the king finally speaks in a clear voice that belies the constriction in his throat. "You were tardy today. Be assured.. I will not forget that!"

Stanley has the grace to bow his head again, saying nothing. The king continues, voice low and level, only not so quiet he cannot be heard by all those gathered around them.

"Although... I am cognisant you kept your honour in the end. We will talk more of this on the morrow, you can count on it."

"Your Grace!" Stanley replies, reverentially, head dipping even lower in silent atonement for his actions.

Turning back, he faces his men, still on their knees around the corpse of his enemy and spies another knight, a familiar figure, sauntering into view across the uneven field. Approaching with a casual elegance that sits at odds with the armour he is wearing, he walks with an ease that belies the rutted and furrowed ground beneath his feet. A helm is held at a rakish angle under his arm, fair hair catching gold in the sun, ruffled by the fresh, rising breeze. Grinning, he wipes his sword on a banner as he approaches the small group clustered around the king. The pennant in his hand appears to bear a red rose, but could equally be blood-stained... and white.

"They are finished!" he shouts, eyes registering both pleasure and recognition as he walks towards the king. "Most of them have surrendered – the rest we have put to the sword! Not many will ask for pardons, most can't even speak the language so who knows if they were pleading for mercy or death! I say we should cram them back into the ships they arrived in and send them back to young Charles. Let him feed and house them for the traitors they are. This war has cost us enough!"

King and knight clasp hands. Both smile grimly in unspoken acknowledgement of a victory shared, but hard won.

"Francis," the king breathes, a measure of relief and gratitude fills his voice.

"God's Grace you are safe! Once again, I thank you for your service and loyalty in the field. We fought with honour and won the day."

Viscount Francis Lovell bows his dark blonde head in deference, blinks away blood running free from a cut above his eye. Turning, he settles his helm more comfortably under his arm. Brown eyes cut towards the kneeling men and with a curt movement of his head, he gestures towards the body on the ground.

"What do we do with him?"

Richard Plantagenet looks down at the body of Jasper Tudor, uncle to the Welsh pretender who had thought to be King of England.

As well as the fatal injury to his head, there are multiple sword and dagger wounds to his torso where the soldiers have roughly divested him of armour and linens. Richard scans the field with practised eyes, taking in other corpses, brow furrowing in question.

"Henry Tudor?"

"Fled, Your Grace, we believe."

Another household knight, Sir Rob Percy, is suddenly at his side. His boyish grin apparent, even though only his eyes show below the upturned visor, allowing a glimpse of a face spattered with blood and dirt. Breathing heavily, he leans on his sword.

"A small group - three, four of them. Ratcliffe is in pursuit, we believe they may be heading back to Sutton Cheney. We will find him."

Richard nods curtly, strips off his blood soaked gauntlets, flexes stiff fingers. He make a grimace as blood begins to flow, restoring a flood of sensation, visibly irked that this particular enemy is still at large, but aware the scale of the defeat has destroyed any threat he once posed. Most of Tudor's men lie dead or dying around the field. The largest part of his army are mercenaries, convicts supplied by the French king. Those not dead already would only fight for the highest purse. They owe no loyalty to a Tudor. Turning back to Rob Percy, his eyes glint hard steel.

"Continue the pursuit – under your charge! I want Henry Tudor captured, living or dead. But I want him in one piece, Rob!" This last delivered with clear edge to his tone, one he knows his friend will understand.

Rob bows his head sharply and turns away, snapping down his visor, mounting his lathered destrier, ready to head back into Sutton Cheney and continue the hunt. That done, Richard looks down at the body lying prostrate before him and lapses into thoughtful silence. He clears his throat, wincing again at the rawness there. By God, he has never been more in need of a drink! Unsure if his voice will sustain a long speech, he speaks carefully to the men still gathered around him.

"These Tudors spread rumour and calumny against my good name, but even knowing this, I will not countenance desecration of the dead. That has no honour and we are honourable men! We won a fair battle, " cool eyes flick carefully to Stanley for a second. "Jasper Tudor lost his life and in different circumstances any of us could be lying there."

The pause is for dramatic effect. Battle hardened stares from around the field fix on him intently.

"Lord Stanley!"

This last, he shouts over his shoulder without removing his gaze from the body. Stanley rises quickly, mud cakes his shiny greaves as he stands beside his king.

"Find a litter, take the body of Jasper Tudor into Leicester."

Not waiting for Stanley to reply, he presses on, with a sudden, desperate need to be away from this field now that the task is done. "Your wife is his nearest kin. Ask where she would like his body interred. I will be happy to comply with her wishes – within reason. She remains in your close care?"

"Yes, Your Grace." There is a moment's pause.

"Good. I was not sure if you would have released her in anticipation of my losing the day." Richard turns enquiring, dark eyes to survey Stanley's face, searching for the most imperceptible of reactions.

"Your Grace," Stanley's voice is silky. "I stood back from the main lines to ensure I could deploy my men and effect the most strategic charge. I saw the tide of battle turn and knew we could finish it quickly. Northumberland..."

Richard raises his hand quickly, cuts off his protestations, but continues to fix him with a fierce intensity from beneath the circlet on his head. The very circlet that had fallen from his own battle helm when he had dropped it on the ground, and which this man, this man who could so easily have turned traitor, had just returned to him from the field. The circlet had marked him out on the battlefield and ensured that Henry Tudor had seen him coming. He had been able to watch Richard charge ever nearer, hacking his way through the pretender's retinue, smashing into and felling his standard bearer with one swing of his battle-axe. With grim satisfaction, he had watched the red dragon of Cadwallader fall under the thrashing hooves of his powerful, white destrier. They had been close enough to read what was behind each other's eyes. Richard saw fear and had raised his sword.

That was when another Stanley arrived, brother to the toadying, grizzled man before him. Well briefed in which way the tide had turned, the field was already won and all he did was deny Richard the victory of killing his enemy himself. A discussion he fully intended to have with both men, there was no doubt of that. He needed to deal with this treacherous and powerful pair, to ensure he had their affinity, but with a light hand on the reins at all times.

"Of course you did," he agrees lightly. "Your strategy worked today – you chose well. As to your motives... I am sure we can discuss those at length back at Westminster. We have more pressing matters to attend to now."

Turning, he steps towards the remainder of his personal retinue who have begun to gather by the body of Jasper Tudor, gratified to see that many of his closest and truest friends are still alive.

"God Save King Richard! God bless the House of York!" The triumphant cries rise in the air. Swords, pikes and halberds thrust up high in joyful appreciation of their victory and their own survival. Richard smiles and walks among the men. Touches one or two of them on the shoulder or arm in familiar acknowledgement of their loyalty and service, exchanges the odd quiet word.

Purposefully, he heads back toward the marsh where he became unhorsed in the heat of the fray. In truth, half hoping to find his destrier unfettered, but still alive, on the field. Unsurprised but saddened, his eyes fall upon a large form, blanketed in his bloodied standard of the White Boar.

White Surrey lies on his side in the marshy ground. Badly mutilated, white coat spattered with blood and gore. A hind leg broken, the bone protrudes at an impossible angle. Another leg sunk deep in the mud, no doubt the cause of the stumble and the king's fall. One eye ruined by a dagger thrust, the other dull and blind. Richard has no doubt that the mercenaries who had failed to hack the rider to death, recognised the animal's livery, then vented their rage on his brave beast. Other than the injury to the eye, the silver white face is unmarked and Richard sinks down into the mud himself, in homage to his fallen steed. He places his hand on Surrey's head, between his eyes, where the protective metal chamfron has been ripped away. He strokes his hand gently down to the nostrils and soft whiskered muzzle.

Three hours ago was it? He had given Surrey his usual treat, a small apple. He could still feel the warm wetness on his hand as it was devoured whole, with just a flash of ferocious yellow teeth.

"My noble friend - sleep well," he whispers quietly.

Tears fill his eyes suddenly, not just for the memory of campaigns fought astride this magnificent animal, but in sadness for the death it has suffered and the realisation of others he cannot share this victory with.

Suddenly, she is there. A bright face, smiling up at him. A small hand, gently placed on White Surrey's muzzle, exactly where his hand is now.

He can almost feel the warmth of her.

"Anne," he whispers under his breath. A short prayer? An exclamation?

He swallows hard. Checks his emotions and brushes his eyes with the back of his hand as he stands. With sustained effort, he gathers himself together and turns on his heel, away from memories.

"Francis! Jack!" he calls loudly. "Gather the men! March the fallen into Leicester to proclaim a victory for York over Lancaster on Redemore Plain."

Men cheer in celebratory acknowledgement. A flurry of activity follows as they ready to ride out from the field. Richard turns towards Stanley's men, watching them loading bodies of the defeated into a litter. Adds, almost absently.

"And a horse, I need a horse."

2. THE PALACE OF WESTMINSTER
August, 1485

Richard sat alone in his privy chamber. The day was unseasonably cold after the heat of recent weeks and he felt distinctly chilled despite the warmth being generated by the log fire burning steadily in the hearth.

Looking up from his endeavours at the writing table, he allowed himself a small, rueful smile, reflecting that some of his current discomfort was probably due to the large wolfhound which had settled itself down in a favourite spot before the hearth. The animal was black, wiry and huge, with long limbs folded under the bulk of it's body; its whip-like tail curled round and tucked under a sleeping head. Blissfully unaware, the hound was unashamedly benefitting from the lion's share of the heat generated by the fire, despite the effect this may be having on any other occupant of the chamber. Shaking his head in quiet amusement, Richard set himself back to the task in hand.

The top of the table in front of him was littered with bills and documents, mostly letters of attainder for proven rebels who had participated in the recent Tudor rebellion. There were also a number of pledges from some of those who now blithely mouthed a fulsome range of platitudes and excuses for not answering his call to arms, or for turning their back to Tudor as he marched across the country unopposed. Now they expected his mercy in order to save their necks from the block, including the not so saintly Bishops, Morton and Rotherham, who were among those seeking to hurriedly distance themselves from recent events. That gave him no surprise at all, only a stunned sense of disbelief that they should have the temerity to expect their lies to be believed.

The ability of certain men to change their colours as often as others changed their boots was anathema to him and one that had certainly affected him in ways he had never anticipated since he took the crown. He found himself questioning how a man could find it in himself to trust any other companion truly, if there were those who could so willingly change sides to save their own skins. What was it, he pondered, that allowed such creatures to progress through life without honour? To swear fealty and cleave to the cause of one man only until a more profitable or comfortable opportunity arose, in one moment declaring undying devotion to a particular cause or house, only to change sides the moment there was either profit or salvation in it. What moral code did such people adhere to? The answer eluded him.

He understood now more than ever that the fickle nature of such men was at the very root of his particular troubles over the past two years. He had been too trusting, too generous and all too willing to believe that others were bound to the same standards of honour and loyalty that were as natural to him as sleeping and waking. When Edward his eldest brother was on the throne, he had given him his unquestioning allegiance. Not just because he was his kin, or his king, but because of the cause he represented and the values he had shown in battle. After the cruel and senseless deaths of their father and brother and the mutilation of their bodies by the Lancastrian army, it had been the sole purpose of everything they fought for.

Memories of that time were sparse as he was only eight when his father lost his life and only later did he find out the true savagery that took place over that festive season in the bloodstained, snow filled fields of Wakefield. Crimson had been the traditional colour of the season and on that sad day it had flowed out of the castle walls to stain the lands all around with sadness. His mother had told him how his father's head was hacked from his lifeless body, how his brother Edmund was cut down on a bridge, his cries for mercy cutting through the cold, winter air. Their heads were then transported to York to adorn the rusted spikes on Micklegate Bar. In a final touch of barbarity, Queen Margaret, the wife of weak and feeble king, had crowned his father's head with straw to give him, in death, the crown he was entitled to in life, yet never attained. A poor jest in truth.

A few months later, after yet another bloody battle in the snow at Towton, the Yorkist army eventually emerged weary but victorious. His elder brother Edward had marched up to those very same gates in triumph, only to find the heads still there, staring out, sightless, over the city. They had lived through victory, defeat, exile and death. Formed bonds forged in blood and steel. How could such be so easily broken? Tossed aside like a broken sword.

His wandering mind checked off each entry on the roll call of the dead he could see behind his eyes, the names written in blood. Their cousins the Earl of Warwick, the Marquis of Montagu. His brother, the Duke of Clarence.

Family.

More recently there were sworn lords Harry Stafford, Duke of Buckingham and William, Lord Hastings, his late brother's friend. So many good men, he recalled with quiet regret as he mused over the names. Now all gone, and some disposed of at his own command.

He had heard that one of the many, and more innocuous, whispers abroad in his court was that the king did not sleep easy at night and he felt wonder that any would be surprised at it. It was easy to take a life in the midst of battle, to kill or be killed, to react to the swing of the sword, the axe. To parry the blow only to turn for a final deadly thrust, almost naturally. Without thinking. It was not so easy when the matter had to be weighed, considered, judged.

Although he felt a measure of regret about those former friends he had sent to their death, he knew his choices had been limited by the actions they themselves had taken. This did not stop him feeling somewhat bereaved by their fate and cursing the fickleness of human nature. He also had to admit that in essence, the rumour about his lack of rest was true. He did not sleep as well as he would like, and certainly not since his wife, Anne, had passed away as spring unfurled its fresh, green hope.

That brought him back, reluctantly, to the document currently held under his hand. Allowing his train of thought to wander far and away from the words he had just been reading was far from accidental. He had digested the content of this particular bill several times and it contained nothing to cause him additional cares or worries, yet the words on the parchment overwhelmed him so much that he felt unable to continue with the task in hand.

His thoughts had begun to meander aimlessly down dark roads which they would do much better avoiding. Rutted, briar-strewn paths he had trodden all too well over the last few months and that had led him down to the very depths of a personal despair. Taking a deep and measured breath, he spread the document out on the table before him. Smoothing his hand across the parchment slowly, he flattened it down with care, the dark jewel in his coronation ring catching the firelight as he forced himself to read it once again.

"For the provision of one alabaster effigy in the likeness of her late, dearly departed Grace, Queen Anne, to adorn her memorial tomb lying in Westminster Abbey... "

He pushed back in his chair wearily, the words still harnessed under his fingers, but held just far enough away so that he could no longer clearly make them out. A nagging pain began to make itself felt throughout the bicep muscle of his right arm, his sword arm. A legacy of many years in his brother's service, the months in the frozen north, guarding the Scots border. Days and nights in driving hail, wind and snow with frosts so hard it made it almost impossible to pitch camp, ropes and canvas stiff and unyielding. Without thinking he raised his free hand, rubbing slowly up and down his arm, applying pressure through the dark blue velvet of his sleeve to try to ease the spreading ache.

As he did, a voice he had been trying to deny for so long now crept easily into his mind. He could still clearly recall how Anne had fretted about this ailment when they lived in the north, at their castle in Middleham, before the yoke of kingship rent their life apart. Her anxious voice echoed around the recesses of his mind, escaping now, filling the very chamber.

"Richard, are you sure it is not a curse? Could the queen have taken against you? There is, after all, gossip that she is capable of such! I have heard say she remarks that we hold a court here in the north to fair rival the king's and that she herself is none too happy about it!"

He could still see her small, worried face; the anxiety clouding her soft grey eyes. How was it that such gentle eyes had the power to burn so deep into his very soul? He remembered looking at her fondly, smiling away her worries lightly. Rumours abounded that the former queen, his brother's wife Elizabeth Woodville, practised witchcraft and cast spells on those she thought to be her enemies. Anne, and her own sister Isabel, had both taken these whisperings more seriously than most. It was the one subject over which Anne would lose her natural common sense.

He could understand this in a way. The Woodville woman had been directly responsible for the death of one of the greatest noblemen the country had ever known. Richard Neville, Earl of Warwick, Anne's father. By enticing Edward into a secret marriage, she had torn apart all of

Warwick's plans for a grand alliance with France. From that very day, the houses of Neville and Woodville had locked horns with a fierce determination to wipe each other out, or die in the attempt. Warwick was a powerful man, the most powerful man in the realm after the king, but he had been no match for Edward's new queen. One by one, the Nevilles had fallen, killed in battle after turning against the king because of his ill starred marriage. Even when Anne's own sister, Isabel, had died after childbirth, she secretly saw the queen's hand at work, even in that.

Richard himself had no doubt Elizabeth was an evil witch - but not of the practising kind!

"Sweetheart," he remembered chiding her with suppressed amusement. "It is nothing. I have been wielding a broadsword or an axe since I was but a child in your father's care and you know that to be true. It is a temporary weakness that is all and worsens with the cold. Try not to distress yourself with court gossip, we are safe here in the north, well away from all of that court...discontent." She had continued to look at him fearfully despite his reassurances and so he had taken her in his arms then, smiling all the while to kiss her cares away.

Ghosts! Today his mind was full of them.

He shook his head slowly, passing a hand across his brow in an effort to clear his thoughts. The old ailment was now only troubling him because of the ferocity of the recent battle. For the rest, he had escaped any major injury, the only blood on his armour being that spilt from others. He knew, without any of his faithful retainers telling him, that he had fought like an animal. He had been totally determined to expunge the Tudor threat and the torrent of grief he had held back over the deaths of his son and wife had been released into such a flood of anger, such a deathly rage, that he hardly knew himself that day.

All he really remembered of the final charge was finding himself close enough to Henry Tudor to strike a blow that would see him dead. He had been able to read the fear in his pale, unbelieving eyes; saw them widen in alarm as he readied his sword in both hands, bellowing at the top of his lungs, felling Tudor's standard bearer with a single stroke. Even as the red and green dragon of the pretender's banner fell to be trampled in the mud, Tudor continued to hide at the back of the field, behind his men. Watching the battle rather than winning it. Infuriated at his blatant cowardice, Richard had taken the battle to him.

Since his victory, he had felt a certain sense of weariness, partly due to his exertions on the battlefield and also, he thought, because of the release of so much tension. He had not truly realised how much of a strain he had laboured under in waiting for the Tudor threat to make itself known. It had hovered over his reign during the past twelvemonth like a noxious cloud and now it was eliminated. Should he not be elated?

He sighed deeply, once again leaning back in his chair.

Jasper Tudor, the pretender's uncle, had been interred in the house of the Greyfriars in the city of Leicester. Margaret Beaufort, Henry Tudor's mother and Lord Stanley's wife, had become almost unhinged with rage on being told of the death of her kinsman and the defeat of her son. Henry Tudor himself was still being hunted across hill and dale by one of Richard's faithful retainers, Sir Rob Percy, with all the frenzy of a rabid dog. The very thought of the satisfaction Rob would be gaining from that chase made Richard suppress a burgeoning grin.

Margaret had been unable, or unwilling, to accept Richard's offer of a choice of resting place for her kinsman Jasper. He had not been able to wait much longer than three days for a decision and so finally ordered the Greyfriars to bury him with all due respect and ceremony. She did not attend. Stanley himself had not even commented to confirm that she even realised he was now at peace. But then that particular lord himself was keeping a low profile, adroitly avoiding any difficult conversations until he got his story straight, but his time would come.

For now, Richard was faced with finalising the arrangements for his wife's memorial and as he sat, the parchment still laid out on the table, it occurred to him that if he had died in battle, his wife, his queen, would lie with no official marker for her tomb. He doubted that Tudor would have signed the bill now in his hand and she would have been consigned to rest forever without the due recognition of an anointed sovereign. It was unimaginable!

A chill swept over him at the thought of her lying for eternity in an unmarked grave and he cursed silently at his inability to once again keep his mind free from the grasp of the ghostly talons of his memories.

Picking up a pen, his hand was poised to sign as he heard the door to the chamber open.

"Your Grace?" His Lord Chamberlain, and childhood friend, Viscount Francis Lovell entered the chamber and paid a quick, but deferential, obeisance. He was dressed head to foot in russet finery, his velvet doublet trimmed with sable. Francis, a handsome and elegant knight, had proved to be a true and loyal friend throughout Richard's early days at Middleham, all his northern campaigns and during the constant troubles of the past two years. Although married, Francis spent most of his time at court whilst his wife Anna, a Neville relative and one of the Fitzhugh family, preferred the domesticity of Minster Lovell, their grand manor house in Oxfordshire. They had no children, even though they had been married for some years, but this seemed not to concern either of them unduly. They had spent most of their marriage apart, at opposite ends of the country, and even now it seemed to be an arrangement which suited them both.

Looking at him now across the room, he knew it was Francis, along with others still close to him, who had given him warnings that he trusted too easily. He could see now that before his recent victory, he had been too blind with grief and despair to see the good from the bad until it was too late. That had cost him dearly. Had almost cost him his throne.

Richard looked up at his friend and smiled.

"Good day, Francis." He waved a hand airily at the pile of correspondence on the table. "As you can see, I have a fair plethora of lords willing to turn back their cloaks and bend the knee. It is taking me longer to wade through these papers than it took me to cut through them personally in the field."

There was a forced jocularity to his tone as he sought to disguise his current morbid mood from his friend. Only, Francis knew him better than most men. He moved over to the table and picked up a few of the documents, surveying the names and seals. His lips twisted in a sardonic smile.

"Some of these men deserve to die twice over. How will you trust their loyalty in the future? Can you really be sure that if battle once again has to be joined, our fair weather friend Stanley will not choose the other side?" He pursed his lips in disgust and threw the parchments back onto the table. "You have given him wealth and titles and still he did not immediately join the fray. The man is a professional dissembler. Always has been." His usually mild brown eyes became fierce. Francis was the most easy-going man in Richard's household but the mere mention of a Stanley could throw him into a rage which would last for days.

Richard stood up suddenly, stretching out his back carefully and walked towards the fireplace, relieved to be away from the table and its burdensome covering. Cautiously stepping around the sleeping wolfhound, he flexed his finger, which were cramped from the amount of signing he had already done.

"I know that the outcome in Leicestershire would have been very different if Stanley had aimed his charge at me instead of Tudor. We were pressing the savages back, but we couldn't have withstood his charge. He would have cut us down – I know it. Do not for a moment think I don't." His thoughtful dark eyes reflected the dancing flames.

"And he is rewarded..?"

"No," replied Richard curtly. "Not rewarded. William will gain nothing from his last minute entry into battle, nor will his brother. Thomas already has his wife's lands and titles, that is all. I feel he would have been due to them anyway as I cannot allow Lady Stanley to retain her wealth as mother of a traitor." Richard reached down and ruffled the fur between the hound's ears. The animal raised a lazy lid to regard him sleepily before returning to its slumber unperturbed. "For the rest, well... we shall see how many of them prefer the noble title of traitor."

Francis turned towards his king and leaned on the opposite side of the mantel, deciding that matters were becoming far too dolorous. He knew Richard well enough to understand how he would have found these past days difficult, his forced levity earlier had not fooled him for one second and he made an attempt to raise the mood.

"How soon you forget, " he began, sarcasm colouring his words, "you were the traitor, remember? That deluded Welsh peasant declared himself king the day before the battle. Totally mad, like his uncle, King Henry! Much good that did him."

Unfortunately, his usually keen aim misfired and he watched in despair as the king's face darkened. Richard moved away from the fire quickly and over to the sideboard under the mullioned window where he filled a cup with wine from a waiting flagon. Turning back, he silently offered a cup to Francis, who shook his head whilst regarding him with a watchful gaze, cursing himself silently for an idiot!

King Edward, Richard's brother, had the old Lancastrian King Henry murdered after the battle of Tewkesbury, to prevent any further uprisings on behalf of the addle-headed former ruler. It had been the cause of one of the rare disagreements between Richard and his elder brother, the king.

"It still bothers you," Francis observed simply, leaning his shoulder against the stone mantel, desperate to make amends for his mis-judgement.

"King Henry's death?" countered Richard, his brows knitted together in concern. "Yes. After all this time it still does. It was not honourable and afforded him no dignity. We were already victorious. The three sons of York. It was a lamentable act."

Francis crossed the room with a stride that told of resolve, ignoring for this moment that this man was also his king. He knew Richard referred to his brother's vision before the battle of Mortimer's Cross, where there had been three suns clearly shining in the morning sky. It was an omen, all agreed, that the three sons of York would be victorious, exterminating the Lancastrian threat. Edward, George and Richard himself. He laid a hand on his friend's shoulder.

"That was your brother's indiscretion," he offered quietly. "Not yours."

Richard turned his head towards him once more, smiling, if somewhat sadly.

"You are a true and loyal friend and I thank you for it." He sighed, and moving away, drained his cup. "Although why I worry about something that happened so many years ago when I have spent the past months being accused of much fouler deeds, I do not know!"

"That will pass now," Francis assured him with a display of his usual confidence. "The country will settle now the threat of invasion is over."

Changing his mind about the offer of wine, he crossed over to the sideboard himself and poured wine into a cup. He was easy in Richard's company, a familiarity bred from years of close companionship, willing to give his life for his friend without question. He had been prepared to do so and more outside the sleepy hamlet of Market Bosworth, although thankfully Richard had no need of it in the end. Yet, still, he could not bear the suffering he had seen his friend endure and wanted to help put an end to it.

"The country will see what a king you are and be glad of it. Look at your affinity with the people of York - Gods, with the whole of the north! No member of your house has ever been able to claim such a feat! Certainly not your brother!"

Richard glanced at his friend from under lowered lids, somewhat ruefully.

"And Northumberland?"

Francis grinned back winningly, sharing the joke and shrugged.

"Well, even you can't win them all!"

The Earl of Northumberland had never taken Richard's popularity in

York, or anywhere else in the northern marches, with good grace. Having been able to wield his power over the region for many years, warring only with the Nevilles for supremacy, he had not been at all gracious when Edward had rewarded Richard after the battles of Barnet and Tewkesbury. Not only had Richard been given most of the Neville family's old holdings in the north, he had married the Earl of Warwick's daughter and gained power and status along with them. After all, he was the king's brother then, and Northumberland owed much to King Edward. He only held his earldom now thanks to Edward's past generousity. But even that had not been enough to salve his wounded pride.

Even at the recent battle, Northumberland had sat back, pretending to wait for Stanley to commit before he engaged his men. Pretending he was acting in defence of the realm, when underneath, his actions were drawn up to one design. Defence of himself.

Richard stared into his empty cup, looking for answers he knew it did not hold.

"At the moment I would be happy to win just a few good, true men - not repenting traitors!" He sighed, ruminating. "Perhaps I should placate Northumberland with some particular commission in the north, now that I will be unable to spend so much time there. The rebellions fermented in the South and in Wales. That is where I need to focus my attentions."

"Perhaps," Francis mused carefully, knowing that he would have to steer the conversation around to the reason for his intrusion on the king eventually, and taking the opportunity this offered him. "But his demeanour could depend on how you resolve our current... situation."

Richard's head came up sharply, brows drawing together. His face wore a puzzled expression.

"Situation?"

Francis moved back over to the table where Richard had resumed his seat. He steepled the fingers of one hand and rested the tips against the table edge, as if feeling his way.

"That is why I am here. Elizabeth, the queen dowager and her daughter wish for an audience. Elizabeth has asked me to intercede. She has been trying to see you since after the battle."

"Francis... " Richard's tone was deep and low with a hint of warning. His dark eyes flashed dangerously. By design, he had managed to avoid direct contact with his brother's queen since reaching an agreement with her when she left the sanctuary at Westminster Abbey, where she had fled with most of the royal treasure and chattels shortly after her husband's death. Her daughter, however, was another matter. The girl's presence at court had caused much gossip and caused Richard to take unprecedented actions to stem the venom spreading through his kingdom. The thought of it made him heave a heavy sigh.

Francis stood his ground and faced up to his friend. The late afternoon sun was streaming through a high window, dust motes circling lazily in its rays. He squinted slightly against the glare, then lowered his head closer to Richard so that he could properly read his expression.

"You have to resolve it, one way or another. Bring it to an end. Restore your reputation and rule the land as we know you can. It has to be done, and soon."

Richard swallowed hard and flexing the fingers of his sword hand, he absently massaged the palm with his thumb, a habit he was like to adopt when undecided. His friend watched closely as he struggled with his innermost thoughts and demons.

"I... Anne.." he began, but his voice broke on the words. He looked down disconsolately at the bill on the table, still unsigned.

"Your Grace," Francis chose his words slowly and sincerely. "The queen loved you dearly. May she forever rest in peace. We must move on."

Richard rested his head back against the chair, his ears filled suddenly with the noise and roar of battle as if he stood once again in the middle of Redemore plain. He closed his eyes briefly and a dozen images flashed vividly against his lowered lids. When he spoke, the tone of his voice had changed markedly and Francis recognised the voice of his king, not his friend.

"Very well, Francis. You may bring them here on the morrow."

3. BAYNARDS' CASTLE
August 1485

Elizabeth Woodville stared, stone faced, at the grey waters of the Thames as she stood by the leaded, mullioned window. The view stretching out before her was not a view she was accustomed to, having visited Baynard's Castle rarely during her marriage to King Edward. The imposing fortress teetering on the banks of the river had primarily always been the residence of his mother, Duchess Cecily, a person Elizabeth very rarely felt the need to either visit or seek out. Proud Cis. The Rose of Raby, wife to a traitor, mother to a king, a fool and a usurper. How proud was she these days?

In fact she could not recall the last time she had been here, feeling it must have been some years ago. To be lodged here now, surrounded by the trappings of a family she had come to despise was repulsive to her, but as she had nowhere else she could stay, she was forced to endure the insult. Grudgingly, she had to admit to herself that Richard was in no way obliged to have provided her with the hospitality of such grand lodgings, especially as it was one of his former homes. That knowledge did nothing to alleviate the unpleasant fact that he and his now dead wife had been installed in the sumptuous royal apartments she had formerly occupied as queen.

Not that these rooms were any less well furnished. Cecily Neville was a duchess of royal blood and she and her son did not tolerate anything other than the highest of royal standards, but still. It rankled. Yet another indication of her fall from grace, inhabiting the space of a woman she could barely speak to and who had never acknowledged her with respect - even when queen. In fact, going as far to provocatively style herself "Queen by Right" in acknowledgement of her dead husband's claim to the throne. As queen herself, this had done nothing to improve the relationship between them, which had remained icily cool throughout her marriage. And beyond.

Elizabeth had been given a country house and a small stipend by Richard once she had agreed to leave the sanctuary of Westminster Abbey, where she had ensconced herself after the death of her own husband. On hearing of Tudor's defeat and despite her reluctance to be seen at court where she had previously wielded such power and influence, she knew that only her presence here could determine the future of her eldest daughter who had been betrothed to the Tudor pretender.

She gave a half silent snort of derision which would have sat at odds with her beauty had there been anyone in the room to witness it. So much for the promises of the dissembler Stanley and his treacherous wife Margaret Beaufort! They swore that the Tudor Pretender would be victorious and that her daughter would become Queen of England! Elizabeth had endangered her own life and that of her remaining family, to participate in their plots and schemes for an outcome they had guaranteed but ultimately been unable to deliver.

Margaret Stanley herself had sent word to Elizabeth that her two sons had gone from their apartments in the Tower. She had eagerly participated in the rumours that her precious sons, the true heir to the throne and his brother, had been murdered at the hands of her brother-in-law. Her face contorted with contempt, but at the same time she could not resist giving her appearance a critical appraisal in the dim glass of the window.

With this unexpected turn of events, Elizabeth now needed to ensure she positioned herself as far away from the Stanleys as possible. She could not afford to be seen to have any type of relationship with them if she was to secure her position at Richard's court. Yet, that would be a distinct pleasure, she felt, rather than a hardship. Her past connections with them had been expedient, knowing all along that their ambitions were directly in conflict with her own. Her sole intention, now that Richard had routed Margaret's son, was to stabilise her position with the king. At least for now.

For, despite a burning hatred of her son's usurper, at heart she was somewhat pleased that Tudor had been beaten. Nothing she had heard about the man made him appear attractive to her either as a king or a son-in-law and she was absolutely sure that any son of Margaret's would be equally as unpleasant and duplicitous as the woman herself. Edward, her deceased husband and king for over twenty years, was too large a presence to block out and neither the current wearer of his crown, or the cowardly pretender who had been defeated so unceremoniously, were suitable replacements. But it was time to put the past behind her and force herself to treat with the triumphal king, as distasteful as the idea may be. She had no choice. Her future, the future of her daughters, and maybe even her sons, depended on what favours she could elicit from her brother-in-law, King Richard. They knew each other well, but it would not be easy and the outcome was far from certain.

Her lips formed a downward sneer as she turned away from the window, leaving behind the depressing view of the river, and at that precise moment her eldest daughter entered the chamber.

Bess found her mother standing completely still in the centre of the chamber, a parchment clutched in one hand - and it was the parchment which caught her attention. She had already listened to a litany of rage about their lodgings, Bess acknowledging patiently that her mother would only be truly satisfied if she had been invited to reside in the royal apartments within Westminster itself.

Steeling herself for a difficult confrontation, she moved further into the room, close enough to be able to look directly into her mother's face. Her instincts warned her that the former queen would not capitulate to the king without a fight of some sort, even though there was no real need and that they had all been incredibly well treated so far, considering her mother's past actions. That was not enough, would never be enough, for Elizabeth.

"Mother?"

Elizabeth turned slowly and looked at her eldest daughter with eyes that blazed from a face set hard with a grim determination. Her pale blue-green gaze could unnerve or bewitch as the owner demanded and it was now appraising her eldest daughter, looking her up and down, noting the rich azure sarcenet of the gown she wore and registering an abject displeasure.

"Not in mourning dress then?"

Bess sighed heavily. She had prayed that her mother would be in a better mood before her forthcoming meeting with the king. It seemed her efforts were to go unanswered.

"Why on earth would I be in mourning mother? Henry Tudor is not dead."

"No, but your hopes of becoming queen certainly are!" Elizabeth's tone dripped acid and she seemed completely unmoved as Bess flinched at the barb. She knew well that Henry Tudor's intention to take her as his bride had been dismissed by Bess with some rancour. Nevertheless, had the positions been reversed, she would now be preparing for her wedding feast!

"It was never my wish to be betrothed to Henry Tudor so I don't see why I should feel any sadness at his defeat. I am pleased for us all that uncle Richard won, as should you be. He is our blood. I am certainly not going to wander round court declaring unhappiness that my betrothal is at an end. Besides, what would the king think?" Bess was fully on the defensive, and her tone softened as she mentioned her uncle's name. This inflection was not lost on her mother who was watching her with the eyes of a hawk.

Elizabeth almost spat, the pitch of her voice rising dangerously.

"The king! Who cares what the king thinks? That man is no king and not all the battle victories in Christendom will make it so!"

Bess eyed the chamber door warily, placing a warning finger to her lips. Her mother seemed to be forgetting they were guests here and not subject to the same privacy of their own residence. "Mother be careful... "

But, Elizabeth was beyond listening and moving swiftly away from the window she swept towards her daughter, brandishing the rolled parchment in front of her like a sword.

"I am going to see this "king" and tell him what I think of him! He has managed to avoid me since we left sanctuary at his request, in order to help him win public approbation, but he will not escape me any longer! He will hear what I have to say! I will let him know what he has done to his brother's family in no uncertain terms and I care not what he thinks as it will all be God's honest truth, which he will now have to live with for the rest of his life. He will rue the day he survived that battle! Damn that traitorous Stanley and his misbegotten wife!"

A polite cough alerted the couple to the fact that they were no longer alone in the chamber. Mother and daughter froze for seconds, eyes fixed on each other and in the deafening silence that followed only the crackling of the log fire could be heard, although Elizabeth could also hear the pounding of blood in her ears as she continued to rage inwardly.

Bess turned slowly as her mother remained rigidly still and found herself looking directly into the enquiring brown eyes of Viscount Francis Lovell, Richard's Lord Chamberlain, no less. His right hand man at court since his return from the battlefield, and also his childhood friend. A small band of faithful retainers surrounded the king daily and guarded his wellbeing closely, protecting him from those who had shown themselves false. Bess also knew that those same men had ridden with Richard on his downhill charge to meet Henry Tudor on the field. Francis was with him on that charge, and had rarely left his side since.

Tudor had fled, and Bess was pleased, more pleased than she could ever express. She had no inclination to marry the Welsh 'dragon' who had hidden away for most of his life in foreign lands like a coward, existing day to day on the generosity of others. What pride would a man like that have? She could not imagine either her father or uncle living such a life. She was familiar with the tale of how they had to flee for their lives to escape the anger of the Earl of Warwick some years ago, but they had come back. Her father could never had settled to a life lived on the generosity of others. He fought back and regained his throne. And Richard had been at his side.

"Sir Francis..." Bess began awkwardly, twisting her fingers in her skirts nervously as her mother stood, stubbornly silent.

Francis bowed his head slightly, extending one leg forward in deference. He was a fair, handsome man and Bess had always liked to see him as a younger, slimmer and more elegant version of her father whose colouring he favoured, apart from his eyes. He looked very resplendent today in York colours of murrey and blue, which had become something of an affectation to him since the victory she had noticed, as if he wished to herald the fact abroad. His long, slim hands were be-jewelled and he rested one of them lightly on the hilt of a small gold dagger at his belt.

"My ladies, I have come to escort you to attend the king's grace."

Bess looked back at her mother pleadingly and getting no response, returned her gaze to Francis who remained unperturbed, regarding them both silently.

"Sir Francis, could we just have a moment? I would wish to speak to my mother before we leave."

Francis's eyes moved from her to Elizabeth and back again, carefully trying to gauge the situation. He had heard every word of what had been said as he entered the room and could see the stiffness in the former queen's posture. It had been interesting to hear how venomously she talked about the Stanleys and that in itself pleased him. As well as which, it only reinforced what they had long suspected in Richard's court, but had little opportunity to prove. Elizabeth Woodville had been plotting with Margaret Beaufort, and by default Lord Thomas Stanley, right up until the day of the battle. Richard was not in for the easiest of meetings today as Francis had no doubt this woman could be notoriously difficult – even in her current position.

"Very well," he conceded gallantly, "but the king cannot be kept waiting. You have moments only. I will wait outside."

After glancing directly at Elizabeth once more and taking in her furious state, he executed a small bow, turned on his heel and left the room. No sooner had the door had closed, than Bess turned on her mother.

"For God's sake have a care! You do not hold the power now! Your actions could destroy us all. They almost did! Can you not stop and leave it be?"

She paused, breathless, waiting for her mother to respond and when she remained infuriatingly silent, she nodded, exasperated, to the parchment still gripped in her mother's tense fingers.

"What does he say? I would like to know before we go to speak to him!"

Elizabeth grunted in disgust and threw the parchment on the table.

"Only that he grants us an audience to discuss matters concerning our future affinity. He writes as if he has summoned me here, not acknowledging that I have insisted on an audience with him! Ha! I have my own demands with regard to affinity! I feel we are somewhat owed a debt."

Bess moved swiftly to the table and picked up the letter, fingering the red wax seal gently. She was used to seeing such seals on all correspondence from her father, but now this bore the seal of her uncle. Placing the parchment back down slowly, she spoke to her mother with a patience unusual in one so young.

"Mother, once again, I beg you! Some of what befell us was caused by your inability to think rationally about our situation. Richard loved father, he was his most loyal and loved brother! He was the man who father sent to do his warmongering when he became too fat to sit on a horse! I remember Queen Anne saying how the Scottish campaign did drive uncle Richard to exhaustion. That it had him falling asleep on his feet, sending him to the verge of illness and collapse at times! It took him away from his family for months and thinking back, how tragic that is now that both were taken from him so shortly afterwards. And all the while father stayed here, safe and sound. Uncle Richard never questioned, never complained, was proud to carry out what needed to be done. Anne told me this..."

Tears filled her bright blue eyes suddenly and she moved forward to grasp her mother's hands in a rare display of tenderness between mother and daughter.

"I loved my father dearly, but even I could see how he could use people to his own ends. He was lucky uncle Richard didn't disown him after our uncle of Clarence was put to death. How would father have managed the north then? Uncle Anthony, taking on the Scots? Making the north safe?" She shook her head in amusement. "Have a care when you demand any debts to be re-paid, Mama, you may find we owe him more than he ever owes us!"

Elizabeth pulled back a little, regarding her daughter coolly and thoughtfully, before rubbing her thumbs across the young girls hands.

"So," she murmured quietly, still aware of the eager ears of Francis Lovell outside the chamber door. Her eyes narrowed and she studied the bright, anxious face before her with a complacent twist to her mouth. "That torch still burns does it? And brightly by all accounts."

Bess said nothing but lowered her head to hide her sudden blush, unable to bear her mother's direct examination. Without a further word, Elizabeth dropped her daughter's hands suddenly and turned to the settle to pick up her cloak.

"Sir Francis! " Elizabeth called out sharply, with the usual air of authority in her voice, of one used to being obeyed.

In seconds, the Viscount was back in the room, leaving them in no doubt that, once again, he had overheard most of everything they had said to each other. Ignoring this, and throwing her cloak around her shoulders, she fastened the fur collar around her throat and smoothed down the folds of heavy fabric. It was very generously trimmed with sable and far richer than her status now merited, but that didn't seem to bother her at all.

"I am ready to go to the king, Sir Francis, however, Bess is indisposed and cannot make the river journey. I will have to beg her pardon from His Grace."

4. THE PALACE OF WESTMINSTER
August 1485

Elizabeth was at least grateful that Richard had agreed to receive her in his privy chamber rather than the less private setting of the audience chamber. This distinct possibility had occupied her mind at one point as she made the journey down river and for a while, in a fit of panic, she had almost asked Francis to turn the boatman back. She knew she still had far too much pride to show obeisance to this man in front of the whole court which was stuffed full of people who had in the past bent the knee to her. It was all too easy to imagine the covered smiles and sneers that would ensue at the sight of the former queen having to prostrate herself before her son's usurper. Her deference had been shown once, if somewhat scantily, when she knew he was unsettled by the imminent threat from Tudor, but this time would be different.

He was victorious, secure on his throne. No matter the level of her fury, her conscience told her that she was extremely fortunate he had agreed to see her at all. Pride, and an innate sense of injustice would carry her through the day, she was sure of that. So angry had she been at being sent to Baynard's Castle, she had forgotten that further humiliation could be afforded to her if the king wished it so. Her sense of relief when she saw this concern was not to be realised was overwhelming, for a few seconds at least.

The fact that she knew the privy chamber well added a different difficulty to her ordeal, but at least one which she could suffer in privacy. She could recall many occasions when she had swept into that very chamber, disrupting Edward's daily schedule. To now have to witness her brother-in-law taking her husband's place in such a familiar setting was causing her rage to rise once again. Even worse than that was the fact that as she entered the chamber and occupied that familiar space, he was not alone. Standing by Richard's side as he sat behind the large oak writing table, the same one where Edward used to complete his correspondence and carry out affairs of state, stood the rigid and regal form of Cecily Neville. The aged and insufferably imperious Duchess of York, Richard's mother, was standing by her son's right hand.

Elizabeth was, however, pleased to note that despite the richly embroidered damask gown and the generous sable trim of her attire, the duchess was not ageing well but as their eyes clashed across the chamber, she became distinctly unnerved. It was some time since they had been in each other's company close enough to look each other in the face. She had forgotten how disturbingly her eyes resembled those of her son Clarence, but she tried not to let her uncertainty show. It was imperative she remained calm and composed. Impenetrable. If she could unnerve Richard, it would be no more than he deserved.

"Elizabeth."

It was Richard's voice and although he looked towards her, he did not stand up as she entered. Cecily's thin lips began to curve upward into a sneer of distaste as she watched Elizabeth approach. Belatedly remembering that the roles had reversed since she was last in Richard's private company, she sank into a deep curtsey. She could not, however, bring herself to call him "Your Grace" - but she noted his sardonic smile at this omission as she rose without waiting for his sanction.

"Duchess Cecily," is what she did say in greeting, passing her glance over Richard to meet his mother's hawk like stare. "I had heard that you had taken vows. It would appear I was misinformed."

Cecily smiled back icily, her face stretched in a rictus grin.

"Dame Grey. I had heard that you had long since gone from court, but it would appear I was also misinformed. I had hoped you would show your gratitude at the mercy my son has shown you by retiring gracefully from sight. Alas, I see you still seek to wander the halls where you wrought such destruction."

Richard shot a sharp, sidewards glance at his mother and then stood up quickly, moving with agile swiftness around the table towards where Elizabeth stood.

As he moved closer, Elizabeth noticed he still wore the darkest blue of mourning and that the cut of his doublet was quite severe, but then she recalled that he had always been one for sombre dress, even if being particularly fastidious and well attired. It is something she had noticed about him from a young age. Once, she had even remarked upon it to Edward, who had smiled sadly and likened Richard in tastes and appearance to their late father. He had, he said, never been one for the peacock's plumes.

Now, suitably drab in her eyes, Richard looked much older than when she had last seen him, which at least gave her some satisfaction. Lines had formed between his brows and were beginning to etch grooves between his nose and mouth. He looked drawn, serious and as far removed in appearance and manner from his brother than anyone could be. How the two could even be brothers she had never been able to understand, so different were they in all things other than blood.

Richard said nothing, aware of her scrutiny, but moved a chair closer to the large table and gestured for Elizabeth to sit. She did so carefully, regarded by two pairs of watchful York eyes, as Richard leaned back to perch on the table before her, folding his arms across his chest.

"I believe you asked for an audience for yourself and Bess, but Francis tells me she is ill?" His deep voice was solicitous and enquiring, even genuine, she reflected. He appeared completely relaxed and although she was loathe to recognise it, completely comfortable in his role. She had always suspected that he had comported himself as an erstwhile king whilst revelling in his estates in the north and his confident bearing confirmed, for her, that she had been right all along. Edward himself had always laughed at her when she broached the subject and had been annoyingly stubborn, hearing no word of complaint against his youngest brother. After Clarence's fate, whenever Elizabeth tried to talk about the dangers Richard's power and influence held, Edward's eyes had flashed dangerously, sparking like lightning and the subject was swiftly changed. He would brook no malice against him. To this end.

Elizabeth looked down demurely at her skirts and smoothed the points of her sleeves. She was very conscious she was not dressed in her accustomed finery underneath the sumptuous cloak which had been divested before she entered the chamber. Notwithstanding, she wanted them to know she was still the same person. Still a former queen, a Woodville, despite the drabness of her outward appearance.

"Yes. " She paused reflectively, her eyes hidden behind lowered lids. "I must relay her apologies. My daughter is sorely disappointed that she was unable to make the river journey today. I am sure you understand, Richard?"

Cecily drew a sharp breath in between her teeth at the constant omission of Richard's true title and her eyes narrowed in a display of animosity. Richard noticed, but merely waved a dismissive gesture in her direction. A shaft of light from the window fell upon the jewelled coronation ring upon his hand and sent a prism of colour dancing along the stone walls. Elizabeth faltered unexpectedly, suddenly seeing that jewel on another, larger, hand.

Plunged down the well of her past, she was suddenly remembering that hand on her bare skin and the pleasure she associated with that thought made her skin prickle involuntarily. She could feel the coldness of the metal as Edward ran his hands over her body and a surge of desire, long suppressed, hit her like a wave, shortening her breath, making her feel momentarily giddy. In one casual gesture of his hand, Richard had found the only chink in the armour she wore each day to guard herself against memories and pain.

She snapped back to the present quickly to find that Richard had arisen from the table and was kissing his mother's hand reverently. He had obviously dismissed her whilst she had been lost in her reverie and she wondered if her face had betrayed her inner turmoil, suspecting, with a flush, that it had. She swallowed with difficulty, not expecting him to be sensitive to her emotions and watched as Cecily swept out of the chamber without giving Elizabeth a further glance. The door closed behind her, leaving the room in utter silence.

Richard returned to his seat behind the table and leaning back, regarded Elizabeth with dark intense eyes full of purpose.

"Now, we are alone and you wished to see me." He paused, seemingly for effect, or to consider his words. "You both wished to see me in fact and yet only you are here. What ails my niece?" His tone was direct, getting straight to the point without preamble.

Elizabeth raised her head defiantly and returned his enquiring stare. There was no trace of Edward in this man's face, which made it so much easier for her. Her strength of will, unbalanced by the sight of the coronation ring up so close, was flowing back.

"Nothing. I felt it would be better if we did meet alone."

Richard smiled grimly, his hand playing absently with a quilled pen on the table.

"I have a feeling that you may have certain - requests?" He inclined his head to one side as he continued to look at her. "Be careful, Elizabeth, as I did grant you many favours after you left sanctuary. It would appear that they were not well appreciated as you continued to plot with Margaret, Lady Stanley to marry Bess to the Tudor Pretender. Is that why she is not here?"

"No, she has nothing to do with this," Elizabeth retorted sharply, "and she gives you far too much credit. Much more than you deserve! I do not want to witness any more of that behaviour than I absolutely have to. The girl is overly fond of you and well do you know it!"

Richard stood up abruptly, the heavy oaken chair skidding against the flagstones with a jarring scrape which broke through the tension. The air in the room was growing cold despite the fire burning in the hearth and the warmth of the day outside. For the first time Elizabeth noticed the large wolfhound curled up in front of the fire place sleeping. At the noise made by the chair, it raised it's head, eyes and ears instantly alert, fixing on Elizabeth with eyes as dark and questioning as his masters

"Tread lightly, my lady," Richard warned, his voice tight, still occupying his stance behind the table. " I will allow you so much latitude but there are limits to what I will take. Especially from you!"

Elizabeth bit back the retort that had risen to her lips. She was unaccustomed to the anger that she saw in his face. It was an expression such as she had not seen for some time, back when she was still queen. Back when Clarence's life hung in the balance and she held the difference between life and death like weights in her hands. The doleful stare of the wolfhound was adding to her uncertainty and the silence between them seemed to last an age.

"Now," said Richard eventually, with an edge of steel to his voice which demonstrated the exertion of an iron control over his emotions. "What do you want from me? I am sure we will both be pleased to see this meeting draw to a close so let us be frank and conclude this business. You are not normally so reticent in your desires and I have other matters to attend to this day. Speak!"

She flinched at the force of this last words which were spoken quietly but heavily tinged with underlying anger and impatience. This was not the young Duke of Gloucester she was facing, not Ned's loyal Dickon. This was the battle hardened Lord of the North, now king of the realm in her son's place. She could feel the implacable force of his will and for one moment understood why some entrusted him with their allegiance and loyalties. Word had reached her ears from others who had told her his spirit was failing since the death of his wife and son, but on this demonstration today, it was obvious that his recent victory had done much to improve his inner strength of will.

"I ask only what I originally asked from your brother, your king, when I first met him. Return of the Grey estates and all that was lost to me on the field when John Grey was killed at St. Albans."

Still carefully watching her, he began to twist a bright gold ring on his smallest finger, his thoughts and emotions impenetrable. He took a deep breath before answering her request.

"My lady, you have been awarded a safe haven and you have some measure of wealth with the stipend I award you. You have held titles, estates and more in the past and used them to make war against me. What has changed that I should trust you now? You still refuse to accept your reduced circumstances and obviously find it difficult to accept me as your king. If it were anyone else sitting there who displayed those attitudes, my next shout would be for the Tower guards."

Elizabeth sat back in her chair forcefully, as if struck. At the same time Richard seemed to realise the weight of his words had hit home. He moved over to the fireplace, stepping carefully over the wolfhound. The hound looked up momentarily but then rested its head back down on its paws, its baleful stare remained fixed on Elizabeth. She almost felt as if she was being judged and found wanting.

Richard leaned against the mantel in silence and stared into the flames, apparently lost in thought for a moment before he heaved a huge, audible sigh. The change in his voice, the softer tone, came as much of a shock to her as the next words from his lips.

"Tell me, have you had any news of the boys?"

Tears stung her eyes suddenly and she looked down at her hands in a desperate bid to hide this further weakness from him. She was determined not to display herself as a pathetic, biddable woman, but she found herself undone by one sentence spoken with care. No matter what she felt, she could not let him see into her inner thoughts. Unable and unwilling to look up, she gave him an imperceptible shake of her head.

The room was flooded with silence and a thousand words unspoken.

"Nor I," Richard mused, dismally, "and I hoped that I would once Tudor was defeated. I hoped whoever is holding them would see that their cause was lost. But then, to be sure of that, I would need to know who is holding them."

There was a question in his quiet voice and when she dared to look up, she could see he was staring at her intently. It was obvious that he believed her connected in some way with their disappearance, a fact she intended to disabuse him of with immediacy.

"My boys were in your care, " she said returning his gaze very carefully. "That you "lost" them is on your conscience. Let us be truthful with one another over this if nothing else, you don't even know if they are alive or dead! The country believes them to be dead, so why do you - of all

41

men - hold out false hope? That should be my pain. I am their mother!"
She did her best to stop this last sentence becoming a cry of anguish. She
almost succeeded.

Elizabeth thought he would retort angrily but instead he crossed the
room back to his seat, his lips pressed tightly together as if to prevent
unbidden words from escaping. Leaning over the back of the elaborately
carved chair, his eyes bored into her face, almost causing her physical pain,
but she was unable to look away as he formed his next words.

"The country believes they are dead because you plotted with those
who wanted to replace me with Tudor. Never has so much dreadful
calumny been whispered in such short time! Tell me, did you or one of your
companions in treason also spread the falsehood that I poisoned my wife?
An evil slander! But then, you had so much enmity to spare for Warwick
and his kin, you would not shirk from profiting out of his daughters death.
Out of my wife's death."

This last was said almost as an afterthought and so quietly she
almost didn't hear it, but she did hear the emotional break in his voice. He
had moved back into his chair and seated himself whilst speaking and as if
finally broken by the burden of his despair, he placed his elbows on the
table and rested his head in his hands.

"*Audacter calumniare, simper aliquid haeret,*" he whispered, more to
himself than any other occupant of the room so that Elizabeth had to strain
to hear what he said. His words hung in the air, neither seeking an answer
or receiving one.

Elizabeth's anger suddenly and surprisingly gave way to a wave of
weariness which came from nowhere and surprised her with its intensity.
She leaned her head back, closing her eyes and breathing in as deeply as
she could. She felt tired for an instant. Tired and old. At that moment she
would have given anything just for her life to be back as it was. Free from
worry, from scheming and manipulating - just able to be content. If she
could only have her sons back, she would want for nothing else. She knew
all too well that there was no proof Richard had harmed them and of the
many emotions she reserved for her brother-in-law, of the many things he
had proved himself capable of, she had to grant that she did not think he
would ever stoop to murder his brother's children.

Although many others had been all too happy to believe that he was
capable of that very act. She felt a small twinge of guilt twist her gut. The
first she had ever felt and it concerned her a little. Not at the pain, but at

the fact she felt guilt at all.

"Richard, Your Grace," she began uncertainly, lowering her head back down to look at him.

His own head had still fallen forward, his dark hair obscuring his face and Elizabeth had another vivid memory of him when he was just a young boy. On the day Henry of Lancaster was brought into London. The young Duke of Gloucester had raged with Edward, wanting vengeance for their father's death, determined to rush from the chamber and avenge himself on the mad old king. Edward and his other brother George, had restrained him, having difficulty in doing so despite his small, slim frame. He had fought fiercely to get to his father's murderer, venting a young boy's rage at his loss.

He was a mere child, eight years old, when his father was killed at Wakefield. His hair had obscured his face in like fashion then as he fought to free himself from his brother's grasp, masking his thoughts from view, only the position of his body giving him away, giving lie to the tension inside.

"Elizabeth. I am sorry." The voice was at first muffled, but he paused, raised his head and looked at her without any trace of enmity. His face was ravaged with grief and he appeared to have aged distinctly even in the last few minutes. The fate of her sons was haunting him, she could see that very clearly, a fact which made her both pleased and uncomfortable at the same time.

"We seem determined to claw at each other like animals fighting to the death, which will only have one result. Leave me to think on this a while. You are welcome to stay at Baynard's Castle as my guest and you will want for nothing whilst I will see what other accommodations I can agree to in due course."

Before she was even aware she was being dismissed, the chamber door opened and Francis once again stood before her. She saw him glance at Richard carefully and a moment of indecision flickered across his face. It betrayed his immediate desire to go to his friend and king who was clearly not himself, but his duty was to escort her back to her lodgings. Or at the very least to pass her into the care of one of his men who would.

Swallowing hard and glancing again at the king, Francis held out his hand to Elizabeth. His eyes met hers with accusatory hatred but his voice was level and cool, revealing no indication of the emotions which were obviously warring inside him.

"Dame Grey - if you please ...."

She allowed herself to be led out of the room, still feeling strangely unsettled, but nevertheless, deep inside her inner core, being able to take some small measure of satisfaction that the king was being left alone. And in distress.

5. WESTMINSTER ABBEY
September 1485

Bess stepped quietly into the solitude of the chapel and halted just inside the door to take in her surroundings, closing the heavy door carefully behind her. She had at first only wanted to find some peace away from her mother's dramatic overtures and in finally escaping the overwhelming suffocation of their borrowed apartments, she had found herself summoning a barge down to Westminster Palace. Wandering around the familiar grounds, she was soon expecting to walk into her father at each turn of the way, on the other side of every arch, every door. His golden laughter drifted out of the open windows in the royal apartments, yet she knew that no one else could hear it, so she headed for the sanctity of the abbey, hoping to still her mind. On reflection, with recent events still troubling her thoughts, she could think of no better place nearby for some peace and time to think. Even thought there was a chapel at Baynard's Castle, she needed to be away from her mother, just for a while.

The nave was dimly lit and cool. Only the flames of several candles and a few flickering torches affixed to the wall sconces, bathed the stones in warm, glowing light. The high vaulted ceiling soared away into the darkness above her head, giving a sense of never-ending space, so that you could almost feel God was up there, in the shadows, listening and watching.

She breathed in deeply with relief, exhaling her weariness, trying not to think about anything at all. Slowly, she moved over to the candle-stand in front of the statue of the Blessed Virgin and picked up a long wax taper which she held to a flame.   Lighting a candle for her father, she held his face in her mind's eye, trying to forget that his golden radiance was buried in due splendour at Windsor some miles away, imagining him smiling, sitting in his privy chamber just a few minutes from where she stood.

Bess desperately wanted to go back and visit his tomb as the day of his funeral had been a blur of fear and despair, but her mother had forbidden it. Had not even been to visit herself.

The small flame sputtered weakly for a few moments before it steadied to a constant burn and then, looking towards the likeness of the impassive Virgin before her, Bess made a deferential bow of her head, crossing herself slowly. The candlelight fractured into a hundred mirrors as she viewed it through her tear-filled eyes. Nothing she could do would prevent them falling now and they darkened the stone flags beneath her feet, like rain drops.

The place was totally silent and she sorely wished that the souls of those departed who surrounded her and were at peace, would help her find restfulness of mind. She moved towards a bench then with the intent to sit a while and think things through in the soft half-light, when she suddenly sensed she was not alone.

There was a sound. It came from a chapel to the left of the nave. Something so faint that she couldn't quite make it out. She had believed that she was alone, had not known that some other lonely soul may this evening be in need of solace and prayer. Straining her ears to hear more, she thought she heard someone speak, or whisper. Something familiar but difficult to comprehend.

Standing cautiously, she even lifted her skirts off the floor so that she could move without causing the slightest rustle of fabric, she made her way towards the source of the noise, although for a moment, the abbey was so quiet she felt she may have imagined it. Before long, she realised that she was approaching the chapel where the body of Queen Anne had been laid to rest. Her mouth went dry. Bess now knew who she was about to encounter in the semi-darkness and she clasped her hands together as she felt them begin to tremble, her skirts falling back to brush the flags beneath her feet, like a whispered prayer. In the chapel, on his knees in the flickering torchlight, one hand resting on the cold brass plate temporarily marking his wife's resting place, was the king.

The dancing light played mischievously on the silver thread of his darkly brocaded doublet, but Bess could see that the top laces were undone and his free hand gripped the throat of his linen undershirt as if he was gasping for breath. His head was lowered, his dark hair fallen forward and covering his face, somehow adding an air of undeniable tragedy to his prone figure. Her throat tightened as she moved forward, ever quietly, still not sure as yet if she would reveal her presence to him or just move away and leave him to his privacy.

Should she go? Every fibre in her body told her she should turn away and leave, but her blood began to race through her limbs like a river in flood. The sound of her thundering heart filled her ears, drowning out what her head was telling her to do, ignoring everything but the longing deep inside her, wanting to see him. Wanting to see him so very badly, even if that meant, selfishly, intruding on his private grief.

Then, from the sorrowful tableau before her, came a sound which tore at her very heart.

"Anne - my love!"

A strangled sob, drenched in grief, rent the quiet air and as she watched, in silence and transfixed, he began to pull angrily at the neck of his shirt. His voice cracked with emotion as he spoke her name over and over again, his head bowing even lower, unable to bear the weight of his despair. Bess stood in frozen silence, her hands gripping each other tightly, torn between wanting to flee and wanting to help him as she remembered him comforting her as a child.

No. That was falsehood, she chided herself. It was past time she began to be honest with herself. She would also like to comfort him as a grown woman. To acknowledge those feelings she had been trying to suppress since he had refused her open declaration of love some time ago, whilst Anne was still alive and very much his wife. For she loved her uncle dearly, even though she had to admit those feelings confused, terrified and elated her all in equal measure. She had been naïve then, foolish enough to let him know how she felt and his reaction to her declaration of love still caused her face to burn with the recollection of it.

He had been shocked and surprised, where she had thought he would have seen all too clearly how she looked at him, how he made her smile. How she always managed to place herself within mere feet of him at every possible opportunity. Only, he had not. But gently, with infinite care, he had made it abundantly clear that any love he may have for her was only as his brother's child. He had been kind, which had made it worse. For if he had treated her contemptuously and callously, as many at court believed he could, she could have recovered, could have moved on. Only, over the following days, he had not appeared to regard her in any less esteem, although he was careful not to be left in her company alone.

Then had come the death of his son. Bess had watched in agony as husband and wife comforted each other, not caring who saw, nor caring who commented and she had turned her face away, unable to bear witness to the love she saw displayed so publicly between them. But now Anne was dead too. Drawn from life, month by month, ravaged by a burning, wasting disease that had consumed her frail body and had all but taken his sanity with it.

Bess had heard men talk about his confrontation with Tudor on the battlefield. They had murmured that he intended to win the day or die, that he had given up all hope of living if he lost his crown, as well as his wife and son. That he rode into battle buoyed up by intense relief at the final opportunity to surrender his life for his cause; to die with honour as an anointed King of England.

As the pictures of the past painted vivid images so real she could believe herself re-living each moment, she watched in utter silence, overwhelmed with emotion as he raised his head to look at Christ on the Cross, looking down on him from the far wall of the chapel. The torchlight lit up his face, revealing glittering evidence of the tear tracks across his cheeks. His hair was disheveled, as if he had been running his hands through it frantically, not a gesture she would usually associate with him. The agony in his face was all too plainly writ and it wrenched her heart.

"Why? Why?" he asked in a broken voice to the un-regarding figure on the cross, knowing that only God could reply and seeking that answer with heartfelt desperation. Both the figure and the chapel itself were silent in response. Bess understood at that moment how deep his despair ran, to feel that God had reconciled with him. Taken his wife, his child, but given him back his kingdom. It seemed an unfair barter and confirmed the whispered conversations of those who had seen him charge into battle.

So unnerved was she by the intimacy of the moment she was witnessing, that she now knew she had to leave. Only as she turned, something, some sound, made him register her presence. Unexpectedly, he sprang to his feet, instantaneously drawing the small dagger from the belt at his waist. Bess's hand sprang upwards to cover her mouth in surprise and fear.

"Who is it? Who goes there?" he called. Then softer - heartbreakingly, almost in hopeful anticipation and wonder. "Anne?"

Bess gathered herself together and, taking the deepest of breaths, stepped forward into a pool of torchlight.

"It's me, Your Grace. Bess. I'm sorry, I didn't mean to..." she stopped speaking when she could more clearly discern the features of his face. Richard stared back blankly as if he didn't know her. His expression looked almost wild, his face contorted and demented. She experienced real fear, a cold, sick dread that pooled in the pit of her stomach and considered if she should run and find Francis, Dick or John. Anyone.

"Bess?" His voice again, his tone completely flat, without comprehension. Repeating the name of a stranger.

Resisting the urge to flee, to find his closest friends and send them to his aid, she moved closer into the light to be recognised, but his eyes were still too full of grief, unseeing.

"Shall I call someone Your Grace? John Kendall... or Francis?" She offered her assistance in a voice gentle and soft, the tone one would use to reassure a scared child. "I believe Jack is still within?" She had named men who were all his close friends as he appeared in very much in need of his closest friends now.

No. Once again she corrected herself for that thought as soon as it had formed. He appeared in need of his dead wife and that no-one could give to him, although she dearly wished that she could. If he could not accept her love, she would happily have him able to gain back the love of his life. Anything to release him from this torture, which, although clutching at her own heart, was clearly ripping his apart.

"Bess?" he asked softly. His tone was a little warmer and he appeared to recover a measure of his composure, his eyes clearing, softening. "I am sorry, I did not mean to frighten you. For a moment I..." Suddenly, he began to sag at the knees and Bess flew to his side instantly. With no other recourse, he clung to her as she flung her arms around him, preventing him from crashing down onto the marble floor, as well as to try and stop himself from drowning in his own grief. His fingers dug into her shoulders and Bess winced, his grip was so strong. She could feel her tender flesh bruising.

"I thought - I saw..."

"I am sorry Uncle Richard. It's just me. It's just Bess."

She saw him frown in the half-light, his straight dark brows drawn together, then, slowly, his eyes began to recognise her, although his gaze became quizzical and confused. He parted from her slightly, attempting to regain his balance, standing up straight before Anne's resting place, reaching a hand out to stead himself against the wall. His glance took it in once more and then moved back to his niece's worried face.

" What are you doing here?"

She closed the small distance he had opened between them, keeping his gaze.

"I just wanted to be somewhere away from mother for a while. She is .... " Bess faltered. She really did not want to talk about her mother now and was sorry she had mentioned her.

His eyes focused completely then and his lips formed a thin hard line at the mere sound of her mother's name.

"She is not happy with me. There is nothing I can do about that. She hates me and I understand why. There is nothing to be done, nothing I can do to change that... " His voice trailed off and he turned away from her again, looking towards Anne's tomb. "I miss her more than ever since my victory," he mused to no-one in particular. "What was it all for if not for her - and my son?"

Bess, in her youth, had no idea what to do when confronted by such raw pain. She had been at court when Anne died and he had been grieving. All of the court had been able to see that, but there had been very little sympathy for him outside his immediate circle, thanks to the evil ministrations of her mother and Lady Stanley. Through all of that, he had remained composed and controlled, apart from the tears she had seen him shed at the funeral mass. When his son died, he had Anne to turn to, he had a partner to help him share the burden of such despair. Only now he was all alone. This tide of emotion was new to her and she didn't know how she felt about seeing her strong, powerful uncle, her king, at the mercy of his emotions.

Almost as though he sensed her confusion and wanted to spare her feelings, he seemed to pull himself together, with some effort, and ran a hand over his face. He gave Bess a half rueful smile in the torchlight, almost embarrassed.

"Forgive me. You should not have to see me like this. I am the one from whom you used to seek comfort as a child. Do you remember?"

She moved even closer towards him, close enough touch his arm in familial remembrance.

"Of course I do! And I always loved you for it! You were my - are my favourite uncle and always have been. It distresses me unbearably to see your pain! How can I help you? How can I comfort you, as you always comforted me?"

She had not quite intended to say those words with such passion in her voice, but she could not prevent it. The question hung in the air between them, unanswered and she became aware that he was searching her face with his dark eyes, but looking for what? They stood, inches apart, when suddenly and without warning, he grasped both of her hands and raised them to his lips. His kiss on her fingers was firm, dry and hot to the touch. It was only as he raised his dark head that she recalled seeing him carry out the same gesture to Anne so many, many times and her breath caught in her throat.

He smiled sadly at her pensive face and gave a downward glance towards the tomb.

"Dearest Bess. You cannot help me, but I thank you. I am in hell and burning."

With those words, he released her hands and leaving his shocked niece standing alone in the chapel, he turned away from her abruptly, striding out of the abbey.

6. THE PALACE OF WESTMINSTER
September 1485

Francis strode across the bailey in the direction of the stables, deeply absorbed in his own thoughts.

A letter had arrived from Minster Lovell the day before, written by his wife Anna, who was being very insistent that matters relating to their estate in Oxfordshire needed his urgent attention. He did not doubt for one moment that this was true. Anna was hardly one to send him letters of longing and regret at their frequent absences, or send pleading requests for him to return home. She had long relinquished any hopes of being at the fore-front of his mind and had, somewhat reluctantly, abandoned him to his duties with the king.

With this in mind, he knew she would not see fit to bother him unless his presence was needed, and he had to admit that due to the uncertainty of the past few months, his attention had been fully focused on other matters and they had hardly spent any time at all in each others company. It was a sacrifice which had become second nature to him, and one Anna no longer tried to prevent.

Their marriage was not a passionate one, having been arranged for them both at an early age, neither of them having any say in the match. In fact, not long after the two had been joined and with no need for any confirmation of the marital bed, Anna being half his age at the time, Francis had been despatched northwards. His wardship, and the wealth he was then too young to inherit after the early death of his father, was held by the king. Edward then lost no time in handing him over to be trained as a knight by the all powerful Richard Neville, Earl of Warwick, at a time when the earl had been a constant presence at the right hand of his cousin, the king. Fortunes changed with the wind during those times and it was in that tumultuous period, three enduring relationships had been formed which had sustained Francis through the years, and none of them was with his wife.

Thanks to King Edward, he had become a friend and companion to Edward's younger brother, Richard, Duke of Gloucester – and by default, a friend of Robert Percy, another of the henchmen being trained at Middleham Castle, a vast stone edifice slumbering quietly in the clean, crisp Wensleydale moors. When a dissatisfied Warwick joined forces with George, another, more mercurial, Plantagenet sibling, the two of them had turned against the king, unhappy at the insidious, creeping threat that was the queen's family. When Edward placed each of his common relatives in places of high rank, elevating them to the status of nobles, Warwick's discontent grew into a jealous beast that had to be slain in order for peace to return to the country.

The matter was settled at the battle of Barnet, where Warwick was killed after George, conveniently, returned to fight within the bosom of his family, turning his back on his former allegiances. At this time, Francis found himself on the wrong side of the king's affinity, which to him had always seemed to him a touch unfair, seeing as he had been given to Warwick by the king himself. He was awarded a pardon which he received, even young as he was, with a sense of ironic thankfulness.

Stepping back off Fortune's Wheel, he was then unable to return to Middleham, something he was none too pleased about at the time. Instead, he was sent to join the household of the Suffolk family at Wingfield Hall, where he befriended Edward's young nephew, John de la Pole, now the Earl of Lincoln. Throughout this time, he had always held the bleak, windswept beauty of Middleham's ashlar walls in his heart and vowed one day to return. His opportunity came when Richard married Anne Neville, Warwick's daughter, and he was awarded the castle for his loyalty and valour in battle. Francis swore a promise to himself that he would not settle until he was back walking those battlements with his friend, riding pell mell along the River Cover, watching his falcon dip and soar against the cristalline blue of the sky.

Since attaining his wish, loyalties and duties kept him close to wherever the duke, now his king, needed him to be. He had been well rewarded, and was now Richard's Lord Chamberlain, one amongst many other titles. He was the man with the power to refuse or grant access to the king's person at all times. Now and then over the years, he had returned to his family home, only to feel the inexorable pull of the north, or the anxiety of his duty, tugging him back to where he felt most comfortable.

He quickly grew restless and bored in the Oxfordshire countryside and Anna, in turn, disliked the formality of court. Her sojourns there at his side were as infrequent as his visits to Minster Lovell. They both knew that their marriage was based more around convenience and old landed ties, than any love which they may bear each other. Francis had to admit that although he was indeed fond of Anna, the emotion between them was more dutiful affection than any form of heart-felt devotion.

They were childless and likely to stay so, a situation not helped by the days he spent bound to his king's service. It was this loyalty which pulled the strongest at this time and if Francis was completely honest with himself, he did not see when this situation would significantly alter. It was a reality that had taken them both some time to accept and now, the marriage bond was as close as it was ever going to be. He fulfilled his obligations as lord of the manor and Anna would walk by his side at royal events, whenever she was requested to do so. It was a bittersweet compromise which they had now both accepted.

He was acutely aware of the value which Richard placed on loyalty and although he knew that his own standing in this respect was not in doubt, since the recent battle, he was finding himself increasingly loathe to be long from his friend's side. He knew, though Richard was unlikely to admit it, that the king was still smarting inwardly for allowing himself to be duped by his cousin Harry Stafford, the Duke of Buckingham. For a short time, that vile traitor dripped poison into Richard's ear and made it sound like the sweetest of music. Richard had listened to his counsel above all, putting a distance between himself and his other close confidantes, so when Harry betrayed him and allied himself with Tudor, his treason was all the more unfathomable.

Since then, childhood friends such as himself and Rob Percy remained very close. There were many others, such as his lawyer Will Catesby, Dick Ratcliffe and in particular Jack Howard, the Duke of Norfolk, whom he trusted, but Rob and Francis were his touchstones. They had silently agreed they would never let him fall foul of such duplicity again.

Although the victory had awarded them a measure of peace and stability, he knew that it would not last long. Richard was determined to put right the wrong-doings of the past eighteen months where the constant plotting and spreading of malicious gossip had almost lead to his defeat on the field. Yes, he had to agree that his king, his friend, had made some questionable decisions in the early, turbulent days of his power, certainly in the weeks following his brother's demise. The execution of Hastings and Buckingham's treason were still the subject of tales passed between many a traveller visiting the city and passing an evening in their cups. That was to be expected, but these were political deaths and would soon be forgotten once Richard had progressed further into his reign. Francis was sure of it.

Most disturbing was the simmering undertone that the king was seen to be a murderer and a tyrant, an image so far from the Richard that

Francis had grown up with, it was almost laughable. But the poisonous sedition that had been spread throughout the London stews had taken root and flourished. It was these more damaging aspects of tavern and town conjecture that Richard was desperate to address, including the more distasteful accusations surrounding Edward's sons and Anne, his wife. Richard' s northern men knew that these tales were exactly just that. Salacious gossip about a powerful and feared man from the untamed north, the land of savages, whispered into compliant ears by the insidious spies working on Tudor or Woodville commands. Much had been said, little of it bearing any witness in truth or foundation.

Richard had, over time, formed his own philosophical take on this difficult reality.

"Audacter calumniare, simper aliquid haeret," he had said, more than once, on hearing each new rumour during the early months of this reign.

"Slander boldly, something always sticks."

It seemed to be a saying that had served Tudor well. Francis knew, without Richard even expressing his wishes, that he wanted to take decisive actions to eliminate these stories and to re-establish his reputation to the levels of regard he enjoyed in the north. To where even Londoners regarded him before he was named Lord Protector, when even those who had never seen him, knew of him as a just and honest man, a brave and noble commander. A loyal brother. It was such ambition that was causing him so much agony and indecision, he could see it in his face every day.

Francis felt the whole situation was eating Richard up and he was determined not to leave it too much longer before bringing the subject up himself, it was just a question of the right moment and this had not, as yet, arisen. He knew Richard well. He would get only one opportunity and both the timing and the words had to be right. The one good omen in the heavens was the fact that France would not be troubling them much for a while. They still had their own house to put in order and Tudor's defeat, which had received their backing only to draw eyes away from their own disarray, would have been sorely received.

Louis, the "Spider King" had died, his webs of intrigue melting away with him and leaving a minor on the throne. Francis smiled to think how they would all be scrabbling to sort out that little problem now that they knew Richard was secure on his throne. At least it meant that their eyes would once again turn inward, away from England, for the time being.

He reached his dappled stallion which had been made ready for his departure, patting the animal on the neck in familiarity. He swung with ease up into the saddle and had been so deep in his thoughts that he had not noticed the cloaked figure hurrying across the bailey towards him. He wheeled his horse around and was just about to spur him into action when a hand was placed on his stirruped foot, fingers closing around his ankle.

He looked down in surprise, checking back on the reins, to see the tense, flushed face of the younger Elizabeth, the former royal princess, turned up towards him. As she looked up, her hood fell back, revealing the burnished gold of her hair, blazing with so much colour that he was, momentarily, startled by it.

"My lord - please... could I have a moment?"

The face that looked up at him was tear stained, her voice was pleading and the grip of her hand transferred a measure of tension which caused him to halt. Francis leaned over in his saddle as he steered his horse away from her, but was unable to prevent it bumping her with its well muscled rump. Yet still she clung on to his ankle, determined not to let him leave.

Francis had never been comfortable in the company of any of the Woodvilles but he had loved Edward as his king. He was probably more accepting of Edward's daughters than any of the rest of the brood, who he felt the devil had spawned with the true intent of sending the country into war. But even then, with Bess, as she was known around court, there were aspects of her behaviour that were a mirror of her own mother. He could not help but remain cautiously distant from her, particularly as she had been the focus of treasonous activity between her mother, the Stanleys and Tudor himself.

Yet, he had to remind himself, it was not her fault. Her scheming mother had been determined to keep her hand on the throne of England, no matter how she achieved it. The two of them were still resident at court like ghosts of the past and he would feel much happier when they had departed. Although he found her family distasteful and was sure that whatever trouble she was experiencing would have been brought on by themselves, he felt that if he did not take the time to speak to her, she may seek out the king. That was something which he wanted to avoid at all costs.

Curious, yet somewhat frustrated that his journey would be delayed, he pulled up his mount and quickly slipped from the saddle to face her. They were of an equal height and as his feet touched the ground, he found himself face to face at very close quarters with the girl who was at the heart of some of the most scurrilous of the recent rumours which swirled around the king.

"Lady Elizabeth," he said cordially, feeling slightly uncomfortable at his closeness to her but unable to do anything about it as he hung on to his mount's reins.

"Please, forgive me," she panted somewhat breathlessly, "but, have you seen Richard this morning?"

His horse, pawed the ground, scraping at the cobbles, impatient to be off. As he steadied him, he fell against her slightly and flushed pink with embarrassment up to his hairline, but she seemed not to notice. A fragrance of rose assailed his nostrils and he stepped back, disconcerted. Unsettled, he was unable to prevent his face folding into a scowl.

"No, I have not. I believe the king rode out to Windsor yesterday." He felt duty bound to correct her by using Richard's formal title. It was this very familiarity which had added to the whole confounded situation in the first place, he reflected sourly whilst trying to keep his expression impassive.

"I don't think so. I mean, I don't think he did. I came across him in the chapel late in the day, " she continued, her voice strained with tears. "I fear he is in torment, Sir Francis. I am so worried. I want to help him and I don't know what to do!"

Francis looked into her distraught face and began to suffer some grudging sympathy for the beautiful girl before him, but he remained increasingly uncomfortable with the topic of conversation. It was a difficult situation all round. He had to feel some empathy with the girl who cared so very much for someone he also loved like a brother. But the fact that her actions had led to Richard almost ritually humiliating himself before half of London so closely following the tragic death of his wife, hardened his heart somewhat.

The vision of Richard addressing the public at Clerkenwell was burned in his memory like a thieves brand on skin. Somehow, a rumour had swept the city that he had poisoned Anne in order to wed his own brother's niece, the girl currently standing before him in such distress. How Richard had even managed to stand upright during that oration was a mystery, he had taken Anne's death so hard. The silent, accusing faces staring up at him, displaying not an ounce of compassion, or belief, made Francis fly into a barely controlled rage, which only Rob was able to calm down.

In the end, even that public debasement had won him nothing. The rumour mill continued to grind away, crushing his reputation into the smallest, powdery grains. Reducing it to dust to be blown away into oblivion. Some believed him, as he had taken the trouble to deny it, but then twisted the knife by adding that as he had not taken the same actions for the deaths of his nephews, that crime must indeed be his. He could not win. He was unable to stem the flow of slanderous words that had been turning the country against him.

After this, Richard had sent Bess to his castle at Sheriff Hutton with the rest of the young members of the family including John and Kathryn, his illegitimate children and his brother Clarence's son, Edward. They were all placed under the guardianship of Francis's friend, and now Richard's heir, John de la Pole, Earl of Lincoln, during the preparations for the Tudor invasion. The last thing they had needed was her return to court after the victory and Francis couldn't wait for her to depart, out of sight and hopefully forgotten.

"My lady," he began coolly, "there is really no need for your concern. It may help if you put some," he paused delicately, ".. distance between yourself and the king. I am sure that this will be easier once you all return to Grafton."

Bess looked shocked and was about to respond when Francis was distracted by the sound of clattering hooves and a cacophony of raised voices and shouting from across the courtyard. Bess, meanwhile, could not believe her ears. Grafton – they were going back to Grafton? Richard had conceded then?

Before she could say anymore, Francis had turned around and recognised the midnight-black destrier favoured by Rob Percy charging towards them at full gallop, the rider vaulting out of his saddle before his mount had even come to a halt. Throwing his reins over the horse's neck, he came over to Francis at a run and grabbed hold of him by the arms, a huge triumphant grin almost splitting his face in two.

"Francis! We've got him! We've got him! Where's the king? Where's Richard? We need to let him know!"

Francis felt suddenly dizzy with apprehension and asked the question, even though he full well knew who Rob was talking about.

"Who? Rob... slow down for pity's sake!"

"Henry Tudor, you dolt, who else? We have him! We've captured the bastard pretender!"

Francis clapped Rob on the shoulder, now grinning himself, albeit more reservedly, at the same time looking over that shoulder into the face of young Bess. Her expression had fixed into a stone mask of fear and disgust, replacing the distress which she had earlier displayed. Rob stood to one side, his eyes taking in Bess and Francis as they stood together, still unable to remove the smile from his face.

"Tudor!" Bess breathed softly. A gloved hand stole up to wipe away a tear track on her cheek.

"My lady," Francis said softly, if a little callously, "you will finally be able to meet your betrothed."

Francis was, at heart, a decent man and as she turned to leave, her fair face a picture of confused despair, he wished he had bitten back his last words. Rob was peering at him, brows furrowed and questioning, his smile disappearing.

"Francis? We need to tell Richard. Will you ride with me to Windsor? We should give him this news ourselves. By God - I can't wait to see his face!"

Francis swallowed with difficulty. He felt like he had a huge stone lodged in his throat as he watched Bess walk away from them to disappear under the arches towards the stairs to the chapel.

"You won't have to wait long, Rob. I believe he is still here."

7. WESTMINSTER HALL
September 1485

Richard was seated at the head of the hall on the King's Bench, framed in the rainbow light from the lancet window behind him. From it's elevated position, reached by several steps, he was sufficiently raised above the assembled throng to watch them as they waited, fidgeting and jostling each other impatiently. For himself, he was completely calm, having waited a long time for this moment. To finally confront the shadow that had constantly darkened the last two years of his life.

As if he had not suffered enough in losing his wife and son, this man he was about to confront had ensured there had been little time to grieve. Perhaps, he mused, as he cast his eyes over the noble gathering, their muted conversations washing over him in a wave of whispers like silk against flesh, that was why his victory had failed to completely raise his spirits. Perhaps now, he could finally find some time to come to terms with everything that had happened. Betrayal, treason, death. He lowered his eyes for a second only, not wanting to miss a single moment of what was about to take place.

The air fair throbbed with anticipation as shafts of early afternoon light, sharp as sword blades, sliced in through the high windows. Searching rays sought out every gilt thread, each precious jewel or chain of gold, causing them to glitter like the crests of rippling waves. It played across the vividly bright silken gowns, sought out the gems on caps and collars, around the white throats of the ladies of the court. Letting his eyes continue their journey and mark the faces that waited in fevered anticipation, he wondered what a marvellous portrait or tapestry this sight before him would make.

Yet, he smiled to himself grimly, if only he could find the artist who could show, within their work, which of those smiling faces masked the snarl of treachery. Sadly, his instinct told him that there were still very few, even within this sparkling, obesiant mass, that he could truly trust.

Above all of this movement, he was immobile. Still. Unable or unwilling to move a muscle, he was not entirely sure which. A restless anxiety being held at bay by the tenacious grip of his inner will, allowing only his eyes to move, his chest to rise and fall with each waiting breath.

As usual he had dressed with great care and fastidiousness. A doublet of dark blue damask and a matching floor length robe, trimmed with sable. The severity alleviated only by the golden collar of suns and roses around his shoulders, the centrepiece of which was a rearing golden boar in accordance with his blazon. The jewelled crown of his kingship encircled his head and he sat ram-rod straight in his seat, appearing completely at ease to all who were present. His forearms resting casually on the arms of the chair, his hands relaxed, jewels glinting on his finger rings. Only Francis and those who had spent so much time with him at Middleham over past years would be able to measure the depth of the tension in his body which was given away by a certain set of his shoulders. No one else would notice a thing.

Next to him on the dais was the throne that had been formerly occupied by his late wife, Anne. Court retainers had tried to remove it after Anne's death, believing it to be more suitable for the king to receive with just one throne in the room as he was now the sole sovereign. Richard had heard word of this and immediately ordered its return, much to the unease of his closest advisers.

Now whenever he received anyone in public, he sat next to the empty throne, on which his wife's crown had been placed on a velvet cushion. He knew it made his Lord Chamberlain and others uncomfortable, could see in their eyes what they wanted to say but dare not, even as they understood his intention. They knew he was making the point that he had loved his wife and that she was sorely missed and still in his thoughts. Contrary to the opinion being mooted abroad that he had wilfully aided her death by poison, weary of the sick and barren wife who had borne him a weak boy for an heir and destabilised his throne.

In this gesture, he hoped to stir some semblance of guilt in those who had worked so hard to besmirch his reputation, or at the very least to unsettle those who thought he knew not what was said, or by whom. This was how he intended to receive Henry Tudor, the former exile he had never met and yet who had been a constant burr under the saddle of his kingship since he took the crown. To some extent, his reasoning told him it was a futile gesture, yet his heart had a louder voice.

His eyes finally settled on the two most important members of today's gathering, Lord Thomas Stanley and his wife, Margaret. Henry Tudor's mother. Garbed in a wimple and barbe which she now donned with an almost irritating regularity to declare her extreme piety to all, the picture was jarred by the opulence of the jewelled crucifix which hung around her neck. It was so heavy it almost dragged down her diminutive frame, making it remarkable that she could remain so upright. Even from his place some feet away from her, he could pick out garnets, sapphires and pearls.

Around her fingers, she was twisting the beads of a rosary in darkest jet. White, bloodless hands, he noticed absently, the hands of a corpse. She was currently a captive, under house arrest and her husband's cognisance because of her treasonous activities on her sons behalf. Richard had allowed Stanley to bring her to court today from their country residence at Bletsoe.

What Richard had actually said, in tones so scathing each word could have stripped the skin, was, "She has waited so long to see him approach the throne, how could I, in all conscience, deny her this opportunity? It will be the first and only time - so she can take it to her grave!" As he had listened to his king's words, Stanley's thoughts on this had been hidden as he kept his head bowed in deference.

The doors at the end of the hall opened then and a herald's voice cut across the sea of whispers, stilling the rumbling murmur in an instant. The shout echoing up to carry around the vaulted beams above their heads.

"Sir Robert Percy! Sir Richard Ratcliffe!"

Most heads turned in the direction of the voice, anxious to see the defeated foe being brought to kneel before his victor. Two liveried men at arms displaying the Blancsanglier escorted in their charge, accompanied by Rob Percy, ebullient, finely attired in green velvet slashed with gold silk. Another trusted companion, Richard Ratcliffe, matching him stride for stride, his dark eyes sweeping the crowd almost suspiciously. Richard smothered a sigh. Ratcliffe trusted very few people and Richard knew he should have heeded his advice more than he had.

Rob kept his gaze firmly fixed on his king's face as he approached the steps, his expression a study in self-satisfaction, as though he had just performed some fantastical mummers trick to entrance the crowd and was revelling in their wonder and applause.

Richard drew himself up a little more in his seat, returning Rob's gaze. He didn't acknowledge the smile outwardly, although he was very pleased that he had been able to afford Rob the honour of presenting his hard won prize. It had been Rob who had shown complete determination to track down their enemy after he escaped in the rout. He had not wasted one hour, one day. It was, Richard thought, only fitting, that he publicly displayed his victory to all.

Behind Rob and Ratcliffe, flanked by attentive guards whose half-armour glimmered with its own light, the thin, brown-haired man approaching the bench came into view. Richard knew Tudor was younger than him by a few years, but noted with some personal satisfaction that he looked much older than his years.

Being more than aware that the burden of power had etched his own face with lines of care and grief, he was somewhat gratified to note that Henry's exile had also done him no favours. The gaunt, sallow face was pinched and drawn and there was a slight cast to his right eye, he noted with interest. A flame of anger burned suddenly. No one had ever mentioned that to him. Why was that? Carefully, imperceptibly, he pressed his own back against his chair. So, they were both marked in some way! The thought caused him to catch the inside of his cheek between his teeth.

Henry was wary. Like a trapped fox, his narrow eyes darting from side to side and he wet his lips with his tongue as if developing a thirst. Richard cut his glance across to the Stanleys, both of whom at least had the grace to appear nervous. Lady Stanley in particular, as she had placed her hand over her mouth above which her eyes were glassy with unshed tears. She had not seen her son in many years and ungracious as it was, he could not deny the feeling of gratification that flooded through him at that sight.

Richard breathed deeply as Tudor stopped before him at the foot of the steps and was prodded to his knees by one of Richard's men. Rob moved forward and placing one foot on the bottom step, he gave a deep obeisance, extending one arm with a flourish. He was obviously enjoying himself immensely, and had no intention of hiding his feelings.

"Your Grace! The pretender, Henry Tudor!" he announced, loudly, to the hall. Richard could see he was making no attempt to hide his satisfied smile as he presented his prize.

"Thank you, Sir Robert," he replied softly and was rewarded by a more familiar nod and a return to formality from his loyal retainer who then stepped back, moving away from Tudor to stand next to Francis, who was accompanied by Jack Howard, Duke of Norfolk. The three of them formed a glittering line of authority and grandeur, ranked at Richard's right hand.

An expectant hush had descended over the sun-drenched hall like a gossamer veil that reminded Richard of the nervous quiet before the command to commence forward into battle was given. It had been the same less than one month ago, as the sun rose over the Leicestershire countryside, staining the clouds rose-red.

"Rise!" Richard's voice was loud, clear and steady, the authoritative tone ringing around the walls clearly like a bell.

Henry Tudor straightened up, pressing heavily veined hands against his slender thighs as he rose to his feet. His simple, homespun garments were a poor fit and had obviously been loaned to him as a disguise. Someone had clearly assisted him, or been duped into believing he was a poor farm-hand. He certainly looked the part in his current disarray and from what Richard had experienced of the French court under Louis, he would have found no cultured mannerisms there. The opaque grey eyes looked quickly into those of the king and just as speedily looked away.

"Why so shy?" Richard smiled grimly to the man kneeling before him, clad in his peasant's finery. "After all, we have already met! On the battlefield, just outside the hamlet of Market Bosworth. Just before you fled the field, I think. However, I could be mistaken in this. I am unable to say for definite due to the tardy arrival of your kinsman's pike-men!" He cast a quick glance over to William Stanley, who stood just behind his brother Thomas. Richard marked his obvious discomfort, but noticed it was only slight. "They did obscure both my view and my aim." The silence in the room was countered only by birdsong filtering in from outside, belying the tension which pervaded the air, bringing in a brief reminder of summer's end. Richard scanned the room again before continuing.

"If not for him, you too would be encased in the cold Leicestershire soil, under stone in the church of the Greyfriars with your uncle. So you have some thanks to express, I would think." Richard slid his arms back with deliberate slowness and pushed himself out of the throne, rising to his feet in one fluid action. Moving with care, he stepped down four of the steps in front of him without taking his eyes from Tudor's face.

"Nothing to say?" He paused, considering the deathly silence across the chamber, flicking his eyes over to Margaret Stanley for the merest of seconds. "I find that very difficult to believe as you have had plenty and more to say of me over the past two years. So, speak up! I am sure we have much to discuss after all this time!"

Henry was looking directly ahead, his gaze level with Richard's belt and the broadsword he wore at his hip. He cleared his throat with difficulty, lips pressed together nervously as his eyes slid side-wards to where his mother stood.

"Your Grace... " he replied, hesitantly, but no other words came. The impasse was broken by a choked sob but Richard refused to move his eyes from his foe, knowing well that the sound had emanated from Lady Stanley, who was now unable to contain her distress. Slowly, Henry looked up and his resigned, grey gaze finally succumbed to Richard's piercingly dark stare. He cleared his throat again, taking a deep breath which belied a summoning up of courage from deep within him.

"Your Grace, I do humbly beg your pardon for all the calumnies which were put abroad in your name. Yet you must know that it was not I who was responsible for either the source, or perpetuation of these infamies. Others did take it upon themselves to undertake this... "

His voice trailed away, seeming to lose either its strength or will. Richard judged him to be in need of a good meal and some rest. It was hard to imagine him as the 'Red Dragon of Cadwallader,' now looking as downtrodden and besmirched as his standard was on Redemore plain as White Surrey had thundered over it with powerful hooves. That memory was still abundantly clear, himself having dispatched Henry's standard bearer, Sir William Brandon, with one single arc of his axe.

"Really?" Richard's voice was redolent with disbelief. "Yet, you named yourself king from the day before battle! Was that not of your own doing? Did others incite you to such treason and force your unwilling hand? I could rightly take your head just for that alone! You are of bastard descent, legitimised only with provision that your line could not succeed. How did you dare to mount an attack on the throne of England, a throne to which you have no right?"

Henry said nothing, but Richard caught a flash of anger that took light in the formerly cautious eyes. Irritated by this and by his refusal to reply, Richard took another step down with his right foot.

"Where is De-Vere?"

The Earl of Oxford had been Henry's most experienced battle veteran, and without him, Richard doubted he would have dared to presume so far in his ambitions. King Edward had held Oxford prisoner, due to his previous Lancastrian activities. It had been yet another of his brother's mistakes which had come back to cause grief to the realm. He was another who had been allowed to escape and flee to the Tudor cause.

Henry dropped his gaze and Richard moved his eyes over to look at Lady Stanley once more. Her earlier distress had melted away and now she stared back at him boldly, her face ravaged with joint emotions of fear and hate, the jet rosary wound so tightly round her hands they now showed red weals where she had constricted the blood flow. She reminded him of another Margaret. Margaret of Anjou, queen to the old Lancastrian King Henry VI - and how she had raged at him after the battle at Tewkesbury when he told her that her only son was dead.

The same hate, the same fear, that same unspoken contempt.

He would have been ready to silence forever the woman who he held partially responsible for the death of his father and brother Edmund, but then he had seen a fragile figure standing forlornly, but defiantly, behind her. In that one look, all his emotions changed, from anger to something else...

"Your Grace?" A deferential voice brought him back to the present. Francis was at the right hand side of the steps, just below him and his words were so quiet they could hardly be heard. The hall had a hushed reverence about it, no one dare utter a word and everyone was looking at their king who was momentarily lost in thought. So many memories he wished he could escape from, just for a while.

He turned his back on Tudor to recover himself, walking back up the steps only to have his gaze alight on the empty chair, the unworn crown. His right arm began to ache, the old muscle memory from Barnet, Tewkesbury. and the north. But his memories were cutting much deeper than swords today.

"Well?" The sudden power in his voice rebounded off the walls of the chamber as he turned back to face them all. Francis saw several people start in surprise and he smiled at the unexpected reversal of Richard's mood. Tudor flinched as if struck.

"I know not, Your Grace. He was in the field, I... did not see him after that. I have not seen him." He was nervous, taking in the furious set of Richard's jaw, the steely glint flashing from beneath his lowered lids. "Nor have I heard from him since that day." A ghastly smile spread across Richard's features.

"Of course not! He was fighting manfully against one of the greatest nobles in the land, whilst you were cowering behind your guard!"

The anger in the pale eyes flashed again and it did not go unnoticed. This was a dangerous man, Richard realised, maybe not particularly skilled in battle, but those eyes held back a multitude of secrets and made him no less a threat for that.

"I am not a coward, Your Grace," Henry answered levelly, with a smattering of indignance, but still he looked down at the floor all the same, to shield what he did not want seen.

"Then tell me this," Richard continued in a low voice, leaning down slightly towards his prisoner, to press home his next words. "Tell me how it felt to be just a pawn in the games played by others. A grown man, a scion of the House of Lancaster, merely a dice to be thrown to see how it fell!"

Tudor raised his eyes quizzically, the anger fled, or more likely cautiously masked.

"Your Grace - I was no man's pawn!" The air in the chamber seemed to thicken, dulling the rays which still filtered through, dancing across the scene.

"No?" Richard raised his eyebrows and looked down at him in feigned surprise. "But you owned no actions that were truly yours. You were the focus of the ambitions of your mother and uncle, were you not, aided by the French who so disgracefully abandon treaties on a whim? You raised no armies yourself, instilled no dignity, inspired no loyalty and displayed no honour. You were moved from place to place. Positioned. Told what to do and when. You were a mere chess piece. Your fate was in the decisions, in the game and play of others." Richard paused again and looked over the assembled faces. "And as you may have guessed by now, I am very skilled in the game of chess." He paused then, resting his hand on the hilt of his sword. "Sir Robert!"

The guard escort fell in beside the dais with a scrape of metal against stone as Rob stepped forward once more and bowed to his king.

"Take our… guest… to the Beauchamp Tower. Guard him well. My instructions will follow when I have considered how best to deploy the board, which I will do at my leisure." The two guards motioned a bewildered Henry Tudor to stand. Grabbing his arms, they turned him to face the great doors and before a silent crowd, escorted him out of the chamber.

Rob and Richard Ratcliffe bowed deeply. Rob's eyes quickly sought out Francis, who gave a sharp shake of the head, and the two knights followed their charge, heels marking time across the stone. They had been anticipating more than this. Where was the trial? The man was guilty of treason and execution was the only way to deal with him, not incarceration. No court in the land would find him innocent of his crimes, and rightly so.

Richard turned his back on the room, overcome by weariness as his strength began to falter. He moved back and leaned lightly on his dead wife's throne, the sudden depletion of his energy forcing him to cut short the audience abruptly. Not that there was much more to be said. The man would undoubtedly have to stand trial, but he still had a further use, which for the moment meant he could not pass any sentence upon him.

The crowds began to filter from the chamber now the spectacle was over, if ending somewhat unsatisfactorily and Richard could hear the discreet murmurings as each one remarked on what they had just witnessed. His head throbbed and his throat was dry, the heat in the chamber was almost stifling. He wanted to turn around and fully regard the impact of events on the Stanleys, but found he had no taste for it. There was a movement at his side and a hand laid upon his sleeve.

"Dickon?" Francis said very quietly, dispensing all royal formality as he knew only a close friend could do. Richard raised his eyes to his friend and Francis was shocked to see the effect that the audience had on him. The ravages of the past two years were painted clearly on his face, shone dolefully out of his eyes. "You must rest. I know you find sleep difficult but we have much to do over the coming weeks. Please – for me – retire to your chamber for some respite, just for a while. I will bring some wine and food there so you can remain undisturbed."

At this last, Richard's lips gave a sardonic twist.

"Undisturbed." He appeared to weigh the word carefully. "How I long for that most unachievable of states. Rest eludes me, dear friend. God help me, but I thought winning our last battle would ease this strife. It would appear this is not to be."

Francis swallowed hard before continuing, sensing an opportunity.

"Do you think this is helping?"

Richard looked up at him questioning, as he nodded his head towards the throne occupied by its delicate, gleaming crown. He exhaled heavily but straightened a little, appearing to rally somewhat.

"At the moment it is. I do think, Francis, that I would not have been able to stand in front of Tudor today, if I had not felt her strength behind me. She did not appear valiant in body, but her spirit was something to behold!"

His friend nodded sadly.

"I remember."

Richard turned back and seated himself on the throne, as he did so, he ran his left hand down his right arm slowly, and back up again, almost unconsciously. Francis frowned.

"Does that pain you? Let me call Hobbes."

Richard shook his head, firmly.

"It was aggravated in the field. It will settle. Francis – I..."

Both men were disturbed then by movement towards the back of the chamber. The room was empty of all company bar two guards draped in their murrey and blue Yorkist livery, standing by the door. Or so they thought. A shadow moved by one of the door pillars halfway down the hall and knowing that the room had gone silent, Bess stepped out from her hiding place, into the sunlight.

"Bess!" Richard sighed as he watched her walk slowly forwards towards him. "I didn't know you were here today." He felt Francis stiffen at his side as he spoke.

White faced, the young girl came to a halt at the bottom step and gave the most graceful of curtseys. For some reason she was garbed in the dark blue of mourning and the velvet train of her dress fanned out behind her on the sun dappled floor. She wore a simple gold chain around her neck and the pendant glimmered in the refracted light. Richard recognised it as the Sunne in Splendour emblem and knew that this had been a name day gift from her father a few years ago, as he had been present when the girl had received it with much delight.

As she raised up from her homage, her eyes locked onto her uncle's face in silent pleading. Richard turned to Francis and laid his own hand on his friend's arm. Francis caught the glimmer of the coronation ring in that one movement and thought briefly how many burdens that trinket had brought with it. Secretly, he yearned for the time when his friend's hand was unadorned and his mind and conscience free of the doubts and cares kingship had afforded him. But now his king was speaking.

"...kindly leave us for a while. I will gladly take your offer of refreshment in my chamber if you would arrange it."

Francis bowed deeply in response and placed his hand momentarily over the hand that wore the burdensome jewel. Turning quickly and with the most cursory of glances at Bess, he left the chamber through a side door which led to the royal apartments.

Richard regarded Bess fondly and suddenly felt a great wash of relief sweep over him, although he couldn't for the life of him work out why. Smiling down at her, he raised his hands and lifted the crown from his head as he stood up. Placing it on the seat he had just vacated, he moved down and extended his hand to his niece. Without any sound, she placed her hand in his, and allowed him to draw her down to sit on the steps with him, her velvet gown billowing in folds around her.

He heaved a tremendous sigh, expelling the tensions of the day and then raised his eyes to look into hers. Her father's eyes. Richard gave her a sad and reflective smile, but Bess was relieved to see it was the smile of the uncle she thought she had lost and not that of her troubled king.

"So," he said quietly, and even managing a rueful grin, "what did you think of your betrothed?"

Bess folded both her hands in the lap of her gown.

"You are teasing me?" she asked carefully.

The sad smile played around his lips.

"A little."

Bess looked to one side, appearing to gaze out into the glorious day.

"You have annulled the betrothal? I have never asked and my mother... " her voice trailed off.

"I have. It was one of my very first acts."

"Uncle..." she began hesitantly, then remembered herself and looked up in trepidation at having uttered the familiarity. When he did not respond unfavourably, she continued. "What will you do with him?"

Stretching back against the steps, Richard considered the question carefully as if he had given it no thought at all before she asked. He decided on an honest answer.

"I don't know. All I do know is I cannot allow any further uprisings to take place in his name. He has committed treason, so there will have to be a trial."

She reached over and touched his hand.

"But it is as you said, there is no-one left to rally to his cause. He is a spent force and his claim to the throne was ever weak which is why..."

"He needed you," Richard finished succinctly, looking at her fair face directly.

Of a sudden, as if discomforted by the subject of their discourse, Bess shifted her position and kicked her feet out in front of her as she was wont to do as a small child, her lips forming a sullen pout.

"I wish my father was here!" The response from Richard was not what she had at all expected.

"So do I!"

She cocked her bright head at him, squinting at the sunlight which still poured in through the windows.

"But, then you would not be king."

Richard looked at her once again and smiled sadly.

"My answer remains the same. So do I," he repeated very slowly.

They looked at each other in the hush of the chamber, both silently accepting their loss and its attendant sadness. Suddenly and totally unexpectedly, Bess launched herself at her uncle and enveloped him in her arms, resting her head on the dark fabric of his doublet before he could respond. Taken by surprise, Richard recovered himself quickly and placed his arms around his niece gently. Then, in acknowledgement the shared succour they could give each other, their grips tightened, but without passion, just the simple sharing of comfort and support.

She felt the rise and fall of his breathing and he in turn could see the crystal tears lining her golden lashes. Both faces were in lost in repose and memories long dead as they offered each other the gratification of their warmth in the present. He inhaled the rosewater in her hair and she could smell fine, fragrant soap, the orris root on his clothes.

As uncle and niece they took each other back in time, without words, as Bess remembered falling asleep in her uncle of Gloucester's lap when she was very young. She recalled loving how dark he was, when all other members of her family were so fair. It marked him out for special attention from her and she had always been fascinated by his eyes, which would change colour with his moods. She had liked the way he smiled whenever her father entered the room.

Or so it appeared to her as a five-year-old.

Their shared reverie was broken by activity at the door. There were voices and footsteps in the outer chamber. Another liveried guard approached from the side door and stopped as Richard looked up at him, for a second thinking that this innocent embrace may be reported back to others as something more than it was. Until he saw the face of the man before him. He knew him. A man of the north.

"Your Grace," the soldier bowed his head. "Lord Stanley is without and seeks an audience."

Bess looked up at her uncle beseechingly, her face shedding her adult years, making her a child once more. He smiled down at her, his first genuine smile in weeks, he felt.

"Thank you, John. Tell my Lord Stanley that I am presently engaged but will receive him in my privy chamber at the hour's turn."

The guard nodded, hiding his own pleasure that the king had remembered his name, turning to leave the chamber and relay the message to the impatient lord pacing fretfully without. It would give him great

72

satisfaction to turn him away.

The chamber was silent once again. Bess moved closer into Richard's safe embrace and she felt him take a deeper breath.

"Uncle Richard, what happens to us all now? What will we do?"

Richard raised his hand to stroke her golden hair and looked over at the jewelled crown which used to adorn his wife's head. He could still picture her face below the jewels, the mixture of joy and anticipation that exuded from her the first time it was fitted to her head. So bright! She had shone, brighter than the crown itself.

"We go on," he said simply, telling his heart what it did not wish to hear.

8. THE WHITE TOWER, LONDON
September 1485

Gathered around a large table within the White Tower Council Chamber, John Howard, Duke of Norfolk and Henry Percy, Earl of Northumberland were taking great pains to prevent any eye contact whatsoever. When it became unavoidable, they sullenly resorted to glaring at each other with open hostility.

It did absolutely nothing to improve the atmosphere within the room which brought its own echoes of meetings gone by. No one was speaking, leaving the hammering of the rain against the windows as the only sound between the group of men who sat lost in their own private thoughts. Even the ravens had been subdued into silence by the foul weather, adding not a single cawing sound as the backdrop to what was about to take place.

For his part, Norfolk still held a great deal of resentment against Northumberland for his late appearance onto the field at Redemore. Yes, he had openly told the king that he purposely held back to watch Stanley's intent and he did finally join the fray once Stanley committed on the king's side. Only in loyal Howard's eyes, that was no certain way to show affinity to your sovereign and he had no problems in making his opinions clear. For years, Northumberland had made no secret of his own feelings regarding Richard's popularity in the northern marches. It was a popularity which had outshone his own and which Norfolk felt gave more cause to his late response last month than any regard for the vagaries of Stanley loyalty. Also, he didn't like to dwell on what would have happened if Stanley had played his cards differently. Or what Northumberland would have done then.

He himself had been hard pressed at the time of Northumberland's intervention and felt lucky to still be alive and sitting on this council at all. His forces had come close to buckling under the constant onslaught of the Earl of Oxford, Tudor's most experienced commander. Many good men, those who had served him for many a year, had fallen due to the lord's late entrance into the melee. For that alone, he had little time for either Stanley or Northumberland, who he considered should have committed their forces from the first, in accordance with the fealty they had sworn. Instead, they chose to sit on the periphery of the field like craven cowards until they could guarantee their own salvation. That he often made these views abundantly clear did nothing for the harmony of the council chamber.

Northumberland himself was not at all happy to be part of this particular gathering and drummed his fingers impatiently on the table, cutting through the tense silence in a way that only increased everyone's anxiety. Richard was currently on his way to Sheriff Hutton, to attend a session of the Council of the North. He had ridden out in support of John, Earl of Lincoln, who, as well as being Richard's heir was also head of the council.

As patriarch of the Percy family, Northumberland was also a member of that same council, which had been founded by Richard and carried out much the same duties in the north as Westminster did for the south. Richard, however, had requested the earl's presence at this particular council meeting instead, and as usual with any commands issued directly by Richard, Northumberland judged sourly that his time could be better used elsewhere. He was making no attempt to hide his resentment at being told to remain in the south.

Francis was standing uneasily behind his own chair, gripping the carved back until his knuckles turned white, an outward indication of his own tension. He surveyed these two elder statesmen, both of whom were vital to the success of the king's government, well aware of the enmity between them. He knew that a wealth of long suppressed anger and emotions would be very easily aroused if he were not extremely careful today and that would be a total disaster for what Richard was now trying to achieve.

He was pleased the king had taken time to go north and although the main reason for his visit was to support his heir in the council, it would also give Richard some time free of the oppressive court atmosphere, one which he had never taken much pleasure in. He was much more relaxed and at his ease in the north, he found it easy to rule and to govern the people fairly. He is approach was direct and forthright, which suited the character of the local commons.

That was much more difficult task when wading, thigh-high, through the political stews which boiled and fermented in London. Even the very chamber they sat in held dark memories from two years ago. It was in this very room that the plot to end Richard's protectorship had come to light. The plot which had resulted in Sir William Hastings losing his head.

Francis looked around the chamber. It was as if those evil portents had soaked into the very stone and he gave an involuntary shudder. Richard had taken Dick Ratcliffe with him, along with his illegitimate son John, daughter Kathryn, and the Earl of Huntingdon, her husband. The two bastard children were now permanent fixtures at court and in some ways this made Francis equally nervous, although he was not quite ready to admit why. For some reason he had expected them to either remain at Sheriff Hutton where they had been lodged at the time of Tudor's invasion, or in the case of his daughter, to return to Wales with her husband. He wondered if Richard was surrounding himself with children to recreate the basis of his informal court as it had been before he became king.

Or perhaps young John just made up for the fact that Richard still missed his legitimate son, Edward, who had never made it to London in the end. After his wondrous investiture as Prince of Wales in the stunning splendour of the minster at York, Edward had returned to Middleham with his mother. Seven months later, he was dead. Snatched away by one of the prurient fevers which had been a constant feature of his short life. Neither Richard or Anne had been with him, both tied down with the bonds of royalty. It was something that neither of them would ever forgive themselves for.

Bishops Russell and Stillington also sat waiting patiently at the table and began murmuring to each other in hushed tones. William Catesby, the king's lawyer and Speaker of the House was also present, regarding the scene before him, steepling his fingers together as he looked over the table with rueful amusement. Everyone was waiting for Francis to commence proceedings, but in the meantime Catesby appeared to be paying particular interest to Bishop Stillington, watching him studiously with his hooded gaze.

Suddenly the door swung open and Rob Percy strolled in, his head bowed, engrossed in a parchment which held in his hand. Belatedly becoming aware of the silence in the room he looked up, grinned amiably at those around the table and crossed to the sideboard to fill himself a cup. Rob may have been the Comptoller of Richard's household, but that elevation had made absolutely no difference to his attitude or indeed his bearing. He would have known full well that the room was full of prickly, irritable nobles, and the fact that they were having to wait for him would have appealed to his sense of humour.

Francis gave his friend a small appreciative nod as he felt his late entrance had brought in a slight thaw to the emotional temperature. Which was exactly the effect he had anticipated.

"My Lords," Rob smiled in greeting as he watched Francis take his seat next to Northumberland, and he crossed the room to sit opposite him. No one responded, Norfolk gave a small grunt and swirled round the contents of his own cup as the candles guttered in the sudden breeze brought in through the open door. A page ran in behind Rob and threw fresh logs on the fire, disappearing just as quickly, no doubt not wanting to linger in a room which was almost airless with unspoken grievances. The sound of the door closing gave Francis the cue he needed.

"Gentlemen," he began in the most authoritative of tones, his voice remarkably steady considering his level of anxiety. "I believe it would be well if we could set ourselves in accord over certain matters relating to recent affairs."

"Are we talking about Tudor lad?" Norfolk's tone was blunt but cordial, although he did not look up from his cup. Francis opened his mouth to reply but was too slow. Northumberland had been waiting to pounce.

"My understanding was that it is the king's marriage under discussion. Or else why would *he* be here!" Northumberland growled disconsolately, gesturing at Rob who raised his brows in mock surprise. "I did not believe we would be discussing Tudor without the king himself being present. We surely need to pick up negotiations with Portugal since these were interrupted by the invasion, but were well progressed. In fact, if I may express an opinion, I feel that the king should be here discussing both of these matters himself or even visiting his prospective bride inside of currying more favour for himself in the north. He doesn't need to do it, he has well enough influence there. It's other matters he should be attending to now. The north needs no persuading. The south, however…"

Rob put down the cup he had been using to screen the amusement he found difficult to contain in front of these serious elder statesmen. Not usually a member of Richard's council, he had been requested to attend at his king's behest. He wasn't completely sure why, but it was not his place to question his king. He addressed Northumberland pleasantly.

"Kinsman, the aldermen of York did request the king to visit and celebrate his victory in the field. He felt in some measure obliged to fulfil the request. You are a member of that council, so I am sure you are more than aware of this? He would not offend the citizens of York, who sent – and lost – good men at Redemore, by a refusal."

Northumberland's eyes flashed a dangerous message in answer. Both Francis and Rob knew that he had little regard for them and other members of the king's closest retinue, in fact most of the men who had formed their bonds with Richard during his dukedom. They, along with Dick, Will, Ralph Assheton, John Pilkington and a few others were now the king's closest advisors, many of them having proved their loyalty either during their formative years or later in service at Middleham. Some were not part of the old nobility of the land and it was that very fact which allowed Richard to invest his trust in them, and at the same time for Northumberland to express his distaste.

Richard had been proven in this trust over the past months. It was his closest body men who had proved their worth time and again in both word and deed. They who had charged with him across the Leicestershire plain towards Tudor's bodyguards without question or hesitation – knowing they would all be killed if Stanley chose to engage for Tudor. Most of the elder statesmen from noble families, Norfolk excluded, had let him down in one way or another, some had even defected to Tudor and Richard was using the people he trusted most to stabilise his position once again.

Bishop Russell, Richard's Chancellor, coughed politely behind a weathered and age spotted hand

"A swift solution to the king's marriage would certainly be of great benefit. We know the death of Louis in France has changed the perception of how England should be treated with, but the country cannot stand another war. At the moment their eyes are looking elsewhere as they squabble over the child who has inherited the crown. We must take advantage of this distraction. After all, they all but tore up the Treaty of Picquigny publicly..."

Norfolk's gruff voice stopped the Chancellor's dulcet tones.

"Aye, well the king saw that one coming a long time ago. Edward was a fool there. Good God, Louis was even plotting with George!"

Northumberland sighed, rolling his eyes heavenwards before he shot Norfolk a contemptuous look.

"Yes, yes, we all know how the then duke was the only one to warn what Louis would do with the treaty. That's done and gone. We will need to enter into some form of negotiations with France when the situation has resolved itself. Do we even know the king's thoughts on this?" His eyes fixed on the anxious face next to him.

Francis reluctantly had to admit to himself that he did not. Only he wasn't about to voice that in this council, so let the question go unanswered and reverted quickly back to the original subject.

"What I can relay to you is that the king is... willing to pick up negotiations for the hand of Joanna of Portugal, if no other suitable match be available. He feels we should send an ambassador to re-open proceedings and this should be done immediately."

If anyone picked up on the slight hesitation in this declaration, no one remarked upon it. There were solemn nods and mumblings around the table, only Francis and Rob remained still and quiet.

"I agree!" Northumberland said suddenly, his mood brightening as he appeared to warm to his subject. "It will also stop those other rumours from resurfacing. Edward's eldest daughter still spends far too much time at court for my liking. That caused enough trouble earlier this year. She should be shipped off to her mother now that she has been granted Grafton. The pair of them are a constant reminder of those unfortunate boys."

The silence in the room was deafening as the words fell into the air like rocks down a well. Francis could hear his heart beating in his ears.

"Unfortunate is a strange phrase," This was Will, quietly spoken as usual for one who could bellow with the best of them in his role as Speaker of the House. His normal tone was much less strident and always came as a surprise. No one else appeared comfortable speaking about Edward's sons.

However, Northumberland was enjoying himself. It was writ plain all over his face and he wasn't about to stop.

"I would certainly call an early death unfortunate. Are we all going to sit around this table and try to convince ourselves otherwise? We may not know who did the deed but surely we can agree that those two boys are dead."

"Percy – we have been here before," said Norfolk impatiently, trying hard to control the anger in his voice. "All evidence points to Buckingham, who is now the lack of a head for it. As to where the bodies are buried if, hear me clear, if they are dead, God only knows! The biggest fear is that someone took them and is holding them ready to try to take back the throne when they come of age – but who? Where would they be? Who could have taken them? I know this concerns the king greatly as he nurtures some vain hope that they are still alive. They were his brother's children after all."

"I again use the word unfortunate," mused Northumberland thoughtfully. "However, perhaps we move too hastily and should think more on this. There would be much to be gained if they could be proven to be dead. Why go abroad for a foreign match when we have some of our very own royal bloodline at court?"

William Catesby turned around in his chair to look Northumberland directly in the eye. His face was a mask of incredulity and disbelief.

"Are you now saying what I think you are saying? Not five minutes ago you were consigning the girl to a life in a country manor well away from court, now you are proposing her as a future queen?"

Northumberland nodded imperceptibly, keeping his eyes studiously averted from anyone else around the table.

"I am reconsidering!" he announced blithely, then rose from his chair and took himself over to the sideboard. He picked up the wine flagon and began to pour without expanding on the reason for his sudden change of heart.

There was an audible grunt of dissent from across the room.

"You have not only been watching the Stanleys, I think you have been taking lessons in dissembling from them." Norfolk murmured in disgust. Northumberland shot him a loaded glare but ignored his words. Rob and Francis exchanged cautious glances as Northumberland turned to face the room, leaning back against the edge of the table. He fixed his eyes on Francis who bit the inside of his cheek, waiting for what was coming next.

"We should declare the Princes dead. If we do that it changes the whole landscape considerably. We could then obtain a naturalisation for the rest of Edward's other children – they are all girls are they not? That would give us some royal blood to offer out for further marriages to Spain, France and Portugal. The king could then..."

"Really?" Rob Percy's tone was sharply scathing as he cut across the Earl's words. "With the greatest respect my lord, are you seriously now suggesting that the king take political and ecumenical actions to marry his niece? A slander he had already been forced to declare publicly as a falsehood?"

Northumberland remained impassive at the sideboard and surveyed them all over his cup.

"A neat solution I think. No one believed that farce at Clerkenwell, so it would come as no surprise. Time is passing gentlemen and the stability of the realm has implications for all of us. I have no doubt that Richard can gain the trust of the south, this may help considerably. It's what he did in York – which was never a Yorkist stronghold and to which I can personally attest." He took a deep draught from his cup. "So. Declare the boys dead, blame

Buckingham if you will, and seek a dispensation, which will naturally be granted. Seems perfectly reasonable to me. As long as the deaths of the boys are not laid at the king's door."

Stillington began to moisten his lips nervously, his watery blue eyes round with concern.

"But are we then not justifying all the rumour and slander which has surrounded the king for most of the past two years?"

Northumberland gave an expansive shrug.

"The board has changed. With Tudor in custody, the Lancastrian threat expunged, Edwards's sons dead - we are dealing with certainties. Royal bastards have been legitimised before. Jesu, that's what gave that Tudor brat the right to invade! Bearing in mind what we have had to wade through the past few months, a little more dissention can be managed surely. If the result be worth the trouble?"

Will leaned forwards across the table, his eyes sweeping the room.

"But, my lord, the death of the boys is not a certainty. Unless someone in this room knows more than the king?"

"Well, if they are alive, where are they?" the elder man retorted sharply. "How did they leave the Tower? Who could have performed such a feat? No, my Lords, those boys are dead. Be it by order or by a mistaken sense of loyalty, they are dead. We just need to accept that, make it clearly known and move on."

Chancellor Russell's busy grey brows reached up to the brim of his hat. "My lord, surely you are not suggesting the king had any part in this?"

Northumberland slammed his cup down loudly and the reverberation echoed around the walls, causing Francis to sit back, startled.

"That would be treason! You think me stupid enough to utter treason in a council meeting? And here of all places? That is somewhere else we have been before! No. I say only that there are - were - those with sufficient affinity to the king to try to resolve a difficult issue for him. He may even suspect this himself."

"If he does," Norfolk growled threateningly, " I think you will find he has distinctly refrained from discussing it with anyone. Therefore, I feel you are on the wrong track, my friend."

Northumberland spread his arms expansively, returning to his seat and slumping down heavily.

"Forgive me my lords, but we cannot dance around these delicate issues any longer. Better to air them out in the open else we shall never resolve the ill's within the realm. There's been a poison festering here for nigh on two years and it is time it was purged. You all know it, some of you are just far too sensitive in your affinity to admit it!"

Francis had said nothing for a while and kept his eyes fixed firmly on the table in front of him. He was feeling distinctly uneasy as some of these thoughts, particularly in relation to Bess, had been clouding his own mind of late, but he had not - would not - ever express them. He had seen at first hand what the disappearance of his nephews, the loss of both Edward the brother, Edward the son, then Anne - and the rumours around his niece - had done to his friend. He had, in his darker nights, considered the situation around Bess and her illegitimacy himself. But he had also considered something else. He had tentatively wondered if Richard had ever thought about taking this same action in relation to his own son and daughter, rather than the children of his dead brother.

He was thinking himself lucky that no-one appeared to have considered the same option, or if they did, they were keeping it close to their chest. To naturalise his own children would give Richard an heir, and John was a healthy boy. Strong, intelligent and favouring his father in all ways. Would this be a route more acceptable to Richard than marriage to Joanna of Portugal and less politically damaging that reversing the position of Edward's children? After all, what did that then say about the boys, about the actions taken against the young Edward?

Grudgingly, and although it left a bitter taste in his mouth, he had to admit that Northumberland was in some sense correct. None of them dare air their true thoughts to Richard at this present time.

His closest advisors, himself included, the men Northumberland resented, were indeed far too sensitive to Richard's feelings on these matters.

Deep down in his gut, Francis could not at this present time see Richard willingly replacing Anne, not even for political security, no matter what Richard himself had said. He kept his eyes veiled, avoiding both Rob and Will, even though he knew they would be desperate to gauge his reaction. His thoughts were disturbed by a polite cough.

"Whom does he feel would best represent his suit in Portugal, if we are indeed still considering that option?" Stillington's voice was steady even though he appeared quite anxious to change the subject.

Rob grinned to himself. All this talk of bastards and weddings must have Stillington almost apoplectic, but he was doing well not to show it, he thought. With his past history in secret troth plights, it certainly wouldn't be him boarding ship to Portugal. He so desperately wanted to point this out aloud and had to remind himself this was a council meeting in London, not the great hall at Middleham, where his friends would have joined in the joke.

Northumberland turned his insolent dark gaze on Francis.

"I think we should send you."

Francis was taken aback, by both the words and implications.

"Me?"

Rob smothered a splutter with a cough. He was having more and more difficulty in hiding his amusement behind his cup and had to resort to using his hand as well. Francis hadn't seen that one coming. He was planning on electing Russell to go.

Northumberland nodded energetically, his face sombre.

"Yes – you. Viscount Lovell, close friend and body man to the king. Our Lord Chamberlain and Chief Butler of England. You have known him from childhood have you not? Who better to present his suit to a prospective new bride. I would think that would meet much approval and regard, much more than sending someone from the body politic. As my esteemed Bishop said, if we have decided that an alliance with Portugal is the way to resolve this?"

He surveyed the room looking at every member of the council with the question in his voice.

Francis followed his gaze around the room in silent despair. He had a feeling the earl was deliberately making things difficult for him in the king's absence as a way of showing his resentment. He was being particularly obstructive whilst giving every impression of participating in the meeting with vigour and interest. So it came as a shock when Norfolk nodded sagely and spoke up.

"Actually that makes a lot of sense. The king has a lot of ground to make up owing to the effective campaign of slandering by the Woodvilles and Tudor. You would make a most convincing advocate. Francis."

His stomach plummeted into his boots. Taken off-guard and trying to recover, Francis toyed with the dagger hilt at his belt and then moved to twist the ring on his finger, reminiscent of actions Richard took when under stress. He could not argue with the logic, even though it had come as a surprise that he would be nominated. What he did know is that he would find it hard to pursue this suit knowing Richard's real feelings, but again he could not let that show.

"Are we, then, all in assent?" he asked nervously, and was disheartened to see the inevitable outcome, as both Rob and Will agreed, smiling at him conspiratorially.

"Let's move on then..." he said, in a distinctly resigned tone.

9. THE PALACE OF WESTMINSTER
September 1485

Francis was crossing the galleried walk above the courtyard, drawn by the noise of the king's party which had recently returned from their sojourn north. Stopping to look down, he could see Richard's horse being led into the stables amongst the melee of stable-hands and servants unpacking baggage carts and taking charge of the various mounts. He also spied the bay belonging to Dick Ratcliffe, standing alongside young John's dappled palfrey. There was a lot of other activity as several men-at-arms were unloading the goods and light weaponry which had accompanied the journey north and were always part of any progress.

He was about to move on in search of Richard when his attention was caught by an infectious peal of laughter and he looked over to the gate where he traced the joyous sound to Kathryn, Richard's illegitimate daughter. She was standing with her husband, William Herbert, Lord Huntingdon, and they appeared to be absorbed in conversation, obviously happy in each other's company. She was an attractive girl, much favouring her mother, who Francis was acquainted with. In fact, he ruminated, he was probably one of only five or so people who knew the parentage of Richard's natural children.

His dalliances before he married Anne had been few and far between, the complete opposite to how his brother had conducted his affairs. Edward had been generous in matters of the flesh and had the services of a plentiful supply of mistresses, enjoyed and sometimes shared with his closest confidantes. There were many tales of paramours shared between Edward, Will Hastings and Elizabeth Woodville's oldest son, Thomas Grey, Marquis of Dorset.

In fact, one of their shared mistresses was now married to one of Richard's lawyers, Thomas Lynom. The woman had been Edward's favourite at the time he passed away, and desperate to retain her place at court, she had slipped easily from his bed into Dorset's – with brief interludes where she had granted the pleasures of her body to Hastings. It was that woman, Jane Shore, who had been used to pass messages between Hastings, Dorset and Elizabeth, who at that time was immured in Westminster sanctuary, plotting to remove Richard from his rightful place governing the realm. Jane had duly paid her penance and was now a respectable married woman.

Richard had been much more circumspect. As with any normal man, there had been visits to brothels, the attentions of camp followers, but Francis was convinced that as soon as he wed, all such associations had become reprehensible to him. He secretly wished that he had been so blessed.

It was no small measure of comfort to him that Richard was able to have this second family close having suffered so deeply over the recent losses of both his son and wife. He felt a lump rise in his throat as although he found it difficult to think about, he knew that his friend felt himself to be cursed. He truly believed that Richard had not expected to live through Tudor's invasion, determined that he would be judged and found wanting. He knew that in his darker moments, of which he had more than his fair share, he had convinced himself that everything he had lost was due to his acquisition of the throne.

It had been difficult for a man as loyal as Richard to betray his brother's trust. It has been a seemingly ruthless decision he took to secure his family's future, yet Francis knew that in Richard's eyes, he had no choice. He had a legal, and moral duty to take the throne.

Had he ignored Stillington's unforgivably late confession, the outlook for the then Duke of Gloucester had been pretty grim. He remembered only too well how difficult the period after Edward's death had been and how for the first time since they met, their own relationship had become sorely tested. He sighed, looking down into the courtyard. So many things had happened in such a short time, they all seemed to run together into one. There had been little time to sit back, little peace. But things were different now.

As he began to turn away from the activity below, his attention was distracted further by a figure running up the stairs towards him. He could see long, dark hair dishevelled from the ride, legs taking the steps two at a time, trailed by a billowing, fustian cloak and his breath caught in his throat. He was taken back twenty years, watching the young Duke of Gloucester returning home after travelling to London with the Earl of Warwick. The young boy of royal blood, who had shown the frightened son of a Lancastrian traitor nothing but respect and friendship. He was frozen in place and time unable to breathe.

This boy was paying scant attention to anything but his haste and almost careered into Francis, just managing to skid to a halt before crashing into the Viscount and causing him bodily harm. He looked up, startled, from beneath his tousled locks, a huge grin breaking across his childish features.

"Beg pardon, Sir Francis," he gasped, breathlessly. "I was hoping to catch up with my father but Harry distracted me with his latest boasts at the quintain. I don't believe him of course, he is about as natural a horseman as Big Walt."

Francis looked down into the smiling face of John Plantagenet, Richard's other illegitimate child, acknowledging that the portly kitchen hand at Middleham was probably the unlikeliest person to ever see on horseback. Although he knew John was permanently at court now, he had not seen him in person since well before he had been taken to Sheriff Hutton where Richard had sent him during Tudor's invasion. Currently, he held the title of Captain of Calais, but had been brought back from France due to the forthcoming invasion. Richard, as yet, had not seen fit to return him to his post. The garrison was currently under the command of Sir James Tyrrell, who was another trusted man. He held the garrison in John's name, and was Francis knew he was honoured to do so.

However, he had to admit that, as ever, he was taken aback by John's startling resemblance to his father. It was like looking into the face of his twelve year old friend, only John's demeanour was much more light hearted than the serious face his father had presented to the world at the same age.

Richard had always been a solemn child, but his early years

had been forged by troublesome times, having witnessed the sacking of Ludlow, forced into exile and then finding himself fatherless on hearing about the death of his father. He was certain that this was the basis of Richard's lifelong determination to be steadfast and loyal. His eyes had witnessed so much treachery and death, only to see his beloved elder brother triumph and avenge their house. Reared to adhere to the principles of chivalry and loyalty, he had built his life around that one cause. Much good had it done him these past two years.

Dragging himself back from the past, Francis surveyed the boy fondly.

"I, too am looking for your father - I am on my way to see him now. How was your visit to York?"

The boy's grin widened.

"The council was very interesting. I would sorely like to be part of it myself one day, they do such good work, and the people of York - they love father so! The aldermen and all the city elders came out to greet him. There were banners and players and mummers and minstrels, all out in the streets and a great gathering at the Minster. People could not get close enough to him! The crowds were pushing and pressing, I thought Argentum would surely rear up in fear, but he didn't! He was as placid and patient as could be. You would have thought he had been father's horse for years and not just..." John stopped, looking suddenly troubled. His words had tumbled out in one long, breathless rush, which made his sudden halt more noticeable.

Francis laid a comforting hand on the boy's shoulder. At Middleham, Richard had often allowed John to ride round the keep on White Surrey, his powerful Syrian destrier, taking turns with young Edward. They were watched by Anne, wringing her hands nervously in the background whilst Richard was much more relaxed and displayed only a cautious amusement at her concerns. Anne had wanted them both to ride much smaller steeds, White Surrey being an instrument of war, a powerful and dangerous beast.

But John was an adventurous child and Richard had tried to

encourage Anne to bring Edward up in the same way – reminding her that he had been subject to these very same concerns as a boy. That he had been encouraged to be brave and daring, to push himself further and harder, a drive which had served him well in later battles as an adult. Francis knew that the brave animal, lost at Redemore, must hold special memories for the boy.

Before he could say anything to reassure him there was a hoarse shout from below.

"Johnnie!"

They both turned to see one of the young henchmen, Harry, in the courtyard below, gesturing frantically for John to join him.

"Tom and I are going to the tiltyard," he yelled through cupped hands, to the amusement of a group of stable-hands. "Come on!"

John looked down dubiously, torn between friendship and duty.

"Go!" Francis encouraged him. "I am sure your father will be busy for a while with court matters. I will tell him you will see him later."

John smiled broadly, his father's rarely seen smile, and made to depart.

"And John…" the boy stopped, suddenly serious, to listen. "Remind Harry he is training to be a knight, not a herald."

The boy laughed as he turned on his heel and flew back down the stairs to greet his friend and Francis continued to watch as they both disappeared into the stables, laughing at some shared joke. Suddenly, he felt a lot older than his years. Had the Earl of Warwick watched over Richard and himself in a similar way, all that time ago? He would not have been at all surprised.

Reminding himself of the task in hand, he crossed the passage quickly and headed to Richard's privy chamber. Two liveried men at arms stood by the door which was partially ajar. Francis entered the room unchallenged, but it was empty, despite the fire burning in the grate and a fresh stack of rolled documents on the table. He frowned and left the room, looking down the passage. There, coming towards him from the opposite direction he saw John

Kendall, Richard's secretary, hurrying along, his arms overflowing with even more papers.

"John?"

"Ah, Sir Francis. There you are!" he panted, peering at him with an abstracted gaze, his thoughts obviously engaged elsewhere. "His Grace is in the solar, if you would care to join him."

Francis nodded and the man continued on his way, heading directly towards the privy chamber he had just vacated. He was mildly surprised that Richard had repaired directly to his private quarters, something he had not done since Anne died. More recently, he had much preferred the austerity of the formal rooms and avoidance of memories associated with places where they had made their home, but suffered such disappointment. He could hear voices as he approached the solar and was somewhat perplexed as peals of laughter broke out just as he entered the room.

Richard was lounging in a chair, legs stretched out before the fire, still in his riding attire although divested of his cloak. He had a goblet in his hand and in Francis's eyes he looked younger and more relaxed than he had seen him in months. Some of the longstanding tension appeared to have melted away from his body. He was smiling easily and for the first time in what seemed like an age, that smile travelled past his lips and reached his eyes; a journey it had not taken for some long months.

Jack Norfolk, Dick, Rob and Will were also standing around the room and he had been so taken aback by the change in Richard's appearance that he had not realised that he himself was the subject of the general good humour in the room.

Richard now looked directly at his friend in greeting, an air of mischief twinkling in his slate blue eyes.

"Ah here he is now! My new Portuguese ambassador! I take it arrangements for your journey are well progressed?"

Rob Percy crossed the room to close the door and slapped Francis on the back. Dick and Norfolk watched in unrestrained amusement.

"Richard, you should have been there!" Rob laughed. "It was

an ambush! Our esteemed Viscount here didn't stand a chance! Northumberland took his flank! I didn't know he was that much of a strategist!"

Francis bore the joviality with good grace, crossing to the sideboard, partly giving himself time to think of a robust riposte and partly out of real need for a drink. Turning back, he raised his eyebrows laconically at the assembled party.

"Gentlemen, you have to admit. It is so unusual for Northumberland to actually engage in combat that he took us all by surprise! I wouldn't have expected him to commit to the Portuguese marriage until a ring was being placed on the fair Joanna's hand. For a change, he pinned his colours for all to see. Who amongst you suspected that of our cautious friend?" He gestured to them all with his cup in an expansive motion "I think, secretly, you were all as outflanked as myself!"

As the group dissolved into humour and spirited disagreement, Francis was watching his king closely. Richard had put his cup down, his face becoming suddenly dark. He waited for the general merriment to subside, but his earlier cheerful mood seemed to have deserted him. For a time he looked down at his hands as he spoke, twisting a ring on his smallest finger, examining it with studied, interest as if he had never seen it before.

"So the alliance was approved then?" he asked once the jokes had run their course. His voice was low and Francis could not judge from his tone how he was reacting to this knowledge.

"Eventually," murmured Rob mischievously. At that, Richard raised his eyes questioningly, addressing him directly without words.

Norfolk moved forwards to rest his hand on the back of the king's chair.

"Lad.., Your Grace," Jack paused uncomfortably, sometimes he struggled with Richard's recent accession as he had known him since childhood, but he quickly recovered himself. Richard smiled at his old friends familiarity and dismissed it, so Norfolk continued. "You need to know that there was also a proposal regarding the late king's daughter."

Richard stiffened almost imperceptibly.

"From?"

"Also Northumberland."

Richard's lips thinned visibly, and he took a drink before he replied.

"I don't think you need say anymore." He got up from his chair suddenly and turned towards them. "Thank you gentlemen for your endeavours. I must retire to my chamber and change."

It was a somewhat peremptory dismissal and one most unlike Richard, who had an easy manner with his close household. There was a moment's pause at the unexpected change of mood, but then everyone began to move out of the room, apart from both Francis and Rob, who had caught their king's marked glance and lingered.

Rob closed the door behind the departing members of the group, leaving the three of them in the room as Richard crossed to the sideboard to replenish his cup.

"So?" he began with his back turned to them, his tone difficult to read, as was his intention. His face was hidden. Richard was no master at disguising his emotions. He had always been an open book and plain to read, something Edward had used for his entertainment at times. Francis was visibly uncomfortable and felt immensely grateful when Rob stepped, in speaking plainly, as he settled himself into a chair.

"As you would expect, Northumberland feels it would be an excellent idea to naturalise Edward's children, in the same manner as the Beaufort line. Only without the bar to accession. Of course," he continued carefully when Richard neither moved or responded, "he is of the opinion that the boys are dead, by person or persons unknown. He feels that this needs to be declared publicly, both to end the speculation and facilitate a marriage that would provide an heir to the throne."

Francis swallowed hard, trying to overcome the perceived obstruction in his throat should Richard turn to him directly. They were moving into dangerous waters now, but if anyone could survive them, it was his closest childhood friends. He hoped, with everything that had taken place, Richard was still aware of that, but for one worrying moment be began to doubt it. Although they saw Richard drink from his cup, he still did not turn to face them.

Rob and Francis exchanged cautious glances, each trying to gauge how far they should go with their friend who was now their king. Richard's perception of loyalties had been severely tested and they were both more than aware that they should not try to second guess him. There was no sound in the room at all and it was this silence that made Richard finally turn to regard them both.

"The man's a dolt," he countered, his gaze level and his voice revealing his frustration. "None of us are fully cognisant of the facts concerning the boys. I only wish we were."

Rob pursed his lips thoughtfully, looking up at the ceiling.

"I have to say, Northumberland was being deliberately provocative. He knows we can't declare the boys dead if we are not sure they are," he paused, thinking hard. "He must have his own opinion that the boys disappearance means they have been murdered. He didn't say any more than that, other than it should be acknowledged and used to stabilise your position."

They saw Richard's shoulders rise and fall, as he leaned back heavily on the sideboard, his arms spread to either side of him.

"So, we announce the boys were murdered, yet not name the perpetrator, or produce evidence of what happened. That clarity will still the murmurings in the realm? To such effect, obviously, that I can then repeal the Titulus Regis and thereby remove the very act that caused them to be murdered in the first place!" He turned away from the sideboard, flinging out one of his hands to the room in disgust. "How exactly does that one play out, I pray?"

"Then there's the matter of Clerkenwell," Francis sighed heavily. "I think we just have to ignore his counsel. The man was obviously irked and took the opportunity to have some revenge at our expense. He made it clear he was not happy discussing either matter without you being present."

"Either matter?" Richard's voice rose on the question.

"Tudor." Rob said simply. The room grew quiet once more

and no-one seemed to know where to take the conversation next so Francis tried to steer them onto safer ground. Not that there was much of this around the particular subject under discussion.

"Richard, can I ask, how do you really feel about the Portuguese arrangement?"

The king responded quicker than either of them expected. He raised his eyebrows high.

"Truly?" He allowed a slight hesitation before he continued. "Numb! It is as if I am arranging a match for someone else." He walked back to the chair slowly and took up his former place by the fire. "It is expedient. I need a wife and an heir. The security of the succession must come first before any... personal inclinations I may have." He stopped, lifting his eyes from the fire to look up at them with grim determination and a certain measure of weariness. "And as you say, we have a Lancastrian pretender languishing in the Tower."

Rob spat out an inappropriate bark

"Gods! He just needs to become shorter by around a foot!"

"No!" Richard said firmly. "Not yet."

His friends both looked at him in confusion but said nothing else. The atmosphere in the room was so charged already that Francis thought he may as well unburden himself now as regret the opportunity later. This sort of discourse in private with Richard was not so easy to arrange of late. As the three of them were already circling carefully around each other to talk of sensitive subjects, matters which were not discussed in general company, he cleared his throat and moved forward to stand in front of the fire.

Once there, he momentarily lost his nerve. He could feel the flames burning the back of his legs through his hose and mentally urged himself to speak up before his clothing began to smoulder.

"Richard, Your Grace, can we speak honestly, without fear of offence, hurt or retribution?" He flicked his eyes over at Rob who was regarding him with interest, running his forefinger over his bottom lip thoughtfully

Richard looked taken aback, slightly shocked at his words and the manner in which Francis was stumbling over them.

"Of course, please!" His voice had a pleading edge which neither of them had heard before. "You are both my oldest and most trusted confidantes. You are as close to me as my brothers were! Good God! You could almost be my brothers and of late I have often wished that you had been. The realm would have been spared much trouble." This last betrayed a slight tremble in his voice. He very rarely criticised Edward. Even with recent events taken into account, his loyalty was still unshakeable. Richard continued, dark eyes imploring theirs in muted appeal "Please, for a while if you can, forget I am your king. Imagine we are back in Rob's chamber in Middleham. Talk as we did then, for how I do sorely miss those days."

Rob needed nothing else. Jumping up he crossed the room quickly and punched Richard amiably in the shoulder

"Thank the lord! Jesus, you had us worried there for a while! I can get another drink now, my throat has been so tight I feared I would suffocate before your very eyes!"

They all smiled at each other in palpable relief as the tension in the room eased. Rob passed behind the chair to quench his thirst and then drained his cup in one.

"All this politicking is thirsty work, Dickon, but I must admit the council meeting was a real revelation. How do you do it and keep some sanity?"

Richard gave a small and grudging laugh as he leant back in his chair, crossing his feet at the ankles as he stretched his legs out before the fire.

"Oh, I lost the sanity a long time ago. Hadn't you noticed? Why else would I trust a Stanley?" His easy manner travelled back ten years, to a time when their cares were much lighter, back to before the yoke of kingship had not weighed him down with the dual burdens of treachery and loss. If they tried, they could almost imagine they were back at Middleham, talking of fortifying the garrisons, planning raiding parties across the border, with Anne having retired and Edward asleep in his nursery tower.

Richard turned his attention back to Francis and leaned slightly forwards in his chair.

"You wanted to say something?"

Francis had seated himself on a small stool at the side of the hearth, drawing it away slightly from the heat of the flames. He took a deep breath and looked directly into his king's eyes.

"There is another alternative, Dickon, along the lines of naturalisation." He paused. "It has been of concern that some may have thought of it and not expressed it but no gossip has reached me. Then the encounter I had just as I came here to find you..."

Richard frowned at that, even if he had been comprehending what Francis was about to propose, he had just lost track of it. Giving Rob a quick side glance, Francis continued.

"I was nearly trampled by John, running up the stairs, in his haste to find you."

Richard's gaze moved back to the flames, once again making his expression difficult to interpret. The nervous twisting of the jewelled band on his finger resumed. Without looking at either of them, he took a long, measured breath. His voice icily cool and devoid of any emotion.

"Naturalise John and Kathryn. Is that what I understand you to be saying?"

"Yes," Francis replied simply, but assuredly. Then stayed silent. Rob filled yet another cup and moved over to hand it to Francis, with a nod and a low aside.

"I think you may need this."

"It had to be said Richard," Francis continued, holding the cup in both hands as if it were some precious possession. "I am sure you have already thought of it? But mayhap, not been able to air your fears, not having..." he swallowed uncomfortably, halted by a spasm of pain which crossed Richard's face, cruelly illuminated by the firelight. He gave a small, desolate smile.

"You are both right and wrong my friend. I have thought of it, have indeed considered it."

He stopped himself, his voice breaking slightly. Francis passed him his own cup and Richard received it without comment, sipped from it and passed it back in the silence between them. In that moment, which seemed to go on for an age, Francis reflected inwardly that he had never expected to share a cup in such a casual manner with a king. There were days when this still amazed him.

Richard resumed speaking, every word couched in sadness.

"Anne and I discussed it. Some months after Edward died and not long before Anne became ill. She, we... had been trying.." The pain became too much and he stopped and bit his bottom lip, lost in some private reflection. His hand went up to shield his eyes, fingers tentatively stroking his forehead.

"She wanted to give me another child. She tried so hard and it was so difficult for her to accept that it would never happen. It was her suggestion, before..." He stopped. Closing his eyes, he leaned back in his chair and his hand fell back down onto his thigh, limply. The gesture in itself betraying a weariness of soul that was indescribable. "She thought it was a solution. That we could still reign with John and Kathryn as our heirs. She didn't mind, in fact she had grown to love both of them, particularly John who was so close to Edward. It was she who brought it up. I still remember the evening clearly."

Francis suddenly realised exactly why this had not been discussed before.

Anne. Brave courageous Anne. Aware of her infertility and at the time probably more aware than her husband of her impending death, she had the good grace to provide him with an option to place a child of his own blood on the throne of England.

Of his blood – not hers.

He wondered if his own wife, or that of any other man, would have been so generous of spirit.

10. ST GEORGE'S CHAPEL, WINDSOR
September 1485

Bess stood, head bowed, in front of her father's tomb and let the silence envelop her like a fog.

In the solitude of the chapel, she knelt down by the black marble slab and ran her hand across it slowly, the pale gold silk of her gown forming a translucent lake on the floor behind her. It all seemed so different from her vague memories of the day of the funeral mass. The chapel itself felt larger, darker than she recalled. She fully expected her mother to turn on her in a rage when she found out that she had delayed her journey home in order to pay her respects here, as so far, the former queen had shown no interest in seeing where her husband lay. Indeed, she had not ventured far from Grafton once the king had allowed her to return to her estate under her own cognisance. Bess had to admit that since receiving the news that she could return back to her former home, she appeared to be a lot more at peace although she was steeling herself for a few pointed questions once she herself arrived back home.

Even when Bess had told her about Henry Tudor being captured and imprisoned, Elizabeth had merely raised an eyebrow and commented that "Margaret must find that very difficult," before she carried on packing her now meagre possessions, ready to leave the court for the last time.

Bess, on the other hand, was far from content. The thought of life at Grafton depressed her. She knew that she would find days on end being constantly in the company of only her mother and other sisters, even though she loved them dearly, a stifling existence. The only ray of light on the horizon was that she had heard that her younger sister Cecily would also be there, even if that had come as some surprise.

Cecily had been wed the previous year to Lord Scrope of Bolton, one of the marriage agreements Richard had pledged to arrange when he had negotiated their release from the shadowed confines of Westminster Sanctuary. Bess reflected sadly that however well intentioned their uncle was, his attempts to settle them into marriages had not been given a particularly precipitous start.

Her sister had been remarkably stoic as she had recounted the private arrangement she had brokered with her husband over the last year of their marriage. Scrope was not particularly enamoured of being wed to a bastard Woodville, no matter how young and winsome she may be. Cecily herself had not wanted the marriage either as although she found him pleasing enough, and with the added attraction that he was an important advisor to the king and a close personal friend, it was still not a match she would have chosen, given the choice. It had not escaped Bess that choice was a luxury which had been taken away from them on the day her father was lowered into the ground at her feet.

Scrope had now been sent north by Richard to attend to some matters on the council, and Cecily had pleaded to be allowed to stay with her mother for the duration of his duties. Bess laughed when reading a letter from her sister in which she admitted that she had never been so fervent in her devotions as she was now, praying several times a day that her husband was kept so busy by the king that he had little cause to venture south. That being said, she knew her reprieve would not last forever, and that she could be summoned at any day to attend him at Bolton Castle. A summons she would not be able to refuse. But for now, she was at Grafton, and for that Bess was thankful.

Bess had not seen Richard since the day Tudor was imprisoned, the day they had both finally been able to share some comfort together over the grief they shared. Those tender moments had done nothing to diminish her feelings for him, which she had long ago acknowledged were deeper than they should rightly be. Just the thought of the coming months closeted away in the countryside had only made her realise that she needed to be close to him - even if it was only to be in his presence at court. All she wanted was to be able to see him, watch him, share the odd conversation. To remind him that they could still be close, without anyone finding cause for suspicion or alarm. She needed to tell him all that and more.

She wanted so much to be welcome back at court without it being an embarrassment for him. Desperately, she even believed she could be happy for him to provide a husband for her, she thought, as long as she could still be close enough to see Richard and talk to him as an uncle. Was that possible? Was it a dream too far? Was she fooling herself? She didn't know. There was only the feeling that her whole being burned to be with him, and that it couldn't be wrong to feel this way about someone. When she thought of those moments in the Painted Chamber, when all had been so innocent and beautiful between them in their shared loss, she missed both him and her father so much her heart was fit to break.

Bess knew her mother would watch her closely, waiting for the slightest sign that her daughter carried any semblance of affection for her king. Elizabeth was unforgiving when it came to Richard, despite his kindness and concern over past months, and his willingness to turn a blind eye to how close she had skirted to danger in courting the Stanleys. She had tried, the evening of Henry Tudor's audience, to tell her how Richard seemed to regret what had happened, the longing in his voice when they both wished, in simple words, that her father was still alive.

Her mother's reaction was burned into her memory and she could see her face now, etched on her closed lids. The haughty features had tightened giving the appearance of a mask stretched across the planes of her face, the ice-blue eyes grew large and appeared to glow with a life of their own. She had pushed away the half empty plate in front of her and risen from her chair, uttering one word before leaving her daughter alone at the table.

"Liar!"

So desperate had Elizabeth been to escape from Baynard's Castle, that she had left a whole week before Bess, murmuring that she had to make the house ready, forgetting that she knew Cecily was already in residence there. It was just one sign of the widening gap between mother and daughter which had begun to turn into a chasm when Henry Tudor declared he would take Bess for his wife. Now it seemed there was no bridge which could re-unite the two sides and Bess knew that life for her at Grafton, would be unendurable.

She had to return to court.

And so, in desperation, even as she packed her chests to leave, she had hatched a plan, identified an ally, gloating inwardly as she thought of it. Guiltily her face flushed as she thought of it. Is this what her mother felt like when she plotted and schemed all those years? Had it caused such excitement and anticipation as she was now feeling? Was it a trait that Bess herself had inherited?

The slow creak of the door at the other side of the chapel disturbed her thoughts. She pressed her fingers to her lips, touched her father's gravestone and then rose to her feet, smoothing her dress down as she picked up her cloak from the floor. Walking down into the nave she saw the slight hooded figure standing just inside the doorway.

As she watched in silence, her co-conspirator raised small white hands, pale blurs in the shadows. Removing her hood, she revealed a thick, dark braid which escaped her cloak as she tilted her head to admire the high windows and vaulted ceiling, her lips parted in wonder. Bess smiled. Of course. She would not have had cause to come here before.

"Bess?" The voice was clear but tremulous as the figure moved out of the shadows and into the chapel. Bess walked forwards with a light, quick step and embraced the young girl warmly.

"Kathryn - thank you so much for coming. You managed to get an escort?"

Richard's illegitimate daughter smiled up at her cousin winningly. "William brought me, but he is sworn to secrecy! I didn't think he would agree, but I told him it was to help Papa and he said yes - as long as we can be back before dark. Before we are missed at supper."

Bess hugged her close once more. She and Kathryn had formed a close bond during their time together at Sheriff Hutton, in the dark hours when Tudor had invaded the land and marched towards a confrontation with the king. Richard had placed all the younger members of the York family together with strict instructions as to what should take place if things did not run his way in battle. Bess, along with her oldest cousin and Richard's heir, John de la Pole, the Earl of Lincoln, had taken it upon themselves to try and reassure the nervous young brood. Clustered around him, wondering what the future would bring had been gentle Edward, the Earl of Warwick, his sister Margaret, and both of Richard's illegitimate children Kathryn and John.

Bess had been very proud that her uncle had taken such pains for all of his children irrespective of their status. She had commented to her mother once about how it must mark the measure of the man himself, but Elizabeth had just looked at her with derision in her eyes and lips pressed so tight she could not make a sound. It seemed that nothing Richard could do would redeem himself in her mother's eyes...but then...

There had been two young nephews who had not been present at Sheriff Hutton and their absence had remained a constant tension. For herself, she had half expected them to suddenly arrive, sent by Richard from whichever northern stronghold they had been placed in for safety. Only they never did. The one time she had tried to engage Lincoln in conversation about her brothers, he had merely shaken his head, unable to tell her anything. Whether that was because he did not know, or could not tell her, she had no idea.

The days leading up to the battle had been difficult for all of them for varying reasons. For the boys, their lives were at risk if Tudor had somehow won the day. Edward of Warwick was a Yorkist heir, only barred from succession because of his father's attainder. He was also not so forward as the other children, having an unusually childish nature, and she feared for him most of all. Lincoln had been named as Richard's official heir after his own son Edward had died and would surely have been a target for Henry Tudor if the worst had come to pass. Being bastards, Kathryn and John were in themselves no threat. But they were still Richard's blood which would not sit easily with Tudor. As for herself .....

She had not seen Tudor in person until the guards had brought him into the presence chamber at Westminster. Not even a portrait or likeness. She had been granted to him by her mother as an enticement to declare war on the rightful king. Treated as some sort of reward... a reward that would have been collected only upon the murder of the man she loved.

Once she had seen Henry in the flesh, she knew she could never have married him and had said extra prayers for Richard's victory. Henry looked cruel, mean in a way, like a man who would not be generous of spirit. She thought this must be due to his many years in exile which had made him an old man before his time. Richard had certainly been right there. Used as a pawn, his mother's chess-piece. Moved across the board of England as it suited the whims of others. She shuddered to think of what might have been and reassured herself by hugging the surprised girl again in thanks and relief.

"What is it Bess? Why did you need to see me? Is ought wrong?" Kathryn was whispering and searched Bess's face questioningly with worried eyes.

"Kathryn, I need your help." Bess grabbed the girl by the arms and looked directly into her eyes. "I will go mad walled up in Grafton! I must come back to court but I don't know how to make it happen!"

Kathryn beamed, her dark eyes catching the candlelight.

"Of course you must! We could be together and go hawking and riding and John would love it! I am sure father would not mind if you did not go."

"That's just it, Kate. Your father thinks I should be with my mother, but she does not need me there now that my sister has come home. I want to stay with all my cousins, as we were at Sheriff Hutton. I want to be with you, and Ned, and Margaret and the others. You are my family now. Can you help me?"

The young girl furrowed her brow in consternation. For a moment Bess saw a ghost of Richard in that expression and her heart warmed.

"Can you not come now? You have your horse outside. We can send your men on to Grafton and you can come back with William and I!"

How innocent, Bess thought sadly, looking at her expectant face, trying to recall when she would have been the same. She had to remember that this girl was only fourteen and very young for her age. It was what made her so utterly charming. She had not been raised in the rarefied atmosphere of court where childhood disappeared early. It made for refreshing company, which made her departure all the more devastating. Bess sighed, sadly.

"I don't know Kathryn. I don't know if the king will let me come back. I need his permission to return first. I cannot just turn up and expect him to welcome me, after all, I have no place at court now. All of my family will be at Grafton."

The girl looked more puzzled for a second, the candlelight flaring in her eyes as they grew troubled.

"Is this because of your Mama?" Then she shook her head, dismissing her thoughts. "But he has forgiven her hasn't he? She was able to return home."

Despite the urgency she felt welling inside her, Bess tried to remain patient and calm. She needed Kathryn to totally understand, she only had this one chance. If this did not work, she was lost.

"It is very difficult to explain, but... I wondered if you could deliver this for me." Carefully, she drew a small parchment out of her cloak pocket and passed it over to the girl. Kathryn looked at the letter for a few moments, then up at her cousin's anxious face.

"For Papa?"

Bess nodded encouragingly, her eyes earnest.

"To him, and him only, and from your hands. Don't give it to John Kendall or Lord Lovell or anyone else. It must come from you Kathryn."

Kathryn took the letter as if it were a most precious burden

108

and dutifully placed it in the pocket of her own cloak, patting it down.

"I will. I will as soon as I see him next. He will be at supper..."

"No!" Bess exclaimed suddenly, then hesitated when she saw the shock on Kathryn's face. "I mean, I need you to be on your own with him when he reads it."

"Why?"

Bess swallowed with difficulty and tried to smile.

"Because I think that he will ask you about what is in the letter and I think he will not be able to deny you anything."

For a second Kathryn looked troubled.

"But I don't know what is in the letter."

"It doesn't matter. He will still want to talk to you about it, I am sure."

Kathryn continued to look perplexed for a short time, then brightened as a consequence of her secret errand occurred to her.

"You could be with us for Christmas! Wouldn't that be wonderful?"

Bess closed her eyes for a second and thought of last Christmas. The sights, scents and sounds of a yuletide court assailed her senses as if she once more stood in the Great Hall herself. The stones of the chapel faded out to be replaced by the walls of the palace. Pine boughs decked the hall with green finery and the windows blazed with the reflected light of a thousand candles as the yule log burned with a ferocity to frighten away the cold outside. Richard, resplendent in damson and blue velvet, his dark hair falling onto his shoulders, as he walked amongst the assembled throng.

Wearing his gold collar, smiling, welcoming, offering his hand, but with his eyes ever watchful. Anne being so ill, coughing, covering her mouth with her kerchief, each breath a labour of love for her husband, her smile bright, eyes fevered and her face flushed. Dear Anne, encouraging Richard to dance with his niece, calling her up to the dais and laughing over the dresses they had both had made from the same bolt of silk. Anne, finally, reluctantly, agreeing to retire, clinging on to Richard's hand like her life depended on it -

which it did.

And all the time the music from lyre, tabor and shawm trilled around the walls, the food platters came in loaded and went out bearing scraps, the ladies danced and twirled in their velvets and jewels, radiantly coloured like light through stained glass. And Richard, and Anne...

Tears came unbidden to Bess's eyes and the candlelight fractured into a million prisms, filling the chapel with light. Once again she enveloped the girl in a tight hug in an effort to hide the tears that were about to fall as well as to show affection.

"Yes " she murmured, a tear tracking slowly down her cheek. "Wonderful!"

11. THE PALACE OF WESTMINSTER
October 1485

John trudged into the bailey feeling particularly disgruntled and annoyed. He was still smarting from embarrassment after a morning at the quintain. His horse had fumbled its footing for a second, causing him to lose focus and he had been whacked on the head by the stuffed, straw head of his "enemy" as it whirled round at great speed behind him. He had been unceremoniously dumped on the ground, much to the joviality of his fellow squires and the anger of the Master of Henchmen. Sore headed, he was just wondering if he should go and seek out his young cousin Warwick, who always usually managed to cheer him up, when the sound of voices raised in anger made him look up to the top of the stairs leading to the Great Hall.

It was the sound of an argument in full flow and although he had not been able to recognise the voices, he was shocked to see his father in some sort of confrontation with his Chamberlain, Lord Lovell. Because of the usual day to day bustle of life in the courtyard, the words being spoken could not clearly be made out from where he stood, but he could tell by the tone of the words that there was trouble afoot.

Straining, his attention caught by a certain set to his father's shoulders, he thought he heard Francis shout. *"We have no choice!"* at one point as his father turned his back on him and hurried down the stairs, but he could not be completely sure. One thing was very clear, the tension between the two of them was unmistakeable.

He had trouble in seeing their faces very clearly from where he stood, but from the way they were positioned on the stairs, there was definitely something amiss and whatever had transpired was leading to a very public display. This was remarkable in the fact that his father was usually so private in his affairs, and in particular that his close friendship with Viscount Lovell was well known. He could not recall them ever sharing a cross word, but at this moment, his father was wearing a heavy riding cloak and looked to be on the verge of leaving the palace, his whole demeanour betraying his eagerness to be gone.

Francis spoke again, something about Burgundy, and whatever it was he said had an immediate effect. His father stopped suddenly halfway down the stairs, taken totally by surprise by whatever turn the conversation had made. His face white with fury, Richard twisted back to glare angrily at his friend and moved so quickly that he had to put a gloved hand on the wall to steady himself.

John began to move a little closer, trying to ignore the small groups of servants who had also slowed down on their way about their chores to watch the startling tableau on the steps unfold. He saw his father answer Francis, turning back and moving up a stair or two, speaking to him in a voice much lowered so that only the timbre could be heard - not the words. Whatever it was he said, John hoped that his father never, ever had cause to speak to him in that way, particularly when wearing that expression, which John could now clearly see. Something there began to make his stomach twist uncomfortably.

Francis was not at all appeased by what had been said and held out both his hands in supplication. At that point, his father seemed to hesitate between continuing down the stairs and retuning back up to the private apartments. Alerted by his hesitation, Francis spoke again, and then was joined at the top of the stairs by another noble, John, Earl of Lincoln, who also looked very grim.

Lincoln was very pleasant company and being the son of King Richard's sister, he was also John's cousin. He usually smiled a lot and had a very easygoing manner. The two of them had become well acquainted as they spent time at Sheriff Hutton whilst the invasion had taken place. Lincoln had been most unhappy that he had not been allowed to fight in the battle, but he had played with the young Earl of Warwick, trying to teach him how to play chess. Even though the boy had soon lost interest and didn't remember any of the rules, Lincoln hadn't got angry with him at all, so it was unlike him to look so anxious.

John had to admit that at times he felt more than a little

confused about his cousin and namesake. He didn't quite understand why a nephew could be his father's heir, but he himself couldn't, and him the king's son! His only son, since poor Edward had died. He knew that his mother had not been married to his father, but to him it seemed so stupid that something like that should make a difference. He understood only that he was of his father's blood, and that gave him a closer relationship to his father than his cousin, no matter how much he liked him.

He had been born before his father married Lady Anne and she had treated him no less than her own son Edward. John's throat constricted painfully on the thought. He dearly missed his young half-brother, more than he could ever tell anyone. And the Lady Anne too, who had followed her young son into the grave. Only Bess knew how he felt. She had listened as they had talked about Edward during one of the long, anxious nights in Yorkshire. She had talked of her own brothers too, how she missed them but knew they were somewhere safe. John swallowed with difficulty as he remembered her words.

He had heard what was whispered in some dark places within the city. It was vile and cruel, and spoken by those who had never met the king. John looked at his father's still figure, standing on the stairway. If only Anne and Edward were here now, his father may not be so unhappy. John missed both of them badly. When they died it had been as if he had lost his real mother and brother, but he refused to let it show. He had to be brave. His father would expect no less.

All these thoughts whirred round in his mind. The scene on the stairs was disturbing him, and he wished more than ever that Lady Anne was here, to step in and guide his father away with her gentle touch. As he watched, whatever was going on appeared to reach an impasse as his father lowered his head and strode back up the steps, retracing his path slowly. He disappeared from view then, followed by Francis, Lincoln, and John thought he saw the bearded form of Lord Stanley at the top of the stairs. He wrinkled his nose.

Something about that particular lord made him feel uneasy.

He had a strange way of looking at people, like he hadn't made his mind up if he liked you or not. Even with people he knew well. John looked down at his boots and scuffed the cobbles sulkily. If only he could spend as much time with his father as these men seemed to. He thought he most certainly would have to if he was named as the king's heir. He would need to know everything that was happening in the realm. Like his cousin Lincoln did on the Council of the North. It didn't seem fair.

A sharp nudge in his back brought him back to earth and he whirled round expecting to see Harry or Tom, but his questioning frown was met by his sister Kathryn who was grinning at him mischievously from the dishevelled folds of her riding cloak.

"Brother," she breathed excitedly, "I hear Harry bested you at the tilt! You really need to beat him soon or you will never be allowed anywhere near a battlefield! You'll be a disgrace to the Plantagenet line!"

John scowled at her from beneath his dark brows. Already feeling sore at his embarrassment, which he knew his friends were going to tease him about mercilessly once they were in the hall, he was also now worried at the scene he had just witnessed. Kathryn looked unconcerned, her long, dark hair escaping its braid, as usual, her skin flushed and glowing. She had beautiful chestnut hair, but could never seem to keep it neatly braided for long, always looking like she ran from one place to another at a hectic pace. She was full of energy and mischief and it drove John to distraction at times.

Like today.

She pinched his cheek which he found irritating for one who was hardly a year older than him, and he twisted his face away as she laughed merrily.

"Come on sourpuss! Remember how Papa said that he had to work very hard and for many hours to become as good a knight as he is?"

That remark did nothing to lighten John's mood. In fact, what it did do was turn his mind back to his half-brother, Edward. He had not been strong, but had been determined to show his parents that he could be like his father. He strove to be as brave and courageous as possible in between bouts of fever. John remembered teasing him with Harry, jesting that he worked so hard that his poor horse, Arthur, probably disliked him for the extra work he had to do.

Lost in his memories, he couldn't resist an outburst at his sister, who he felt had no business being so happy whilst he was feeling so wretched.

"Well, it didn't do Edward any good did it? No matter how long he practiced, he will never ride off and command an army to glory!"

Kathryn's face darkened and the merriment melted from her eyes and turned into hurt. Although she had the same dark colouring as John and her father, she had her mother's cool green eyes. Now they darkened with sadness.

"Don't John - not even as a jest! I miss my Lady Anne and poor Edward, as does Papa. It is not fair to talk about them in that way." She looked at him for a second, scrunched her face up in thought. "Why are you so dour today?"

John twisted on his heels uncomfortably and thought a change of subject would help as he did not like to see his sister unhappy and had not meant any harm. It was just that some days, things around him seemed so wrong.

"Father has had an argument with Sir Francis," he blurted out suddenly. "They both looked fit to punch each other at one point." He kicked a stone across the courtyard. It skidded towards a horse being led into the stables and earned him a reproving look from the stable-hand.

Kathryn's face registered shock and disbelief.

"Now, John stop this! Enough jesting, you are no longer very amusing, if ever you were. Your mood is most hurtful. What is wrong with you?"

He looked at her face earnestly and he noticed that she was at least now, in some measure, interested about what he had said.

"I am not jesting with you," he replied somewhat indignantly, "I saw it myself on the stairs over there." He gestured towards where the confrontation had taken place. Kathryn's eyes followed the direction of his hand and frowned.

"What was it about? Was it Tudor? France? What, John?"

He shook his head slowly, shrugged and looked up at her from beneath his lashes, happy to now have her full attention and feeling relieved that she had for the moment been distracted from his earlier selfish outburst.

"I don't know, but he had stern words with Francis. Lincoln and Lord Stanley were there and whatever was said, it made Papa so angry that he did not go on his journey but turned around and went back inside. Argentum is still waiting - look!"

It was only then that Kathryn saw her father's destrier, saddled and ready to be mounted, waiting patiently across the other side of the courtyard near the stairs. A young squire stood holding the reigns, kicking his heels and absently chewing on a stick of straw, obviously used to waiting on the whims of kings.

"Whatever it was," John whispered, drawing closer to his sister conspiratorially, "it was bad enough to make Papa white with rage." He paused. " Do you think Francis will lose his head?"

Kathryn rolled her eyes. Now he sounded suspiciously like their cousin Edward Warwick, whom she loved dearly but who viewed the world in such simple terms. Although he grew in body, he seemed to prefer to keep the ways of a child. He was fast being left behind by everyone else, and seemed to spend an awful amount of time alone in his chamber, preferring the company of children younger than him.

"God's blood John!" Kathryn exclaimed, adopting one of her husband's favourite curses and feeling terribly adult when she did it. "He would never send his friend to meet the headman's axe!"

John pulled a pugnacious face and knew his next words would annoy her even more but decided to speak them anyway.

"But he did! You know what cousin Cecily told us about the old lord Hastings.... "

The young girl suddenly felt older than her years, her face grew stern as she stepped closer towards her brother.

"John, enough! This is folly and Papa would be most hurt if he could hear you talking this way." Her fingers curled secretly round the letter concealed in her cloak pocket. Bess had trusted her. Her older, more beautiful cousin trusted her and it made her feel very grown up. Which was more than she could say for her brother. "Besides, whatever made him angry will soon pass."

She reached up absently and plucked some horse hair from the shoulder of his doublet. Although they were very close in age, she felt very protective of her younger brother, not least because of the resemblance to their father.

"And we are bastards remember, of no account, so matters of state need not worry us. That is one thing of certainty that we will never be a cause of concern for the king."

John looked at her mutely. That was half the trouble, he thought, but caution warned him to keep that to himself.

12. THE PALACE OF WESTMINSTER
October 1485

Kathryn was awake early.

Her husband William was travelling with a small party to conduct some business for the king over in the West Marches and she had slipped on a robe to watch him and his men depart from the courtyard as a pale dawn crept into the sky, blotting out the stars one by one. Grooms and pages scurried round in a fever of early morning activity under the waning torchlight and the sound of banners fluttering in the late autumn breeze.

The smell of bread wafted over from the bake-house, and her stomach grumbled. How she wished for Mass to be over so that she could have breakfast! Her adventures of the previous day had left her feeling exceptionally hungry even though she had supped well the previous evening. Shivering, she pulled her fur lined cloak around her tightly wondering how she could best accomplish the task that Bess had charged her with.

Kathryn both admired and was in awe of Bess. She had seen her as a distant, golden-haired beauty at her father's court, feted and fawned over by men of all ranks from the highest Lord to the lowest page. Everyone seemed to love her, either for her beauty itself or for her parentage, as many still talked about King Edward daily and crossed themselves sadly at his loss. This last gave Kathryn a pang of regret as it felt like a rebuke against her own father, who she felt was just as good a king as Edward had been.

She knew he was in no way like his shining, golden, elder brother – in neither stature nor personality. Only, as she knew him, as her own father, she loved him dearly, even if she was slightly cowed by him at times as his changes of mood could be frighteningly swift. His face could cloud over in an instant, without warning and his anger could be devastating to behold. It was odd, she reflected, that she felt exactly the same way about Bess and her father, but for different reasons.

The courtyard began to fill as the palace awoke and she told herself that she needed to go back inside before she was discovered in her nightshift and slippers. As she turned, in the corner of her eye, she caught sight of a figure turning into the archway down the end of the passage which lead to the chapel. Even in the half-light, and cloaked, she recognised her father from his determined gait.

And unusually, he was alone!

Recognising this may be her only chance, she ran back to her chamber and dressed as quickly as she could. She brushed her hair, but having no time to braid it, she hoped that she could conceal this fact in her hood. It was not seemly to be seen at her age, now a married lady, with her hair unbound. That privilege should be reserved only for her husband's eyes, but she was so desperate to reach her father whilst he was on his own, she decided she would have to take the risk. Once the day dawned in full, she would not get the chance to even approach him. As the general melee of the court caught up with the hour of the day, her father would be lost to her in constant attendance with lords and retainers, carrying out the business of state. She could ask for a private meeting, and may still have to do so if she could not catch him now, but that thought made her nervous and caused her to hurry even more. It was no good. She had to catch him now.

Throwing her cloak back round her shoulders, she pulled up her hood and hurried out of the room. Down the corridor, through the great hall, up the stairs and through to the entrance of St Stephen's Chapel she flew on soundless feet. Her heart was pounding in her ears, her hand anxiously grasping the letter in her pocket, but her thoughts of sharing the holy season with Bess spurred her on.

The chapel was in half light itself, with a few torches burning, waiting until the sun reached the stained glass windows and filled the space with glorious colour. She looked around and could see her father kneeling at the altar rail, his head bowed. The majestic figure of Christ on the Cross seemed to look down dispassionately in the flickering, sombre light. She caught the faint smell of some incense she could not recognise, and looked around. The chapel was, thankfully, empty.

Having reached her goal, she was now undecided as to what to do. Her father was lost in his devotions and she had no intention of disturbing him, but she couldn't stand here all day like some lost waif. The parchment rustled in her pocket as she flexed her fingers absently and she moved towards the end of the nave, thankful she had forgotten to change out of her slippers. Silently, she slipped onto a nearby bench, sliding herself along until she was at the other end, and as close to the kneeling figure as she was likely to get, and waited.

As she did so, his bowed head raised. The torchlight glinted on the suns and roses collar which sat on his shoulders, similar to one she remembered fingering gently and in awe as a child, sitting on his lap during one of his rare visits to her mother. The memory of the serious dark man who had held her on his knee stayed with her for many years. It was not until she had been taken to Middleham Castle, to join Lady Anne's household as a lady-in-waiting that she began to understand how important her father was. Now, she marveled in the quiet, she was the daughter of a king.

So distracted was she by her memories, she did not notice that her father had risen from his devotions, crossing himself reverently. He had then turned to see his young daughter, hair flowing loose over her shoulders, sitting in the place reserved usually for the most esteemed worshippers, gazing up at the vaulted ceiling completely absorbed in her thoughts.

"Kate?"

Startled, her head jerked down and she saw the figure of her father standing before her. She didn't realise she was staring at him, her mouth open in surprise and trepidation and in the dim light of the chapel, she also did not notice that he was struggling to hide his amusement at both her appearance and surprise.

"Papa! I saw you come this way and wanted...." she stopped suddenly, considering her manners. "I have not disturbed you?"

He moved a step closer, looking down at her with mock sternness, his jewelled hand resting on the hilt of a dagger on his belt.

"No, you did not. What do you do here this early? Does Father Doget know of your early morning visits? He will be delighted you are so devout. As am I." She did not see the slight curl of his lip. Kathryn frowned on hearing the name of his stern faced chaplain, not understanding that he was jesting as his face was in shadow and his voice was serious. For his part, deliberately so.

"I came to see you. William was off early and I watched him leave, and I saw you come this way..." She trailed off breathlessly, aware that all her words were running into one and she clenched her fingers around the parchment in her pocket. Oh why couldn't she be a cool and detached lady like her cousin, she asked herself, not the excited, stammering child she could hear talking!

"And are running around the grounds of Westminster with your hair loose like a hoyden and..." he paused looking down and arching his brows, "for the lack of shoes!"

She glanced at her feet as if startled, unconsciously pulling more of her abundant hair loose from the hood, then looked up again.

"No – I – Papa..." becoming more flustered by the second, she still had not caught the amusement in his tone which he could no longer hide.

Richard could not bear to prolong her agony any longer and moved over to sit beside her. She looked up at him wonderingly as he tenderly began to pull the rest of her hair from the constraints of her hood so that it covered her shoulders in its full glory. He loved his two children, both born of indiscretions when he was much younger and when marriage to Anne had all but seemed lost.

Kathryn's mother had not been high born, but respectable nonetheless, one of his mother's ladies who also spent some time at court serving Elizabeth. He had suspected at the time that she was there to take back tales to his mother of the queen's indiscretions, but if she was, she never discussed that with him. He had admired that, it suited his standards of integrity, and so he had questioned her not. Her daughter was the best of both of them, he felt.

Pretty as her mother had been and fearless as he had tried to be as a child. He had seen young Kate face fear on more than one occasion, and master it, trying to make sure that no one saw. She was a brave child, and a happy one, which he had to acknowledge she owed to her mother, not to him.

"So, what is it that presses you to charge around the palace half dressed? What could be so urgent or important that you could not find me in the solar later in the day?"

Kathryn looked at him steadily, trustingly. It was a look to break his heart.

"I have to give you something."

Richard sat back indulgently and smiled, puzzled by this sudden intrigue. Slowly, she pulled out the now crumpled parchment and catching hold of one of her father's hands, she lifted it, turned it palm upwards, and placed it in his hand. When he just continued to look down at her, she curled his fingers around the letter and then returned her hands beneath her cloak. The early morning chill was still holding firm.

Shaking his head slightly in bemusement, but keeping his eyes on his daughter, he unfolded the small letter. The nave was beginning to fill with dawn light, but it still made the neat script difficult to read. He got up and moved over to the nearest torch, standing beneath its flames, reading the contents in silence.

Kathryn watched him hopefully. Her heart beating slightly faster than normal. Her eyes wandered over the carved prayer stalls and empty pulpit, her mind already full of the gaiety they could have when Bess returned to court. She knew just how to dress her hair, and had let her use some of her own perfume... she felt a flame of excitement burn.

"Where did you get this?" These were the first words her father spoke, his head still bent and intent on the letter in his hand, even as his voice was slightly strained. Kathryn stayed seated, pouting a little at his tone.

"Bess sent a message before she left court. She asked me to meet her at Windsor. I did not know why, but I so love Bess and wanted to see her again. I miss her so much. This place is full of boys." The last came out so sullen that Richard raised his head and gave a small smile at the petulant set of her face. She looked so young and innocent, yet she was wed. He bit the inside of his cheek thoughtfully, trying to diminish the sudden stab of guilt. It had not been easy, handing one so tender into the hands of a young man who would take her into his bed. Yet, it was a good marriage. Will had shown his loyalties in Wales, even if in the end, Tudor had progressed further than any of them ever intended.

"Windsor," he said coolly, his tone giving nothing away.

"Yes. Her father, the king, King Edward is buried there. She was visiting...." Kathryn trailed off uneasily. This was not as easy as she anticipated and she couldn't work out why, but was astute enough to feel some tension between them since he had read Bess's missive. Her heart began to beat harder as she feared she may have incurred his wrath by meeting Bess without his knowledge. William had known, and had been happy enough to escort her. Surely he would have protested if she was doing something wrong?

Richard re-folded the letter and turned back towards his daughter, his face a mask to his thoughts. As he didn't speak, Kathryn became worried and decided to fill the silence. She drew up her shoulders haughtily to help give herself courage. She was a married lady now, she should act like one, with dignity.

"She asked me to give you the letter, to put it in your hand. I have done so." This last uttered proudly, almost defiantly, realising that her father may not be best pleased with the contents, although not knowing why.

"You have. Your task is accomplished," Richard agreed seriously, crossing the stone floor to stand in front of her. Kathryn stood up, pulling her cloak around her and made ready to leave. There was not much more she could say and it seemed her father preferred not to say any more or share his thoughts. She wondered what there was in the letter to make him act so. What it was Bess could have said.

She moved away from him then, making for the main door to

gain her exit. Bess's face suddenly shone before her eyes, her lips moving in a silent plea. Her heart began to feel heavy. She couldn't let her down! She stopped and turned around, pulling her cloak around her protectively once more. Her father was staring up at the figure on the cross before the altar with a strange look on his face.

"Bess only wants to come back to court, Papa. There is nothing wrong in that, is there?" Her plaintive voice echoed across the chapel as the sun finally brought light to the windows.

She saw his shoulders move as he took a deep breath before he turned and walked toward her.

"No – no there isn't. Come, the day begins, and you need to make yourself respectable before half the court see you in state of undress."

They both smiled at each other. Kathryn's face shone radiantly as she looked up at the father she adored. She had done as Bess had asked and was now going to walk with her father, spending rare and precious time in his company.

Richard's smile was much more reflective. How he ached to be as young as she was once again, to be free of the cares and troubles that now clouded his thoughts. As he linked her elbow through his, she leaned her head against his arm and his heart leapt.

He knew there were difficult times ahead, possibly more difficult than those he had left behind, and at all costs he had to protect his children and so was pleased that this young girl was blissfully unaware of the political storm that could be brewing around both herself, and his beautiful niece.

13. THE PALACE OF WESTMINSTER
October 1485

Rob Percy cantered through the gateway to the palace reflecting that he had never been so relieved to end a journey. He was accompanied by his squire, a bright young lad called James, who had preceded him through the gate and already dismounted, taking the time to catch the attention of one of the laundresses, who was labouring over her abundant load of linens.

James had proved to be amusing company over the past few days. He had an innate quality for mimicry, which Rob found extremely appealing and which had lightened a particularly difficult visit. He had told the lad, with a raucous laugh, that he should consider a change of occupation as he would earn a far better living as a mummer after hearing him speak with Lady Stanley's voice. His imitation had been so lifelike, the hairs had stood up on the back of Rob's neck, and he had needed to check that the lady herself had not followed them back from Bletsoe.

The two of them had just returned from a meeting which had been carried out at Richard's request. Lady Stanley had written to the king making a fervent appeal for the release of Henry Tudor into her safe keeping. Richard had openly shown Rob the missive wherein she was making all sorts of assurances for his future affinity and behaviour which, in reality, it was highly unlikely she would be able to guarantee. Preferring not to deal with her personally at this time, Richard had dispatched Rob to visit her at their country residence, where she currently resided under her husband's cognizance. He was charged to listen to her case on the king's behalf.

Spending time James's company had given Rob some slight difficulties when finally greeting the lady herself face to face. Never one who found it easy to remain totally serious, it had taken a great deal of self control, more than he thought he possessed, to block the squires mimicry out of his mind once he was standing in the solar of their palatial home.

They met in the presence of her husband, Lord Thomas Stanley, who was a constant, if silent, spectre in the background. He didn't utter a word in support or argument, only to add a small comment about the fact that he would have expected the king to have granted his wife a private audience to discuss a matter of such importance.

"Importance?" Rob had queried, looking directly into Stanley's florid face and frowning. He would have sworn you could see the alliances shifting behind his rheumy eyes.

"The fate of a Lancastrian heir," Stanley had replied smoothly, glancing at his wife over Rob's shoulder.

"The fate of a pretender from a bastard line." Rob had replied tartly. That retort cost him the best part of an hour standing there before them with no offer of hospitality from the furious mother of the prisoner. Of course, she couldn't vent her fury, a fact that gave him immense satisfaction, despite his dry throat and urgent desire for a drink. She wanted the king's favour, and the best way to get it was to avoid annoying one of his closest retinue, no matter her personal dislike, which Rob knew he had. That worried him not at all. The feeling was mutual.

Margaret had sat before him, trying her best not to allow the malevolence in her glare escape, and failing miserably. Dressed in the deep red of congealed blood with a white widow's barbe covering her head, her fingers constantly reached for the crucifix which hung from a heavily jewelled chain around her neck. She fingered it absently at times as she spoke of her son's willingness to pledge allegiance to the king, how he would repent of past injustices and treasons, how she would personally vouch for his good behaviour, and how he would abase himself before Richard and become a true and loyal subject.

She would even offer money, she had said, as surety for his loyalty. Looking at the quality of the gold cross, it appeared there would be no shortage of funds to procure this agreement, even if, at the moment, her husband held all of her fortune in his hands. Rob still didn't believe a word of it and knew exactly what Richard's reaction to a surety would be, knowing he would never allow them to buy Tudor's freedom based on a standard he could never attain. He had been glad to finally escape the dark confines of their private chambers, and out into the cold, fresh air.

Stanley had walked Rob out into the autumn gloom, shoulder to shoulder, talking very quietly, his head lowered and inclined towards Rob, who had busied himself with pulling on his gloves.

"My wife is very - passionate about this matter. I feel if she could present herself to the king in person, he would be more inclined to be disposed in her favour. She did, after all, carry the queen's train at the coronation and was very close to her for a time at court." His words had been silkily smooth, almost slippery Rob had thought.

James had walked towards them then, leading Rob's glossy black stallion.

"That was before she committed treason," Rob remembered retorting sharply as the squire passed him the reins to his mount. Stanley was still playing the supplicant and faithful servant.

"His Grace has been most merciful," he had murmured, but the telltale eyes were lowered as he spoke.

"Tell me, Lord Stanley," Rob had continued in a clear voice, chafing to be away from the cloistered atmosphere which Lady Stanley appeared to occupy. "Has your wife visited her son?"

Stanley had looked up then, his grey brows knotted together, either to indicate he was unsure of how to answer, or in a show of concern for his said wife.

His retort had been indignant. Falsely so, in Rob's eyes.

"Of course not! You would know if she had, I am sure. The king has not allowed him to see anyone as I understand it."

Rob had nodded curtly, as he gathered the reigns of his harness together and readied to mount. Sir Percival had picked up on his mood and began to paw the ground, snorting impatiently.

"Then permit me to say, but I am at a loss as to how Lady Stanley can possibly vouch for her son in the manner she has indicated if she has not spoken to him since his defeat at the hands of the king." He had paused, appearing to turn his attention to calming his horse, but watching Stanley's urbane face all the while from the corner of his eye. When he did not reply, Rob had continued in a matter of fact tone. "Unless, of course, the lady was in correspondence with him after he fled the field?"

Without waiting for a response, he had launched himself into the saddle, and pulled back the reins. Sir Percival reared slightly, then calmed.

"I will relay Lady Stanley's case to the king as I have been charged. She should be comforted by the fact that he has troubled himself to send me on this errand and she will have to await his pleasure. I can offer no more than that."

Wheeling Sir Percival round, he had touched his heels to the glossy flanks, and galloped away from Stanley, who had watched him leave with coolly unreadable eyes. James had also watched his departure, and with a quick nod of courtesy, he too had kicked his horse into motion, noting the expression on Stanley's face so that he could report back the reaction to his master during the journey back.

So as he returned to the palace, Rob was in sore need of a drink and an hour of his wife's company, to drown out the taste of this afternoon's work.

He pulled up and dismounted, causing James to turn his gaze away from the flustered young servant girl, who was very fair and decidedly flushed from her efforts. Smiling, Rob began heading inside to find Richard when he saw Francis standing by his own mount in the centre of the yard. He was cloaked and appeared ready for a journey. Fides was saddled and harnessed and Francis was fussing with a stirrup, his head down, hair covering his face. Rob nodded to the squire and crossed over the courtyard to join his friend, as he did so he gave the waiting animal's neck a gentle pat.

"Homeward bound?" His question was friendly and jocular with a hint of sarcasm. He knew it had been some time since Francis had been back to Minster Lovell, his family seat. He also knew that his wife, Anna, had been writing to him and expressing her dissatisfaction in no uncertain terms. That last morsel came from his own wife Joyce, to whom Anna also wrote at length to obtain all the latest gossip from court. She complained regularly that Francis was more than happy to neglect his wife, leaving her at home to run his affairs. She very rarely ventured to court these days and Joyce was her only conduit to understanding her husband's life. Francis himself, however, seemed more than content with the arrangement, although sometimes, he did admit to the odd pang of guilt.

Francis glanced up from his fumbling with the leather straps and Rob saw that he obviously had it wrong. The expression on his face was a mixture of anger and weariness, much more than he would anticipate to see if he was just making a long delayed trip back to his home. It sat ill on him.

Anger was not an emotion which visited Francis regularly, and it took much to rattle his placid nature, so there was obviously something seriously amiss. Rob wondered what could have occurred whilst he had been at Bletsoe. He also wondered if Francis was still smarting from Richard's reaction to their discussion last week. Although the conversation initially appeared to have gone well, bearing in mind the sensitivity of the subject, distinct rumblings of unease on Richard's part had become apparent since then, and it was Francis who appeared to be taking the brunt of the king's change of mood. When Francis didn't respond, Rob tried to provoke him into talking.

"If you are eager to break your neck within five miles of the city walls, I would continue worrying that stirrup just the way you are. You never were good squire material at Middleham as I recall. If Fides has any sense..." He stopped abruptly as it became obvious that this ruse was not likely to have any beneficial effect on Francis who appeared to be well beyond casual amusement. His mouth was set and his expression completely closed down. However, he did immediately drop the offending item in disgust with a curse.

"I tell you Rob, I would much rather be going back into battle than make this journey. I wish to God that Richard had charged someone else with this duty. It is certainly not an honour I would seek."

"Why? Where are you bound?"

Francis finally raised his gaze and looked at him grimly, his eyes betraying his misgivings.

"Grafton."

"Grafton?" Rob almost spat the word. "What in Gods name are you..?" He stopped abruptly at Francis expression.

"I am escorting Bess back to court."

The silence between them was filled with a thousand words which neither of them would voice. The familiar noises of the courtyard filled their ears as they both looked at each other, knowing exactly what thoughts occupied each mind, being able to accurately predict what the other would say, if words could be spoken. Rob lowered his voice and drew Francis to one side so that they were shielded by Fides bulk from the nearest group of squires who were busily tending to their work.

"Did he give a reason?"

"Only that Kathryn needed more female companionship and had requested her cousin's return."

Rob bit his lip pensively.

"And do you believe him?"

Francis looked mildly shocked - either at the thought that he would ever disbelieve something Richard had told him, or that Rob would voice it. He cleared his throat.

"I do, Rob. I do. I just don't think he should bring her back. Not after all the rumours last year. Not that there was any truth in it as we know," he added hastily, determined to reinforce his loyalty to his friend.

Rob passed his hand over the stallion's mane thoughtfully.

"Not on his part at least. But you can't deny that declaration he made at Clerkenwell wasn't particularly edifying." He paused, reflecting. "You do know about the conversation that she had with Jack?"

Francis nodded slowly. He remembered it all too well. Bess had asked Norfolk if he thought it would ever be possible to obtain a papal dispensation for an uncle to marry a niece. This was at the time put down to the work of her mother, planting ambitious thoughts into her daughter's impressionable head. There had been one point last year where Elizabeth tried to out-Stanley the Stanleys and play both sides of the board at once. With little success as it happened. However, it led to a rising tide of rumour abroad that Richard had poisoned Anne in order to clear the path to wed Bess. Anne's death had been agonising enough to them all, and this repugnant talk had just poured salt into a gaping wound. Enraged, and made rash by grief, Richard had made a personal declaration to the populace to deny the rumours and clear his name.

It hadn't worked. Londoners were a strange mix and viewed Richard with some suspicion and not a little fear. Not for the first time Francis wished they could administer court from the north, where everything seemed so much more straightforward and simple. With the success in battle, the rumours had subsided somewhat, but not disappeared in entirety. To bring Bess back - who knows what the people would make of it? They loved Edward's daughter in London, but would that not just serve to remind everyone about her brothers?

He shook his head in exasperation.

"What does bother me is that the girl still harbours hope in that direction now that the seed has been planted and Richard is safe on his throne. As well as which..." Francis tailed off. He looked up to the top of the stairs leading to the keep as though hoping to see someone standing there, or making sure they were not.

"I know." Rob said, watching the track of his gaze. "With all of this talk of the Portuguese marriage, he seems to be withdrawing. He hasn't said any more to you about John or Kathryn?" Francis shook his head again.

"Not since the other day when he walked out of the council meeting." Francis sighed and fiddled with the reins nervously. "I really didn't mean to tell him about what was being said in that way. I could kick myself for it, for he was shocked to the core. I was just trying to make him see, one way or another, he has to decide on the match and I knew all too well what he was going to do. We would have lost him for the day had he continued down those stairs," he smiled sadly. "That habit of his drove Anne to distraction in Middleham. She told me that she made an effort to always put herself between Richard and the chamber door if they had difficult matters to discuss."

Rob ran his hand through his unruly hair and looked around the courtyard, watching James still trying to woo his way into the young girl's bed.

"It's not your fault Francis. You had to let him know the rumour was circulating. If people are beginning to say the princes are to be found abroad, they have to admit then that their king cannot have done away with them!" He sighed irritably, picking up on Francis's mood. "It's this place. He was never this indecisive in the north."

Francis sighed and heaved himself up onto his mount. Much as he appreciated his friend's comments, he still felt bad about blurting out yet another rumour which was circulating in the stews of London. There was talk of Edward's sons being harboured in Burgundy, in the house of some rich - and anonymous - nobleman. Francis had secretly placed men in the local taverns trying to find out more, and he was eagerly waiting for their reports. He had in fact not wanted Richard to know what was being said until he had more information, but it had slipped out in his desperation to try and make Richard stop and focus on the matter of his succession.

Lincoln had been a fine candidate as a temporary solution in the circumstances, but things were different now. Richard was young enough to sire more sons, if only he would take the final step to agree to the Portuguese match. Either that, or take other actions with regard to the son he did have. The ploy had worked, but things were now difficult between them because of it.

Rob was looking up at him carefully, his blue eyes clouded with concern

"Richard worries too much about what people will make of his decisions, he still fears the weight of popular opinion is against him. I keep trying to tell him that he will never fully win over the south and should stop trying so hard. Jack told him as well - he just can't see it! He can't understand why they don't love him like they did Edward." He heaved a resigned sigh. "He shouldn't care so much."

"But he does." Francis answered grimly. "And it will torment him for the rest of his life and for her part in that I would willingly put my hands around Elizabeth Woodville's slender throat and snap it. So help me God I would!"

He nodded towards his friend, and hauling on Fides reins, he pushed his mount forwards and they cantered out of the gate into the late afternoon sunshine.

14. THE TOWER OF LONDON
October 1485

The guard unlocked the thick wooden door, the jangling of his keys jarring in Richard's ears, echoing round the ancient walls. As he walked through the darkened passageway, his way guided only by torches arranged on the walls and the footfalls of the tower guard, his thoughts came thick and fast.

He was trying not to think about George, but it was strange the way being in the precincts of the Tower brought back more memories
of him than anyone else, all things considered. The execution of his brother had been difficult to reconcile for many, many reasons, foremost amongst them being Edward's complete inflexibility when it came to any other option other than death.

George. Charming, humorous, irascible George, his companion through the many trials of their young childhood when their father raced across the country trying to wrest power from King Henry and his French Queen. The sack of Ludlow, exile in Flanders, all leading to the eventual death of their father and brother. He could still remember George's rage contorted face as they were told of their deaths, particularly the fate of their brother Edmund. It was a hatred Richard was to see in different forms many times once Edward joined their house to a Lancastrian widow. For George, it was the ultimate betrayal, and the golden glory that was Edward's triumphal attainment of the crown, became tarnished and dull in the span of a day in May.

Then there was the matter of King Henry.

Henry had been killed here by Edward's command, and as Francis said, Richard had not been party to that or responsible for it. These days, that didn't seem to matter. He had been Constable of the Tower at the time, and the duty he did have was to ensure that the order was carried out. That, and to ensure the body was laid out for all to view, in as dignified a way as possible. He should have realised how brutal was the mantle of kingship then, as he looked down on that weak, frail body of a man, who just happened to have been born a king.

He had remonstrated with Edward, but his brother had been implacable.

"No more rescues," he had snapped in anger. "The Lancastrians have no focus if he is gone, so gone he shall be Dickon. See to it!"

Edward's boy's. They had also been a focus for rebellion, and still were, where ever they were, if they were still alive. It was those thoughts that had brought him here today to exploit an opportunity that now presented itself to him in the form of the erstwhile usurper. He wanted to look Henry Tudor in the face and find out if he knew anything of their fate. He had invaded his kingdom on the basis that he was the legitimate heir to the throne, so he had to know something about those boys, or else why risk the enterprise?

Richard had told no-one he was coming here. Leaving it as late as he could to ensure the Tower precincts would be quiet, he had been accompanied only by two of his northern men-at-arms who were posted at the foot of the tower stairs. They would surely have guessed his intent, but no word of it would pass their lips, of that one thing he was certain. Consciously aware that Francis had him under close scrutiny since their recent disagreement, he had to admit he had been slightly duplicitous in sending him off to Grafton to escort Bess back to court.

He was well aware Francis was not at all happy to be sent on such an errand but at the time Richard had found a twisted humour in it. Francis had never trusted Elizabeth, and had no time at all for her daughter, so the mission would irk him greatly. It had been either that, or send him to Portugal as suggested by the Council to pursue the marriage proposal. That had been a step too far for Richard.

Although he was currently at odds with Francis, he didn't want him more than a few days ride away. He was one of the small band of men whom he could trust completely, and he wanted them all close at hand. He knew their current breach would heal, but in the meantime, it allowed him some freedom to carry out his intentions this evening without scrutiny or question.

The argument three days ago had arisen out of nowhere and if he was completely honest with himself, Richard had to admit that he was being more than unreasonable. For the first time in their relationship, there was a palpable tension between them which made Richard feel uncomfortable and also made him react impulsively. It didn't help that Francis had voiced what he and Anne had already talked about with regard to his son John.

For some totally inexplicable reason, he was uneasy that Francis had made those private thoughts and discussions an option, that he had made them real by talking about them. He didn't even know why this was, as on the evening in question, it had not troubled him at all. It was only later, in the confines of his lonely bed, that he turned everything over in his mind. Anne, his son Edward... John. And the question of remarriage. His uncertainty during the night had transformed into irascible anger by the morning, and even he didn't know why.

Those same conversations had continued, guardedly, over the next day or so to the point where Richard felt an enormous pressure to make a decision he felt totally unable to make, despite the inevitability of the situation. The breaking point had been a few days ago when a number of members of the Council visited his chamber to press him to act on the Portuguese arrangement or announce an alternative solution. This was the point where Richard had displayed the behaviour that his late wife would have recognised all too well. He left the room, calling for his mount to be saddled, determined to ride away from both the clamouring voices and the utter hopelessness of the situation facing him.

He knew he had to re-marry. Of course he knew, more than anyone, why he needed an heir to secure the stability of his throne. What he couldn't work out why he was in such a turmoil of mind over it and so had felt the burning need to escape the confines of the court and ride out, as he used to do at Middleham. He had fled from the chamber, leaving all behind in a state of shocked consternation, hearing voices remonstrating behind his departing form. He had been half way down the stairs on the way to his horse and escape when he had heard Francis say, clearly and concisely.

"Those boys cast a long shadow Richard. There are rumours that at least one of them has surfaced in Burgundy. We have to know your wishes!"

That stopped him as readily as if the blood had frozen in his veins. He knew his face had drained of all colour. Alive? The boys had been found alive? His head had whipped round and he shot Francis a look of pure rage at how he had relayed this news, how he had casually thrown the remark down the stairs as an after thought. He had strode back to the Council chamber with both rage and fear in his heart, along with no small measure of hope.

Hope.

Above all he truly did hope that his brother's boys were alive. As bastards they were no threat to his rule as long as they were in England. He would welcome them home, support and provide for them, in the same way he had ensured that their mother was taken care of. But whilst they remained abroad, there were still those who held out for revenge, who would want to unseat him on the pretext of placing Edward on the throne, with Henry Tudor also waiting in the wings. And if the boys were alive, why, then Tudor's life would be shortened by many years. Once that mystery was solved, with Tudor's help or without it, the block was his only redemption.

The atmosphere in the chamber had been tense and heated. He had stood rigidly while Franics informed him of rumours circulating that at least one of the boys was abroad. It had even been broached that he was at Richard's sister's court in Burgundy. It was very unclear as to where this information had come from, but the whispers were there.

Whispers, rumour, gossip - he was sick to the very stomach of it. The only saving grace of this latest item of tavern gossip is that it could put an end to the very worst that people thought of him. He would give much for that alone - to be vindicated in the eyes of those who viewed him with suspicion, called him monster, murderer. Tyrant.

He stopped. The dark thoughts seeping away into the walls of this ancient building. The Tower guard was standing in the inner corridor, waiting to unlock the final door to Tudor's cell. This man, his hated enemy, may be persuaded to tell what he knew. May even be prepared to barter information for his life. Richard nodded to the guard curtly, and the man placed the key in the lock and turned.

15. GRAFTON MANOR
October 1485

Francis waited in the solar at Grafton Manor, doing his utmost best to hide the rising tide of his impatience. The house was large, and very well appointed, light streamed through the leaded windows and flooded the room, which was well furnished, the walls covered with rich tapestries depicting a range of heraldic scenes. He remembered Elizabeth's mother had an eye for elaborate tapestries and he grinned to himself, thinking back to how she had stolen old Cooke's tapestries and had the unfortunate man thrown in the Tower. With her daughter's help.

The Woodvilles had, from some time back, endeavoured to lever themselves as high up the noble rankings as they could and everything about this room screamed their ambition. Francis ruminated that even though he was descended from the old nobility of England, his own manor house fell far short by comparison. He was only too pleased that his wife, Anna, could not see the Woodvilles surroundings.

He heard Fides whinnying outside, almost in boredom. He was probably making a protest at now long he had been left in the hands of Francis's new man, Geoffrey. Finally, he had replaced his former squire who had lost his life on the field at Redemore. Geoffrey was young and willing, but for some reason, Fides had decided to make the boy's life as difficult as possible. The noises he could hear now emanating from outside were just one of his mount's protestations.

Francis grimaced at the floor ruefully, and scuffed the toe of his boot amongst the rushes. He had been waiting now for over half an hour whilst Bess readied herself for the journey. With raised voices coming from above, he could judge that Bess's mother was not entirely pleased at this turn of events. No more pleased to obey Richard's wish than he was in having to fulfil the task.

He was trying valiantly to regain his good humour, which he was finding very difficult as he suspected that Richard had sent him on this mission as a form of punishment, and he had taken to wondering if he had been too familiar in recent days. Richard's emotions had been swinging like a pendulum since the battle in a way Francis had not witnessed since the death of his brother. There had been days then when Francis feared for the repercussions of some of his actions, and to a degree that had come to pass. Things had settled, eventually, and he had regained his usual sense of perspective and judgement. It was only since August, or perhaps more accurately, since Anne's death, that he seemed to be having difficulty once more.

The man Francis remembered, the calm, tolerant, shrewd Duke of Gloucester, Lord of the North, had been infested by the ravaging disease that was kingship. It was changing him, and Francis was fearful for Richard and for the realm.

A small cough brought him back from his reverie. A slim, dark haired girl dressed in rose silk stood before him, small, slender hands curled around a flagon.

"Sir Francis," she smiled, and her face lit up as radiant as the sun itself. "Forgive us for not offering you some refreshment after your travels. I am sure my sister will not be long." She held out the silver flagon towards him. The girl was slightly smaller than he was, enough to take advantage of being able to look up at him coquettishly from underneath her lowered lids.

Francis's breath caught in his throat. Could this be? He knew Bess's younger sister had been wed to Ralph Scrope, but did not recall her looking so womanly for her young age. In the company of her more radiant, elder sister, she always seemed to be in shadow, which at this moment completely confused him as to why. Remembering himself, he reached out his hand and took the cup from her, his fingers momentarily touching hers, and he felt the warmth of her skin, a touch that somehow seemed to burn. Her eyes flicked up for a second in surprise. Had she felt it too?

"My lady Cecily," Francis said, cordially, feeling slightly discomforted by his reaction. "I thank you for your consideration. The journey was indeed thirsty work, despite the lateness of the year the sun is quite warm today."

He took a deep drink from the cup, regarding her with his eyes over the rim. All the time, she returned his gaze, a slight smile curling her lips, her mother's lips, full and sensual. The wine coursed down his throat pleasantly, and he became aware that Cecily still stood watching him.

"I did not expect to find you here," he said more confidently than he felt. "Ralph, Lord Scrope is with the council in the north, is he not?"

Cecily nodded, colouring slightly.

"Yes, my Lord. He agreed that I could spend some time with my mother rather than alone at Bolton. I thought at the time it would be an ... agreeable alternative." Her face looked pensive and she slid a sideways glance towards the door, as more angry words drifted down the stairs. She smiled quickly. "I am sure Bess will not be long. At the moment, she is trying to convince mother that uncle Richard has her best interests at heart and will not marry her off to a stable hand."

Francis smiled at the young girl, pleased that she had referred to Richard as her uncle, recognising that above everything they were still connected by blood. He leaned forward conspiratorially.

"Well, as it happens, I do have a new squire myself. And quite a handsome chap at that. She may yet be swayed."

Cecily laughed out loud, revealing perfect white teeth.

"Yes, I have seen him. I think he may be a trifle - em - young, for Bess's taste."

Francis drew his brows together and was wondering if she was really directly referring to Bess being attracted to her uncle, when an imperious voice interrupted them.

"Sir Francis, you have a party of men with you I take it? Enough - fitting for the guarding of a person of my daughter's status?"

Elizabeth Woodville sailed into the room in a trail of pale gold velvet. Her beauty was still undeniable but of the ice-cold type to which Francis had never been enamoured. Neither was he in awe of it, and never had been, even when she was seated next to Edward on the throne. He had possibly been one of the only men at court who could not understand why the king had been so besotted with her for so long. Her pale blue gaze flashed over to her daughter and she frowned.

Francis bowed slightly, more out of politeness than any deference.

"I have a squire and two men-at-arms. I am not sure exactly what you consider to be fitting for someone in your daughter's position. A full royal guard perhaps?" This last was said sarcastically, which was not lost on Elizabeth.

She turned from her errant daughter to glare at Francis.

"Do not play the wit with me!" she began imperiously. "Bess is the daughter of a king and should be attended as such. How else can I be confident that she will be given due status at court if she travels there with only a farmhand for protection?"

Francis was not sure if the farmhand reference was aimed at himself or his squire but ignored it anyway.

"The king," he paused as he saw her mouth form a sneer at this, "the king, who restored your own estates to you and provides for your keep, is more than aware of the entitlement due to Lady Elizabeth, which is why he sent me rather than someone like Lord Stanley."

This last was a lie, but Francis had been riled by the temerity of this woman. His eyes flicked to Cecily who he could see was struggling to hide her amusement. He sensed an ally and was pleased by it, a lot more pleased than he expected to be.

"And you are..?" she began disdainfully, her lips curling, but Francis interrupted her sharply.

"His Lord Chamberlain."

Elizabeth stopped. S he was more than aware of the closeness of Francis to the king. He had been honoured with the same office as William Hastings had been granted to her husband and they were the closest of friends. She was both irked, and sourly satisfied at the same time.

"Very well," she announced, seating herself at a table without offering similar to her visitor. "I am happy that you have made adequate arrangements."

Francis said nothing, fixing her with a direct look, dark brown eyes fencing a frosty gaze.

"However...."

Francis went to open his mouth to speak - there was no "however" this was the king's command. She saw this and carried on regardless.

"I wish my daughter Cecily to accompany her so that she will have a friendly face at court and company befitting her rank." Francis shifted his hand onto the hilt of the dagger at his belt unconsciously.

"Madam, court has not changed remarkably. Your daughter will see many friendly and familiar faces there. The king's own daughter - Kathryn - has interceded for the girl's return. She misses her companionship. They formed a close bond whilst in each other's company at Sheriff Hutton...."

"A bastard girl" Elizabeth spat dispassionately, before he had finished speaking. Cecily gasped audibly at this outburst.

"Mother! Please."

Francis considered the girl in the rose-silk dress carefully before he replied.

"They can comfort each other with like status then. And Lady Kathryn has also made a good marriage, which should go some way to reassuring you, as has Lady Cecily here." He paused, and thought he saw the smooth young face wince at the reference. "I am sure the king's intentions for your daughter will be given no less consideration."

Elizabeth studied her hands, bare of the jewels she had been so accustomed to wearing, tracing the indentation left on her finger by many years wearing the coronation ring.

"My daughter deserves more than marriage to some hedge knight."

Francis felt his tolerance slipping away with his humour. He wanted to be gone from this place, his task accomplished. He wanted to spend his time repairing his relationship with Richard, to reassure him of his loyalty and service, not act as nursemaid to this harridan's daughter. Just a few moments in the presence of this dangerously political woman made Francis feel that he needed to ensure the king's protection now more than ever.

"Then I am surprised that you ever betrothed her to Henry Tudor. For I can assure you any match the king will make will be far more compassionate and advantageous than that," he replied in suitably clipped tones.

Elizabeth's head shot up and she placed both her hands in her lap underneath the table where they could not be seen.

"Henry Tudor still has a legitimate claim to the throne. Locking him in the Tower does not change that." Francis moved towards the table easily, setting down the cup that he had forgotten he was holding. He rested his hand back on his dagger but regarded her with a look of flint.

"Madam, that is treason," he began in a very low voice. "However, for the sake of your daughters I will overlook your...indiscretion... this once. But please, have my lady Elizabeth ready to leave without further delay, or I may feel the need to call in my men-at-arms."

Elizabeth had been avoiding his gaze, but now raised her eyes back to his and he could see them register a defeat, albeit a very small, grudging acknowledgement.

"Thank you, Sir Francis. You must forgive me, but any focus on the eventual destiny of my daughters does all the more require me to think upon the fate of my sons."

Francis's face turned to stone. He had no intention of discussing the bastard Princes with her. Elizabeth saw this, and was obviously satisfied enough that the barb had hit home. She continued, her voice steady and as cool as autumn rain.

"Whatever happened, wherever they are, in this world or the next, I take comfort that they are together." Francis nodded sternly, the only concession he would make.

Elizabeth stood up, looking every inch as regal as she had at

Edward's court, smoothing down the folds of her skirts.

"With that in mind, it is my wish that Cecily accompany Elizabeth, or I shall have no option but to refuse the king's request." Cecily gasped again loudly.

"What? Mother, I...!"

A lightening glare from her mother killed any further exclamations, and Cecily's complexion burned hotly. Francis thought this made her look even more attractive but he looked back at the girl's mother quickly.

"My lady, you are more than aware that this is a command and not a request? "

Elizabeth drew herself up to her full height, unperturbed by his serious tone.

"Sir Francis, I think you and I need not play games. King Richard knows full well how I feel about the security of my children. It will surprise him not in the least when you arrive with not one Woodville bastard in tow, but two. After all, he did not stop at commanding the presence of just one Prince. Why should my daughters be treated any less? "

Francis swallowed hard - well aware to what she was referring. Richard had sent him with instructions to secure Bess only. Would he be angry or just acquiescent if Francis returned with two girls? He looked at Cecily who seemed to be staring at him beseechingly, but to what end he was not sure. Did she want him to agree or refuse? She had her own husband away in the north who believed she was housed here, Elizabeth obviously had no regard for his opinions either.

He had to admit, the thought of Cecily's company on the road was most attractive to him, feeling more affinity with this warm, smiling, guileless girl than he had ever felt for her sister. Bess was a curious mix of her father and mother, and both made Francis uncomfortable.

"Very well," he agreed finally, "as long a we can leave within the hour."

Elizabeth smiled and nodded her head.

"Both are already packed. Unless I can persuade you to rest the night here and commence your journey on the morrow? "

Anxious to be away from this scheming woman, Francis shook his head.

"I thank you but no. We have adequate accommodations along the way. The king expects my imminent return. "

She nodded her head archly

"Very well. I can see why the king would need his closest advisors with him at all times." Smiling archly, she moved away. "I will send Bess down. Cecily, go bring your cloak, you can travel as you are. John will bring your chest." These last words were tossed casually over her departing shoulder dismissively.

Cecily looked down at the beautiful rose silk in dismay. Then back at Francis's concerned face. He could see she had been taken completely by surprise, but felt she was not altogether displeased by the outcome. He smiled.

"I will wait, my lady, if you would rather change for the journey. One favour deserves to be returned, especially if you would pour me yet one more cup whilst I await your readiness?"

Cecily's face showed a mixture of shock and embarrassment. She said nothing as she refilled his cup from the wine sitting on the side table, crossing the room in silence apart from the rustling of her silk skirts. She placed the cup in his hand, momentarily resting her fingers on his arm. He felt the warmth of her through his sleeve.

"Thank you, Sir Francis," she almost whispered. "I will delay you for only the shortest of times as I am as desperate to be away from here as are you. I will write to my husband once we reach London."

With those words she left the room.

16. THE TOWER OF LONDON
October 1485

Henry Tudor lay on the hard narrow bed in his cell, his eyes closed as the ceiling had nothing new to offer in the way of a view.

On the whole, he had to concur, he had been treated with a great deal of respect. A level of respect he knew that he would have in no way provided had Richard Plantagenet been the occupant of this cell and the positions reversed. He twisted around, trying to get comfortable, and lay facing the door. After what he had witnessed on Redemore plain, he grudgingly had to admit that Richard would never have allowed himself to become his enemy's captive. The memories of that bright August morning were burned into his brain, although he had tried fruitlessly over the past few weeks block them out.

He had been given books to read, decent wine - not to his particular taste, but decent. Yet nothing had been able to blot out the memory of that armoured figure on the huge, white warhorse, charging up and down the battle lines, his sword raised, the early morning sun glinting on the gold circlet he had placed on his battle helm.

"Lunacy!"

He could still hear Jasper's incredulous voice in his ear as they had stood at the back of the lines, watching this one man army regroup and redirect the men under his banner.

Henry had silently agreed, although he had not expressed it to his uncle at the time. He was both ashamed and envious as he realised he could never have put himself so at risk on the field of battle. There he sat, surrounded by his meagre household, letting French mercenaries do his fighting for him. He was not a soldier, had never commanded a battle, not like Jasper or De Vere. And Richard Plantagenet... his reputation in battle was to be feared. He was his brother's war monger, and he had never failed him.

Henry knew the day lie with the Stanleys. He knew his forces could never hope to defeat this man without their intervention. He too keenly recalled the looseness in his guts when he suddenly saw that Richard had charged back up the hill and harried together his own household and he had watched with increasing fear as he began to realise what was about to happen.

Richard had wheeled round, circled his men and appeared to be instructing them. Then they all turned as one and began to charge down the slope in his direction, heading directly for him. Around two hundred men, mounted on armoured warhorses, banners streaming showing the white rose, the silver running hound, and the raging white boar of the Blancsanglier, the king's own, came closer, and closer - cutting through the swathe of men at arms before them. Hacking, stabbing, cleaving limbs from bodies, bloodied hooves crushing through bones, blood-speckled foam flying out from studded harness. Closer and closer, the very ground shaking beneath the onslaught of so many charging hooves.

Henry shook his head, and sitting up, reached for a cup on the side table by his bed. His hand was shaking as he raised it to his lips. This memory was haunting him incessantly having no other thoughts to occupy him during his captivity. He passed his hand over his face and breathed deeply. The relentless vision returned, and he had watched in frozen horror as the armoured cavalry came nearer and nearer. The monster in the gold circlet, spattered in the blood of men he had killed, bore down on him, raising an arm and slicing his standard bearer almost in two. Henry watched the Dragon of Cadwallader fall in the mud before the rampant, raging white boar.

The ground had begun to shake then with an additional rumbling, like the noise of a raging sea and suddenly there was an additional cry, out from the flanks of the field.

"York - York and England!" Stanley had betrayed him. Jasper had looked round in alarm, his eyes wide.

"Henry – retreat! Flee! Head back to the village!"

With that he charged forwards and was lost in the red tide of the Stanley attack. That river of armour also cut him off from the king's fury, and he thought, or may have imagined, that he saw pure rage blaze out from the dark eyes behind the visor. It had given him the chance he needed. He had wheeled round his horse and headed back to Sutton Cheney at a murderous gallop, unable to shake the vision of that vengeful stare.

The sudden turn of the key in the lock made him jump, bringing him back to the present with a welcome jolt. The guards in the Tower were nothing if not regular. He was not expecting anyone to attend him for a good while yet to bring his evening trencher. Something was about to happen. His mouth grew dry as tinder. His heart began to thud painfully against his chest.

The door opened, and a figure dressed in black stepped into the room, invisible hands closing the door behind him.

Henry Tudor sat up and and found himself looking directly into those same dark eyes, and the expression in them had not much changed.

17. LEICESTERSHIRE
October 1485

Francis lead the small travelling party through the late autumn sunshine. It had been a particularly bright year, and the leaves were turning through every shade of auburn and amber before floating to the ground and lining their route with a carpet of flame coloured glory. Bess rode next to him on a dappled grey palfrey, and he had expected this journey to be somewhat uncomfortable for that reason. But what was actually occupying his mind was the presence of Cecily, her sister, riding in silence behind him. He couldn't swear to it, but he had the distinct impression that her eyes were settled on the back of his head, his shoulders, every part of him, and he was both slightly uneasy, but also somewhat pleased at the thought. What he would have preferred, in order to satisfy his curiosity, and vanity to be honest, was for Cecily to ride alongside him, and Bess to trail behind.

That may have eliminated some of the feeling that made him constantly want to look round and see if she was, indeed, watching him. He had heard her on occasion speak to Geoffrey, the humble squire who she was riding alongside. At first, when he heard her gentle laughter at some comment the boy had made, he thought how kind it was of her to entertain him, or even talk to him. It showed a common touch that her mother, even as a commoner, did not appear to share. It also confirmed to him that Cecily was probably more comfortable with her current status that her mother would like, or approve of.

They had passed the previous night at an inn and he had managed to avoid spending any time alone with Bess, other than making sure she was comfortable, and was happy with her lodgings and repast. He then visited the stables to ensure the horses were being looked after by his new squire, a fact which very much surprised the young lad who had not expected to see his lord wandering the yard after dark. After partaking of refreshment himself, he then took care to ensure that he bade the ladies good night before both he and they retired to their rooms.

He had a feeling Bess was desperate to speak to him, and was taking great pains to avoid it. He had no doubt she knew it too. His position as a close friend and confidante of the king meant that many people often sought his ear or opinion. This he did not mind, in fact was honoured by it, but on this particular occasion, he really did not want to enter into any discourse, fearing where it may lead.

However, Bess, as expected, had been awaiting her opportunity and as they rode slowly, slightly ahead of Cecily and Geoffrey, she turned her head and began regarding him curiously with Edward's eyes. His stomach lurched upwards and he groaned inwardly waiting for her to speak. Her first words were a surprise.

"You don't like me much, do you?"

Francis stared directly ahead wishing it was Rob sitting here not him. He would willingly have exchanged his recent altercation with the Stanleys for this experience. He remained silent for a space, not wanting to enter into this conversation, but also not wanting to upset the girl. She was Richard's niece after all, she could still complain to him and in his current mood, who knew how he would react. Finally, he decided on a response, and made the error of turning to look at her.

"My lady, I don't really know you all that well so that is hardly a fair judgement." Still watching him from beneath the folds of her hood, she smiled. Her mother's smile, disconcerting with those eyes, which threw him off balance this close.

"Even so, I think it is a correct one." He could hear the laughter in her voice. She was obviously finding this an amusing distraction, whilst Francis really just wanted to squirm in his saddle. He tried to smile back, only managed something weak and half-hearted.

"We barely met at court, my lady, you were much in Queen Anne's presence amongst her ladies. My wife, I would imagine, is much better acquainted with you, having been in her service at the same time."

Bess was having none of the deflection.

"True. But I also spent a lot of time in my uncle's presence." She paused as if for effect. "You were there, more than most. You and Will Catesby, Dick Ratcliffe, Rob, John, Secretary Kendall... but mostly you."

"Yes." Francis desperately tried to adopt a tone that was completely non committal. He thought he heard hoof-beats from behind moving closer, picking up pace. Was Cecily watching this exchange? Did she know what her sister was going to say, to ask? Had they discussed it last night as they both shared a chamber?

Bess laughed loudly all of a sudden, a joyful peal which resonated in the clear, crisp air and Francis, taken by surprise, raised his eyebrows and gave her an uncertain look. She was no longer looking at him, her head facing determinedly forwards, her perfect profile set against the sunshine casting dappled shadows through the leaves. But she was smiling, her lips curved with amusement.

"As I said, you do not like me. That is a great shame, for we have a great deal in common, if nothing else our concern for my uncle's welfare."

She stopped smiling, thought for a minute, her face becoming serious and still without turning her head asked quietly.

"How is he, my uncle, the king?"

Francis swallowed hard. Here we go, he thought, cursing under his breath. He was not known for his diplomacy, which is why the whole Portuguese matter had caused such merriment. He would have to take extra care if he did not want to say something that would either cause offence, or trouble. He stayed safe, deciding the less words he spoke the better.

"The king is well." But he could not help himself, adding, "and considering a marriage proposal." Bess did not flinch. She was ready for him.

"Joanna of Portugal." She paused for a confirmation that was not forthcoming. "Has she visited court yet?"

"Not yet." Francis admitted in clipped tones. "There has been much to do. The king.."

"My uncle does not wish to marry again," Bess announced

clearly and confidently, cutting through his reply and still concentrating on the road ahead as if she could see her future there. "Not yet, at least. He very much loved his wife and she will not easily be replaced. Not in his realm, or his heart."

Francis was feeling both annoyed and frustrated but was desperate that either emotion didn't show. He gave himself time before answering so that he could appear casual and light hearted whilst the complete opposite was true.

"What you say is true, however, the king knows his duty. So, I do not know what else would bring you to that conclusion. The negotiations are well advanced, an envoy..."

"Loyaulte me lie!" The words stopped Francis with the same effect as a slap across his face. He was also getting slightly annoyed at her constant inability to let him finish a sentence. In that, she was acting exactly like her mother.

"My lady?" At this, they both turned to look each other in the eyes across the silence broken only by occasional birdsong and the plodding of horses feet through the leaves.

"Come now, Sir Francis." Bess's manner was coquettish, her eyes full of mischief mixed with a hint of seriousness that Francis could not avoid. "You know full well what I mean. My uncle's motto. Loyalty, chivalry, honour. He won't remarry until the rumours around Anne's death have completely disappeared and his honour is restored in the eyes of the people. He can't, he won't, betray her. He didn't in life, contrary to popular opinion, and he won't in death. He has to restore his own honour so that she can rest in peace as his queen who died of consumption, a family disease. Not poison, by her husband's hand."

Francis could feel himself hurtling towards trouble. He silently agreed with everything she was saying, but at the same time resented being lectured on the king's character and intention in so personal an area by this young girl. A thousand words were filling his head, none of which should be voiced. But his own loyalty was just as binding as his friend's, and would not allow all of his feelings to be suppressed.

"All of which will not be helped by your own return to court, Madam. I am sure you have not forgotten the king's declaration at Clerkenwell. That was a most unfortunate necessity, and it did more harm than good. Tudor's agents did their work with extreme efficiency, showing they have much more prowess in gossip than in battle." He paused, still watching for any change in her expression. "Something I know that certain members of your family had a direct hand in. Particularly your half brother, Dorset - and your mother. I still to this day do not understand how Richard ever forgave either of them."

Bess continued to look him directly in the face, but her amusement dimmed slightly.

"See - I was right."

Francis thought of a retort, re-thought it, and then spoke.

"It is not your good self that I - dislike,' he began carefully, "it is the damage you can do, the hurt you can cause. Without even trying, without even being aware of it." Something in her eyes flashed, and Francis became more reckless. "But you are aware of that, aren't you?"

Bess shook her head suddenly, and her hood fell back revealing the golden splendour that was her hair, braided into thick ropes and coiled around her shoulders.

"If you are asking if I love the king, the answer is yes," she replied turning away from him to look directly ahead once more, now unsmiling, her jaw set tight. Francis pulled on his reigns and Fides moved closer to Bess's palfrey.

"What I am really asking, is do you love your uncle?"

Without missing a heartbeat, Bess turned her gaze back to his. Her eyes were brimming with tears, and she was struggling to maintain her composure. She looked more like her father than ever, a true golden descendant of York. And her reply gave him not only the answer to his question but a confirmation of his fears.

"Yes. Yes, Sir Francis. God help me, I do."

Francis pulled Fides up so suddenly that the animal reared up on his back legs, startling Bess's palfrey who danced away to the side of the road.

"Bess! Sir Francis! What is it?" Cecily's voice was full of alarm, and she pressed her own mount forward to place herself between them.

Fides was back under control, but Francis's tense grip on his reins was making him nervous, and his hooves pounded the ground, beating the leaves into a muddy morass. Neither Bess nor Francis spoke to Cecily and her alarmed face turned from one to the other for answers. Both of them stayed relentlessly silent, focusing on calming their mounts.

"Bess?" Cecily leaned over and grasped her sister's hand, her tone pleading. Bess looked at her and smiled sadly, then turned her eyes back to Francis.

"Sir Francis?"

Francis flicked a quick glance over his shoulder. Geoffrey and the two men at arms wearing silver hound livery were keeping well back, and he wanted to make sure they were out of earshot. Geoffrey looked most wary, but Francis gave him no reassuring sign to signal that he should move or take any action.

He looked back at the two women beside him. One dark, wearing a perplexed and puzzled expression, the other fair, far too fair, and sombre. Tears still moistening her eyes. When he spoke again his voice was low and almost threatening.

"You cannot return to court. Please!" He turned to Cecily "Did you know about this?" Cecily looked from one to the other, totally uncomprehending.

"Know what? What is wrong? You are both frightening me!"

Francis's brown eyes were boring into Bess's, even though it was Cecily he spoke to. Bess, bravely or brazenly, held his stare, but her expression did not change.

"Know you why your sister is returning to court?"

Cecily looked at Bess, still trying to work out what had caused this sudden tension. She shook her head in confusion.

"The king, he commanded it. Bess is to be welcomed back to court - to spend time with Kathryn, John and Edward. Our royal cousins. Bess?"

Bess said nothing at first. She moved her eyes away from Francis's face and surveyed her sister's perplexed countenance. Cecily was flushed and worried, her eyes darting between the two stony expressions.

"It's alright Cecily," Bess murmured gently.

"It is not alright!" Francis growled angrily. "You cannot do this! You cannot surely hope...." he trailed off, too angry to even put his thoughts into words.

Bess finally began to regain her composure, and straightened up in the saddle.

"Sir Francis, please. I mean no harm. I need to be at court. I have to be close to him, even if he never even notices I am there. That will be enough for me." Cecily's face dissolved into understanding.

"Uncle Richard? Bess, is this about Uncle Richard?" Neither of them answered her, but she didn't need them to.

"And watch him remarry?" Francis retorted cruelly. Bess avoided his gaze.

"If necessary."

The autumn air was crisp and fraught with tension. The leaves almost crackled with it. Francis took a deep breath.

"I am asking you one last time, please return home. I will tell the king you are ill, indisposed, that will come to court when you are much improved."

"He has asked for me," she replied simply.

"Or you have designed this in some way,' he retorted heatedly. "He had no reason to send for you!"

The young girl drew herself up using every ounce of the former regal bearing she had enjoyed.

"I think, Sir Francis, that the king would be most unhappy if you did not escort me to court. Besides, I will give you an undertaking."

Francis frowned, he was both furious and trapped, like a snared hare. He could not disobey a direct command from Richard, particularly not at present whilst their relationship was so tested. Bess could end this, by turning her palfrey round and heading home. She could disobey the command, and suffer no consequences. He could not force her hand, or disobey his king. All he knew was that in taking this beautiful girl to court, he was single handedly assisting in adding to his friends recent troubles. Unless...

"An undertaking?"

"Yes."

"Go on" He gave a quick look at Cecily's face, she still stood by Fides forequarters and had remained silent throughout this interlude. He was satisfied that she was innocent as to her sister's motives, although it appeared that she was fully aware of her feelings with regard to her uncle. That pleased him in a perverse way, he would have been terribly disappointed if she had proved to be part of Bess plan.

"I promise that I will maintain my distance from uncle Richard. I will not seek him out, I will only attend the events and functions appropriate to my status. I will not make myself stand out to him in any way. I will play my part as companion to Kathryn. If you witness my breaking this agreement, you can inform Richard of this discourse, of a supposed plan to entrap him if you wish, and I will return to Grafton or to whatsoever place he should see fit."

It was something and nothing, he thought grudgingly, watching her sitting there, bathed in sunlight. How could Richard not notice her? Not know she was there? However, if he had no attraction to her, if he did not return her feelings, which Francis hoped he did not, and if he kept a guarded watch on her, maybe she would meet someone else at court and be distracted. Or he could persuade Richard she would be better off married as soon as possible. He grinned grimly to himself. That would work.

"Very well," he agreed." But I will be watching you my Lady. I cannot allow you to stir up old tensions. I am duty bound to protect my king. " Bess nodded, giving a small smile.

"So, we have an accord."

She touched her heels to the palfrey and it moved forwards at a pace. Cecily watched her go, and turned to look at Francis's worried face. Her eyes were the most open and honest he had ever seen in a young girl, but her quiet words wrapped a chill around his heart.

"And if the king seeks her out? If my uncle seeks the company of his niece, his beloved brother's daughter? What good will your accord do you then?"

18. THE TOWER OF LONDON
October 1485

Richard Plantagenet and Henry Tudor regarded each other across the small, dimly-lit tower cell, each trying to assess the measure of the man in front of them without giving any thoughts or feelings away.

Uppermost in Richard's mind was the thought that he should probably enquire after his prisoner's welfare - but he couldn't bring himself to be so generous, remembering the shadow this man had cast over the last months he had spent with his wife and son before their death. That tragedy alone had been more than enough to bear in such a short space of time, but to know that this man's presence had been the subject of additional fears and worries, over and above those events, stripped out any concern from his soul.

Henry was more taken with the difference he could see between the man who stood before him and the one he had seen charging towards him fully armoured. This was the first chance he had to view the king, as all he could really recall about the day he was dragged into court was seeing his feet as he had been kneeling on the floor. All else had passed in a haze of confusion and fear, he knew well what had happened to Hastings, and feared no less a retribution. He waited for the king to speak, which before too much longer, he did, in a voice much deeper and authoritative than Henry expected.

"The Lady Stanley has been interceding for you." A pause. "Constantly."

Henry licked his dry lips. He would have liked to have taken a further drink from the flagon on the side, but dare not. He became aware that he was still seated on his narrow bed, and rose slowly, out of respect for the crown rather than the person.

"My mother is a generous and pious woman, Your Grace, but a woman non the less. She will find great difficulty in my current situation."

"No doubt," Richard rejoined smoothly. " But she would find greater difficulty if your head was not still adjoined to your shoulders. She has at least been spared that." Richard stopped for a beat, watching Henry's face carefully. "For the moment."

"I thank you for your mercy." Henry said with difficulty, his throat annoyingly parched by an anxiety he did not want to betray, trying to navigate the waters of this conversation with great care. Richard began to look around the room with seeming disinterest, noting the unmade bed, the almost untouched wine.

"You say Lady Stanley is pious. God-fearing too, I understand?"

Henry nodded slowly.

"More than any other person I have acquaintance with. She believes it is her destiny to be the mother of a king."

Richard smiled grimly for a moment.

"Then perhaps she should have been on Redemore Plain that day. She may have had her beliefs - altered - somewhat." Henry flushed, which looked all the more noticeable given his usual pallor, but did not reply. "Lady Stanley now assures me of your loyalty. Of your willingness to bend the knee to a Yorkist king and pledge affinity. Do I understand this to be true?"

Richard had his head turned, as if appearing to gaze out of the small window of the cell. However, he had Tudor firmly pinned in his peripheral vision, watching every blink, every nuance of expression.

Henry had to think quickly. Whatever strategy his mother was employing now, he had to play along. She had never failed him, that had been his doing. He had lost the field, squandered the opportunity she had built for him. He had to take a care not to do that again. If she was in communication with the king, seeking to bring about some form of reparation between them, he needed to take advantage of that. Pride had never been an issue with Henry, he had spent too long taking advantage of the hospitality of others to show the slightest wound at bending the knee to this man. Revenge could come later.

"You do." He replied simply, looking at his hands.

Richard leaned back against the wall and crossed his arms over his chest. The suns and roses collar shifted slightly against the velvet as he did so. His face was blank, not a hint of belief, understanding, humour or any other emotion was present.

"And how does she know this? As far as I understand, you have had no contact with her or any of Lord Stanley's men? Unless some of my own tower guards are acting as messengers, at risk of their own treason?" He regarded his prisoner thoughtfully waiting for a response. "So how does she know this?"

Thinking quickly, looking up at his interrogator, Henry replied succinctly.

"Because she knows me."

"Ah." Richard was smiling, still giving every appearance of being relaxed and at his ease. "The pawn is moved once again. She is so sure of your acquiescence to whatever action she wishes you to take, you do not even need to discuss it. What a comfortable bond that must be between the two of you." He stopped, considering carefully. "I envy you, truly. I was never able to understand my own mother's motives for some of the actions she advised, and she certainly never took to interfering with any of mine. Although, I must say, our family appear to have had considerably more success without such a maternal connection."

Henry did not know how best to respond so he stayed silent.

Richard continued in his quiet tone, but Henry, with the practice of years of attuning himself to political undercurrents, could pick up the menace in his words.

"As you are so connected to a lady who has been at the centre of my court for some time until I discovered her duplicitous nature, I was wondering what you would be able to tell me about the disappearance of my brother's sons?"

Henry struggled to hide his surprise at the question. To give himself time, he repeated word for word.

"The disappearance of your brother's sons?" He shook his head slowly, grimacing, feeling the pull on his damaged eyelid. "What would I know about that?"

Smiling dangerously, Richard responded, fixing him with eyes that were darker than the midnight shadows in his cell.

"What would Lady Stanley know about that is more the question, is it not?"

Henry took a deep breath, carefully considering his answer.

"Then perhaps your enquiries are best made of Lady Stanley herself."

"I choose to enquire of you," Richard replied immediately, "bearing in mind the close - ah - connection that you both enjoy."

The cawing of ravens outside on the green raked across the silence. Once again, the two men were regarding each other carefully, eyes intently trying to search out each owner's intentions.

"I know nothing of these matters." Henry eventually offered, with an air of detachment he did not feel. "I was in Brittany, I believe, when the boys disappeared."

"Now I hear they may have surfaced." Richard noted the surprise which registered on Henry's face. "If these new rumours be true, that is." Again he left a tense pause, began to remove and replace the jewelled ring on his smallest finger, studying it as he did so. "But you know how rumour spreads. Saying something hardly makes it true. Even if one repeats something enough times, to a great many people, and they all believe what is said. It still doesn't make something a fact." Richard fixed him with an intense stare from lowered lids, making his eyes appear as they had behind his visor slit, causing a shiver to crawl down Henry's spine. "You would agree?"

Henry nodded silently, trying to work out which trap Richard was trying to get him to fall into. Treason, murder, or just bribing guards to pass messages. They would all lead the same way, it was certain.

Richard now moved slowly and seated himself on the chair next to the small table under the window, and he gestured to Henry to sit. Obediently, he slowly sank back onto the edge of the bed. There was a jangle of keys outside and Henry wondered how much the guards could hear through the oaken door. Perhaps not just tower guards. Richard could have other men-at-arms out there, waiting to take him anywhere. He had heard about the Rivers men being dispatched north to be tried and executed and in comparison their actions had been in no measure as presumptuous as his own in the king's eyes.

"You were indeed in Brittany when I discovered that my nephews had been spirited away. But you were also at that time plotting with both Lady Stanley and the Duke of Buckingham. Now, I know you are an intelligent man. You would not stake all on an invasion unless you yourself were to grasp the crown, and to do so, my nephews were an inconvenience. So why did you? What did you know?"

Henry cleared his throat, coughing into his hand. Buckingham. How he hated that name. The man had been a useless, craven, fool.

"I had been told that you yourself had the Princes murdered. The deed had been done on your order."

Richard chuckled softly in derision.

"That I had murdered the offspring of my closest and dearest brother, to whom I had always been steadfastly loyal. My nephews? My own blood?"

"Yes." Henry regarded him levelly. "Your loyalty did not stop you from declaring them to be bastards, so that you could take the throne. What is one more step to secure your claim?"

"Telling the truth about their status due to a pre-contracted marriage falls a long way short of murder. The boys are my kin, " Richard rejoined smoothly.

"The boys didn't know you well, I believe. How could you be emotionally connected to two children you had hardly seen?"

Richards sardonic smile left his face briefly, and Henry was not comfortable with what replaced it.

"Blood. Blood and loyalty. I have two bastard children. Plantagenet blood runs through their veins as it does my nephews. I do not feel any less for them than I feel for my own son born out of the marriage bed. As you have neither issue nor marriage I cannot expect you to understand this." After a short silence he began again, with his former composure regained.

"It is true that I had not seen either of the boys on a regular basis, and that the elder child Edward had been encouraged to view me as a threat. That is something I would have been able to overcome, given time. However, that opportunity was taken away from me, and I will find out by whom - I can assure you. And when I do, there will be no mercy." He paused. "For anyone."

Henry looked down and clasped his hands together firmly. He felt suddenly weary.

"Then I wish you luck in your quest for the truth," he said quietly, raising his eyes back up to look at the king. Richard leaned forwards then, his eyes glittered darkly. Those eyes. Back again, shining out from behind a visor, below a gold circlet, blotting out the early morning sun.

"Truth?" he said quietly, pinning Henry to the spot with that intense stare "What understanding do you, Henry Tudor, have of the truth? The taverns and brothels have been redolent with your "truth" for the best part of my reign. I mostly blame Savage, but he fell at Redemore or else he would be feeding the crows. Then there is Rotherham, Morton - but you know all this. They act as mere puppets, more pawns, whichever game you wish to compare this to. What I am seeking are the facts, and I will not stop until I possess them." He paused, breathing heavy, but his steely gaze remained. '"And I truly believe that you can help me resolve this. Until you do, you will remain here under your current circumstances, and if you have to surrender your mother to save your own life, what will you do then?"

"My mother?"

"Who plotted with Buckingham to take my throne. Who plotted, with you, to take my throne. Who would have had to take actions, to remove obstacles, to take my throne. I was one obstacle, you ruined my reputation, albeit in the south mostly. There were two other obstacles and I would know how they were removed. You would still be hiding in the French court if they had not been done away with one way or another. Someone with affinity to you removed them, and I will hold you responsible until I find out who that was, and what was done."

On these words, Richard stood abruptly and moved to the door. He gave a sharp rap on the oak with his knuckles, and keys jangled obediently, turning in the lock. He placed a hand on the door as if to open it, and then turned back.

Henry was still sitting on the bed, digesting his last words.

"There will be no contact with Lady Stanley. There will be no opportunity for your release from your current imprisonment. Not until one of you gives me the information I seek. I know you have it, and nothing will change until one of you admits your part. When you do, we shall see."

With that, he opened the door. Henry managed a quick glance of the passage outside, which only contained the figure of his usual gaoler. Richard had visited him alone. Relief and disbelief coursed through his body.

He needed to think, about the conversation and the measure of the man he had just truly met for the first time. He also needed to think what his mother would do next, especially if Richard gave her the same options he had just expressed. If he hadn't yet, he was sure he soon would, and it was what his lady mother chose to do next which could influence the eventual outcome for both of them, and for the country.

19. THE PALACE OF WESTMINSTER
October 1485

Rob watched the scene in the courtyard below as Francis rode into the bailey with his Woodville charge. He had been anticipating his return and wondered what mood the errand would have left him in, having to admit a slight feeling of amusement, despite the troubling circumstances and the current rift between Francis and Richard. It was then he noticed that his friend appeared to have returned to the city with slightly more baggage than he had been sent to collect.

He recognised young Cecily at once, as soon as she had had thrown back her hood. She was darker than some of the other sisters, although she seemed to have grown up considerably since he last saw her before the death of the queen, when she had been much more visible around court.

A sudden rustle of fabric and the fragrance of his wife's favourite perfume assailed him and he smiled. Joyce had been a close friend of his first wife Eleanor, who had died in childbirth a few years ago. Over the course of the intervening years he and Joyce had formed a close friendship, which had eventually led to their own marriage. Now, she leaned over his shoulder to see what could be absorbing his attention and gave a small laugh which caught in the back of her throat.

"She's back then?" she whispered with a mischievous note in her voice. Rob looked at her sideways. She was an attractive, ebony-haired woman and Rob always considered himself fortunate that he had been free to choose his own bride once he had wished to re-marry, subject to Richard's approval, unlike Francis had been. Fortunately for him, she also had a quick wit coupled with an almost dangerous sense of the humorous. He could see right now that she was finding it hard to mask both that and her contempt.

"And brought another one too! Woodvilles do like to do things as a family! That will be two husbands to find rather than the one at present then?"

Rob returned his attention to the activity below. Bess and

Cecily dismounted with gallant assistance from Francis and his squire, who readied to gather up the horses for stabling. Francis appeared to be instructing Geoffey in just this duty when a blur of blue fabric hurtled into view, stopping him in his tracks. Kathryn had obviously also seen her cousin arrive and ran headlong to greet her, almost knocking Bess over with the enthusiasm of her welcome.

Cecily stood back and exchanged an amused smile with Francis, whose tense expression relaxed some at the sight of the two cousins embracing. Rob could see that the pair exchanged words, although he couldn't make out what was said, but whatever it was made Francis grin as they watched the girls greeting each other.

"Hmnnn!"

Rob turned his head towards Joyce as she made a low sound which he didn't understand, but did recognise that it was not at all complimentary. She was also looking at Francis who was now in quiet conversation with Cecily as Bess and Kathryn linked arms and began to walk slowly across the courtyard, both lost in animated conversation with one another.

"Interesting!"

"What?" He did not mean his retort to be sharp, but something in what he observed gave him a niggling unease. He just wasn't sure exactly what it was. Joyce nodded to the figures below.

"I haven't seen Francis that engaged with a woman for a long time!" Then she laughed mischievously. "And certainly not with Anna, his own wife!"

Rob whipped his head round to look again, grinning at his wife's apparent naivety.

"The girl Cecily? She has more sense than that. So has Francis come to that. He despises anyone with Woodville blood for what they represent, as well as the trouble they have caused. The realm would be better off without any of them. Pity Richard was only able to dispatch Rivers and Grey." He stopped, realising he had been stung into a reply without thinking. "Anyway, she's Ralph Scropes wife now!" Joyce continued to look past him into the courtyard, keeping her voice low, but unable to keep the smile from dancing round her lips.

"Not so happily, I hear... which, makes two of them you could say."

Rob's brow furrowed, as he shook his head.

"No. Francis may not be close with Anna these days, but that is down to his duties here. He would never woo a Woodville, even if that were not so."

Joyce raised her eyebrows archly and inclined her head, her blue-grey eyes twinkling.

"If you say so, you know him best." She gathered up her skirts and made to move on gaily. "As for me, now I go to welcome a Woodville back to court. It was so good of he king to think of me for this honoured duty." This last comment was uttered with restrained amusement and more than a little irony!

"He wants you to make sure she is well looked after," Rob countered, still looking at his friend below. "It is an honour to be one of her ladies. She still has royal blood." Joyce snorted in a most unladylike manner which made Rob turn and grin.

"Of course! And if I watch her very closely at the same time, it will not go amiss?"

"Maybe... " he said thoughtfully. "This could be a mistake, having her back at court so soon."

"Bess or Cecily?" Joyce asked mischievously. He turned to face her then, the look on his face slightly admonishing.

"Bess of course. There was so much rumour last time she was here."

Joyce sighed heavily and laid her hand on his.

"You can't move around here for rumours most days. Admittedly it has improved some since the battle, but just as one story fades, another springs up like weeds on a grave. Now it's the boys again." She stopped then, watchful of the concern on his face. Standing on her toes, she gave him a sudden and affectionate kiss on his lips. "Watch out for him, Rob. I still fear he is not the Richard he was."

Smiling back in fond acknowledgement, Rob drew her to him

and rested his hands lightly on her waist.

"No. he is not. These past two years have not been kind to him. I would that we could give him some time for himself in the North. Middleham perhaps." He watched Joyce's face change. "Or Barnard Castle. Just a week or two of peace. Time to breathe, to grieve even. He has had scarce chance for that. He still misses Edward terribly, perhaps more than Anne."

He sighed himself then, lifting his hand and tucking a stray lock of hair behind her ear gently.

"Edward had Richard to consult and advise him, to charge off and array men for his causes. I think Richard misses that companionship, that connection. He and Anne, they were so close."

Joyce took his hands from her waist and squeezed them tightly as she returned his gaze earnestly.

"Then you and Francis must do for Richard what he did for Edward. Be loyal, steadfast, tell him the truth, but defend his honour at all costs."

Rob's eyes became suddenly moist.

"With my life, you know that!" he whispered. She seemed to be searching his face, looking for something lost as she answered him carefully.

"Does he?"

Rob closed his eyes then and swallowed deeply. Things had been in such upheaval, there was barely time to think some days. All the business with Harry Stafford, the conspiracies, the days of sadness...

"I don't know - I hope so. He did, in the north."

"I must go," she whispered, kissing him quickly once again and dropping his hands, nodding over his shoulder in the direction of the courtyard as they parted.

"And I would put a stop to that, before things get even more complicated than they are already!" And with that, her trim figure clad in green damask swept away down the gallery to meet Bess and Kathryn as they arrived at the top of the stairs.

Rob's eyes followed Joyce as Bess called down to her sister to join them so that she could show the girls to their chambers. Cecily mounted the stairs, closely followed by Francis, who bowed his head to her as she walked away with the small group of ladies. Francis watched them go, then turning his head, he finally saw Rob. Grinning, he walked down the gallery towards him, stripping off his riding gloves as he approached.

"How did that happen?" Francis shook his head in bemusement at Rob's question.

"Elizabeth would not sanction Bess to come to court without her sister. She made reference to the two boys being together, at Richard's command, so said he could not refuse." He paused wearily. "I don't know what she is up to, but there will be something, I vow."

He appeared to be avoiding Rob's eyes, paying undue attention to his gloves, twisting the leather this way and that. Rob knew those mannerisms of old, had seen them at Middleham when the young Francis was worried about something. Most memorably when he had heard the Earl of Warwick castigating the king to George. Francis had not known if he should tell Richard what he had heard, and had spent the morning in the tiltyard twisting his gloves at every opportunity, until Rob tore them from his hands and beat him about the ears with them.

"And?"

"And what?" Francis looked up. Rob said nothing, but snatched the gloves out of his hands with a determined look.

"You know me too well" Francis replied grudgingly, but with a resigned grin. He looked around him warily, checking for anyone in earshot. "It is as we feared, this was not a good move. We will have to be vigilant Rob, the girl is still fond of Richard. She admitted it on the road."

Rob was so taken aback, that he swallowed the desire to tease Francis about Cecily. He was about to question him some more when he saw the figure of John Kendall turn into the far end of the gallery, and head directly for them.

"My Lords, my Lords," he gasped as he hurried towards them

"The king was enquiring as to your return Lord Lovell. He requests your attendance in his privy chamber. Yours also Lord Percy."

The two friends exchanged cautious glances. Kendall looked flustered, but gave nothing away and bustled on down the gallery.

20. THE PALACE OF WESTMINSTER
October 1485

Richard stood looking out of the window, hands clasped behind his back. Norfolk was already in attendance, seated at the table looking his usual gruff but amiable self and glanced up expressionless as the two men entered the room.

"Your Grace!" Rob intoned deferentially, as both men made their obeisance to the figure by the window. Richard turned, his face also unreadable, with a worrying pallor. He gave Rob a swift glance, looked at Francis more searchingly and then gestured for them both to sit.

"Francis. Good journey?" The words were quite tersely spoken, but it was obvious to all that his body was rigid with tension.

"Yes, Your Grace," he answered. He was then made even more uncomfortable as the king poured wine from a flagon at his side into two cups and placed them in front of them, there being no cupbearer in sight.

"You are no doubt in need of refreshment. I am more than aware that you will want to wash the taste of that particular task from your mouth." He glanced at Rob. "And I have never known you to refuse a drink."

As Rob grinned accepting the cup, Richard's face relaxed slightly, but he remained unsmiling as he seated himself opposite them. Francis felt a little of his tension release, but was still aware of the atmosphere in the chamber. He gratefully accepted a cup, drinking deep, noting that Norfolk was also making every effort to keep his thoughts to himself, his eyes lowered. Rob tipped his cup towards Richard in acknowledgement, and then took a drink himself.

"How is your charge?" Richard asked almost absently, regarding Francis intently, his own drink left untouched on the table between them. To anyone else, his tone would seem totally polite and uninterested. All those in the room knew him much better than that.

"Well." Francis thought it expedient to keep it brief.

"More than well!" offered Rob, mischievously and Richard raised his eyebrows, exchanging glances with Norfolk, who remained silent. Francis cleared his throat, shooting a grudging look at Rob for opening this up. Particularly in the current mood.

"Dame Grey requested that Cecily accompanied her sister to court. She said you would not refuse Bess the company."

"Or something in that vein," Rob offered under his breath. He was desperate to break the tension between his two friends, and the only way he knew to do this was by uniting against a common enemy, and the only weapon he had was humour.

Richard looked at Francis in stern anticipation, waiting for him to explain. Francis sighed inwardly. At that moment he could have willingly run Rob through with his dagger. Things were difficult enough at present, he just wanted to complete his duty and move on. Richard raised an eyebrow in surprise that he had not yet spoken as Francis glanced around the room, looking at anything but at that implacable stare.

"She said that as you had insisted that her two boys be together under your care, you could not refuse to do the same for her two daughters."

There was a stunned silence in the room. Francis held his breath. Rob smiled at Richard over his cup, watching as he pursed his lips, thoughtfully.

"She was right, for once. In fact, her judgement is most visionary. Anne always thought she was a sorceress." The room fell coldly hushed at both the casual reference to Anne and the thoughts she had about Elizabeth. All present knew this to be true, but no-one had heard it admitted so frankly from Richard's own lips. "I didn't realise the girl was at Grafton, I thought she was with Scrope."

Richard surveyed the small group carefully and continued.

"Well, I have been discussing Bess with Norfolk here, among other things." Jack still gave nothing away to the two younger men who were now both looking directly at him. "You were right, Francis, as always. It is time to take some actions to secure the succession. I cannot, would not, lie to any of you, and you will all be aware how sensitive a subject this is for me." He paused, considering how to go on. "My first marriage was not a political one in a certain sense, and I was able, through the benevolence of my brother, to marry a woman for whom I had real affection." Rob and Francis exchanged glances as he paused, his voice breaking slightly. "A future marriage will be an entirely different prospect."

No one else spoke, waiting for him to continue. He leaned forward across the table to his two closest friends.

"I am sorry that you may have found my demeanour intractable over these last weeks. You were kind enough to give me your honest counsel, and I am very thankful to you for speaking to me so frankly, although it may have seemed different at the time." Rob stretched back in his chair expansively.

"Oh, don't worry Dickon. It was only Francis who thought he was on the way to the block. Although I do feel that would have been preferable to a visit to Grafton."

All four of them burst into spontaneous laughter, finally breaking the tension between them. Francis felt a sense of relief that was overwhelming. He had truly feared that his bond with Richard had been compromised, and was extremely gratified to find out that it was still in existence and as strong as ever. He would never doubt it again. It was at this point Norfolk spoke.

"Grafton or Bletsoe? By God, I bet you both thought you had been sent to purgatory!" Richard smiled broadly, although Francis noted that the merriment never quite reached his eyes.

"Nevertheless, both errands were necessary, if not exactly pleasurable, and there was no one else I could have trusted to carry them out in such an exemplary way. But that did also mean that you were not available to carry out other representations which I have recently undertaken."

Francis played with his cup ruminatively, his eyes lowered.

"Do any of those representations involve the Pope?"

"No." Richard answered carefully. His fingers toyed with the stem of his silver cup, but he still drank nothing. "Ratcliffe has been dispatched to Portugal to escort Princess Joanna and the Duke of

Beja back to England to visit court for the Christmas festivities."

"Manuel of Beja?" Francis was quizzical, his gaze shooting up to meet Richard's. He didn't understand. Why would Manuel be accompanying Joanna on a visit to a prospective husband? He did not have to wonder for long as Richard answered.

"It is my intention to strengthen the alliance by offering Bess in marriage to Manuel, if he should be so inclined after meeting her." He stopped for a moment, chewed the inside of his cheek in thought. "Of course, Elizabeth may have her own thoughts on the union, but it is a respectable and suitable marriage for the girl."

"Which is the real reason you sent me off to bring her back to court?" Francis said with caution. The tight knot he had been carrying in his chest for the past few days began to loosen.

"Partially. That only really fell into place later. The main reason was because Kathryn had asked me to bring her back." He smiled fondly, thinking of his daughter. " I do find it difficult to refuse her anything. Strangely enough, she reminds me of Anne when we met again after Tewkesbury, brave and fearless, yet still very vulnerable."

Norfolk then interjected, steering the conversation back onto firmer ground.

"Catesby has also been sent to Flanders to find out what he can about this rumour concerning the Princes. He will also visit Burgundy, to speak with the king's sister, as we think she will have spies or knowledge that may be useful."

"Catesby?" Rob exclaimed in surprise, thinking of the introspective lawyer in Richard's service. Most of the time, unless on matters of the law, you could be hard pressed to get a word out of him. To send him as an investigator seemed an odd choice. Or so he thought.

"Lincoln has gone with him," Richard assured him quickly, reading his face. "As my nephew, he will report back to me and he also knows how to handle Margaret. I am not entirely sure I have her full approval for ascending to the throne. Correspondence over the years has been a little cool." He allowed these facts to sink in before speaking again taking a deep breath before his next words.

"I have also been to visit Henry Tudor in the Tower."

Time seemed to shudder to a halt inside the room. There was anticipation in the air. As if someone should speak, but no-one wanted to say the words, whatever words there were to say. In the end, it was Rob who broke the silence with his usual irreverence.

"You have been busy, Your Grace. And how was his Highness?" Francis grimaced.

"I heard it was his intention to be called "Majesty" if he became king. "Grace" wasn't grand enough." Richard nodded peremptorily.

"Yes, I had heard that too. But one hears many things these days. I have warned him that he will stay in the Tower until he offers up any information he has about the fate of Edward's sons. He is to have no contact with his mother, no visitors of any kind. This has been relayed to Lady Stanley."

"Hopefully, then, the truth will out," Norfolk grumbled. " Either Tudor or his mother will finally admit to their part in the matter, or confirm Buckingham's guilt."

"If Buckingham was guilty, there is no doubt they were still involved, I am sure of it!' Rob added angrily. "He would never have thought of something of that nature himself, never mind have the intelligence or resources to carry it out. He would not have been able to resist bragging about it for a start!" He paused, shaking his head slowly. " I am sorry, Dickon, I know you grew close to him, but he really was the most shallow and vainglorious of men."

Richard smiled at his friend, and he and Francis exchanged an acknowledging glance.

"I was close to him for a time. I admired his loyalty to me, not realising that it was false. I will never forgive myself. How could I allow myself to be manipulated in such a way? It will not happen again." His eyes sought out Francis once more. It was an old wound, now healed. The glittering figure of the Duke of Buckingham, Henry Stafford, had placed himself firmly between Richard and his closest friends, stopping at nothing to ensure that their counsel went unheard or unheeded.

"He took advantage of your grief, Dickon," said Francis in answer. "You could not see it. You could not be expected to, and so much was happening so quickly."

"Yet you saw it." Richard response was quick and direct. Francis turned to Rob and then lowered his head, stared into his cup thoughtfully.

"Yes." Rob agreed. "Yes we did. And even if we had burst through the men-at-arms outside your chamber, held you down in your chair and told you that he was entirely false, you would not have listened. Unfortunately, you had to find that out in the hardest way."

The chamber filled with shared memories, words not spoken, decisions taken, each man alone with his own individual recollections in the silence.

"I do regret Hastings, of all of them, " Richard said suddenly, his mood changing.

"Hastings became jealous, lad," Jack moved forwards and placed a hand on the king's shoulder. "He couldn't wait to see what you would do, feared being sidelined for Buckingham. Only that could have forced him to countenance the crowning of an illegitimate boy, Edward's son or no. I do think that had Buckingham not attached himself to you so closely after Stoney Stratford, he would not have turned his coat. If only he had waited before joining the Woodvilles in their plotting. Buckingham would have still travelled the same road to his end, that was his ambition. Hastings should have seen through that, he should have come to you."

"Edward didn't trust Buckingham. He never gave him the offices that should have been due to him. That was my mistake, and I paid heavily for it." Richard admitted. "In more ways than one."

"Tis done, lad." Norfolk muttered. "You are surrounded by friends now, men you can trust. We will help you build a new succession, a new realm, one to equal Edward's years."

"God willing." Richard said absently. He appeared to be lost in thought and Francis noticed he was twisting the ring on his smallest finger, round and round...

21. THE PALACE OF WESTMINSTER
November 1485

Cecily stepped into Bess's chamber and was astonished by the scene which greeted her.   The room was awash in a sea of silks, velvets and damask, kirtles and hennins.   Her sister stood in the middle of the chaos and appeared to be in a state of some excitement, heightened when she saw Cecily enter the room

"Cecily! ' she cried." Thank the Lord! I need you to help me!"

Cecily moved further into her sister's chamber, picking her way carefully over the cast off garments and surveyed a further pile of gowns thrown haphazardly across the counterpane on the bed.

"You need to help me pick a gown!" Bess breathed desperately, standing in the middle of the room, half in and half out of her plain wool day dress. "Quickly, quickly! Which one suits me best? One which makes me look the most regal, the most grown up? Oh Cecily, I don't have all my very best gowns here – what shall I do?"

Her sister picked up the skirt of a sky-blue silk gown which she remembered Bess wearing at court some months ago. It was identical, she remembered, to one which Anne, the queen had worn on the same evening. Whether by mistake or design she had never discovered, but she did recall the uncomfortable gossip which had followed, and was fearful that Bess had either not heard what had been said, or more likely, had chosen to forget it.

The fabric was beautifully stitched and embroidered with golden thread and trimmed with the finest Italian lace. She rubbed the silk carefully between her fingers, it felt gloriously smooth and sumptuous. Fit for a queen. She wondered what it felt like to wear such a grand gown, as, although she had worn some beautiful dresses as a Princess, none had been quite so beautiful, or as high quality, as those her mother had worn. This one itself, was only so fine because it had, indeed, been made for a queen. Richard's queen.

"Why?" she asked calmly, considering the scene before her

with a casual indifference. "What has you in such a bother?"

Bess stopped and turned to face her sister, now only clad in her kirtle. Her face was flushed, her eyes sparkled with joy.

"Uncle Richard has sent for me. He wishes to see me in his Privy Chamber."

Cecily dropped the skirt of the blue gown as if it burned her skin.

"Well I wouldn't wear that one!" Bess looked puzzled as she stared at the gown. Obviously the significance had long passed from her memory, much as Cecily had suspected - or in truth, the incident had been so innocent as to not raise any memory with her. She pursed her lips and looked into her sister's face. She could be so innocently beguiling and yet so used to manipulating people to get her own way, a trait she had inherited from their mother.

A warning bell sounded deep within her. Bess never stopped to think, not when she was as excited as she was now and although she wanted to see her sister happy, she felt the situation needed cooling down somewhat. Francis Lovell's concerned face rose in her mind, and not for the first time since they had returned to court.

"What about your agreement with Sir Francis? The accord you made with him not three days ago? You promised him, Bess."

Bess was suddenly absorbed with looking down, sorting through the gowns at her feet and refusing to meet her sister's searching gaze.

"What of it?" she replied lightly. Cecily couldn't see the arched brows feigning an innocence which did not exist, but she knew they were there.

"Isn't this breaking it - and with alarming speed?" Cecily paused to more closely examine her sister's reaction, noting her averted eyes and flushed face. "Francis Lovell is an honourable man, and a close friend of our uncle. You should not play him false, never mind going back on your word so easily. Does that not trouble you?"

Bess raised her head back up and with a hint of obstinance, she reached over and picked up a gown of violet velvet, shaking it out the better to view its beauty. Trimmed around the neck and sleeves with miniver, it was rich and luxurious, another gown from her earlier days at court. The skirt had a cloth-of-gold panel which would accentuate her small waist. She wanted to appear demure, but grown up. She wanted to appear beautiful.

"This one?" she asked artlessly, looking at her sister for approval. Cecily merely inclined her head, waiting for an answer to her earlier question. Her question going unanswered, Bess sighed, and folded the gown over her arm, smoothing the velvet slowly. As carefully as she now spoke.

"The king has sent for me. For me! I promised I would not seek out the king. This means the accord still stands. Sir Francis cannot reproach me for obeying a command." Cecily frowned in annoyance and frustration. She still had a small suspicion that this meeting had been contrived somehow.

"Are you sure you have had nothing to do with this? You, or Kathryn?"

Bess merely smiled again and shook her head.

"No. Not at all. I was going to keep my word. I was going to avoid bumping into him at every available opportunity, which would not be easy here as you know. You can't miss the king in his own court. Yet, I was happy to try, as hard as I could." Cecily shook her head with resignation. Her sister was headstrong, and for most of her life had been used to getting her own way. It was only in the last two years she had begun to even comprehend that life did not always serve up your every wish on gold plate. Sometimes, you were presented with dishes you did not expect. Betrothal to Henry Tudor had been a lesson which she seemed to have easily discarded from her memory.

"I still think Francis will be uneasy. I wonder if he knows?"

Bess shrugged with indifference and stepped out of the day dress, kicking away the cast off gowns on the floor. But then she stopped suddenly and looked directly back at her sister for the first time in a while. The smile on her face widened conspiratorially.

"Francis now is it? I thought I saw you making puppy-eyes at him on the way to London. Do you really like him?"

Cecily flushed, her face turning as red as the dress she was wearing. She had believed, up until that moment, that she had masked her feelings for Francis very well. She had crossed his path before, at court, after they had been released from sanctuary, but it had been such a difficult time then that she had hardly had the chance to notice him, never mind actually get to speak to him. Then, he had been constantly at the king's side, or in his company, whereas she had spent most of her time as one of the queen's ladies, and she had been concerned more with her future marriage plans.

She had then been cast into the whirlwind which was her marriage to Ralph Scrope. She sighed thinking of her husband. Her uncle had indeed done as he promised, had been as good as his word, and she was now wed to one of his closest noblemen with his own estate in the north. Therein lie the main difficulty. Cecily had no desire to venture into the wild north, and she had a suspicion that her husband was not displeased by this.

He was the younger brother of Lord Thomas Scrope, from a family of northern gentry who had long served the king when he governed from his castle of Middleham, and although they were only a few years distant in age, in character they were miles apart. Ralph was serious, a man of very little discourse. She blushed as she recalled their wedding night, when even then, very few words were exchanged. There was just the memory of fumbling advances, some pain, discomfort and embarrassment.

Since then, he had remained polite, courteous, but distant, preferring to exert his time and energies on his service to the crown, especially if that took him back to his beloved north. She recalled somewhat wistfully that this had been the only time she had seen his face light up with anything that resembled affection or love. When he spoke of his home. It had only happened once, the day after their wedding feast. After that, the turbulence of the realm had caused them to spend a lot of time apart, and she could not help feeling that it was something that was a relief to both of them.

The expression of relief on his florid face was clear when she asked if she could spend time with her mother whilst he was abroad on the king's duty. She had no doubt he would find his ease there with other women, and she found this did not bother her one whit. For a while, she had been fearing his summons from Grafton, but also knew that she could now press on her sister to insist she stay with her at court, for as long as the king desired it. She was sure the contentment she felt at this knowledge was not appropriate for a wife, but still she could not help being secretly pleased.

It was only when Francis had visited Grafton that she really saw him for the first time, to see him up close. To speak to him and judge his manner. She had been surprised at the excitable fluttering feeling in her stomach as they had spoken and exchanged greetings, looking into each others eyes directly. He was very handsome, very charming and she knew of his undoubted loyalty to her uncle. Something her mother had always made a mockery of, calling him the king's glittering lapdog, in reference to his badge of the silver running hound. She struggled to keep her tone even as she responded to her sister's teasing.

"I thought he was a very pleasant and agreeable man, yes. He has a sense of humour, which appeals to me. I can see why our uncle favours him as a close companion. "

Bess began to step into the violet gown, making more of a struggle of dressing herself than was necessary in the vain hope that her sister would come to her aid.

"But you would like him to be your close companion, would you not?" This last question was delivered with her eyes cast down and her back towards her sister. Cecily didn't answer at first, but finally moved towards Bess to help her dress, seeing that the girl was in such a high state of emotion she was in danger of tearing one of the only two very best gowns she currently had with her from Grafton.

"Yes. I do," she admitted, helping Bess into the sleeves of the dress and pulling the fabric firmly around her shoulders. "I do find him very handsome. But he is married, if you recall, we met his wife Anna at court last year. He is married, as am I."

"Well then!" Bess beamed over her shoulder as Cecily began

to pull at the laces at the back of the dress. "We must see how that stands now, as she is no longer at court I believe. You yourself have admitted to me that you are not enamoured of Scrope, and I have also heard that the Lovell match is not a happy one."

Cecily began to tie up the laces of the gown, tighter than was strictly necessary and needing to push her sister's golden braid out of the way. A tight lump rose in her throat. She knew Bess was only trying to make amends, to repair their earlier discord over the promise she had made. Yet, the very thought of what she was saying caused her heart to beat a little faster, for just a few delightful seconds before her natural common sense cast the dream away. That is all it was, a fanciful dream. Someone like Francis Lovell would never be interested in a royal bastard, married or not.

"Back at court mere days and already listening to gossip Bess?"

"Sometimes gossip is the truth!" Bess exclaimed happily and twisted round to view herself in a looking glass, picking up her braid to tidy it into place. Cecily let go of the last of the laces with a sigh, and watched her elder sister admire herself, turning this way and that, pinning her hair into a coil at the base of her neck.

She did indeed look beautiful. Truly stunning. Cecily admired her golden beauty, and often wondered why she herself was so much darker in colouring. She believed that it may have come from the York side of the family, as their uncle the king was dark where his brothers had been fairer. If their uncle was any sort of man, he couldn't fail to appreciate her radiance, which was why this was such a dangerous game that Bess was playing.

She knew that Bess harboured feelings for Richard. She also knew that Bess had long been their uncle's favourite niece, back from when she toddled around the passages and halls of this very palace. What she was not sure of now were her uncle's feelings for Bess, if they were any other than the natural affection for his brother's daughter.

Earlier this very year he had shocked the city by making a public declaration that he was not planning to marry her, to avert the gossip coursing through the Southwark stews. He had even sent her away to prove his lack of intention, which had shocked Bess to her very core, and caused days of weeping and sleepless nights, and during that time, Bess had gained another, sinister suitor. Henry Tudor.

"If you stand by that belief," Cecily answered in a matter of fact tone, "how does that sit with the rumours saying our uncle murdered our brothers then? That gossip still pervades I notice."

Bess whirled round on her sister in anger, the cloth-of-gold taking light suddenly as it turned towards the chamber window.

"Cecily, no! How dare you? That is cruel and unkind. He would never have done such a thing!'

Cecily shrugged, being deliberately difficult, now seeing the vision that her uncle would receive in his privy chambers, and her earlier concern began to gnaw at her, like a toothache. Although she herself could not countenance that Richard would ever have harmed his brother's sons, she could not resist repeating her sisters own words back at her.

"But gossip is sometimes the truth?"

22. THE PALACE OF WESTMINSTER
November 1485

Bess gathered her skirts together, took a deep breath and entered the privy chamber, feeling the hot gaze of the guards at the door on the back of her neck. She was confident in her appearance and knew full well how her dress flattered her figure and colouring. Her bearing was still that of a princess and now she was back at court she intended to use that to her full advantage.

Keeping her eyes demurely downcast, she moved forwards, immediately feeling the warmth from the flames in the hearth, adding to the fire she knew was already burning inside her. This may be her one chance, her only chance, to make sure that she regained a position as close to Richard as she could. She was not entirely sure how she was going to do it. There was no queen at court, no ladies-in-waiting, but most of her hopes lie in Kathryn, and she knew she could trust her to be her advocate.

Whilst Kathryn was at court and close to her father, Bess intended to be at her side. Her biggest fear lie in the possibility that her husband may suddenly whisk the girl off to his estates in Wales. If she could influence Kathryn to prevent that, she would, without hesitation. Bess knew the girl was fond of her, an she intended to use that to her full advantage, as she had already begun to do.

Inside the chamber, still without looking up, she could hear Richard talking quietly to someone, but that was the only sound, not even the rustle of paper or crackle of a burning log could be heard above it. The pounding of her own heart assailed her ears and almost made her want to turn and run. Almost.

Richard stopped speaking as she came further into the room. Finally - six paces in, but feeling more like she had travelled a league, she stopped and sank into a low and graceful curtsey, her head remaining bowed, summoning every inch of her royal training. Her mother had taught her well.

"Elizabeth." His voice was low and melodious to her ears. "Come girl, you may rise."

She did as she was bade, lifting her head at the same time and her heart, now thudding completely out of her control, lurched inside her chest. She was sure he would be able to see it, beating hard and fast above the neckline of her dress, threatening to break through her skin. For a second, she couldn't breathe. She had truly not realised how much she wanted this.

Richard was seated, dressed in crimson cloth-of-gold and black velvet. The colours were severe but suited him, and any severity was lightened by the golden collar that was so familiar to her. She had a sudden urge to rush towards him, to throw herself at him in abandon the way she did when she was younger, when it could all be so innocent, when neither of them cared who knew that they loved each other.

She thought he looked a little better than when she had last been in his company, not so careworn, not quite so sad. It would ease her heart greatly to know that he was finally getting over Anne's death, that he was finding something else, someone else to live for. He smiled at her, the smile creasing his dark grey eyes and, relieved, she knew he was pleased to see her. Genuinely pleased. Making a conscious effort, she pressed her heels hard against the floor to stop herself from moving, frightened of the depth of her feelings for him.

It was vital to her to remain watchful, detached, but despite knowing this she was hungrily devouring his face with her eyes. As she tried to burn every inch of him into her memory, she suddenly noticed the figure standing like some sort of protective sentinel at his side. Francis Lovell, dressed in plain blue, a departure from his latest variations with murrey and blue. He was regarding her with no visible expression at all, no matter how hard she tried to read his eyes.

"Are you well?" Richard's voice, full of warmth and concern, brought her eyes back to his face.

"Yes, Your Grace. Very." She paused for a breath, trying to keep her voice clear and steady. "Thank you for welcoming me back to court. I have missed Kathryn, John and Edward so." She stopped, flicked a glance at Francis who was not even looking at her, his gaze fixed into the distance. "I have missed everyone."

He nodded slightly, as if pleased, he was regarding her intently.

"And Dame Elizabeth?" Bess smiled conspiratorially

"My mother retains her youthful vigour, Your Grace." That made him smile again, albeit ruefully.

"Please Bess. We are family. You may address me as such."

She rose then, rapt, but nervous, smoothing down the skirts of her dress with her hands, needing to have something to do whilst she thought of what to say. Why was she so anxious? This was her uncle, her uncle Dickon!

As if sensing her awkwardness, he rose from his seat and moved around the table. Bess's breath caught in her throat as he stood before her and took her hands, leaning forwards to kiss her cheek. She could smell the fragrance of fine Bristol soap, a hint of some other perfume, unrecognisable, but heady. Keeping hold of her hand, he led her to a chair by the fire and bade her sit. Her eyes fixed on his every move as he seated himself in the chair opposite and continued to keep her gaze, his face registering pleasure at the sight of her, she was sure of it. She knew him so well.

Francis hadn't moved, he stood like a sentry at a postern gate. Guarding. Waiting.

"I am pleased you are well and were able to come back to us. Kathryn more than most, and I must thank you for the friendship that you show her," Richard continued, leaning forwards so that he was as close to her as he could be despite them sitting on separate chairs. "I am also pleased to be able to give you some glad news."

He watched her continually, speaking slowly and deliberately. Every word he spoke in his low, caressing voice felt like a balm to her heart. He broke off for a moment, and gave a quick glance towards Francis, then he reached over once again and placed a hand over hers. His touch was warm and dry, she felt a heat spreading up her arm towards her chest. She felt flushed, faint. Oh dear lord, she thought, please let him love me! Please let him allow me to make him happy again.

"I have sent a message to Dame Elizabeth so she is aware of what I am about to tell you."

Those words brought her back to the present with speed. Her mother? What did she have to do with this? Bess looked around the room as if expecting to see someone else there for some reason. Yet, all she could see was the object of her desire, studiously regarding her, and Francis, who now fixed his attention on her with a steady and unnerving gaze, like a cat with it's prey. There was something happening here, they both knew what it was whilst she could only guess. Concerning her? Concerning her mother?

"Is this about my brothers?"

Richard was taken aback, his hand left hers swiftly as if her skin burned and he sat back in his chair, his face whitening slightly.

"No. Why would you think that?"

Bess considered very carefully before she continued. She had no intention of bringing up what was being discussed at Grafton, what she had also heard confirmed in her few days at court. People seemed happy to go out of their way to tell her what they had heard. Many who passed on this story were happy to speculate about her brothers having turned up abroad, yet no-one then went on to admit that if this was true, the king was not the tyrant he was being made out to be in the taverns and brothels of the city and further abroad.

"I have heard a story, about some boys. About Flanders..."

She stumbled on the words, not wanting to change the way Richard was looking at her, or to raise the spectre of her brothers claim to the throne. What good would that do? She became more acutely aware of the silent brooding presence of Francis Lovell and it began to irritate her. Why could he not just leave the room and let them speak alone? She pounced on that thought as soon as it entered her head and lacing her hands together whilst looking down, she spoke very quietly.

"If we are to talk about this uncle Richard, would we be able to do so in private?"

She thought she heard a small chuckle from Francis, but when she looked at him, he appeared not to have moved an inch. Richard also now directed his attention to his friend.

"Francis, would you mind? I think we could both do with some wine."

Rather than leave, he turned to one side and poured out some wine from a waiting flagon, crossing the room to offer a cup to Bess. At this offering, she tilted her head and looked directly into his dark gaze. His eyes held a warning, a reminder her of their agreement, but her heart had no intention of heeding. She didn't want to drink but she took the offered cup and nodded her head in thanks, unable to voice any words to him. Instead he then turned to Richard.

"Would you prefer me to leave, Your Grace?" Richard shook his head at his friend's question.

"No. We will not be talking about the rumours abroad. That matter is being dealt with." Bess didn't understand, but knew enough from his mood that the subject was not to be discussed. So, if not that then, she mused, what?

"So what is it then? What is it that could concern both myself and my mother?"

"Your marriage."

This came quickly from Francis, and Richard tilted his head towards his friend with a disapproving look.

"Marriage?"

Bess held her breath. Marriage! Was that it? Marriage, to Richard? No - it couldn't be, could it? Why else would he bring her here, to his Privy Chamber with only his closest friend and confidante present! Why else would he have suddenly agreed to her coming back, sending Francis to bring her, telling her mother. It all fell into place! It explained why his closest friend and companion was looking so dour, having seen his hopes dashed, thrown to the winds.

Tears of pure joy filled her eyes and began to fall down her cheeks. Her throat constricted, she couldn't talk or breathe. Overwhelmed with emotion, she lunged forward and fell at Richard's feet, her face turned up towards him, beaming with love, adulation and joy. She grasped his hands with her own and looked up into that strong stern face she had loved since she was a small child.

"Oh, Richard! I can't believe it! I f only you knew how I have wished for this moment. How I have dreamed ... even though my mother said you would never consider it, even if she approved! How I was so frightened that she still kept me tied to that Tudor pretender, when she all the time knew my heart, knew it better than anyone else."

Richard was regarding her with astonishment, which Bess did not notice through the tears in her eyes. So overwhelmed with emotion was she that she lowered her head to kiss his hands so she did not see him make a motion to Francis with his head, his eyes communicating what didn't need to be said. Francis, reluctantly, departed from the room leaving the King and his niece alone.

The last image he saw tore his heart apart. Bess, surrounded by violet velvet, was outlined by the firelight in the darkening afternoon, prostrate on the floor before her uncle, her lips pressed to the fingers which bore the coronation jewel.

And Richard, his face filled with an agonising despair, was lifting a hand to gently stoke her sun-bright hair before he told her of his plans.

23. THE PALACE OF WESTMINSTER
November 1485

Outside the chamber, Francis had to admit he was feeling slightly more at ease, and to some extent, a great weight had suddenly lifted from his shoulders. Knowing that Richard has finalised his plans for remarriage, he did not feel the need to witness the girl's embarrassment as he explained what her future role would be. He now had no doubt that Bess was totally infatuated with her uncle and would have not ceased to strive until she had found anyway possible to back Richard into a corner, no matter what the consequences. By securing his succession and at the same time solving the problem of what to do with Bess, Francis felt that to leave them alone for this short while could cause no real damage.

He walked down the passage planning to go and oversee some new horses that had recently been acquired from Middleham. It had crossed his mind that he could select one to send down to Minster Lovell as a gift for his wife's name-day, as well as a form of consolation for his lack of presence on his own estates. Anna still showed little interest in coming back to court but was unfailingly insistent in her pleas to get Francis to return back to the manor house for a while. It troubled him that he would have to write back and tell her that with the impending visit of the Portuguese party, he would still be needed by the king.

It troubled him, but also gave him a small measure of relief. Although he still felt a strong affection for his wife, their marriage had been something of a tragedy for them both. They had married young, and Francis had immediately been dispatched north, eventually finding his feet in a Yorkist household, much to his own surprise. He had tried to love his wife and failed. Just as they had failed to have any children, and Francis felt that she blamed him completely for their lack of issue. Being totally honest with himself, he was not unhappy that current affairs prevented his return to Oxfordshire and it was this guilt that caused him to hope a name-day gift of a fine palfrey would suffice as form of apology.

He was making his way towards the stairs when he caught sight of Cecily sitting alone in a window seat.   Her hands were folded in her lap and she appeared to be totally absorbed in her own thoughts. Her head was bowed, the light creating a silken sheen on her darkly coiled braid.   The sight caused him to pause momentarily and every fibre of his being told him that he should continue on his errand, but the picture of stillness she made as she sat, seemingly unregarded, made him stop in his tracks.

Since the ride back from Grafton, he had been unable to completely erase her from his mind.   Her small heart-shaped face, with the soulful yet mischievous eyes, seemed to occupy his thoughts more than he would ever have thought possible.   He was also a little alarmed, if he could admit it to himself, that he felt an emotional response to one of the Woodville women, and a married one at that!   It was a fact he would have laughed at a few weeks ago. Only he found something in the way Cecily bore herself, the way she seemed to separate herself from the main focus of Woodville behaviour, that was very attractive.

That didn't stop him finding that fact difficult to acknowledge but in the end, he couldn't stop himself.   He walked over and stood before her as she sat in quiet contemplation.

"Lady Cecily?"

She raised her dark head and on seeing his face, a smile crept slowly from her lips up to the very corner of her eyes.   In that one simple act, Francis became sure, as he had never been before, that this girl also felt something for him.

"I am waiting for Bess." She sighed, looking in the direction of the privy chamber where she had watched her sister disappear earlier. Her expression was almost shamefaced, her eyes beseeching.   "He sent for her Francis – honestly! Please don't blame her." The smile wavered, becomingly so he thought. "But I do admit, she was very eager to go."

Francis was overcome with enormous sympathy for the girl. He wondered what it had been like to walk in the shadow of her golden-haired sister for so many years. For a second, he was reminded of Richard; smaller, darker and quieter than his tall, fair brother. He looked down at her, his face relaxed.

"I know," he informed her. "I have just come from the chamber myself."

Cecily stood up suddenly, she was slightly shorter than Francis and was able to look up at him from beneath a crescent of dark lashes. She examined his face for a moment, then nodded, as if resolved.

"I will return to her chamber then, and speak to her there. " As she moved to depart, Francis placed a hand on her arm.

"No need - she is still with him, and may be some time." Cecily looked at him searchingly then, an expression of concern crossing her brow.

"Are they alone?" The furrows on her forehead deepened as Francis shook his head, momentarily distracted by how the light from the window caught the fair down on her cheeks and coated them with a soft, luminous glow. But Cecily's expression set hard with rage.

"Francis - how could you let...?"

He placed a finger on his lips swiftly and stopped her words in mid-flow. Francis looked over his shoulder and back towards the stairs, but then taking Cecily's hand, he led her into an empty drawing chamber off the passage. The room was dark and cool, only one or two candles burned from sconces on the wall and the fire in the hearth was unlit.

Breathlessly, she looked up at him, even though she had followed him without resistance, her face was full of question. He could faintly trace the outline of her cheek in the dim light and although he was still holding her hand, she showed no intention of pulling away.

"Francis?" Her voice was a ghost in the stillness. He took her other hand in his so that he was cupping both of them loosely and looked down into her upraised face, the candles bathing them in their inconstant light.

"Cecily, the king has arranged a marriage for Bess. He is

telling her now. A messenger has been sent to Grafton to inform your mother, and who knows how she will take that news! However, I am so glad you came to court with her, although I swear I did not know about this plan until we arrived back here. There was no artifice on my part in removing her from Grafton, and I think the same can be said for Richard. It would appear young Kathryn may be at the root of this somewhere. Only now, your sister will need you here, you will be able to help her prepare and also be able to reassure your Lady Mother that all due consideration for her is being undertaken. Richard has no desire for Dame Grey to return to court, I am sure you understand?"

For the next few seconds he desperately tried to determine her expression, but found it difficult in the shadowy confines of the chamber. Now that he had finished telling her his news, he became aware of the warmth of her. His senses were filled with her fragrance, but he couldn't work out how she would respond to his words. Finally, when it seemed like she would never speak again, she whispered,

"Please tell me that ..."

He immediately knew what she was thinking and although annoyed, he kept the emotion out of his voice.

"It's Manuel of Portugal, the Duke of Beja. It is a good match, Richard is planning to marry his cousin Princess Joanna. They are on their way to court to visit and finalise arrangements."

There was silence again at these words. He knew she was thinking hard, but still she made no move to remove her hands from his, which he was glad of. Her face was still tilted up towards his, although he could not read her eyes, their darkness lost in the gloom. He forced down a desire to touch the upturned cheek which was lined in gold by the nearest candle, and the overwhelming urge to seek out her lips in the soft darkness, her words soon prevented him from succumbing to temptation.

"How did Bess take this news? I am thinking she will be very surprised, she did not expect to be married so soon." She paused. "Portugal..." It began to dawn on her that this would mean her sister would leave court, leave the country. He thought he saw her eyes glisten. Francis swallowed hard then, his grip on her hands tightened.

"I think she will be upset rather than surprised, Cecily. She misunderstood what Richard was saying. She thought that the proposed marriage..."

"Was with him." She finished his sentence in hushed tones.

"That is when I left the room, at Richard's request. He is breaking it to her as gently as he can I am sure. He is very fond of her you know."

"Oh I know that of course." Cecily breathed, releasing a further wave of intoxicating fragrance. "They have always been as thick as two thieves, smiling and jesting with each other, sharing private jokes. All innocent on his part I am sure. I think she just reminds him so much of my father, of all that he has lost. I see the same look in his eyes sometimes. A form of admiration, of worship almost. A different type of love than that Bess would have from him."

Francis raised his brows. He was astonished that this young girl could have seen and understood so much and his own admiration for her grew as he listened to her explain what Francis himself should have so clearly seen. Richard's feelings for the girl had always been innocent. A connection with the brother he loved, and the life that was gone.

"She will need you," he said softly. "She will be glad that you are here." After what seemed like hours but was only seconds, she whispered his name.

"Francis? "

"Yes, Cecily" His own voice was low and hushed.

"Are you glad that I am here?" There was no pause before he answered.

"I am," he admitted, his voice breaking slightly.

"For Bess's sake?"

"No. For mine." Without further hesitation, he gave into the desire which had been mounting for so long now, and lowered his lips down to hers. For an instant, in the candlelight, he saw her eyes searching out his before they closed.

24. THE PALACE OF WESTMINSTER
November 1485

Richard's head felt tight, as if his crown had left an indent which would never be erased. His sword arm began to ache dully, and he silently cursed the changeable weather. Bess still had her head laid on his hand, and he could feel the dampness from her tears. He needed to speak to her, but his voice seemed to have dried up, despite the wine he had been drinking.

How? How in all goodness had he come to this?

His marriage to Anne had been fortunate. From a young age he knew that they were affectionate to one another, although nothing formal was ever said. They spent time in each others company, searched each other out, found comfort in talking quietly to each other, encouraged by her parents.

When Warwick turned against Edward, their paths forked, but she was always there in the shadows of his life. He had sired two bastard children, but deep down he had always known that somehow Anne would return, and after the victory at Tewkesbury, everything had fallen into place.

It was a marriage of more than convenience. He gained wealth and titles, Anne gained royal status, and both of them gained the devotion of like minded souls. He would no more have betrayed Anne than he would have acted against Edward. Their years in the north were happier than either of them would ever have anticipated, and he knew that others had envied their close marital bond. It was simple. Their love had grown, helped because they knew each other as well as their own selves and it was not surprising that part of him had died with her. The small part of him that had remained after his son's death. Now he was left to try and rescue what was left of his living soul, to remarry and restore the succession of the Yorkist dynasty - and find a way to maneuver his way out of this emotional and complicated situation.

It would have been easy if he felt nothing and he would have much preferred it if he could remain detached. For a while after

Anne's death and before the battle, he had his wish. The long, dark passages in which he dwelled had twisted and turned, preventing him from escaping their inevitable gloom. Only recently had he begun to walk back into the light, to notice the brilliance of the sun, the smell of autumn burning its way towards the year's end.

But with that re-emergence came the exposure to more pain. Was there truly no end to it? To see this young girl prostrating herself before him clawed at his soul. He had to break her heart, and he feared that his own may bruise all over again, even though he had thought no further pain was possible, that he had suffered all the tortures Hell could spew up at him this side of Heaven. She was Edward's daughter, he could see him in her every movement, and when he couldn't see Edward, he could see his brother Edmund.

And then, there was Elizabeth herself. He loved her. He knew he loved her, but as to how that love was framed, he was no longer at all sure. Was it as his niece or as something more carnal? The very thought made him ashamed, but he had to admit the truth of the confusion to himself. His throat protested as he swallowed, and taking a deep breath, he began a conversation which he had no idea how to conduct.

"Bess, look at me!" Her tear stained face, alight with joy and tinged with relief, shone up at him. The radiance from her gaze was so fierce it could almost burn his soul. She looked joyously happy, despite the tears, and the earlier brittle tension had disappeared. It was as if those few words had dispelled her fears and doubts. As if she felt - safe.

"Richard. I can't believe... that you did care! I have loved you for so long, but I ... I was so sorry about... about Anne..." she stammered, breathlessly, desperate for him to understand, her eyes pleading with him to know her innermost feelings. "I loved her. I loved her truly and I never would have done anything to hurt her, despite what people said."

"Hush, child. Please!" his voice was hoarse, from a mix of anxiety and emotion. "Please, get up. Come Bess!" He moved forwards to grasp her arms and raise her up from her knees and she allowed herself to be lifted from the floor, keeping her eyes fixed firmly on his face as if she feared he would disappear, and regained her seat by the fire. From inside his sleeve, he produced a fine linen kerchief and pressed it into her hand.

Bess folded it between her fingers and pressed it to her face, inhaling deeply whilst Richard pulled his chair closer to hers, so that their knees were almost touching, but he kept his hands folded in his lap as he leaned forwards.

"Bess, you must listen to me. You must not doubt that I have love for you." Her face was a burning candle in his eyes, bright and hot.

"Oh I know!" she cried, her tears falling once again." I always knew!" She reached out again and placed a hand on his knee, and he looked down at her small, slim fingers.

"This is very difficult for me" he began, raising his gaze again to meet her eyes, feeling them bore deeply into his, so deeply he wanted to avert his gaze once more but dare not. He had gone this far, now he needed to see it through. His head was throbbing dully, his throat tight. He paused to take a sip from the cup at his side aware she was watching him closely.

Damn Francis, he cursed inwardly. This was not going the way he had planned and his friend's unfortunate interjection had changed the whole course of events. He knew how worried Francis was and that he just wanted Bess married off sooner rather than later, but Richard didn't want to hurt her. Not more than he had to. It was obvious this news would be a severe blow to her, and he wanted to cushion that as much as he could. For quite some time, he had been aware of her feelings for him, she had admitted them herself whilst Anne was still alive, and he had tried to dismiss it as childish infatuation.

It was only when she returned to court, after being holed up in sanctuary during the early part of his reign. When she walked into the hall, it was as though Edward had come to life in a female form. Her humour, her laughter, the colour of her hair, rich and golden like his, not the icy gilt of the Woodvilles. Guiltily, he had found himself comparing her to Anne, who by this time was beginning to become as frail as a wraith.   So it was no surprise to find out that others were carrying out the same assessment, and using this to twist the thoughts of anyone who would listen.

Yes, he had danced with her, and listened to her sing and play the lute. They had smiled at each other, and spoken together in private on more than one occasion.   But in comparing her to his wife at that time, he was only experiencing an acknowledgement of how much his kingship had cost him. He could count up the expenses like entries in the house books. What he saw in her then, he longed to have back, but not with her.   With Anne, with his son, with his life as it had been before.

But now they were gone, and he was a man changed.   Soon, he would be forced to marry a woman he had never met, and to expose to her what only a few close acquaintances knew.   When she, a royal princess, saw how he was made, would she be reviled? And if she was, what then?   Anne had known him for years, before his affliction was visited upon him, and it had mattered not, so comfortable were they with each other during their shared youth. Somehow, it felt different now he was older, more... pronounced. He sighed, dragging himself away from the deep well of his thoughts and he looked back into the smiling face before him.   The love he saw there humbled him so much, he felt weak.

He also had to admit that to send her away to a foreign land would also be a final wrench from his brother's memory.   And all the time he was weighing up her future, she was adoring him silently, trustfully, with Edward's eyes. How much more torture could the devil serve up for him? He cleared his throat decisively, setting his mind to the task once more.

"I have to remarry Bess, for the succession and for the country. You know more than most how hard this is for me, how much Anne meant to me." He explained all this carefully, but seriously, whilst holding her gaze. "In truth, if I had an heir, I would not remarry, but that is not the position here and a king needs a son."

Bess, who had been eager to speak for some time, seized her opportunity.

"You know I would never try to replace Anne! That is why this is such a wonderful solution! We both knew and loved her so much and I know she would want us to be happy, more than anything would want you to be happy. She loved you so much - as much, if not more, than I do." She smiled at him coyly, all tears gone now. "If that could be at all possible."

Richard groaned inwardly. He was making a complete mess of the whole thing. There was only one way to go now, he had to end this overwhelming display, so he did.

"Bess, we cannot marry." He tried hard to keep any sharpness from his voice, but in the end he knew the words came out cold. Shock registered on her fair face, he could have slapped her hard and received a similar reaction.

"But, Richard, you – Francis - I don't..." she stammered desperately, in true confusion. "You said we were to marry!"

"No - Francis stopped me saying anything. He said we were here to discuss your marriage."

Bess sat back in her chair, a hand raised to her face as she covered her mouth, thinking, eyes fiercely bright above her fingers. Suddenly, Richard could see Elizabeth Woodville staring at him with an accusation that seared his skin. That made him very uncomfortable and he shifted in his seat. To his relief, she cast her eyes down then and began to twist the linen handkerchief between her hands.

When she looked up at him again, her face had hardened somewhat. That in itself surprised him, he had never seen any kind of edge to his niece - believing happily that she had escaped the Woodville stain. But there it was, staring back at him and his heart plummeted.

"Then - if I am not to marry you, who else?" A thought came to her and she continued with disgust. "Please God, please don't tell me you have pardoned Henry Tudor and I am his prize for bending the knee and pleading undying loyalty?"

Richard couldn't help himself, but he laughed out loud. A laugh that had a hard sardonic edge to it.

"God's blood child! Henry Tudor? You think I would trust a Beaufort?" He shook his head smiling. "That was a lesson well learned. No, never Henry Tudor! The man will be lucky to keep his head." The next words came as a knife thrust in the dark, the blade flashing in her eyes.

"I know you have been to visit him," she said quietly watching his face for a reaction. At those words, his blood ran cold. How?

Silently furious inside, Richard managed to keep his emotions in check. How on earth had she come across that fact? She hadn't even been at court. Once again he had proof of how few he could trust, but he was determined to remain cool under her constant surveillance.

"Really? How?" He hoped he sounded much more matter of fact than he felt. She shrugged her shoulders carelessly, as if it was of no great importance.

"People talk to me. They tell me things. They don't care if I need to know them or not, they just seem to gain a certain pleasure from seeking me out." Her face finally began to reflect some of the despair she was feeling. "Some seek my approval because I am your niece, others because I am Edward's daughter. " She stopped briefly, appeared to be weighing her words. "Some because of my brothers..."

He sighed heavily, witnessing what a burden was being placed on both of them.

"In these circumstances then, I think your marriage comes at a most prudent time. Men will always try and use you to their own ends, Bess. Men who still, despite honour and rewards, cannot see their way to remaining loyal to me. They wait for the next best opportunity to undermine my cause, and if one is not sufficiently apparent, they create one."

Slowly, as if the weight of those words dragged at his heart, he rose from his seat and moved back to the table. He surveyed the pile of parchments littering its top with distaste, red wax seals gleaming like newly congealed blood.

"I hate the court, Bess. It is a vile and malicious stew of greed and malcontent. Men, sometimes even women, all out for their own ends." Bess knew to whom he referred but made no response. "I tried to stay away as much as I could whilst serving your father in the north." He gave another rueful chuckle. "By God, I tried to stay away after I was crowned! I don't think any other anointed king saw quite so much of his country in such a small period of time! I yearn for peace, for wide open spaces," he broke off, his face displaying all his emotions quite clearly now. "I long for Middleham." Stopping, he recovered himself enough to raise his head and regard her with fond concern. "I cannot regain that peace, but for you, with a new husband, you can get out of this treacherous atmosphere into something better. You can create a new court Bess and learn from your father's, and indeed my own, mistakes."

"I could do that with you," she replied simply, her head still bowed, intent on the fabric in her hands. "We would work together to heal the wounds of the past. We would throw out the Beauforts, the Stanleys, the Mortons - all those who conspire and wait for us to trip up. We wouldn't. We would be such a force, Richard. The blood of Old York. Stronger, basking in the Sunne in Splendour. We could make our reign glorious!"

She was looking at him now, sitting high in her chair, straight backed as if on her very own throne, her eyes blazing with passion and determination. For one small moment he began to wonder, if, how? It hurt to watch her bare her soul. He could see how much she wanted this and he felt unworthy of how much she invested in the power of his love. Bess rose from her own seat as he watched and took a few steps towards him.

"You misjudge me Richard. You think I am my mother. You think I plot and scheme and want this union just for what it will bring me. You should give some thought about what I can bring you. Yes, there would be my father's affinity, and those that spy against you would not spy against me. But aside from all that, I love you, with a depth you will never understand. We could be so happy, so happy -

we could have children, beautiful children. But you do not trust me, even in this, I suspect you think I am my mothers creature."

"I do not," he replied quietly, looking at the empty cup on the table, which he had no desire to refill. "And I have always known you to be strong willed and am fully aware of what value your marriage would have to any suitor lucky enough to win your hand."

"Despite my bastard status?" He sighed and swallowed hard, looking at her from beneath lowered lids. His own heart began to pound now, uncomfortably.

"I would change that if I could." She took a further step towards him, her eyes blazing.

"So do it! Is it not in your power? You are the king. You can do this, can restore what has been taken from me. How much better would my marriage prospects be then? How many alliances, how much loyalty would that buy you?"

Richard pressed his hands flat on the table , leaning across its cluttered surface to regard her. She was so young, so dreadfully young.

"Your mother's marriage was clandestine. My brother, love him as I did, was a past master at wooing women into his bed and counting the consequences after. I feel sure he only embarked on this pursuit because Warwick was against it and Edward wanted to prove he was king, not the earl's mammet. If Warwick had not been so angered by your mother's common status, Edward would have had her bedded and wed to a convenient nobleman before the year was over, as he had so adroitly done in the past. But no, Warwick made a fight of it. Chaos ensued. We are still reeling from it all these long years later." He tilted his head back up to stare at her fiercely. "To reverse your status negates my claim to the throne. How can I declare that? What I did, I know was right in the eyes of God and the country, although damn knows they don't see it! As for your brothers, I know not where they are, living or dead, and pray constantly that they are found - God willing - alive somewhere. What then? How long would it be before some of these men who kneel at my feet fly to their aid and raise an army against me?

Christ, Bess, what would you have me do? Betray my self before God? Have me admit that I ascended on a lie, that I was anointed with the chrism knowing it was all false?"

He all but threw himself down in the chair, resting his head on his fist and staring into the flames. The air in the room became redolent with tension. Bess moved towards him slowly and placed a hand lightly on his shoulder, giving it a slight squeeze.

"In just a few seconds you have vindicated yourself of any guilt on those matters to me. Others may doubt you, may doubt your claim, I do not. I never have, you know that. I also know that you have no idea what happened to Edward and Richard, or these rumours and gossip would not trouble you as they do." Richard showed no response to her words, his mind was racing as he felt the flames warming his face, wishing they could burn deeper and warm his soul. "All you have to do is bar the male line from the succession, similar to what happened with the Beauforts I believe." she murmured quietly. For a few seconds, her hand seemed to burn through the fabric of his doublet, scorching through to his skin.

He turned his head towards her. His face had regained its weary, careworn mask, and he looked tired, exhausted.

"Enough, Bess. You are to be married. We are both to be married. But not to each other."

The chamber was in semi-darkness now, and the Vespers bell was chiming. Bess moved round to stand in front of her uncle and sank to the floor in a deep curtsey, the rustling of her gown the only sound against the metallic chiming of the bell.

"Then there is nothing more to say. May I have your permission to leave, Your Grace?"

Richard did not reply, but held his hand out to her. She grasped it, and placed her lips to it, lingering just a little too long. His stomach contracted at the touch. Rising elegantly, she moved to the door of the chamber when Richard's voice stopped her.

"Bess? You haven't asked me the name of your betrothed." He had difficulty with the words, his voice was hoarse with a hundred emotions. Bess stopped with her hand on the door latch and smiled to herself. She knew his internal torment, and was pleased that it matched hers. Turning her head slightly, she looked over her shoulder.

"No. It is of no consequence to me. I will marry whomever you have chosen Richard. If I am not to marry the man I love, then it matters not whom I take to my marital bed."

With those words, Bess left the room, leaving Richard alone with his thoughts.

25. BURGUNDY
November 1485

John de la Pole, Earl of Lincoln, was studying the richly coloured marble tiles under his feet. The castle of La-Motte-au-Bois was where they had finally arrived and where the Dowager Duchess of Burgundy, King Richard's sister had requested they meet. The chateau was now one of her favourite residences taken up after the death of her husband, Charles. It was a particularly grand palace, even by Burgundian standards and John has been exceedingly impressed by the sheer display of wealth and splendour. Having himself stayed in some of the most prestigious houses in England, he still had not experienced such sheer opulence before.

He had also only met his aunt once before, when he was younger, and although he wasn't particularly looking forward to it now, Richard seemed to think he had the measure of her. The journey by sea had been uneventful, which they were particularly fortunate in taking into account the time of year, but his companion, William Catesby, one of his uncle's chief councillors, as well as being Chancellor of the Exchequer, was pretty poor company. Mostly he had his nose stuck in piles of correspondence and didn't care much for talk, or for partaking in the odd cup of wine, both of which John enjoyed immensely. It made for an exceedingly staid journey.

Will stood at his side now, nervously tapping his fingers on a dagger at his waist and looking around the chamber uncomfortably. Although they were closeted in sumptuous surroundings, the room itself was somewhat dark and oppressive, all the hangings and furnishings favouring dark tones which added to an air of heavy solemnity. It was also very cold.

"Do you believe this boy could be one of the Princes?" Will's question came so suddenly that it took John by surprise. They had travelled all these miles and his companion had not uttered one single word about their mission. Now, seconds before they were due to see this boy, he decided to start talking. Priceless!

John had just opened his mouth to reply to that effect, when the door opened and two liveried men-at-arms entered the room flanking a slim, dark haired figure striding forwards purposefully, clad in purple cloth-of-gold.

Margaret of Burgundy favoured her father in the same way that Richard did, but was slightly taller. As she swept almost imperiously towards them he remembered that although she was not traditionally beautiful, she was rather what John had heard some refer to as a "handsome" woman. He did notice, however, before he bowed his head, that she still had the merriest dark grey eyes, set in a face that appeared wreathed in good humour. Her features told the story of her life in Burgundy, a testament that she had made a good marriage and been happy with Charles, until his death a few years ago.

"No- no!" she exclaimed suddenly halting, "let me look at you!"

She grabbed his arms and forced him upright, none too gently, as he began to bow, her searching eyes scrutinising his face minutely. John, somewhat taken aback, found it hard to keep a straight face. Her grip was fierce, reminiscent of Richard's, and on that thought he couldn't help but begin to smirk.

"Heavens!" she exclaimed. "But you do favour Dickon, I see no Edward or George, which is no bad thing!" she murmured under her breath. That made John face finally collapse into a smile. He felt he was going to become quite fond of his aunt, but although she continued to grip his arms firmly, she had now turned her attention to John's companion.

"And you are..?" She was looking shrewdly at Catesby and John was even more amused to see the complete discomfort on Will's usually expressionless face. In stiff response, Will bowed sharply, so sharp his spine almost made a cracking noise.

"Your Grace - William Catesby,"

"Ah - the kings lawyer! Well, there could well be a pretty constitutional tangle for you wrestle with here! Dickon certainly picked his envoys with care... if not a little irony." John was not completely sure what she meant and his dark brows drew together quizzically as he looked from one to the other. Margaret smiled at him ruefully. "His heir and his lawyer, to identify a missing York heir?"

John felt slightly stung but he didn't quite know why. He was very loyal to his uncle, who had always done the best for his welfare and was now grooming him to be the next King of England should he have no further issue. John himself was not ambitious, and sincerely hoped that Richard would remarry and get himself a son before much too longer. Having seen the burdens that kingship brought, he wasn't exactly too eager to take up that mantle, he enjoyed his freedom and thought he would find the yoke of kingship far too restrictive. Not that he would dare broach that with his uncle. This was a matter of duty, but soon Richard would remarry, and the situation would resolve itself, he was sure.

"Your Grace," John began in as respectful a tone he could muster, "the boy we have come to see, if found to be who we think he is, has been declared illegitimate."

Margaret was regarding him with watchful, if smiling, eyes. She had relinquished her firm grip on his arms but he could still feel where they had encircled him as if they had left a mark. He felt sure that if he peeled back his sleeve he would see either bruises or red welts. She remained directly in front of him, topping him by a couple of inches in height and folded her hands in front of her, fingers laden with jewels which winked darkly in the sombre surroundings.

"Yes, that is true. But what has been done can be undone, if there is a will." Margaret walked away a few paces towards a chair which sat on a raised velvet dais. She made no attempt to sit, but paced back and stopped before them. Placing her hands on her hips, she turned her eyes back onto Will, who seemed to shrivel under her gaze.

"Lawyer - what did you make of this pre-contract story? There are many who say that Dickon did make it up to take the boys crown. Not that I would entirely blame him I have to say. Elizabeth Woodville is a rare breed - a woman with too little heart and too much brain. I can understand how my brother would have needed to guard himself against her ways. I am not surprised at what he planned, just non too happy about the way it was executed." She smiled then, with pursued lips and said as if to herself. "An unfortunate choice of words. You were Hastings man were you not?"

Will composed himself, proudly drawing up to his full height.

"I was. I was also witness to his plotting against the king, and able to ensure that he was made aware of the treachery abroad against him. I was also able to speak to the Bishop of Bath and Wells who informed the king of the whole pre-contract situation. I feel that my advice was of assistance to him on both these occasions and enabled him to take the most appropriate course of action, as circumstances dictated."

"You certainly did that." Margaret turned, her rich skirts rustling and sweeping the floor behind her with a silken slither as she moved over to the heavily carved oaken chair up on the dais and seated herself. The two men watched in silence as she settled down and arranged her skirts around her feet with almost careful deliberation. "I have to be certain of my brothers intentions for this boy. His record in this respect goes against him."

John stepped forward quickly - although he was still enjoying certain aspects of this discourse, and in particular Will's discomfort, he would not brook any calumny against his uncle. He had heard far too much gossip and rumour in London and he was determined not to countenance as much here.

"Madam Duchess, my uncle, your brother, has been accused of murdering his nephews. He did not. At worst, someone else did, at best someone unknown spirited them away. If you are as protective of this boy as you appear to be, I believe you favour the latter, therefore your remarks seem somewhat unfair."

Margaret's lips curved upwards. Lifting her left hand, she snapped her fingers and a cupbearer appeared from nowhere to rush to her side. She took a goblet from him and took a slow sip, carefully regarding John from over the rim. After drinking, she rested the goblet on the arm of the chair, whilst the cupbearer hovered expectantly at her elbow.

"I can see why Dickon would choose you as his heir. Fairly burning with loyalty and chivalry are you not? You take me back some years and it could be my brother himself standing there, he was always a fool for courtly values - much good it did him in the end. How many of the men he trusted paid him back in false coin? Too many to count – that's how many! Half of his "trusted" followers pledged themselves to that Welshman Tudor." She almost spat the name, sweeping up her cup as if the very word tasted foul. After taking another sip of wine from her cup she continued.

"Did they capture him, by the way, after the battle?" It was Will who answered.

"Yes, Your Grace. Henry Tudor resides at the king's pleasure in the Tower." Margaret continued to cast an appraising gaze over Will.

"Ah, really. Is he to stand trial?"

"No, Your Grace. Not at present. The king feels he may have information on the fate of the two missing boys."

"One missing boy." Margaret replied curtly, swilling her wine round in her cup. Will Catesby coughed politely.

"Your Grace, you seem very certain that this boy is one of your brother's sons. Can you tell us why you would be so sure? I believe you have not seen the boys for some years, your last visit to court being some five years ago?"

Margaret fixed steely eyes on the lawyer, but Will seemed to be gaining confidence in her presence. He kept eye contact with her without flinching or looking away, and became the man that John saw at court and who he was much more familiar with. His calm objective manner is what Richard sought out in him, finding his insights invaluable as he was able to remain detached from highly charged situations.

"You are making me feel tired." Margaret suddenly exclaimed curtly. "Sit."

As John and Will took their seats to one side of where she herself was seated on the dais, Margaret again gestured her cupbearer, who this time hurried forward with wine for the guests. John took his gratefully and immediately slaked his thirst deeply, whilst Will regarded his cup suspiciously, sipping only once, before putting it back on a table.

Once the young lad who was her cupbearer had re-filled John's cup, Margaret dismissed him, and at the same time barked something in Flemish to the men-at-arms who bowed deeply and left the room. She settled back in her chair then and licked her lips almost nervously. For the first time her facade seemed to falter and her face became slightly anxious as she turned her gaze back to the waiting faces in front of her.

"Very well. There is no easy way to tell you this, and I know exactly how my brother will react when hears what I have to say. However, there is no other way of assuring you of the validity of this young boy's lineage."

"Your Grace," William interrupted before she could continue. "Do not think to second guess the king. He is much changed since you last saw him, so many events have occurred in so short a time. We, his closest retainers, and who know him well, have difficulty in predicting what he will do or say on any given day. It may be that whatever - fears - you have, are misplaced." Margaret listened, nodding sagely as Will spoke, but not meeting his eyes.

"Very sad," she murmured when he had finished, her left hand plucking at the fabric of her skirt absently. "Our brother, Anne, Edward... all so quickly. I have heard so many things..."

"False things!" John was rapier quick in his response. He knew where this was going and was not about to countenance it. "Malcontent gossip! Instigated and spread by southerners with no trust of anyone who hails from the north or who bears the confidence of the king. Tudor gossip, Beaufort lies, Woodville..." He stopped when he noticed her face suddenly harden.

Margaret began to chew her bottom lip anxiously, in exactly the same way John had seen his uncle do when ruminating over a particularly tricky issue. From the moment she had entered the room, she had shown them such an assured manner that this sudden display of anxiety seemed out of place. Her fingers began to drum restlessly on the carved armrest and as she did so her face regained its normal composure, indicating she had settled her mind upon something. The dark eyes, so reminiscent of John's uncle but burning out of a feminine face, fixed on his.

"I know that this boy is genuine, because he was sent here with Thomas Dorset two years ago. He was sent here by Elizabeth Woodville, his mother."

26. BLETSOE
November 1485

Thomas Stanley strode swiftly through the solar heading for the stairwell which led to his wife's chambers where she had blatantly decided to spend the majority of her time after being confined under his custody when the king had ordered her house arrest.   Since the death of Jasper Tudor and the imprisonment of her son, she had remained almost exclusively absent from any part of the household's daily routine, appearing only for devotions and to break her fast.

She had been due to join him this very morn, but after a full half hour of waiting at the board, he had discarded his own repast and, in exasperation, decided to go in search of her, cursing under his breath at her inability to spend any effort in returning to anything resembling a normal life.   Having lived so long, driven by the sole purpose and intent of ensuring her son ascended to the throne of England, she was unable - or unwilling - to participate in a life where this was no longer possible.

Servants going about their daily duties knew from the scowl on his bluff features that to get underfoot would earn them a swift and painful punishment, and they scattered hastily in different directions, clearing his path. As he climbed the staircase, Stanley silently raged at his own situation which had lead to a frustrating inability to regain the former closeness he had with the king. This had been very much on his mind whilst he had waited for Margaret to appear, and her disinclination to honour him with her presence, along with his current frame of mind, had resulted in a simmering fury.

He was still smarting from the meeting where he heard a rumour that the missing boys may well have re-appeared abroad, and from the upstart Lovell of all people.   After that revelation, the council chamber door had virtually been slammed in his face, excluding him from the meeting which followed. He would swear that jumped up courtier smirked at him as he closed the door.

His own thin lips curled into a ghastly smile above the

peppered grey and russet of his well groomed beard. Dolts! Let them believe it, fools that there were! They could then waste months running around the Duchy of Burgundy to no avail. He formed a silent prayer that Lovell would fall off his horse and break his neck in the attempt. Or drown crossing the channel.

On reflection, he knew he should not be too surprised at his current isolation, but when he had handed the golden circlet back to his anointed king in the middle of the battlefield, he thought he done enough to avert suspicion and certainly enough to retain his status with the king. Very few people at court, and then only those closest to him, including his own son Lord Strange, knew his real intentions on that scorchingly hot day in August. He had sat on the edge of the field, keeping his own cognisance and watching as battle was joined, as the two opposing lines of armed men had thrown themselves upon each other amidst a hail of arrows. He had sat back and waited for the right moment to make his move and declare for Henry Tudor.

It was the taste at the back of his throat that had done it. A certain burning of bitter bile as he had watched the two very different camps from his vantage point. He could clearly see Henry, a battle virgin, seated on a black mount only just visible behind the powerful form of his standard bearer, Brandon. Looking totally ill at ease in his German plate, probably the first he had ever worn, he appeared to be focussed on watching the banner bearing the Red Dragon of Cadwallader fluttering and unfurling in the breeze. The sworn men at his side, Jasper being one of them, were all looking intently, and somewhat uneasily, in a totally different direction.

When Stanley followed the direction of their gaze, his face broke into a hard edged grin borne from a mixture of satisfaction and grudging admiration. No wonder Henry was looking away! Stanley had fought alongside the king when he was the young Duke of Gloucester, and the man was many things, but neither a coward nor a fool. He had a natural gift of being able to command a battlefield, a strong, inbuilt instinct that enabled him to analyse the lie of the land, take the difficult decisions swiftly and make them well. So what he was seeing then, although slightly out of character, did not do anything to change his opinion of his king's prowess.

Richard, ever the warrior, had ached to fight the French in the campaign that sputtered to an end on a bridge at Picquigny, with Edward signing a French accord, taking gold and pensions instead of glory and prisoners. It had caused a bitter, if temporary, enmity between the brothers and was the only time that the two had really been at odds over strategy.

After that disappointment, and with England peaceful, Richard had turned his energies into reiving the borders and keeping the Scots in their place in King Edward's service. He had laid siege to both Berwick and Bamburgh, in order to return the fortress which had been handed to the Scots by Margaret of Anjou. He had burned Dumfries and marched a triumphant army into the very heart of the Scottish capital. There was no doubt that the green-sick Henry was facing a formidable warlord, and what Richard had been doing at that very moment, was making that fact hit home - hard.

In his own inimitable style, Richard had taken care to ensure that he was totally recognisable on the field. He had made himself a mounted target for every Lancastrian soldier or ambitious French mercenary who fancied taking him on. Astride his usual, fearsome, Syrian warhorse, he was clad in burnished Italian armour, with the gold circlet of his kingship circling the silver helm upon his head. And in direct opposition to Henry, he was a fury of activity.

He had charged at speed up and down the battle lines, maneuvering his steed with a deftness one could only envy, riding down into the fray and back out again, his battle-axe slicing through men as if they were over-ripe fruit. Stanley could see the two young striplings of Richard's retinue, Lovell and Percy, trying their best to act as close body-men, but Richard had them outdistanced and outpaced. He had seen him many times in battle, but it never ceased to amaze him how someone so slightly built could carry armour and wield weapons with such power.

Then, movement on a nearby ridge had caught his eye, taking away his attention from the field. The banner of Henry Percy, Earl of

Northumberland, a northerner, if another somewhat uneasy bedfellow. His power in the north had waned as Richard's had waxed when, as Duke of Gloucester, he governed the north under the patronage of his brother the king. Richard won power and influence by actions which gained him the respect of the people of the north, whereas the brusque Northumberland had demanded it as an indication of his status. People had seen the difference between the two and had made their choice, which had left the earl feeling distinctly affronted.

As to be expected, he had called his men for Richard, but now they sat on the ridge behind their lord, just watching him. Stanley had no reason to think that the earl intended to betray his king, only the suspicions of his usual shrewd intelligence. He was keenly aware that as he himself watched and waited - Northumberland had done the same. Like pieces on a board, if he moved, Northumberland could move against him. Or with him.

Seeing no sense in trying to second guess Northumberland, he had turned his attention back to Richard at that point, who had spurred his horse back up the hill and dismounted amongst a group of knights. There was a pause, then a flurry of activity, with the men of the household running, shouting, changing horses. He saw Richard swing into his saddle once more and draw his broadsword, the blade catching the early morning sun. Frowning for a moment, he had looked around. His horse had pawed the ground impatiently, sensing his anxiety. Then he had seen why.

Henry had made a fatal error. He had become distanced from his retinue and was clearly visible to his enemy, with only his standard bearer at his side. In the instant Stanley saw this, there was a shout, a roar, the thunder of hundreds of hooves above the field of battle. Richard and his household were charging down the hill, mud, grass and banners flying in their wake, making directly for Henry.

Stanley had reined in his horse nervously. Up until this point, he had intended to join the battle for Tudor. Not that he was ill-used at Richard's court, in fact he had been exceedingly well rewarded for his service. He had titles and wealth to go with it - and more lately his wife's fortune was added ti the pot, thanks both to her scheming and Richard's cautious restraint. Since the executions of Hastings, Buckingham, Rivers and Grey, Richard had become somewhat reluctant to take further such actions, showing much more mercy to those he discovered to be acting against him. No - he had been comfortable at Richard's court and Henry Tudor was an unknown entity. However, it was one thing to be a friend of a king, another to be married to a king's mother. How well would he have been regarded then, what power would he be able to wield as a king's right hand man? A relative with the king's ear - it had certainly worked for the Woodvilles who had flourished mightily from being related to a king by marriage.

Across the plain, he saw the massed ranks of his brother's army, waiting to see which way he himself moved, waiting to join together either on the side of Tudor or the king. They had already discussed two nights before, that at the very least, William would join with Tudor, and this decision had, unfortunately, reached Richard's ears. But actions spoke louder than words, and at that point, there was still all to play for as they viewed each other across the stretch of the field before them.

His scheming wife had assured him of the levels of power and influence he would gain, would, as his step-father who had helped him to the throne, be a close confidant. Only Thomas had retained a niggling doubt that the only person whispering in Henry Tudor's ear, would be Henry Tudor's mother. That thought had unsettled him more than he liked to admit.

In an instant, with those thoughts swilling across his brain, feeling the grudging admiration of Richard's ability in battle, and the threat of the ever watchful Northumberland, Stanley gave the order to charge. He led his pikemen across the plain and crashed into the battle lines with a thunderous roar yelling, as much to his own surprise as to Henry's. "A' York, for York and England!" and joined battle on the side of his king.

The rest was now history and well documented. His men had joined with Richard's charge and swept over the Tudor forces like a red tide. Richard by this time was unhorsed, and Stanley saw him arcing his broadsword to the left and right, scything through men with ease, his feet planted squarely in the mud as he swung and swung again. Henry had turned and fled, his eyes full of fear and hatred. Stanley got close enough to see that, got close enough to deny Richard the pleasure of splitting his enemy's vitals by placing himself between the king and his quarry. If he couldn't join him, at least he could give him an opportunity to escape, to fly back to France. Now he wasn't sure if it was just such an action that had resulted in his current predicament.

He was not exactly ostracised at court, but was no longer a close advisor, no longer a member of the inner circle, as it were, and he was finding it very hard to be involved in any meeting of the council or any gathering where key decisions were being discussed or made. Unable now to hear a whisper of what was happening with regard to the rumour surrounding Edward's sons.

And now, his own wife was deliberately avoiding him, obviously deciding to breakfast in her chamber, rather than have the courtesy to spend time in the company of her husband. Snubbing him blatantly, in full view of the servants! It was totally unacceptable.

Margaret was a difficult woman. Pious, but in a way that almost made him want to throttle her with her own rosary beads. He found himself unconsciously clenching his fingers at the thought. Even before their marriage of convenience, he knew that she was completely fanatical on the subject of her son and the English throne. Her dreams of destiny had been bound up with the Tudor line for so long, even the death of Jasper seemed to have unhinged her slightly.

With all her hopes thwarted, she had shunned her husband's company more and more often, leaving him to eat meals alone with only the company of household servants. Not that they had ever shared a bed, but during the early years of their marriage they had often sought out each others company. Long evenings spent before the fire with wine and conversation, or if he was being completely honest, plotting and politics.

She had, however, lost her appetite for scheming since Henry had been dishonoured, either that, or she was seeking out the company of advocates she deemed more reliable than her husband. The rift caused by his actions at Redemore appeared to have brought disaster to both his marriage and his political career, and his wife preferred the solace of her ladies and her prayers to that of her husband. He was no longer prepared to stand for it, and it was well past time for it to stop.

Reaching the door to her chamber he swept in, throwing the door wide without being announced, ready to confront her and demand she attended to her household as she should, only for his feet to stop dead as the heavy door swung back on its hinges.

The chamber was empty. There was no sign of any breakfast, the bed was untouched and no fire burned in the hearth. The room gave every appearance of being unoccupied, and not just from the previous night. Stanley turned one way and another, trying to work out what could have happened, when he heard a slight noise behind him, the sound of feet shuffling on the floor.

Turning swiftly on his heel, he encountered the slender form of Reginald Bray, Margaret's close servant and their current Master of Household. Bray bowed slowly from the waist, in deference.

"My Lord?"

There was a hint of insolence in this simple action which left Stanley infuriated. He was in no mood to be condescended to. These bloody Beaufort people, he thought to himself furiously, always considering themselves far superior to normal human beings.

"Enough of the innocence, Bray!" he barked, brusquely. "Where is my wife?"

Bray's hooded hazel eyes regarded him carefully. It was obvious that he was much more aware of Margaret's daily activities than her husband was, which only served to stoke his anger, causing it to burn with more ferocity. Bray licked his lips quickly, as if to consider his choice of words before he replied.

"Lady Stanley has gone to London, my Lord."

An astonished silence filled the space between them. Stanley struggled to stop his jaw from gaping, and instead succeeded in grinding his teeth together in pure frustration. He seethed visibly, his next words spoken with the sharpness of a honed dagger.

"May I remind you that Lady Stanley is under house arrest. The king could have my head for this if he finds out she is abroad and I have no knowledge of her whereabouts!"

Bray stroked his chin, nodding sympathetically, his expression bland, a blank canvas.

"Indeed my Lord."

Stanley moved forward quickly, his patience spent. He was already out of favour and this woman's stupidity could be the final straw, giving Richard the excuse to repay Stanley with the same coin. Exiting through the door he pushed past Bray, who lost his footing momentarily, but his face remained impassive as he steadied himself against the door frame.

"Ready my horse and some men, and you had better tell me where I can find her! The truth Bray mind, or I will not account for my actions!"

Reginald Bray recovered himself fully and walked away from the door moving further into the chamber before turning slowly to face the irate Stanley. His manner was calm, masking his thoughts, but his eyes were steely and his lips formed a slow, supercilious, smile.

"My Lord, Lady Stanley has gone to Westminster. She has gone to see the king herself to plead for her son. She feels not enough has been done since Sir Robert Percy's visit. She feels that as you have not been able..." he paused, shifted from one foot to another, "or willing, to intercede for her son, that she needs to speak for him herself."

Stanley's face turned the colour of sour milk, all blood draining from his cheeks.

"Lady Stanley is under house arrest," he repeated, through gritted teeth, the words sounding like a low, animalistic growl, "by order of the king, and subject to my will." Bray nodded sagely, his head cocked at an angle.

"She is aware of that my Lord."

Stanley cursed, and pounded the door frame with his fist.

"Jesu, man! My head could roll for this!"

The curve on Bray's lips extended.

"She is also aware of that, my Lord."

27. THE PALACE OF WESTMINSTER
December 1485

Margaret pushed her way impatiently through the crowds thronging outside the chamber searching the room for a familiar face.

She was uncomfortably aware that she presented a somewhat unkempt appearance owing to her haste, as she had ridden hard and travelled the miles from Bletsoe in half the usual time. Steadfastly moving between the press of bodies, it soon became apparent that she was attracting the interested glances of many of those who recognised her and were well aware that she was not supposed to be at court.

The small ripple of whispers began, and she could not disguise the grimace that twisted her thin lips at all the mealy-mouthed sycophants who believed her to be secure under the tenure of her husband. Even with his wily reputation, she had no time for anyone who considered such a man to be a worthy gaoler for her. Stanley had far too much self-interest in her cause to merit that reputation. In her sour disposition, she reflected that the very least Stanley could have done was detain her at one of her London houses and not that hellhole that Bletsoe had become since her arrest. It was, after all, his fault that she was subject to the indignity of her straightened circumstances in the first place.

Not that any of that mattered now.

Her sole purpose this day was to find Richard's closest lackey in this heaving melee and her hawk-like gaze scanned the room hunting for a certain face. At that very moment she achieved her aim, locating that one particular person further up the hall, standing a few feet away from the main door to the privy chamber. She stopped, frozen to the spot, skirts gathered anxiously in hands still gloved from her ride, her full attention fixed itself on the glittering form of Francis Lovell, Lord Chamberlain of England. The sour grin extended.

Francis was splendidly dressed in murrey velvet, jewels studding his collar, belt and hands. He inclined his head, talking animatedly to John Kendall, the king's Secretary, an occasional smile playing around his lips, whilst all the time watchful eyes roved the assembled faces. His handsome, if arrogant, face did not disturb her; the cause for the halt in her step was the woman who she could see standing beside him.

Positioned very comfortably to his left, leaning slightly inwards so that her arm rested almost inconspicuously against his, was the former Princess Cecily, who was doing her best not to look adoringly into his face. And failing miserably.

Margaret was very familiar with Cecily, having spent so much time at King Edward's court where his children had been very prominent, apart from the eldest boy who had been closeted at Ludlow under his uncle Rivers tutelage. The girl was now almost an adult, and very pretty. It was obvious to Margaret, as it must have been to most of the occupants of the chamber, that there was a closeness between these two which was both intimate and interesting. All the more interesting if you considered what their respective wife and husband may make of their display.

Of more immediate concern to Margaret was what that naive young girl may be whispering at night into those searching brown eyes, and if those words would include any tales from her time in Westminster sanctuary. She had been witness to much, including the constant passing of letters and correspondence which had flown between the hands currently knotted in the folds of her own skirts and the slim, white fingers of her mother Elizabeth. Yes, some of what had occurred then had led to her being immured in splendid isolation, but Richard did not know it all, she was absolutely sure of that. If he did... well, she herself would already be in the Tower. Or dead, at the hands of the tyrannical usurper. The thought made her snort inwardly.

Tyrant?

They had done an excellent job there! The man could no more be a tyrant than he could turn pewter into gold. The fact that most of the population thought differently was a testament to their herculean efforts. Not everything may have gone as well as they could have hoped, but that particular scheme had reaped its rewards. And whilst her son was still alive... She swallowed almost painfully, her throat dry from the hard journey, thinking of Henry, immured in his cell. The thought was unendurable.

Not yet noticed by the small group under her observation, she continued to watch, waiting for an opportunity to arise where she could approach Francis and speak to him before he had chance to react. As she watched, there was a flurry of noise and activity emanating from the main entrance to the chamber. The crowds parted like a forgiving tide to let Cecily's elder sister, Elizabeth, pass through the doors and into the throng. Like the entrance of a queen herself, despite her recent fall from the royal descent.

Bess traversed the room grandly, smiling and acknowledging several of the assembled lords and clerics, all of whom she was more than well acquainted. Margaret could see the adoration brimming in the eyes of several doddering old fools and she covered a sneer with leather clad fingers. With a natural regal air, Bess wove her way through the room, step by step, moving ever forwards to join the small gathering forming around Lovell.

Favourites of the king, to a man.

Bess, gowned as richly as her mother had ever been, wore a dress resembling the the darkest claret damask, embroidered with gold thread, and she was attracting admiring glances from all around. A wry grin clothed Margaret's face as she acknowledged this fortunate development which caused the court vultures to forget about her own presence completely and set their gimlet eyes on this vision of beauty, bastard status or no. The young girl should have been a glorious sight, her strawberry blonde hair perfectly complimented by the colour of her dress and the rich rubies adorning her throat that burned hot in the torchlight.

However, this perfect picture was spoiled, like a smudge across a painting as she turned away from the crowds. Duty done, her face became rigidly set and cold as stone once she had completed her court pleasantries. Most occupants didn't see her expression change as she turned her back on them to glide towards her sister, but Margaret did. Her grin stretched somewhat. Some terse words were spoken and Margaret was intrigued to see the reaction her arrival had on Lovell in particular, happily noting that there was little love lost with that particular sister.

Cecily and Kendall both greeted Bess warmly, their smiles welcoming and grins broad, but for Lovell, it appeared that this was a far from welcome encounter.   The veneer of wariness on his face now became tinged with unmistakable distaste. Margaret's remaining hand gripped her skirt tighter, her raised hand now resting on her breast. Her chest constricted as she acknowledged how much she missed being at the heart of this nest of intrigue and gossip. The realisation of how far detached her husband had allowed her to become caused the gorge to rise in her throat. Her inward fury was almost murderous and she swallowed it down bitterly, determined that things would change before too long. She would see the destruction of all of them, if it took the rest of her life.

Whatever words were exchanged, Margaret would never know, and she watched in desperation as any opportunity she may have had to gain Lovell's attention begin to slip from her grasp. The group was further expanded by the arrival of William Herbert and his wife, Richard's bastard daughter, in the company of a younger boy. He was not immediately known to her but judging by his looks, she knew him to be one of the Yorks.   He had that same dark glower that she found so annoying.

Margaret had already pushed past Sir Robert Percy, who had been standing at some distance talking to a group of court ladies, chief amongst them being Margaret, the Duke of Clarence's daughter. From what she could ascertain, as she considered them all distastefully, the only people missing from this chamber were the traitor's son, simple minded Ned Warwick; Richard's heir, his sister's son, the Earl of Lincoln and Jack Howard, the Duke of Norfolk. And Richard himself.

It was only after reaching this conclusion there came the dawning awareness that everyone around her was garbed in their best finery. Colourful sable-trimmed cloaks, Italian silks and velvets, damask, feathers and glimmering jewels. The air was permeated by a heady mix of perfume which suddenly assailed her senses, bringing an unwelcome reminder that she had ridden hard and eaten little. The room began to perform a slow and lazy spin around her, colours merging and blending into one vivid tapestry, so bright that her eyes were forced to close against the glare. A thousand voices filled her ears with a cacophony of sound that roared and ebbed in her head. Sweat began to bead her brow, the back of her neck uncomfortably damp beneath her braid and barbe.

"Lady Stanley?"

The deep voice sounding clear in her ear was accompanied by a guiding hand on her elbow and she willingly allowed herself to be led into a side chamber, where a chill breeze was filtering in from an open casement. The firm grip steered her to a seat and in short order she found a goblet of wine being pushed into her hand. She grasped it unsteadily with annoyingly shaking hands and took a sip, the Malmsey stinging her throat as she tried desperately to clear her vision and identify her saviour.

Standing before her, Henry Percy, Earl of Northumberland, had unsheathed a small dagger and was twirling it round, its point embedded in a small table. He wasn't looking in her direction and appeared to be quite at ease, showing no hurry to return to the outer chamber. Margaret steadied herself and took a deep breath.

"Thank you, my Lord. I am most grateful." She stumbled over the words once her senses had finally returned, keeping her head down and unable to look at him, feeling both foolish and embarrassed by almost collapsing at his feet.

Then, and only then, did he raise his eyes to hers. Percy eyes. Untrustworthy, she thought dispassionately. Like my husband's, a small voice inside her echoed. Percy slipped the dagger back into its sheath casually, but with a firm click of metal against metal.

"What are you doing here my Lady? I was most surprised to see you today, and without your husband."

Margaret cleared her throat and fought desperately to regain her composure, cursing herself for appearing so weak in front of this man who she was more than a match for in normal circumstances. He would never have dared to question her attendance at court in the past and had she the energy, she would have been seething that he did so now.

"I wish...I need to speak with King Richard. It is a matter of great importance." Percy made a grunting sound and shook his head. "You have picked the wrong day I am afraid. Did you not notice the great and good assembled outside?" She frowned, affronted at his tone and not understanding what he was talking about.

"I did, what of it?"

Northumberland gave a sudden explosive laugh that was half shout half bark and stroked his beard with his hand as he smiled at her.

"The king is entertaining his prospective bride. Joanna of Portugal. He has finally acceded to the council's plea to marry and beget an heir, which believe me was somewhat like pulling a lame horse uphill." He was clearly enjoying her discomfort and continued with his education of recent court events. "What is more, it will be a double celebration. Young Elizabeth is betrothed to Manuel, Joanna's cousin." There was a brief silence before he continued by uttering a sentence which almost had her flying out of her seat in anger. Almost.

"You have been too long away from court my lady." Margaret's senses began to clear, like sun breaking through early morning fog. Northumberland was circling her chair like a predatory animal. "Ahh, if I recall, you did think his intentions lie elsewhere?"

Margaret was not as completely recovered as she thought, and unusually for her, spoke her next words without thinking.

"Of course not. That was Rotherham's work."

Northumberland said nothing, but continued to be watchful of her every move, every expression. He continued to pace the small chamber like a restless bear.

Margaret was becoming increasingly irritated. She had very

little patience to play games with this man, she had come to see the king, and no matter what else was taking place that day, she had to find a way to achieve what she had set out to do. She doubted Stanley would give her the opportunity to escape again should she fail in her task this time. The breeze which had been so welcome moments earlier now left her feeling distinctly cold. She wondered if she was becoming ill but shook away the fancy and spoke to break the silence.

"Is it official then? Or is this just cod diplomacy before he finds a reason not to go ahead with a marriage?" She posed the question but did not wait for an answer, carrying on with her train of thought. "Personally I will believe it when I see it. He used to trail after that insipid Neville wife of his like one of those damnable wolfhounds he takes everywhere. I can't believe he will replace her willingly." Percy shrugged as if he cared not.

"He seems serious. It took a while, other options were considered and dismissed. I feel that he was more comfortable with other paths than this one, but we need an alliance if we are to stabilise our position against France for when they have finally resolved their own succession issues. What with that and this Burgundy business..." Percy lips pressed together thinly as through his slitted eyes as he saw her brows draw together in question.

"The boys?" he offered with an air of innocent comment, inferring that she had already heard the latest gossip, whilst knowing that she had not and enjoying her discomfort. He had always found Margaret Beaufort insufferably smug and pious when she had been a favourite in old King Henry's court before wheedling her way into successive York courts. To say he was taking an inordinate amount of pleasure out of her current circumstance was somewhat of an understatement.

"Boys?" she repeated, stopped in the act of brushing some dust from her skirts to hide her increasing annoyance. She was aware she sounded imbecilic but unable to stop the words escaping her lips.

"You have been away too long," he repeated, his voice

dripping with sarcasm and marked amusement. "There is a rumour that the Princes have turned up, safe and sound and with their Yorkist aunt in Burgundy."

"Impossible." Margaret whispered, eyes wide and now focused intently on his rough, weather-beaten features. He nodded, slightly, his head inclined to one side, lips pursed in consideration of her reply

"It's a rumour. No more. But Richard has sent his nephew to find out the truth. You must admit he has a sense of the ridiculous." When Margaret looked at him blankly he explained. "Sending his heir to find the missing, deposed heirs? But who knows what will happen if he can parade those two young princes through the streets of London, clad in silk and velvet, smiling fairly and alarmingly healthy – that is - for two dead boys. All those stories about their murder, how he had them put to death. By Jesu, think of it! Think of the high moral ground he will be able to conquer! He may even become as popular in London as he is in York! Now, my Lady, imagine that!"

Only those last words, steeped in rancour, revealed the fact that this man continued to remain jealous of the king's popularity in his own northern strong hold more than he liked to admit. The Percy family had spent years fighting the Nevilles for supremacy over the territories, and once Warwick was dead, he thought the war was won. Until Edward sent his little brother north...

Margaret shook her head slowly and rubbed her brow with her hand, her eyes closed. The rigours of the day were taking their toll and although tired to the bone, she had no option but to stay and see this through after taking such a risk. Her husband was no doubt either seething back at Bletsoe and plotting his revenge, or galloping into London as they spoke. And as for the king. If she didn't get the chance to speak to him personally, his pandering courtiers would certainly be only too eager to inform him she had been here, and without the opportunity to see him, to plead, it would all have been for naught. The very thought made her feel sick.

"It won't happen. Those boys are no more," she sighed

wearily. "I may not be up to date with court gossip as it stands today, but I can assure you, there is no-one who has better recall of the events of last year. No-one, Lord Percy." Those last words held a frost that caused the earl to raise his eyes to meet hers, whose hard set chill matched the timbre of her voice.

They had both been so engrossed in their private conversation that neither of them had noticed the figure standing in the shadowy arch of the doorway. It was only when a low voice invaded the soft dimness of the room that they both turned, incredulously, to confront the intruder.

"That is very interesting indeed Madame. In that case, I think we need to talk."

Taking one step into the chamber, Richard emerged from the shadows and closed the door behind him.

28. THE PALACE OF WESTMINSTER
December 1485

Richard continued to stand in front of the closed door, his face impassive, his dark reflective gaze registering Percy's unease before moving on to look at Margaret. Although taken by surprise, she had recovered quickly enough to slide off her chair and perform a hasty curtsey. He tugged at the sleeve of his purple brocaded doublet twice, almost nervously as he watched her, but internally he was extremely calm.

For the first time in a long while he began to feel a glimmer of hope, a beam of bright light revealing the end of the long, dark road he had been travelling and he was wondering if he dared to believe that he would finally be able to kill the beast that had stalked his reign. If Margaret had the information he suspected, and confirmed his suspicions around her involvement in certain affairs, it may finally allow him to redress the balance. To be vindicated in the eyes of all those who did not know him, but had judged him on the evidence of rumour and gossip and found him guilty. To move away from the agony caused by the death of his son and wife, and the unhappiness all of this had caused them. To finally and completely remove the blight from his kingship. If that could be achieved now and with the current arrangements for his re-marriage being finalised, maybe, just maybe, he could begin his rule anew.

Richard, a man in previous years known for wearing his emotions like his Blancsanglier badge, betrayed none of these feelings as he continued to view the two conspirators in silence. It was Percy who spoke first.

"Your Grace. Beg pardon, I did find Lady Stanley in the outer hall seeking to gain an audience with you. However, she became faint and I brought her into this chamber to recover."

Richard's eyes did not move from the prone figure in front of him. He had given her no leave to rise and so she remained at his feet on the floor. That began to make Percy feel distinctly uncomfortable as he well knew it gave a more accurate indication of the king's mood than his face did. The past few months had changed him greatly, and it had not gone unnoticed on his old adversary.

"That was most gallant of you, Henry." The king's clipped tones finally confirmed Percy's fears. "However, she appears most recovered now so you may leave her in my care." Percy saw Margaret's lowered head move slightly, before he bowed to the king and made for the door.

"Henry!" Richard's voice brought him to a halt as he reached for the latch, his hand poised in mid air. "Find Lord Lovell on your way out and ask him to attend me here."

"Your Grace!" Percy gave a further bow of his head in assent and departed from the room, relieved to be escaping the tension left behind, but smarting nevertheless at the ease of the dismissal. He knew Richard was still making him pay for holding back his men at Redemore. In the end, they had not been needed, but still, the stain was there and proving difficult to remove.

Behind him, the chamber was as chill and silent as a tomb until Richard's voice cut through the quiet.

"You may rise, Lady Stanley."

At those words, Margaret pushed herself up from the floor slowly until she stood, straight-backed, in front of Richard, but felt momentarily unable to raise her eyes to look at him. Now that she was here, that he was here, it was difficult to look at his face and meet his gaze.

The last time she had seen Richard anywhere near as close as she was now, was before his wife Anne died, but after their son had been laid to rest in the cold ground. At that time he had been ravaged by grief, and she was sure, a great measure of uncertainty. She had worked diligently in the dark recesses of the court to bring about his downfall, and he knew, or thought he knew, everything she had conspired to achieve. Having no comprehension of what she would see when she finally dared to look in his eyes, she raised her lids.

He was waiting. His eyes were as dark and intense as she

remembered, but now there was something else there. A hardness that she had not seen before. Yes, there was still some sadness, and even regret she felt, but it was that look of flint that chilled her down to her very bones, adding to the winter breeze. Recalling now some of her husband's conversations, she could see why he no longer had the ear of the king. That king was dead. The one standing before her looked totally changed, and most of that change came from somewhere far behind the deep grey stare. What she saw there had her in fear of this man for the very first time in her life.

The atmosphere between the two of them as they stood inches apart, was indescribable. For Richard, there was the anticipation that he was close to finally resolving so much that had mystified him for the past two years. For Margaret, the fear of where her actions would now take her after witnessing in person what her husband had been trying to articulate for months. Richard had their measure and any vestige of malleability had gone, forever.

There was a quick rap at the door, which then opened to admit Francis Lovell. He expertly swept the room with his gaze and as the door closed behind him Margaret was sure she heard the scrape of metal on stone. Men-at-arms? For her? Her heart began to beat hollowly in her chest. Francis broke the silence as he turned to greet Richard with a quick but hard smile.

"Princess Joanna has retired for the evening. She sends her felicitations and will join you at chapel and then to break fast in the morning." The words were delivered to Richard, but the contemptuous gaze was fixed on Margaret. Richard nodded in acknowledgement but began to twist the ring on his small finger. Margaret recognised that ring, having been close to Anne for a time when she was queen, she understood its significance to him. Perhaps he was not as calm as he appeared, or the mention of his prospective bride made him think of his last one.

This would have amused her sense of humour in the past, but today she was too concerned with her own fate. She could do Henry no good in the Tower, and Stanley... Stanley still had all her wordily goods at his fingertips, unless Richard should find reason to take them away from him. She tried to suppress a rising smile of satisfaction. Whatever her fate, if she could at least engineer that, it would be some form of recompense.

"And Elizabeth and Manuel?" Richard was talking to Francis, enquiring after his guests.

"The Duke has also retired, but Elizabeth is without." Francis hesitated. A look passed between them which left a wry smile touching Richard's mouth.

"Very well." He turned back to Margaret and took a deep breath. Before he could speak, Margaret impetuously broke in.

"Your Grace, I hear congratulations are in order. May the good Lord bless your forthcoming union." She was able to go no further as she watched Richard's formerly set face transform into a mask of pure disgust, a fact reinforced by the calm, if cold, voice which then carried across the room.

"You wish the Lord to smile on me? Have you been taking lessons in coat changing from your husband my Lady? I think perhaps you had many other words to utter about my previous marriage, and blessing was not one which you would have chosen to use."

Margaret had expected venom, anger, rage. She had not expected to be spoken to with such measured, if icy, stillness. Richard's voice was deeper than she ever remembered it, and she did not know if this was a sign of yet another change, or his way of containing his emotions. Either way, it was a formidable weapon and one which truly left her unnerved.

"You misjudge me, Your Grace." It was a pathetic attempt, but all she could think to say at that moment. Her mind was furiously scrambling to mount a defence to the attack that she knew was on its way.

"I do not," he replied sharply, "but perhaps you have misjudged me. To your cost."

The sun was going down now, and the room was becoming uncomfortably cold. The breeze which had been so welcome earlier was now causing Margaret to shiver. For some unaccountable reason, this made her brave enough to spit out a biting response.

"It is said that York does not make war on women. Do you tell me this has changed?"

Richard's chameleon voice became almost silkily smooth.

"Would it surprise you if it had? Could not you, who has, how did you put it - such recall of what has happened over the past two years - understand why?" Margaret didn't like this tone of voice any better than the previous version. She stumbled for words.

"I was speaking out of turn, Your Grace, I was speaking of..."

"You were speaking of my nephews!" Richard's sudden shout of rage was so unexpected it even made Francis, still standing by the door, flinch, his eyes widening in momentary surprise. Margaret moved back a step as if struck by the force of his words and she began to shake, from both the cold and her fear.

Richard strode across the room almost impatiently and closed the leaded casement window with a bang. He continued to speak throughout, although she could no longer see his face, which was a measure of relief.

"I can see you are still the ultimate dissembler. Marrying Stanley was a match made in Hell, devised by the devil to visit the seven plagues at my door. You plotted and schemed to destroy my reputation, murder me and steal my throne. Well you succeeded in the first, and I do suspect that only a last minute volte-face by your husband made you fail in the last two."

By this time he had turned, and moving to a nearby chair, he rested his hand on the back, his fingers gripped the oak tightly, turning his knuckles white and causing his rings to embed into his flesh, leaving angry red marks.

"I still do not know why your husband decided to fight for me on that day, I am only sure that he did not intend to until the very last moment. I am also certain that as you should be under house arrest at my command, which is incredible taking into account your presence here tonight, I expect Lord Stanley is currently thundering his way towards London at full speed to limit the damage you have caused." He broke his conversation for a second and flicked a look at Francis who was still watching events impassively. He appeared to be turning something over in his mind. "We are in for a long night, Lady Stanley, and we will talk, but not here. There are men-at-arms outside who will accompany you to my privy chamber and wait outside to ensure you do not leave. I have another matter to attend to and then we will continue this conversation. So if I were you, I would spend this time ensuring your "recall" is all you believe it to be. Think yourself lucky you are not already occupying a cell next to your son, although that is still a distinct possibility."

He turned his head towards the door with an assured jerk.

"Francis. See that Lady Stanley is taken to my privy chamber and is put under guard." He paused momentarily. "And see that she has food and wine. I will not stint on hospitality as she has made such efforts to reach me. We have much to discuss."

Francis nodded his head in assent, and opened the door. There were indeed two cloaked men-at-arms outside bearing the royal arms, and as they moved into the room, Margaret could see there were still a few people beyond milling about in the outer chamber.

A new indignity was about to be visited upon her and she began to feel her face burn despite the cold. Never before had she been escorted by armed men, and it was now to be done in full view of a range of courtiers and nobles. She knew there were many out there who knew her well and would be happy to see her misfortune and as she strained to identify their faces, her eye was caught by a flash of ruby and gold.

There, pacing in front of the door, and casting anxious glances inside as she was waiting to enter, was young Elizabeth Woodville. Francis made a gesture, signaling Margaret to move between the waiting guards, a smirk of satisfaction narrowing the brown eyes which spoke of a long awaited ambition achieved. Margaret ignored him, and picking up her skirts, moved forwards to stand between the armoured men, the sound of jingling mail and metal ringing in her ears as the small party moved out of the room into the passage outside.

29. THE PALACE OF WESTMINSTER
December 1485

Richard was feeling the cold himself. The day had been a long one, and he was desperate to continue his conversation with the woman who was now leaving the room, flanked by two of his trusted men. No fire had been lit in this side chamber, and the open window had led to loss of any heat which had passed through from the press of assembled bodies who had clustered together to watch todays spectacle. He took time to gather his thoughts as someone, he didn't see who, entered the room to light candles as dusk fell and shadows began to darken the corners of the room.

Joanna. He didn't really want to think about the events of earlier that day, and much of it had passed in a blur if he was honest with himself. She was fair enough, gracious, devout most assuredly, but he didn't know her. In all of his other close relationships, matters had only become intimate because he first ensured he got to know the person concerned, unable to commit to the full exploration of carnal sin until he knew he would give himself no cause for regret after the event. For his sake and for theirs. And Anne... they knew each other so well they were almost one before they even wed.

Only now it was another woman well known to him who was taking up his thoughts. Bess. She was still not happy and she had taken great pains to impress this on Francis earlier, insisting that she see the king immediately the Portuguese contingent retired.

That demand had been circumvented by the arrival of Lady Stanley, which had caused a distinct surge of excitement in the crowd, ripples that had reached him courtesy of John Kendall. It had been a welcome distraction and had led to an earlier than anticipated retirement of the court party. Richard had assured them easily as he begged their leave murmuring, "Affairs of state....." and with a casual gesture he left the room to find his uninvited guest.

With all eyes outside fixed on Lady Stanley's fall from grace, he doubted many had seen Bess slip quietly into the room. But here she was, looking beautifully grown up in a gown made especially for this occasion. Her hair was bound and braided, held back in a net scattered with amethysts which added a pleasing foil to the rubies which flashed at her throat. He had taken pains to see that she was garbed fit for a foreign prince. Her mother had no doubt raged that she had not been invited to this momentous event, which is why Richard was indeed happy that Cecily was here for the girl.

Cecily, who seemed to seek out the company of Francis more than he would have expected. He could not be sure, the girl was so young, but he meant to talk to Francis about it when all of this business was out of the way. A talk now further delayed by the actions of Margaret Stanley, whose interference tonight he could have well done without, despite what he had just overheard. He sighed heavily, twisting his thumb ring agitatedly, Was there never to be any peace now? No moment to reflect, to go out and ride until his thoughts were cleansed?

"Uncle Richard?" The familiar soft voice brought his attention back to the matter in hand.

"What is it Elizabeth?" Richard pulled himself out of his reverie irritably. "It has been a long day I am sure you agree, and mine is not over yet. As you can no doubt imagine."

For a moment she appeared taken aback. Her hands played with the points on her sleeves, but as always she kept her eyes fixed on his face. As if she couldn't stop looking, as if she was afraid she would forget what he looked like if she did.

"Am I not Bess now?" she asked quietly, and turning to her in the dimness, he could see the hurt in her eyes. He shook his head impatiently but his tone remained terse. He had no time for games or for trying to salve her bruised emotions.

"Bess, please, you can see what is happening here. I need to speak to Lady Stanley. I think she actually realises that she may now be held to account for her actions and I cannot allow her the luxury of time to find a way to extract herself from her current situation." The young girl continued to look at him, but her voice was tinged with scorn.

"You don't really think she will tell you the truth do you?"

He shrugged as if it were a matter of no consequence.

"I have her son in the Tower. What else would she do?" Bess gave a soft snort of derision.

"Before you get into any lengthy conversations with Margaret, I would speak to my mother." Bess watched the expression of sheer incredulity spread across his face as she continued. "I know you will not like it, but she has had experience of both sides of that woman's duplicity and feels that Lady Stanley is directly responsible for her current situation."

Richard was secretly more than impressed that this young girl spoke so eloquently and had always believed that she had an understanding beyond her years, but he didn't let this show as he expressed his contempt.

"Your mother is more fortunate than she deserves to be, considering her conduct after your father died. I don't think she can tell me anything about Lady Stanley that I don't already know. But I thank you for your concern. Now - why did you want to see me?" This last question was asked of her even though Francis had already alerted him to her concern. There was no going back. This meeting was a formality only. A kindness. Bess hesitated, still fiddling with her sleeves, unsettled by his obvious impatience.

"Perhaps it should wait. As you say, you have urgent business to attend to." Bess turned to go and Richard suddenly had a sharp pang of conscience. He chided himself inwardly for constantly choosing to forget how young she was, barely out of her childhood. It was not her fault that he veered between viewing her as Edward's young daughter, his beloved niece and then a captivating, beautiful young woman. This, depending on his mood, could very easily influence how he reacted to her. Understanding that in this instance he was being a little unreasonable, he moved forward swiftly and placed his hand on her arm.

"No, Bess..." She halted immediately, and her head went

down as her eyes were drawn to the fine boned hand resting on her sleeve. She didn't speak, but also didn't move any closer to the door. "It has been a long day for both of us. We have been constantly on our best behaviour because our guests have seen fit to pay us such an honour as to visit personally and discuss the marriage proposals. I think this is fairly unprecedented and displays quite openly how desirous of this match their family are. I found Joanna to be most charming, and certainly very modest and pious." He halted for a moment, wondering if he should carry on, but decided to initiate the conversation which he knew she wanted to have. "How did you find Manuel? He seemed most charming, and very attentive. He is a very good match, and will one day rule. You could be a queen, Bess."

For a moment he thought she had either not heard him or was determined to ignore him, but then felt the imperceptible tremor in her arm, saw the slight shake in her slim shoulders.

"Bess?" his tone was soft, concerned. Her hand came up and covered his as it rested on her arm. It was warm, invitingly warm, and the movement released a waft of her fragrant perfume, redolent of roses in a summer garden. Still she didn't lift her head but she spoke. So low, that he had difficulty in hearing her at first.

"Please, uncle, please don't."

"Don't?" Misunderstanding her, he thought that she did not want him to comfort her, and so tried to extract his hand from her arm. She tensed at first, but then allowed his hand to slip from beneath hers. Finally, her face turned up to his and he could see tears welling in her eyes, could see the golden down which covered her fair cheeks which were flushed pink.

"Don't send me away. Don't make me marry Manuel and leave everyone behind." Her voice was emotional, pleading, her eyes harnessing his with their intensity. "I have lost too many people, please don't take me away from everyone else I love. Please! I will go away from court, I will live quietly with mother, I would even go to Bermondsey if you will. I will do whatever you wish, just not this."

The room fell silent and all that could be heard was the musical ringing of the bells calling the monks to their prayers, the light in the chamber was dimming further despite the candles. Richard was struggling for words. He had thought that Bess had finally accepted her fate, had seen what an excellent opportunity it was. Manuel was prepared to marry her even with the stain of illegitimacy, the pairing of these two houses of significance to both countries in their future dealings with France. The difficulty he was having was rooted in the fact that what he wanted more than anything was to sympathise with her, to tell her that he didn't want to marry either.

He wanted to let her know that he was more than happy for John his nephew to remain named as heir, and to just live out his years as a widower. It had taken all his willpower to agree to his council's advice when his whole soul was crying out to be left alone. Just for a year or so. But such was not the luxury of kings, he knew that in his heart. Fleetingly, he had wondered if just such pressures had led to his brother Edward's unfortunate marriage. It was that thought that had drenched all other considerations with a tide of ice cold water. His brother had swum against the tide, and look what that had wrought.

His right arm began to ache again and he pulled it tightly into his side to try and numb the sudden pain. His mind raced to find the right words, the words which would make her understand that however hard this appeared to be now, it was the right thing to do for both of them. Suddenly, he remembered something which had escaped his mind when the news of Margaret's arrival had reached his ears. He had been in such a hurry to make his excuses and leave the hall, that he had forgotten what he had planned.

Carefully, he reached into the pouch hanging from his belt and retrieved a small object wrapped in purple velvet, drawn close with silken ribbons. For a few seconds he turned the soft fabric between his fingers, feeling the outlines of the contents.

"I have something for you," he said, his voice breaking the silence. Bess continued to watch his face for a moment, then noticed the object in his hand. "I intended to give it to you earlier this evening, but of course events overtook me." He held out his hand with the small velvet pouch resting in his palm, the ribbon ties dangling between his fingers. "This is for you. So that you always remember your uncle kindly when you are a grand queen in Portugal."

She looked at his hand and, glancing back at him quickly, took the token from him. Richard watched as Bess untied the ribbons carefully and shook the contents of the velvet pouch into her hand and a small beautifully crafted brooch fell into her palm. She picked it up with her fingers and held it up in the candlelight. It was a fine silver boar, with rubies for eyes, obviously made by a master craftsman who had taken time to replicate the finest detail. It was beautiful, delicate - despite the boar not being the most attractive of beasts, the jeweller had done his work well.

"It was made especially for you." Richard said quietly. "Especially for this occasion." Her head was bowed now, as she turned the brooch around and around in her fingers.

"It's beautiful," she murmured quietly. She appeared to have composed herself since her earlier outburst, one that Richard knew was heading his way, but which he had no recourse but to try to resolve. "It is kind of you to do this for me." Her voice was halting as she took time to consider her next words. "And, I do have a gift for you as well."

Richard inclined his head down towards her, a slight smile curving his lips. He was genuinely pleased at her reaction.

"Do you?" he asked, watching as she nodded her fair head. Then, the benevolent smile vanished as she raised her head and looked him full in the face and even in the dimness the resolute fervour in her eyes unsettled him.

"I do. My love." Her eyes shone out at him like stars, tears welling, adding to their sparkle as he felt his chest tighten. But he could not weaken now, the deal was done. For both of them.

"Bess..." his face hardened, despite himself, but she was ready for him.

"No, don't "Bess" me in that voice! You know I love you! Have known it for some time and chosen to ignore it.   You could keep me here, you could! You could marry me to an English nobleman, like you did with Kathryn. You could find someone compliant and we could be together, then I wouldn't have to be queen. I don't want to be queen, I never have done! That was always my mother, not me. My father kept Jane Shore at court..."

"Stop!" Richard shouted, aghast, his face a mask of incredulity at her implied suggestion. "Bess, stop this right now!"

She ceased speaking obediently, but her eyes continued to blaze defiantly, the small brooch turning and turning in her hand, the ruby eyes winking in the flickering light.   When Richard had controlled his emotions enough to resume speaking, it was in a voice was full of astonishment and edged with anger.

"You would compare yourself to that harlot Shore? The woman who wantonly dragged your father towards an early grave? Even if the affection I felt for you in any way matched your own, it would be impossible! I can't countenance this, Bess, truly I can't. Can you imagine your mother's reaction? She already views me as the Devil incarnate! You well know that she would only countenance a relationship with me if you were to be my queen! And it is just because of this, that you need to be away from here, for whilst you remain, there will always be those that doubt my intentions towards you, and to cast unflattering aspersions on your honour. Christ, girl! They have already done so - have you forgotten?"

Richard wheeled round towards the mantel with its bare black hearth and rested his head on it in despair.

"You were not there, you did not see what it cost me to cast you aside, but take my word on it, it was far from pleasant!" Memories of his public address at Clerkenwell came flooding back like bile to the back of his throat.   The unbelieving faces, the words spoken from lips still numb with grief after the last touch from his wife's cold lips.

A small smile played over Bess's mouth, as she heard only the words she wanted to hear.

"So you have thought about it. I thought you may have, despite your protestations whenever I choose to bare my soul to you." Richard drew himself up to his full height, he was finding it difficult to breathe, the air seemed thick and he felt unable to draw it down into his chest. He closed his eyes momentarily with the effort.

"Of course I have considered it. It was put to me by my own council some time ago, along with many other options to beget an heir, including marriage to Joanna, including marriage to you." Biting his bottom lip suddenly, he realised he had said too much as the smile on her face grew imperceptibly. "What are you smiling at?" he bit off his words angrily.

Bess did not change her expression but busied herself by carefully pinning the small silver brooch to the neckline of her gown, close to the creamy skin of her breast. When finished, she raised her head back level with his and folded her hands in front of her at the waist of her gown.

"You. I am smiling at how hard you are finding it as you try to deny that you have feelings for me." He began to shake his head slowly, the room was now stifling, the earlier chill departed.

"Of course I have feelings for you - you are my niece!" He was becoming increasingly bad tempered. The girl could be the image of her mother when she so chose. The marriage he was arranging could give her immense power and wealth, it could give her a life she may never have hoped to achieve from the moment Stillington rolled out that pre-contract. Not for the first time, Richard wished he had just separated the Bishop's nodding grey head from his body and seen an end to it. Perhaps he would have been able to live with Elizabeth as Queen Regent, perhaps she would have left his family alone... perhaps, perhaps...the uncertainties rolled back down the years.

"No." Bess shook her head slowly, her voice cutting across his thoughts as she raised her hand to stroke the precious metal of the brooch. "No - it is more than that.."

"No.." his protest fell on deaf ears, she was no longer listening to him.

"And if you would be honest with me, you would admit the truth of it. That marrying Princess Joanna, no matter how pretty, pious or devout she is , or how profitable and expedient the match may be, the fact remains that you don't really want this marriage. I know that. I know you. You won't lie to me. You may dissemble and evade and change the subject by offering me gifts, but you don't want to marry her. Admit it, please Richard, be honest with me and with yourself. Let us admit that to each other, if we agree on nothing else."

Richard was beaten. He knew, with terrifying certainty, that he could no longer hide his feelings from her. However much he thought he had become a master of his emotions over the past three years, her words had sliced through that confidence in a single stroke. Bess was an intelligent woman, had spent her life in court circles, had seen and been involved in court politics and intrigue, and for a good part of her life, had become very familiar with her father's youngest brother. Astutely, she had spotted his weakness. He could recall her being present at many of his meetings with her father, showing what he thought was an almost endearing interest in what her elders were discussing. He could now see that she had in fact been doing much more than that.

Looking around the room, he was also conscious that she was waiting for an answer. In days now lost to him, back in Middleham, he had often found himself in the throes of such difficult conversations with Anne where they had disagreed over a matter. His eyes fixed on the chamber door longingly, wishing he could just exit the chamber, remove himself from the need to continue with this discourse, but Bess was strategically placed. Seeing the amused expression on her face as she followed the track of his gaze, he also knew that this strategy was something else she was familiar with, no doubt relayed to her by Anne when she was a lady of her chamber. As much as she was Edward's daughter, she was Woodville too. Understanding he had no way out, Richard raised his hands before himself in supplication and frustration.

"Enough, Bess, enough!"

Turning from her he found his way to the nearest chair and slumped down upon it, leaning heavily on his right arm, which was still paining him somewhat. Bess remained where she was, hands still folded, displaying her enigmatic smile, radiating self satisfaction, but not saying a word. The silent victor on the battlefield of his emotions.

"I am too tired to play the mouse to your cat, and far too wise to think that you are going to leave this room without my telling you what is in my heart." He didn't look at her, instead stared off into the middle distance, but as he began to speak he absently grasped the upper part of his right arm, flexing his fingers to try and find some relief. "You are right. I am not as desirous of this marriage as I portray. But do not think that you now hold some tantalising secret which will help you get your own way with me as you are not the only person at court to know it. In truth, I would be happier not to marry at all. I have secured my crown on the field of battle, I have an heir of royal blood, I have some measure of peace in the realm. If I have to go to war against France, I will, and be victorious. The match with Portugal suits their needs more than mine and although an expedient match, I have no real appetite for it. So there - you have it. You have what you want, so what say you now?"

Bess walked slowly towards him, one step placed carefully in front of another, her hands still folded before her, and came to a halt before his chair, the smile gone from her face, which now wore an expression somewhere between solemnity and sadness. As she did not speak, Richard continued to do so. It was as if she had pierced a troublesome blister which had been throbbing and pulsing with pain, and now he spoke, albeit unguardedly and with relief. He forgot for the moment the real reason Bess had wanted him to admit his reluctance to marry, and spoke to her as he would have to his brother, her father.

"The Privy Council want this match in preference to the available alternatives," he was halted by her sudden quizzical expression. "Legitimising you and then marrying you. Or legitimising

John and Kathryn and naming John my heir. The former of course is complicated by the exact whereabouts of your brothers, as to legitimise you does the same to them, but a bar to succession could be introduced" He looked at her wryly. "As you are aware. When Lincoln returns from Burgundy, I should be more informed as to that situation, but whatever the outcome, it will not change my mind with regard to my marriage."

"Burgundy?" Bess still stood before him, now looking dumbstruck and he suddenly saw that in letting his guard down he had gone too far. Damn it! What was it about this girl! His conversations with her never went where he intended them to go and he constantly found himself thinking furiously to recoup lost ground.

She didn't know. Why would she know? There were very few at court who were party to the rumour itself, and even fewer who knew why his nephew John had been sent to Burgundy. He had been trying to maintain an appearance that he did not take the rumours seriously, whilst taking actions to determine the truth. He didn't want anyone suspecting what he was doing, and taking their own actions to snatch the boys away, if indeed they even existed, especially at the home of his sister, who seemed to have declined to mention it.

The matter was something now so closely guarded that he was also certain that Dame Elizabeth Grey was not aware. The closest they had come to it being spread abroad was when Francis threw the comment at him down the keep stairs, but he was as sure as he could be that only his close courtiers had understood what was happening. Even Stanley had been kept at arms length on this one, for if it was true, Richard didn't want anything going awry. If it was true, it was his intention to bring them home. And now, amongst everything else going on this evening, he would have to explain himself to her on this account. His heart sank in his chest, he shivered and not just because of the lack of heat in the room. He gave a heavy sigh and gestured towards her.

"Bess - sit down."

Watchful of the sudden darkness on his face, she sat herself down carefully in the nearest chair without a word.

"You know there is a rumour that there are some boys in Flanders who could be your brothers. It has now transpired that these boys are actually in Burgundy, with my sister Margaret. Their aunt." These last words seemed superfluous. "As soon as I heard, I dispatched John - Lincoln - to go and see what the situation is. As far as anyone else is concerned, he has gone on a political visit with William Catesby. It is not a remarkable journey. He will reassure Margaret of events since the battle, and at the same time sound out the situation. He will send no correspondence, I dare not allow the risk that it would be intercepted. I will find out the truth of it when he returns. Whenever that may be. He will stay as long as it takes him to be certain of the situation."

The silence formed a chasm between them, but he could see from her face that her mind was working furiously. Eventually, she fixed him with a stare that was pure Woodville.

"Then I am sorry uncle, but until this matter is resolved I do not see how I can possibly enter into a marriage contract which would involve my leaving England, no matter how profitable it be. We need to either agree to abandon the idea all together, which I have to admit is my preference, or we postpone any ceremony until the outcome of your ministrations in Burgundy are known." She paused only fleetingly. "By that, I mean for my brothers to be identified, secured and back here either at court or with my mother at Grafton. I appreciate this will take time, but I do not see how you can expect me to leave my mother and the rest of my family at this time."

Richard tried hard to suppress a sardonic smile, but was not completely successful and saw her mouth tighten.

"I am sure your mother can cope with finding her sons alive and well. That would be the ultimate outcome of this surely and would be a relief for her I am sure, as well as a surprise. She already suspects they are dead, were murdered two years gone. At least, that is what she wanted everyone to believe."

He tried hard not to pay close attention as she inhaled deeply, her chest rising and straining at the neckline of her gown, where the rubies in the boar brooch glittered balefully. She was truly beautiful, a product of both York splendour and Woodville coolness. A stab of pain shot through his arm.

"It is not just my mother, there are my sisters to think about, and indeed myself. If they learn that our brothers may be alive and then we find out this is all some hoax, or mischief, the disappointment will be all the greater. Surely you can understand that? I know I am the strongest one amongst them now, that became apparent whilst we were in sanctuary. I need to be here - whatever the outcome." Richard had begun shaking his head part way through her discourse and continued as she stopped.

"They cannot know about this. They cannot know anything until John comes back, and maybe not even then, it will depend on what he has found out. This would be so much easier if he were able to correspond with me in the usual manner. He could well be on his way back now. But as I cannot trust this information falling into the wrong hands - I - we, have to be patient and wait."

The rose stained lips set in a childish pout, her hands folded once again in her lap in a gesture of resolution. He noted these actions, trying not to smile, seeing once again the very young girl in the woman before him. But the actions belied her words.

"Then Manuel can also wait. If I am such a catch, it will not be an issue."

The pleadingly passionate girl of moments ago had disappeared, and Richard was not sure he was comfortable with the demeanour of the person who now sat before him. Bess was either her mother's daughter, or trying desperately to play a part in a game she could not win. He did not blame her, she had been around court enough to see how these political games were played, how the board changed as the pieces moved, how you always needed to be two steps ahead. Her father had been excellent at that, whereas Richard was much more instinctive and often guided by his gut. It was such a feeling now that was telling him that this was not the real

Bess, not yet, but so easily could be if the course of events took a certain path.

For one strange moment, he felt he was seeing the person Bess would have become if he had been slain on the field and she had married Henry Tudor. The very thought un-nerved him and coloured his tone.

"No. There will be no postponement." He was twisting the ring on his small finger again, an action he found helped him think. " I have admitted my innermost feelings to you regarding my own marriage and let you into my confidence. That is a huge burden to bear and I am sorry but you pressed me into it. The marriage arrangements go ahead, for both of us. I will ensure that you are kept fully briefed on matters concerning your brothers."

Before the sentence was finished, he could see his judgement was correct. Her face had already begun to soften, the posture of her whole body changed and appeared to collapse downwards slightly, her hands began to twist and fold the fabric of her skirts.

"Then, if I must marry, once again, I entreat you to match me to an English nobleman - at least then I would be away from court but not out of the country?"

"There is no one suitable Bess, if there was..." Richard sighed desperately, but was interrupted before he could say much more.

"John Plantagenet."

One name - uttered with an aim which hit home true enough to make Richard sit back in his chair as if struck. Whatever turmoil Bess had been experiencing had now been overcome as her hands rested calm in her lap once more. Knowing her as he did, he realised that she was aware of the effect this announcement would have on him, and had been reluctant to say the words. Once spoken, the decision was made. Richard opened his mouth to speak but Bess was quicker. After all, she had known what she was going to say.

"John. Your natural son, John. Yes - I am older, but he is growing, and I am quite fond of him, and I think he is of me. It is not as.." her flow of conversation halted as she reached for the right words, "inappropriate as some of the marriages my mother has arranged in the past.   In fact, it could also help you resolve your own - difficulty."

Richard was listening incredulously.   If he didn't know better, he would have sworn she was speaking a script which had been prepared for her, word for word, by her mother. However, looking at her face, he had no doubt that this plan was entirely of her own making, and so he knew what she was about to say even before she uttered her next words.

"If you legitimise John, as your council have already discussed, you could name him your heir.   If you then allow us to marry, you unite the tensions that have existed since you took the throne from my brother. If my brother is still alive, you have no need to concern yourself with succession, as he is already declared illegitimate, as am I. I don't think there are any legal or ecclesiastical issues - but if there are - I am sure they can be resolved.   Your son would be king after you, I would be his queen. If my mother could marry a king, why not I?"

There was an almost unholy silence in the room, but for him it was filled as Bess's words continued to resound in his ears. And he heard what she said next.

"And you would have no need to marry Joanna."

Richard stood up abruptly and moved across the room to the window he had previously closed. Darkness had completely settled over everything now and it was impossible to see out.   There was nothing on which to fix his gaze, no view, no fire in the hearth, no lazy hound slumbering the day away. Only the beautiful young girl sitting serenely in the chair, offering him temptation, hope or damnation, he wasn't sure which. Perhaps all.

He felt he had already had a taste of damnation, and it was this he was trying to recover from. Turning again, he retraced his steps to stand in front of her.   She herself remained seated, but raised her face to his. He saw in her eyes how desperately she wanted this.   They had become lucent, liquid pools that a man could lose himself in forever, drinking deeply as he sank to his doom but without a care. All worldly possessions forfeit just for that one fleeting pleasure. In a few well chosen words she had presented him with his hearts desire. A genuine way out of marriage to a woman he did not love or want, a method of remaining faithful to the memory of the wife he had loved beyond life itself. A living son and heir, a chance to renew the Yorkist line of succession and a opportunity to heal old and festering wounds.

She was right - he could think of no immediate impediment legally, although it would be unusual. The Pope could be persuaded to be acquiescent if need be. Laws could be re-written, Acts enabled. More wrangling, more politics, but the result? How much legislation was he prepared to draw up to further secure himself and his succession. Why could it not be easier?

He could see some of the faces in the council and Parliament now. Would he not still be seen as some sort of despot, changing the natural order of things just to strengthen his claim? He didn't have an issue with legitimising his children, he loved both of them dearly although he still keenly felt Ned's loss. But for this? On one hand it was a ideal solution, on the other hand it smacked of nepotism.

No, he told himself. He had to resist the temptation she was offering. Marriage to Joanna was simple, straight forward and already had approval. His own personal happiness had to take a lower priority, he would learn to be happy with his new wife. She would bear him sons. All he had to do was sign a marriage treaty and arrange a ceremony. Easy. Simple. Clear. Honourable.

"No." All these thoughts had crossed his mind whilst he remained motionless in front of her, and on his word she rose from the chair. They were inches apart. Roses. The sweet heady smell of roses overwhelmed him. "You are to marry Manuel. It has been agreed. I will not break that accord, not even for you. Now go, Bess, and with a warning. Tell no-one about this conversation tonight, and I mean no one - not any part of it. If I discover you have, you may find yourself in Portugal a lot sooner than either yourself or your prospective husband ever anticipated. Go, and I will see you in the morning."

Bess said nothing more, but his heart ached as he watched the tears well, only to remain steadfastly unshed. Slowly, but with immense dignity, she moved away from him and went to the door. Richard began to relax, the muscles in his back were aching from tension and the effort of holding himself erect. He was about to exhale with relief, when he once again heard her speak.

"It will be a shame to leave, and not meet my new cousin." Her head turned back towards him as she passed through the open door. "You did know Kathryn is pregnant?" The door closed behind her with a heavy thud leaving Richard alone and speechless.

Elizabeth crossed the outer chamber, which was now empty apart from the usual men-at-arms who stayed in close proximity to the king. Reaching the far wall, she opened a window and flung it wide. Carefully unfastening the silver brooch which was now warm from the heat of her skin, she tossed it from the window and out into the murky depths of the fast flowing river outside.

As she closed the window and turned back, she caught sight of Francis as he returned from his duties to join the king. Giving her a cursory glance, his steps slowed only momentarily before he regained his former impetus and knocked on the chamber door. Then he entered and was gone from sight.

30. THE PALACE OF WESTMINSTER
December 1485

Cecily was nervously pacing the corridor outside the Painted Chamber, where the door to the small ante-chamber which had unexpectedly become the focus of so much activity remained resolutely closed. It was quite some time since she had seen her sister and could only now assume that she had achieved her wish and obtained a private meeting with their uncle. That very thought sent shivers down her spine.

Margaret Stanley had recently been marched unceremoniously through the assembled throng in the direction of the privy apartments, accompanied by two men-at-arms, to the astonishment of most, and the undisguised pleasure of a certain few. Francis would have been one of those with his sheer pleasure on show if he hadn't been so absorbed in the other events of the evening. Not only was he playing a key diplomatic role in the visit of the Portuguese party, but he had been one of the first alerted to Margaret's appearance by Kendall, as well as the one person Bess has sought out to vent her fury on.

Cecily had watched patiently from the sidelines as Francis calmed and charmed Joanna and Manuel in turn, entertaining them after the king left the chamber, until they decided to retire. No sooner had that duty been discharged than a more than surly Earl of Northumberland had literally stomped across the room and informed him that the king requested his attendance. He had duly answered that call, giving Cecily's hand a quick, secret squeeze as he left. It was a silent form of language between them that she knew meant, "Wait for me - I will be back."

Until then, it had been such an exciting day, one such as Cecily could not recall since her own father was on the throne. Not only had she been seated close to foreign royalty, the festivities had given her the ideal opportunity to spend time with Francis, in close company, without anyone thinking it unusual, or remarking upon it. In the shared company of Bess, Kathryn, John and Ned, no-one noticed if they stood too close, spoke too quietly, or exchanged glances of longing and smiles of affection.

Bess had been the first note of discord in an otherwise perfect day. The court fair glittered with an array of jewels and the richest of fabrics, tables were laden with an abundance of fruit and wine. A banquet of five courses consisting of heron, venison, swan and an abundance of different fish, followed by almond pastries, spiced, baked apples and a marchpane castle based on Joanna's home was given pride of place on the table.

Joanna spoke very little English, but was attractive enough, having black hair and deep, ebony eyes. To Cecily, she seemed very exotic as she had smiled delightfully and paid attention to everything that was going on around her, even though she must have understood very little. Manuel, her cousin, was not as dark in colouring, and although not as handsome as some at court, he was pleasant enough to look upon. He mastered the language more than his cousin, engaged Bess in conversation and she played her part beautifully. No one would have guessed that she was resenting every minute of the time she spent in his presence, and fully intended - still - to avoid the marriage at all costs.

No - Bess had adapted to her role well, as her mother and uncle would have expected of her. Only Cecily noticed the small tell tale signs that gave her away, whilst everyone else was remarking on what a perfect match they made. She had no doubt that Manuel himself was completely charmed, although Cecily had to admit she did not envy Bess and the position she now found herself in.

The meal and dancing over, Richard had been conducting some private business with the couple when Bess had sought out Francis to insist that the king see her before retiring. When Francis had raised his fair eyebrows in question, Bess had launched into a low-voiced tirade of reasons why the marriage could not go ahead. At one point, Kathryn had tugged on Bess's sleeve and aimed a warning "Sshh!" in her direction. It had slowed Bess down, but it had not changed her intent. It was at that précise moment that John Kendall had re-appeared by Francis's elbow and whispered in his ear and the pair had disappeared into the inner chamber without a further word.

The next time she saw him he was following in the wake of the two men-at-arms flanking Margaret Stanley, and now she watched him stride purposefully down the corridor towards her, having ensured that his charge was safely ensconced in the king's private chamber. Her eyes devoured him from his fair head, down to his booted feet, a delightful tingle coursing down her spine just at the very sight of him. Only very recently, they had lain together, finally succumbing to the clamouring demands of their yearning bodies, and even though they both knew it was a sin, nothing had ever seemed so perfect.

As he came to a halt before her, they stood inches apart, but she ached for his touch and a wave of desire overcame her once more, flushing her cheeks, her heart beginning to quicken. Noticing a lull in proceedings, as many of the courtiers had now also retired for the evening, Francis took the opportunity to raise her hand discreetly to his lips. They were trying very hard to keep the confirmation of their relationship away from the eyes and ears of the court, but it was not proving to be easy to find time alone together.

Cecily had welcomed Francis back wordlessly, merely looking up at his face with questioning eyes. She could see how pre-occupied he was and she longed to reach up and smooth out the small indents between his brows. It was nothing new for Francis to wear his feelings for the king on his sleeve, and Cecily was beginning to learn just how deep those feelings ran, and how much it cost him to serve this king.

"She's been talking about the boys. Your brothers." Francis had said quietly, consciously aware he knew much more than he could tell her. He continued to hold her hand, his fingers squeezing hers, hiding the contact in the folds of her pink velvet skirts "She made it clear she knows what has happened to them."

He looked down carefully, aware his words were bound to have an impact on her. It was a sensitive subject, and one which had for too long caused speculation and unrest but Cecily remained stoically calm.

"Does Bess know?" Francis shook his head doubtfully in answer.

"I don't think so. She has other matters on her mind. She slipped in to see Richard as I escorted Margaret out. No one saw her - I don't think - they were all too busy watching Lady Stanley. Richard is desperate to talk to her, that was his reason for abandoning the festivities, he won't want Bess to hold him up for long." Cecily pursued her lips thoughtfully at this.

"Bess has other ideas."

"I know, I know," said Francis with a distracted air. "And now I have also received a letter for him. Lincoln has landed and is heading back to court."

"Lincoln? The Earl? You mean John?" asked Cecily keenly. It was only then that Francis realised his error. He turned to face her fully, keeping them in the shadows of a window alcove.

"It's nothing. He has been on a mission for Richard. It is just - well, I wish Richard could have a bit of time..." he trailed off, not seeming to know how to finish the sentence, his concern clouding his eyes. Cecily raised a hand to his face, gently cupping his cheek.

"And you. When do you get time? The king has you at his beck and call daily, you are his right-hand and his conscience, but when do you get some time? For you...for us?"

Francis raised his own hand and covered hers, smiling ruefully.

"Now you understand why Anna left court. It was a frequent source of argument that I was constantly unavailable to her." He stopped and inclined his head to one side for a moment. " But to be honest, most of that was my doing. I didn't seek out her company as much as I could have done, indeed, should have done." Cecily couldn't resist a gentle retort, with a beguiling curve to her lips.

"And yet tonight, with all that is happening around the king, here you are!"

Francis moved his head down, lowering his lids over his eyes and added softly.

"Here I am, indeed."

She stretched up her neck and their lips touched, gently, but their eyes were open and locked upon each other. They dared only the briefest of exchanges, and parted quickly, aware someone could round a corner at any time and catch them out. Francis straightened his back, and looked down the corridor towards the closed room. His brow was furrowed with worry.

"How is the king?" Cecily asked as his attention continued to be focused over her shoulder. He sighed wearily in reply.

"Fine, in the main. I know his arm pains him somewhat, I noticed that this evening. If we can just get through these next few weeks, I think we may be able to make some real progress with popular opinion. The wedding announcement will help - the London folk love a good reason to celebrate. Let's hope we can fill the fountains with enough wine to wash away the fouler memories of the past few months. However, he will also need to travel back north. It is a balancing act, this country. Who in God's name would ever wish to be king?" So distracted was he that he completely missed Cecily's stung expression, so intent was he on watching the chamber door before them. He didn't look at her until she spoke her next words, in a tone loaded with mild reproof.

"He did. He decided to become king. He took the throne, Francis. We have all had to pay a price for his actions. This is his."

Francis took a backward step away from her, unsure as to her intent with those words. He wasn't sure what to say in response. It was too difficult a subject to be discussed hurriedly, and he was far too aware that in his current state he may say the wrong thing. The last thing he wanted was to spoil their relationship through a lack of tact, as his fondness for the girl was growing by the day, deepening into something much more serious. He had already decided not to answer her when he saw a flash of colour cross his vision. Bess had left the chamber and so the king would be alone.

"Wait here," he said quickly, and left her side as Cecily turned to watch him stride down the corridor and disappear into the chamber at the end of it. Although she was left uneasy at how they had parted, she didn't regret what she had said, even though she knew that it would have pierced the armour of loyalty that Francis wore daily, underpinning his court dress.

She was a Woodville, daughter of the previous queen, sister of a deposed and supposedly murdered young king. For a fleeting second, she understood Anna Lovell completely, understanding that no matter how deep their feelings for each other would become, she had become entangled with a man whose first duty would always be to his king. The fact that they had fallen in love was always going to bring them difficulties taking everything into account. Even without the constant shadows of Anna and Ralph.

At that moment, the regal figure of her sister Bess swept out of the entrance to the Painted Chamber and moved determinedly in Cecily's direction. So grim faced and determined did she appear, that she did not even see Cecily standing to one side watching her approach with trepidation.

"Bess?"

Her sister stopped immediately and turned her head in the direction of the voice, but still appeared not to see her sister. Her face was flushed, and her eyes, moist with unshed tears, were blazing with an unspoken anger. She did not speak, but remained frighteningly still and her chest was rising and falling, straining at the neckline of her gown, as if she was struggling to breathe.

"Bess!" Cecily repeated, in true astonishment at her appearance. "What has happened? What did the king say?"

Although she could not have failed to hear the words, Bess stared at her uncomprehendingly.

"Bess!" Cecily's voice became insistent, almost strident, echoing up to the vaulted ceiling, and she moved forward to grasp her arm, giving it a firm shake.

"Not here!" Bess hissed in harsh response, and recommenced her unrelenting progress down the corridor. Cecily watched her leave, and then glanced back in the opposite direction to see if there was any sign of Francis returning back to her. She was torn between wanting to comfort her sister and needing to spend precious time in the company of the man she loved.

In the end, she had to admit to herself that Francis would not let the fact that she was waiting for him curtail any meeting where Richard needed his counsel. She also recalled that as he left, on that occasion, he did not squeeze her hand, knowing instinctively that he would be some time. It pained her greatly that they had parted with unresolved words between them but sadly, she had to acknowledge that she would probably not see him again that evening. With some reluctance, she followed her sister's footsteps as they echoed into the distance.

31. THE PALACE OF WESTMINSTER
December 1485

By the time she reached Bess's chamber, Bess herself was sitting on the end of the four poster bed, staring into space. Cecily closed the door behind her and stopped a few paces in.

"You look cold. Frozen!"

With those words she crossed over to the hearth and threw another two logs onto the already roaring fire. The flames licked up and devoured the wood hungrily, throwing out more heat into the room as Cecily looked down into its glow, waiting for her sister to speak.

"He has changed." Bess said finally, her whole body displaying her desolation. "The old uncle Richard, the uncle he was before he became king would not have been so cruel." Cecily turned her attention away from the flames, somewhat startled by her words.

"Cruel? He was cruel to you? How?"

Bess folded her arms around herself, as if to offer comfort to her own body. Comfort she could not obtain from the arms she most desired.

"He insists that I marry Manuel. Insists that I leave England, leave my family and everyone that I care for, the way of life that I know. He is happy to hand me over into the care of strangers, into a foreign land. At least if I had married Henry Tudor I would still be able to stay in England!"

"Bess!" Cecily's stomach lurched into her throat, her sister's words shocking her to the core. "Sshh!" she whispered urgently, crossing the chamber swiftly to stand before her disgruntled sister. "You are saying you would prefer the king to be dead! I cannot believe that is what you really think! You are upset and tired. It has been a long day and a very difficult one for you I am sure. Let's get you undressed and into bed. I can send down to the kitchen for a posset to calm you. Tomorrow, things will look different, I am sure."

Bess was in no mood to listen and began to display behaviour that Cecily had seen a thousand times in her own mother, to her own rising despair.

"He is using me as currency.   To barter with the Portuguese and annoy the French.   This is all politics, he doesn't care for that pious Princess, he as much as admitted it to me - but I could see it, he didn't have to tell me.   You noticed it too, I am sure," she paused, nodding at Cecily, seeking her agreement. "The way he used to sit at table with Anne? He was so attentive, even throughout their long marriage. You remember? Remember how it was? And tonight? Well - he hardly looked her in the face at the table. Oh yes, he smiled, and was gracious, and fawned over her hand.   But his eyes..."

Cecily became impatient, and not a little worried at her reasoning. That it was all true could not be argued, but still, it was to no avail.

"He hardly knows her Bess. He had known Anne a long time, you know that. Their relationship was different to most..." her voice trailed off and she was surprised to feel tears choking back her words. Suddenly all she could think of was Anna, Francis's wife, and although she knew that their marriage was in no way the same as Richard and Anne's had been, the fact remained that she was still his wife. What Cecily had done was become his mistress, a fact which when taken on its own, shamed her down to her very core, even before consideration of her own husband who now seemed so remote he no longer existed.

"Still," Bess continued, flatly refusing to give in. "He doesn't love her and will never love her, as I will never love that insipid cousin of hers. I'll not do it, Cecily. I will find a way, I will! There is too much at stake."

Cecily's thoughts cleared at her words.

"There is nothing you can do. Richard is the king and you cannot disobey a command. What will you do, run away?"

"Maybe..." she replied, thoughtfully, but calmer now, her brow furrowed and lips set in a pout. Her hand suddenly raised to the neckline of her dress and she gave a small exclamation before burying her face in her hands. Perplexed, Cecily moved quickly to her side, and placed her arm around her slim shoulders which were now shaking as her anger gave way to tears.

She stroked her bright hair with one hand and spoke to her as she would one of her younger sisters. No matter how brave and sophisticated Bess tried to be, Cecily knew her true heart.

"Are you going to admit to me what is really going on here Bess? To me and to yourself? You may feel better if you do."

Bess raised her tear stained face which was full of desperation and distress. Cecily acknowledged, with a sudden sense of prophetic fear, that this was exactly how she would look if Francis ever decided to put her aside and return to his wife. The thought made her feel nauseous.

"He gave me a gift." Bess sobbed softly. "A brooch. A silver brooch inset with rubies. It was a boar, his badge, the sign we see all over court. Worn by those who serve him, who have pledged loyalty to him. Richard's men." Her voice was low now, and she stumbled over some of the words as she swallowed her tears. Cecily said nothing, just stroked her back soothingly and let her continue, to purge her agony with her words. "I told him that I love him, for I do. I told him tonight as I have told him before, and each time it is as though he does not hear my words. As though something stops him hearing me say the words, and, and I am sure….really sure, that he has feelings for me, even as he denies it. I know I shouldn't love him the way I do - but I cannot help myself. It is just there - every day - burning a hole in my heart until I fear it will be completely consumed and I will no longer have a heart left to beat. And if he will not love me, I long for that day. Long for a day when I can see him, and not have to force my feet to the floor to stop them running over to him, can stop my eyes from watching his every move, stop myself from imagining what it would be like..." she stopped suddenly and raising her tear-stained eyes, a flush crept up from her neck to cover her face.

Cecily removed her arm from her sister's shoulders, but continued to regard her studiously, not anticipating her next words.

"What is it like? To give yourself to a man you love?" It was now Cecily's turn to blush, and she felt the heat of it spread across her face, made more intense when matched with the direct enquiry from her burning gaze.

"I..I -Bess, how could you ask such a question?"

"But you are so lucky! You love Francis - I know you do! You now know how it feels to be desired by a man you also have feelings for! Think of it - a choice between Henry Tudor and Manuel - that is all I have had to consider! Even now I am declared bastard, I still cannot be allowed the freedom to choose my own path. I can't bear it, I can't...!" Once again her sister dissolved into tears and she could only watch, lost for words, unable to defend the truth.

Thinking carefully, she pulled a handkerchief out of her sleeve and pressed it into Bess's hands.

"I think you will have to come to terms with the fact that no matter how much you care for uncle Richard, no matter how much he may care for you, it is an impossible situation Bess. And it is not his fault." Bess sniffed into the linen, her sobs once again subsiding.

"Do you think he really does love me?" Cecily rubbed her temple with her fingers. She was developing a headache, and she desperately wanted to feel Francis's strong arms around her. She thought for a while on the question that hung in the air and began to think of times, such as tonight, when she had seen her uncle and Bess in the same room. He was always very attentive around her, he did not seek her out, admittedly, it would be nigh impossible for him to do so. Only, since she and Francis had been intimate, there were certain glances, certain smiles which passed between them, things which secretly allowed them to share their feelings in plain sight. She had seen such expressions pass between Richard and Anne.

But when Bess was in the same room as Richard, there was something else, something she couldn't put a finger on, but it was some elusive quality in the way Richard looked at his niece. Almost, she struggled with the idea, almost as if she was something far too precious to behold. As if, no matter how he felt about her, she was not to be sullied by profane thoughts or actions.

It was not that he didn't love her, she thought he most certainly did. It was more about the way he loved her, as if he was in no way worthy, as if she was beyond his reach. She didn't have the words to explain this to her distraught sister, and so she replied simply.

"Yes, Bess. I think he does. And I think knowing that will have to be enough for you." When she didn't respond, Cecily continued. "Where is this brooch? I should like to see it."

Bess raised her head, and her eyes were full of a deep hopelessness.

"I was so angry - so angry with him. I gave him a way out, a way for us to be together, more than one way in fact, and he rejected me." She stopped, and twisted the handkerchief this way and that. "I took it off and threw it out of a window. Into the river. I wish I hadn't done it but I was so angry and upset, but now I have nothing of him, nothing!" Once more, her head went down and her body shook with the force of her sobs.

Cecily took her in her arms once more, and began to rock her backwards and forwards, thinking.

32. THE PALACE OF WESTMINSTER
December 1485

Francis rapped on the chamber door and entered without waiting. His first thought was how cold the room was, and then he fixed his eyes on the king.

Richard had both hands braced against the mantel and was leaning forwards, his head bent low below his shoulder blades. Francis waited, aware that he would have heard his knock on the door, his mind lost in a maelstrom of thoughts. He gave himself a moment to restore some calm before the next events unfolded as the day was undoubtedly proving to be much more demanding than he ever envisaged.

The visit of the prospective bride and groom would have been enough but with the added complication of Margaret Stanley and an recalcitrant Bess, he was finding his diplomatic skills, such as they were, sorely tested. Then there was Cecily. Beautiful, doe-eyed Cecily. He longed to spend time with her, having tasted the delights of passion, he found himself counting the hours to when they could dissolve in each other's caress again. He had never felt this way about any other woman in his life, and all he wished for was the ability to spend more time with her. Time being the one thing that close associates of the king always had a dearth of. He hoped, that once Richard repaired to his Privy Chamber to tackle Margaret, he would finally find that time for himself, and for her.

"Francis?" the voice was initially muffled, but he watched as Richard straightened up carefully. Saw the imperceptible flex of the right arm and hand, reflecting that this day needed to be done and over.

"Your Grace, Lady Stanley awaits...." he trailed off as Richard turned towards him with a face like death and waved a hand to indicate he did not want to hear the rest of the sentence.

"Did you see Bess?" The very tone of his words confirmed that the meeting with his niece had not gone well. Francis fumed inwardly. He had tried stop Bess from getting to see Richard tonight, and would have succeeded if it had not been for Stanley's wife. The girl was an incessant nuisance, and he wondered if he should suggest her return to Grafton until she departed for her marriage.

"I did, briefly," he answered carefully. "From her appearance, I am guessing that she was unable to persuade you of the error of your ways."

Richard laughed sharply.

"I have a feeling she did not share with you everything she had to say to me. She certainly made some... interesting suggestions." Francis bit the inside of his cheek, his mouth twisting in thought.

"Surely nothing better than you are already offering her. She should think herself lucky that you are going this far bearing in mind her reduced status."

He watched as Richard gave a contemptuous shrug, but noticed that there was something not quite genuine in the gesture. It seemed almost forced, fake in some way that left him feeling uneasy.

"She feels the answer to my dilemma is for her to marry John."

Francis felt stupid for a moment, he had been too busy trying to read Richard's expression in the dim candlelight.

"John?"

Richard met his eyes finally and Francis was not at all sure what he saw there. He felt he knew Richard better than any man living, but there was something else taking place here, and whatever it was, he was trying to avoid sharing it with him. His discomfort increased with the realisation.

"My natural son, John."

Francis suddenly felt sick to his stomach and in some way understood why Richard's eyes were unreadable. To do this, he would have to legitimise John, the exact conversation they had some time ago. There was a certain irony in hens coming home to roost here.

"I take it you refused this suggestion, hence her mood."

"Hmm?" Richard appeared distracted, lost in his own

thoughts, he was twisting a ring on his finger absently. "Yes, of course."

The tone of his answer left Francis far from convinced. Something she had said must have obviously struck either a chord or a nerve with him, but whichever it was, he was currently not of a mind to include his friend on his ruminations. So he decided on a change of subject, of sorts. All such subjects seemed intertwined of late, like sticky, gossamer strands of a spider's web. Francis took a deep breath.

"I have also had a message from Lincoln. He has landed and is a day away. Should we not wait to hear what he has to report before you talk to Lady Stanley?" Richard stared into the middle distance giving the matter some thought, or at least giving the appearance of doing so.

"Lady Stanley will be staying with us longer than she anticipated then. But we will still see her this evening, after all, we have kept her waiting too long, and I never again intend to give a Stanley the opportunity to breathe easy if I can help it."

"We..?" Francis asked quietly, now understanding with some disappointment that his evening was far from over.

"Is Rob still here?" Francis shrugged at the question. "Somewhere around, I would imagine."

Richard finally cleared his mind of whatever was bothering him.

"Find Rob please Francis, and bring him back to my privy chamber. I will require some witness to what Lady Stanley has to say this evening. It may be, depending on what she knows, that I will need at least one of you to prevent me from taking actions I will later come to regret."

Francis nodded, and left the room in search of Rob. It was obvious that Richard was now focused on his meeting with Lady Stanley, which in one way was fortuitous, as he felt that it would have been more dangerous for him to be dwelling on the words of his niece overnight. At least this would force that meeting to the back of his mind, even if it made the interminable day drag out even further.   As he went in search for his companion, he noticed that the corridor where he had left Cecily waiting was empty, and he sighed tiredly.

How long would it be, he thought, before, Cecily, like his wife before her, decided that sacrificing time together for his duty to his king, and his friend, was just too high a price to bear.

33. THE PALACE OF WESTMINSTER
December 1485

Richard approached the door to his Privy Chamber and marked the small group gathered outside. He had given Francis some time to locate Rob and in doing so they also appeared to have sequestered the services of Norfolk, whose large frame he could see dwarfing the two younger companions. Aware he was keeping them all waiting, he had still felt the need to pay a brief visit to the chapel where he had knelt for a few moments of quiet contemplation.

Well, he grudgingly admitted to himself, that and seeking the wisdom of the Lord, if any were forthcoming. Despite his clear-headed refusal in front of Bess, and his determination that his own mind was resolutely set upon its course, he found that no matter how much he tried, his mind kept re-playing aspects of their conversation. He hoped that a spell kneeling on the cold, hard floor of the chapel may refocus his thoughts. So far, success in that was limited, but he had no further time to spare. Three pairs of eyes fixed on him as he stopped before the chamber door, the two men-at-arms straightening slightly to attention as they acknowledged his presence.

"Jack." Richard said curtly to the older man, still looking decidedly uncomfortable in his best court finery "I did not expect to see you here."

"No, Your Grace," he responded gruffly " but I was with Rob when Francis came to fetch him. Not to put any words in the mouths of babes, but I think they both feel it may be of benefit for me to provide further witness this evening. If you consent that is?"

Richards eyes moved from Rob to Francis, who were both surveying him calmly but with anticipation. They were his closest companions, but he was well aware that in a complex political situation, there could be no man of better use to him than Jack Howard. The two younger men had known this and ensured that he would be in attendance to act as both witness and advisor. He returned their gaze solidly and allowed a flicker of a smile to register on his lips.

"I thank you Jack, you are most welcome. Your counsel on anything we may find out this evening will be most valuable to me." The older man nodded in appreciation, although his eyes appeared also to be reflecting the length of the day.

"Yet I hear young Lincoln is due back any time. Would it not.?." Richard was already shaking his head.

"No, let's do this now. The Lady has been allowed to cool her heels for longer than I anticipated, much longer than I would have desired. I wish to ensure that she understands the severity of the situation she now finds herself in, and I would like to do that before Stanley arrives in hot pursuit of his errant wife. I will also then need to deal with him and his perception of "care"."

Turning on his heel, he nodded to the nearest man-at-arms who twisted the latch on the door and threw it open. The heat from the chamber washed out into the cool passage and greeted the men as they entered the room. Francis, being last in, crashed into Rob's back with a muttered curse as the group in front of him halted unexpectedly, and he tried to look over his shoulder to see what had happened.

Margaret Stanley was kneeling before the fire with her hands clasped and head bowed in silent prayer. Her back was rigidly straight and she portrayed the very picture of piety, with her profile sketched in light from the fire. Francis, regaining his balance, saw the line of Richard's jaw tighten, and a muscle flexed in his cheek. He had no doubt himself that she had heard the voices outside the door, and had "arranged" herself in this tableau for dramatic effect. She was now, it seemed, trying to appeal to the more devout side of Richard's nature, knowing that this had been one of the reasons why he had stayed his hand against her over past actions. He also noticed that the food and drink which he had earlier had placed in the room was untouched, and he was glad of it because he felt sorely in need of some strong wine himself.

"My Lady?"

Richards tone was courteous, but slightly chilled as he moved closer towards the kneeling figure. The rest of them followed, now able to fill the room and close the door behind them. Margaret's head raised slowly at the sound of his voice, but she did not turn in their direction until she had slowly crossed herself and pressed her lips to the heavily jewelled string of rosary beads she held in her hand. In the firelight, they glittered like darkest jet. Richard took two paces forwards and held out his hand to help her rise.

For the longest of moments it appeared that she was going to refuse either to stand or decline his assistance, but after a tense pause she placed her hand into the one Richard offered to her and rose in one smooth practised motion. Francis nudged Rob's shoulder and cocked his head towards the wall.

In response, Rob moved around the back of the group to the sideboard.

"Wine, Your Grace?"

Richard nodded wordlessly as he guided Margaret to the nearest seat, and Rob began to fill three cups.

"My Lady?" he asked courteously, cutting his eyes over to her as she carefully smoothed her skirts before the fire. Fixing Rob with her shrewd dark eyes she shook her head.

"No, thank you." Rob had no particular love for this lady and so gave a matter of fact shrug of the shoulders. He found her current status quite amusing but knew he would need to disguise any irreverent humour this evening for fear of incurring Richard's wrath.

"Gentlemen, be seated," Richard said as he grasped a cup himself and took time to take a swift, deep drink.

"Forgive me, my Lady," he continued, aware he was paying more attention to his thirst than to his guest for the moment, "but it has been an eventful evening, one way or another." On these final words he locked eyes with his adversary. The ones that met his were small, shrewd and calculating, he could almost liken them to those of a predatory animal and he noticed them register his unease as she gave a small, tight smile.

"I can imagine, Your Grace. I saw your niece waiting without."

Rob gave a small whistle of indrawn breath, and looked at Richard whose face remained closed. But Margaret had not finished, her gimlet gaze still fixed on Richard. "I only mean that I would imagine that it is in no way easy for you to accommodate the bastard children of Dame Grey. That you commit to do so does you credit." Rob bit his lip to prevent the rejoinder that burned there.

"And it is the bastard children of Dame Grey that we are here to discuss, Madam, is it not?" Richard's rejoinder was swift and decisive. "You therefore appear to have led us directly to the point, whereas my intention was to handle the matter with more," he paused and inclined his head towards her, "delicacy."

Silence fell around the room as Richard moved back to a table, which was, as ever, piled with letters and documents. He pushed them aside to perch on the very edge of the table, giving him a certain height advantage over Margaret. Norfolk interjected at this point, his voice low and gravelly in the hushed chamber.

"Madam, I think the king's wishes are abundantly clear in this matter. You must tell us what you know, there can be no profit or advantage in hiding the truth of it. And you do know, don't you? You do know what happened to the king's nephews?"

Margaret's back stiffened and she sat up very straight in her chair, the rosary beads pooled into a glittering heap in her lap. Her gaze moved in turn to take the measure of each man's face with an expression which belied her years, making her appear much older than she was. Her examination of her interrogators completed, she rested her gaze on Richard.

"My son..."

"What of him?" Norfolk interrupted brusquely. "He only keeps his head because of the mercy shown him by the king's grace. You endanger him further by any prevarication on your part."

Her attention shifted between Norfolk and Richard. Richard was inwardly now very pleased that Jack was here, and silently admired his companions wisdom. Jack's position as one of York's elder statesmen was obviously having an effect, and one which he felt could not have been imposed by Rob or Francis. Margaret didn't regard them as serious threats.   Even with the gravitas provided by Norfolk's presence, Margaret was unbowed and as she settled back in her chair but her chin jutted slightly in defiance.

"I would need certain guarantees with regard to my son, Henry."

Richard said nothing but watched her carefully. He didn't think he had ever been in the company of a woman who could convey such an iron will as Margaret Stanley, not even his brother's wife. It was difficult not to have a certain measure of admiration for her, but that was tempered now by his distrust and dislike. He was about to answer when a dispassionate voice sounded from across the room.

"You are in no position to ask for guarantees!" This came from Francis, who was seated in a chair against the far wall and whose outline could only just be determined by Margaret in the dimness of the chamber, although both the fire and the candlelight picked up on his jewels, causing them to burn darkly.

"Yet I do ask them," she insisted, turning to Francis as she spoke, eyes narrowing as she tried to read his expression in the half light. "I do have information which I have kept to my conscience over these last months, and could freely name those who you may, or my not, be surprised to find out know more than you would think. I would be a fool to give such away so freely." She stopped only to turn back to Richard. "And you know I am not a fool."

"Are we talking of your husband?" Once again, Francis's voice, tinged with anger, came out of the gloom. Margaret's eyes remained fixed on Richard.

"I am talking of many people." Her reply was cold and contemptuous, confirming, for both Richard and Francis, the distaste she had for the king's younger confidants. When Richard rejoined the conversation, his voice was dark and melodious, quite in contrast to Francis's cold anger. By design.

"What "guarantees" do you have in mind, my lady?" The question, though pleasant, was couched in a voice which rippled with undercurrents of danger. Margaret gave a small half smile which did nothing to relieve the hard, carved lines of her face, only succeeding in cloaking her with an air of superiority.

"Well, for one, that he keeps his head."

There was a muttered gasp, but Richard refrained from shifting his gaze.

"This is no matter for amusement, madam." Rob Percy's voice was tinged with astonishment. "Your son is a traitor, plain and simple. As my lord of Norfolk reminded you, it is only due to the king's mercy that he still breathes in this world."

"Calm yourself, Rob," Richard interjected, smiling to himself, his hand turning the empty cup absently. "Lady Stanley is more than cognisant of her son's precarious position, which is why she has risked her own freedom to come here today. It also proves what I long suspected - that both Lord and Lady Stanley act independently of each other when it comes to matters of self interest and that their marriage was only ever designed to achieve one aim. Am I right, Lady Stanley?"

Margaret bridled inwardly but had no intention of putting her emotions on display, particularly to this group of people. If she had a weak point, it was Stanley, and the marriage she believed would cement her position had turned to ashes in her mouth. Stanley was not under discussion, yet. Until she chose to offer him up as a bargaining tool, something she would have no hesitation in doing if circumstances demanded. She must save her son at all costs and no price was too high. She readjusted her shoulders in an unconscious show of defiance.

"My marriage is not under discussion, and so I would ask that we return to the matter in hand, if it please Your Grace."

Richard allowed his face to register some grudging pleasure in her response, but was stopped from answering her immediately as Rob shifted forward in his seat.

"Tell me, Lady Stanley, is it true that your son had all address him as "His Majesty?" And if this is so, why would you ever believe that the king could allow him to keep his head? Would we have been subject to the same mercy from "His Majesty" had the fortunes of war been different?" The room fell silent as the occupants appeared to ponder on Rob's words until he spoke again, his words underscored with a dangerous chuckle. "I think not."

Dismissing Rob's question, and at the same time ignoring him in person, Margaret cleared her throat and continued employing the imperious air which had been well developed over many years.

"I would also wish for him to receive a pardon, for which he would swear allegiance to Your Grace." Jack raised eyebrows high up into his greying hairline as Francis and Rob exchanged incredulous glances. Unable to hold back any longer, a bark of laughter escaped as Rob studied his feet, shaking his head in amazement, only to lift his head in shock as she continued. "And I would also wish for the return of my chattels and fortune, that is to be released from the hands of Lord Thomas Stanley."

No one spoke. The fire crackled and burned fiercely, fighting a war of its own against the December chill. Francis desperately desired another drink, but dare not move. He picked up one of the chess pieces from the board laid out on the table next to him and weighed it in his hand. It was a black knight. Richard himself leaned further forwards from his perch on the table, his eyes narrowing as he scrutinised her face closely.

"Are you asking for your marriage to Lord Stanley to be dissolved madam?" Seemingly unafraid to return the keen stare, Margaret pursed her lips as if in thought.

"If that is what it takes, then so be it."

"Lord Stanley now having outlived his usefulness." Richard pondered aloud. "Thus answering my earlier question."

"You ask a great deal for someone in your position my Lady." Norfolk's voice was quiet and concerned but Margaret answered without looking at him, her eyes remained on the king's countenance.

"Not too high a price when you consider what is at stake."

Francis, irritated into action, stood up from his chair noisily and walked closer towards the immobile form.

"Do not for one moment think your knowledge keeps you safe.

The price you ask far outweighs what ever evidence you could reliably impart. How would we ever know the truth of it?" This last was said as he turned in appeal to the rest of the room. "We have always known never to trust a Stanley - I don't see how that has changed."

Margaret smiled at Francis thinly.

"There are other advantages to my proposals, if you would care to consider them."

"Really!" Francis spat sardonically. He took the opportunity to move over to the sideboard to obtain the drink he felt in dire need of. He didn't see her nod, again returning to watch Richard.

"My son is still the heir to the Lancastrian line. He could still ascend to the throne albeit through a more peaceable route."

Francis stopped mid-action and turned, flagon in hand with a look of sheer disbelief on his face. Jack had difficulty in stopping his mouth from gaping but managed to recover to utter uncomprehendingly.

"Are you seriously suggesting that a traitor be named as the king's heir?"

Rob gave up all pretence and slapped his thigh, laughing roundly.

"Ye Gods Francis, pass me that flagon! Don't bother with the cup, I'll drink it dry as it stands!"

The smile was fixed rigidly on the otherwise impassive face as she remained intently focused on the darkly glittering form of the king. The firelight danced playfully over his golden collar, warming the severity of his dark doublet. She could never work out why the man always dressed as if he was either in mourning, or about to be so.

"These are difficult times my lords." The thin hands left her lap and spread expansively. "How much uncertainty could we overcome if we tried to work together on the matter of succession. When I have imparted my knowledge, you will be better able to see how this arrangement could work to the weal of us all."

The room fell deafeningly quiet broken only by Richard as he stood, turning his back as each one of them in the room tried to read his expression, something which he did not want them to do as he knew he would have difficulty masking his feelings.

"There seems to be no end to the number of people who feel they can offer me advice on who should be the rightful heir. Completely forgetting that the past incumbent of that position has not long since been laid in the ground, that another of my blood has also been named so and that there is yet another young prince who, some would still insist, could have a claim, if his health improves as the years pass." He spoke this line softly, but every member of the room heard him clearly. The spectre of Clarence hung in the room, like his laughter used to after he had moved on. Richard turned slowly, and regarded Margaret with clearly determined eyes.

"You have given me nothing this evening, my Lady, other than food for thought and my time is pressing. Tomorrow I have marriage contracts to draw up, and no doubt your embarrassed husband to deal with at some point. I therefore feel you have given me no option other than to keep you here under guard. This will give me the time to consider your proposals further."

Pausing, he removed the ring from his smallest finger, examined it, and replaced it promptly.

"It may be that I have heard enough, as the price you demand for any information you have is not only exceedingly high, but is also repugnant to me. Until then, we can make you comfortable." He looked over to Francis. "Have Dick notified that Lady Stanley will be spending time as a guest in the Tower. I believe the Wakefield Tower has comfortable appointments, King Henry was afforded a certain level of hospitality there some years ago. See it done."

Francis tried hard to suppress the smile rising to his lips but was unable to do so, he turned with a nod to Richard and left the room to carry out the arrangements.

Margaret's whole body was rigid with shock. Captivity and arrest, and in the very apartment where King Henry lost his life. She was convinced the irony was not lost on any of these men, but she was determined not to give her captors the satisfaction of witnessing her anxiety.

"As you wish - Your Grace" she said, but despite her efforts Richard could hear the fear in her voice and see the anger in her eyes, and was glad of it. His mouth curled with a dark humour that reached no further than his lips.

"You are a skilled courtier madam, and a consummate player of the game of politics. You must sit and hope that this time, you have not overplayed your hand."

34. THE CITY OF LONDON
December 1485

John de la Pole was immensely relieved to finally lay eyes on the city gates. He felt he had been too long away from court and although his mission had been fruitful, he was finding it exceedingly hard to come to terms with what he had learned from his visit to Burgundy. The sheer splendour of the duchess's welcome, her sharp wit and cautious approach, and the ensuing revelations had left him reeling at the implications they were now faced with. He also had to admit that he had his own position to consider, even though he had not uncovered anything which he deemed would cause Richard to alter the fact that he had been named his heir.

It had always been a double edged honour. He had taken the place of Richard's own dead son, had been given the authority of the Council of the North, much to the chagrin of the Earl of Northumberland. When Tudor invaded, he knew that had Richard been defeated, he could have expected to face the executioner's block. As a Yorkist, a Plantagenet and Richard's heir, he could not have thought to receive mercy at the pretender's hands.

Richard had refused to let him fight at Redemore. He had insisted he stayed closeted with the children of the family at Sheriff Hutton, playing nursemaid with his cousin Bess. The resentment had been deep at the time, but he knew that Richard had needed someone there who could take action had the battle not gone well. He had been given his instructions, which, thankfully, he had not needed to put into play.

He was also keenly aware that when Richard re-married, as he surely must, a new son would naturally become heir to the throne. But that was some way off, and there was the possibility of daughters before sons. He had time to build his reputation and cement his relationship at court and in the north long before that happened. By giving him the Council to preside over, a role that was nominally given to his young son before his death, Richard had granted him the opportunity to serve him as Richard himself had served his king. Indeed, this recent mission displayed how much trust was invested in him now.   And to his uncle, trust and loyalty were as food and drink. He could not live without them, and those who provided it were valued beyond gold.

He was turning and turning these recent events over in his head when finally, William, riding ponderously by his side throughout, decided to speak, which took him somewhat by surprise.

"So - how do you think the king will take this news?" Lincoln was so astonished by this sudden question that he pulled on his mounts reins and brought his bay to a sudden stop.   Twisting his body round in the saddle, he turned towards his travelling companions and motioned them to stop.   Catesby who had walked his mount on regardless, suddenly realised his journey had continued alone. He stopped and turned back over his shoulder, his face a quizzical mask.

"Lincoln? Is aught wrong?"

Spurring his horse on once more, he drew level with the lawyer and stared at him in undisguised amazement.

"Is aught wrong? Christs' blood Will, we have travelled by sea and land this past few days and not once have you been willing to enter into conversation about what we have witnessed.   You have dissembled, evaded, avoided any opinion on the matter, despite my pressing! Just shaking your head and lowering your eyes, and now, now before the very gates of London you decide the time is right to talk? In God's eyes, man, what are you thinking?" Lincoln's agitation as his words spilled out transferred down his leather reins, and the horse snorted fitfully.   William held a sanguine expression as he surveyed Lincoln with doleful eyes.

"In matters such as this, I often find it more prudent to keep my own counsel first, until I am sure I have appropriate advice to offer."

"In matters such as this?!" Lincoln repeated, just as incredulously, his horse crabbing sideways as the tension increased, causing the rider to re-adjust his hold on the reins. "Just how many times can you have been required to give counsel in matters such as we have just seen? What if the king had been present? What if he had need of your counsel ten days back - what then? Would he have been met with mute stares and silence?"

Will gave every appearance of being totally unabashed by Lincoln's exclamation and continued to regard him with no change of expression.

"If pressed, I would have given the best advice I could at the time. I cannot guarantee that it would have been the best available, just the best at that time of pressing."

Lincoln turned his head towards the City and exhaled loudly. It had been a long journey and arduous both concerning its delicacy, its outcome and the nature of his companion.

"God save me from lawyers!" he muttered under his breath, but loud enough for Will to hear, and touched his spurs to the bay's flanks. Will watched him move forward and with only a suggestion of a smile around his lips, then pushed on to follow him.

Back with his own thoughts, Lincoln continued to consider what they had learned, more than aware that his uncle would want every detail. He was now even more certain that Will would just stand by nodding sagely and interjecting as he thought fit, leaving him to be the bearer of their tidings. Not for the first time did he wish that he had been accompanied by another, more amenable companion - Rob Percy for instance.

Now, he would have made for fine company, John reflected, grinning to himself. One with many a tale to tell, who liked his Rhenish and smiled constantly. By heaven he would have liked to have seen Margaret and Rob joust with words! Would indeed have laid a purse down for the privilege!

The duchess's revelation that Elizabeth Woodville had full knowledge that her sons had been hale, hearty and alive when they were smuggled out of the country would hit Richard hard. In her defence, at no time had she openly accused Richard of the murder of her sons, but once those rumours were abroad and she had finally agreed to relinquish the privations of Westminster sanctuary, she had offered not one word to scourge the vile gossip which had plagued the king's reign for the best part of two years.

An acquiescent observer to events, she had allowed that open wound to fester and had watched as a malicious poison threaded its way throughout London and the rest of the country. It had spread like a plague, invading every part of the land until it had the sovereign in its grasp, clinging on to him like the hand of a rotted corpse.

Richard had tried, more than most kings, to let his people see him for who he really was, but everywhere he presented himself, the whispers and malcontent permeated amongst the crowds of watching faces like some noxious odour. Murderer, tyrant, devil in ermine - the underlying current of lies swept before them into every village and vale.

Henry Tudor himself had joined the throng, cloaking his lack of a claim to the throne by fostering every seditious rumour that crossed the Channel - stories no doubt embellished by the Dowager Queen herself as she negotiated her eldest daughter's hand in marriage to the Welsh milksop. And all the time, that former Queen of England knew the truth and had the power to make it stop. Instead she had lingered in sanctuary for no good reason other than to embarrass the king.

Then in a remarkable volte-face, she agreed to come out, on the promise that Richard would do no harm to her or her kin, find noble marriages for her many daughters, give her a place to live and a pension to maintain it with. She accepted all of this as if it were her due, and said not one single word to deny the falsehoods being bandied abroad.

Lincoln's rage had been so complete that on landing back in England, his first instinct had been to bypass London, travel to Grafton and put his hands round that slender white throat until the artlessly smiling face above it turned blue. That was the only time he was thankful that he had Will with him, who would in no way have countenanced such a detour.

That, and the fact that he had been unable to let Richard know anything of what had transpired, had forced him to turn his mount's head firmly in the direction of the capital. He deserved to know, needed to know without delay. However, he suspected that had Rob been with him instead of Will, they may well have gone to Grafton anyway, if only to see her face when she was told that her secret was exposed.

In the end, it should have been obvious what had happened, if not for the swirling maelstrom of rumour and deceit. Sir Edward Woodville, despite trying to raise the whole fleet with his half of the treasury gold given over by the Dowager Queen, had finally escaped with two ships when Richard first entered London as Lord Protector. It was on such ships that had made the crossing. One Prince in each for safety and to avoid detection.

What was going to be even more difficult for Richard was the total involvement of his sister in the events of that summer two years ago. She also had the power at her fingertips to remove the stain from his character, or at the very least to have let the man know what she had got herself involved in.

Christ, he thought sadly, when you look back. The lies and deception that surrounded him! The very worst stink of putrefaction that was aimed at his character and which had mired him with its filth to this very day. Sickening at the thought, he also acknowledged to himself that there would have been those who smiled secretly when he lost his son and heir, and then his wife - all nodding sagely and declaring it the Good Lord's judgement on a despotic ruler. At this he laughed out loud, it's bitterness jarring in the cold, and Will gave him a quick and strange stare.

Richard - despotic! Lincoln shook his head as his horse plodded on through the grey afternoon. As the gates draw nearer, he shifted in his saddle, his breath misting the air before him like fog. The thing that disturbed his sleep and had kept him sweating at night, tossing and turning in the finest linen sheets, was the thought of what would have happened if Richard had been slain outside the village of Market Bosworth. Who would have spoken up? How would the truth have been uncovered?

How easily would Henry Tudor have sat on the throne with a Woodville bride at his side when at least one brother was alive and well and casting eyes over the channel from Burgundy. Tudor's intention to wed young Elizabeth had been very clear, he needed the blood of old York to justify warming his backside on the velvet cushion of the throne. For this to happen he would have needed to repeal the Titulus Regis, making young Elizabeth, and her brothers and sisters, legitimate once again. This destroyed the matter of the pre-contract, and in one stroke, threatened his own claim to the throne.

What exactly had Elizabeth Woodville expected to happen once the usurper found that his main rival for the throne was not only still very much alive, but alive and then with a better right to England's crown than him? Exactly what double dealing game had she been playing and with whom?

And what of Richard? Left to lie cold in his grave. Marked down in history as a usurper and murderer of children for all time? Jesus God! The thought caused his blood to run cold in his veins and he wished again that he had been with Rob and could seek out the nearest tavern. His thoughts haunted him and he felt in dire need of a good strong drink, to just get right royally drunk, before he relayed this tale to his waiting uncle.

Then there was Duchess Margaret. Clever, calculating Margaret who seemed to have learned so much from her deceased husband in the art of politics. Not exactly lying. Not telling the truth, just not doing anything other than provide a haven for her dead brother's sons at the request of their mother. Margaret, corresponding with Elizabeth and Henry Stafford, the erstwhile Duke of Buckingham, a man always with an eye out for the best chance of improving his own self interest.

At least his impatience meant that he had already been dealt with, which Richard had done in short order once he had been so roundly betrayed. His sardonic expression sliced from his velvet shoulders to roll in the mud. But how Richard would react to his sister's machinations was anyone's guess. Imperiously cool, she had informed them that she had been so unhappy on hearing of the whole pre-contract story that she felt duty bound to help her sister-in-law when it became obvious that the Princes were in danger.

In danger from whom he had asked and the list was long and predictable. Buckingham, Morton, Stanley, Beaufort, Tudor - Richard, her own brother.

There was a further matter which left Lincoln uneasy. That was a direct question over Margaret's motives and one he was still struggling to resolve. She had also let slip that she had knowledge of the pre-contract story before Richard did. It would seem that brother George had informed her - chapter and verse - when he was hoping to become Prince Regent and marry Charles's daughter, Mary, after Charles himself had died.

Frustratingly, she had also declined to enter into any conversation around why, if she knew of the pre-contract, she would help Elizabeth and allow her remaining living brother to be so roundly vilified. The whole affair was a knotted skein of plots, secret correspondence and betrayals, which ultimately could have led to Richard's death. He was still struggling to put together all of the pieces, to make some sense of it all.

"Think you the king will be disinclined to return the boy to his mother, considering her involvement in this subterfuge?"

Will's voice pulled Lincoln out of his reverie as they were entering the gates and were assailed by the familiar sights and attendant stenches that brought home the fact that they were inside the city precincts.

"It is one thing to return something lost to its owner," Will continued, looking quickly over his shoulder to ensure that their small retinue was far enough behind to be out of earshot, "it is quite another to just remind someone where they have left something hidden, even though the owner may be fully aware if its location and need no reminder."

Lincoln did not reply. He listened intently to what his companion was saying but felt that by keeping quiet he may finally get some conversation out of the man as it had certainly been a long time coming. He continued to fix thoughtfully on the space between the bay's ears. The horse was perking those ears forward, as eager, it would appear, to reach home as its rider. Will was in full flow now, as if the press of familiar streets had restored a confidence he had been deserted of abroad.

"Of course, the difficulty is that wherever the boy is finally settled, the old problem remains. He is a focus for rebellion and uprising for those who were loyal to Edward and see the Titulus Regis as invalid. Those who then realise that there is still a living issue from Edward - well - I don't think enough time has passed for us to be out of those particular woods."

Lincoln continued to watch his animal's head rise and fall with the plodding movement of its feet. Despite resting at a tavern in Sandwich, he was both bone weary and desperate for this journey to end. After such a long time silent, Will now appeared unable to stop talking, even though he was eliciting neither agreement or dissent from his companion. His next sentence changed that.

"Of course, the answer to that is to deal with those who would be the most likely to take such actions." Lincoln's head came up sharply at that.

"Are you saying what I think you are saying?" Will looked at him questioningly.

"Has Oxford been captured yet?" Lincoln shook his head at the mention of Tudors's most experienced commander in the field. As far as he was aware Oxford was still in hiding somewhere after Tudor's defeat. No one had as yet given him up.

"Shame," continued Will matter of factly, as he adjusted his reins in his gloved hands. "I was thinking, certainly Stanley and his wife..."

"Will," Lincoln signed heavily, "Richard is not going to imprison the Stanleys, much less wreak the punishment for treason on a woman. That's a different kettle of fish to Tudor deserters." Will nodded sagely at that, but pressed on.

"You would think so wouldn't you? But, we have hopefully leaned a lesson from Buckingham's actions. His plot was to free the princes but his loyalties were pledged to Tudor I believe - it is currently still very difficult to separate the two causes because of the age of the boy, but no matter. There are those still abroad whose actions could be said to have defined them as traitors, if our king were not so generous of mind."

The wily fox face of Stanley flashed across Lincoln's mind, quickly replaced by the bluff, wind chiselled features of Northumberland.

"The whole things a bloody mess if you ask me," Lincoln grumbled irritably. "I can well see Richard insisting that his sister get herself over here on the next sailing and explain herself. It's still not certain she will hand the boy over to him anyway. She didn't seem keen."

His thoughts were still in Burgundy and he had the vision of Margaret's face firmly fixed in his mind. She was shrewd and intelligent, that woman and if she could not see a good reason to hand the boy over into his uncles safekeeping, there would be no persuading her. But, he knew that Richard needed the boy in England. To prove his own innocence and to prevent any further uprising and despite what he had said in reply to Will, there were certain members of the king's court who may just have to be subject to imprisonment...or worse...man or woman alike.

He kneed his mount forward more determinedly, desperate now to reach the edge of the city and progress along the road to Westminster. He felt an urgent need to be rid of this burden and call his duty discharged.

35. THE PALACE OF WESTMINSTER
December 1485

With the marriage contracts arranged and terms agreed, the Portuguese contingent made their elaborate farewells and taking advantage of the unusually clement weather now sailed back home. With a sense of some relief, Richard found himself turning his thoughts away from the impending nuptials and forcing his attention once again to the pious and learned lady who currently occupied a somewhat comfortable, if reluctant, presence in the Tower. Especially with the knowledge that Lincoln was due back in the city at any hour.

Uppermost in his mind now, however, was a matter of a more personal nature which needed to be attended to. Bess's words regarding his bastard daughter two nights ago were no doubt meant to deliver a surprise, as sure as if she had withdrawn a dagger from her sleeve. He was both annoyed at her, and disappointed in Kathryn at the same time.

He wondered idly if she had even told her own husband, as Will had not mentioned the fact at all, despite being at court daily. These musings were churning through his mind like unsettled seas, as he crossed the galleried hall swiftly, with his head slightly lowered in thought. With his level of preoccupation, he was taken by surprise when he almost collided with young Cecily, who suddenly hurtled round the corner at great speed, blue skirts gathered in her hands and her hennin flying. He stopped short as the young girl managed to halt within inches of the toes of his boots but in complete disarray, now tinged with alarm.

"Your Grace!" She mouthed apologetically in shock as Richard deftly grasped both her upper arms to prevent her stumbling headlong into his chest. "I - I..!"

"My, my, my Lady, you are in a great hurry," he drawled, holding her at arms length as amusement danced around his lips. Looking down into her flushed face, he had a feeling that he both knew where she was heading and who she was anxious to see, something which caused him consternation of a different kind.

"Beg pardon, Sire, I am - I mean I ..." she tried to bob to a small curtsey but his firm grip on her arms prevented such movement, which only served to increase her discomfort. Richard observed the small heart-shaped face as she struggled vainly to regain her composure whilst he spoke.

"I have had a letter from your husband, Lord Scrope. I must apologise that the duties I assign him keep him longer in the north than intended, but he has accepted my assurance that you are well settled at court with the Lady Elizabeth." During these words she had now steadied herself, lowering her eyes demurely, which still could not prevent the slow, pink, colour which flushed her neck and cheeks.

"That is most kind, Your Grace. I thank you for your hospitality, and I know my lord husband is only eager to serve you as best he is able."

"Good." He replied somewhat perfunctorily, inclining his head as he paused to consider his next words. "Lord Lovell is in the courtyard. I have just left him there."

His tone was cool, his face impassive, which took some effort on his part and which only served to force the bright flush to increase in intensity. Looking up quickly, her eyes registered both surprise and fear as she stared back at him lost for words. Richard checked a sigh. Although not entirely approving of the dalliance between his favoured courtier and the bastard daughter of his brother, he could see that they were entirely taken with each other. He knew that Scrope had not been deliriously happy with the match he had made, despite the generous dowry Richard had provided as part of the agreement forged to winkle Dame Grey out of sanctuary.

He was less concerned for Scrope, who he knew would find his ease elsewhere, than for Francis, whose own marriage had been entirely out of his control and not a blessed union by any stretch of the imagination. To which, he had to recognise his own contribution, knowing full well that he had always relied on Francis, but that this burden had been laid more heavily on his friend's shoulders since Buckingham's treachery.

Anna Lovell was descended from a long Lancastrian line, as had Francis been before his own father's death. That he had become close quartered with the then king's younger brother had caused him difficulties with his own kin for many a year, culminating in a final reluctance for his wife to even be present at court, once Richard himself was crowned and Francis became his chief minister. Thinking on it then as he did, it suddenly struck him as a strange irony that the two close friends were now both childless, and wanting for a loving and settled wife.

Shaking his head quickly to clear his thoughts, he mentally reprimanded himself that he had still not addressed the matter of Cecily with Francis before both of their reputations were completely tarnished. Momentarily, he thought of Anne once more and how he had felt on hearing she had been married to Edward of Lancaster, and his mood softened as his own heart constricted painfully. Suddenly sympathetic, he leaned forward, closer to the girl's expectant face.

"Before I let you go to him," he whispered, "would you happen to know where my daughter Kathryn is at present?"

He watched her swallow nervously, unsure how to respond to his mood.

"In the solar, Your Grace." Keeping his grip on her arms he leaned further forward gently and whispered into her ear.

"Your secret is safe, for the present. Now go - he is as eager as you are and I don't want him bounding round the courtyard in search of you should I cause a delay. Your paramour can act like an unruly colt at times!" So saying he released her and with a incredulous smile and quick curtsey she fled the gallery.

He was still smiling to himself when he entered the solar, framing in his mind the conversation he would later have with Francis, only to find that his daughter was not alone. Kathryn sat on a settle surrounded by samples of marten, miniver and velvet and appeared to be trying to work something onto a gown which was gathered around her feet in a bright silken wash of gold.

John was also there, seated on the floor, his head bent over a piece of parchment on which appeared to be drawn something resembling battle lines. Sprawled out opposite him on the rug was young Ned of Warwick, legs laid out with ankles crossed, his bright head bent over the parchment and his small white hands clutching wooden figures which he was moving back and forth between the drawn lines with great deliberation.

Watching those heads bent together in play, one darkly sleek and the other shining like a saintly nimbus made him catch his breath in his throat painfully, recalling a memory of the great chamber at Middleham. He swallowed it down with difficulty and his eyes then travelled upwards from where John was sitting, following the green folds of velvet to find Bess sitting comfortably in the window seat. She appeared to have a prayer book in her hand and for the second time he checked himself. The book was well known to him, being Anne's book, which he had given to Kathryn upon her marriage.

The children all looked up as he entered the room, and he quickly waved a hand to dismiss any formality as Bess made ready to rise. Ned, totally unaware of Richard's sudden presence, was babbling away as the others all fixed eyes on the king.

"Crash, clang, arghh! That's the end of you! The Silver Swine has been killed in battle! Long live my victorious father the king of his kingdom!"

John smiled slightly at his own father, shaking his head and he glanced down again at the impromptu battlefield.

"Silver Swan - Ned. Edward of Lancaster was The Silver Swan!" He grinned even wider at his father standing in the doorway.

"We are acting out the battle of Tewkesbury, Papa." Richard moved further into the room, his dark brows had drawn together inquisitively as he looked down at the parchment battlefield.

"Forgive him, Your Grace." A soft voice drifted over from the corner where Margaret, Ned's sister, sat with her embroidery frame. Although she sounded embarrassed, her face showed no sign of it, only a gentle, calm resignation. "He gets confused at times." Her sad gaze recalled George, Isabel and Anne all at the same time and he swallowed again, just as quickly, to shake the memories that today, once again, appeared to be threatening to swamp him.

Completely ignorant of his sister's excusing, the boy continued to crow proudly.

"It was a fine victory for the House of York! " Finally, catching his uncle's amused smile, he rolled onto one arm and looked up, his fair face clouding. "Were you there?"

"Of course he was you ninny! I told you before!" John groaned as he playfully tweaked the boys falling curls. "The king was Duke of Gloucester then and fought valiantly with the king to give a great victory and end the Lancastrian threat to England."

Ned proudly brandished one of the figures high in the air before placing it triumphantly, in the midst of the battle field.

"And then my father became king!"

John's smile disappeared instantly, but his quiet tone spoke of a patience with his young cousin which belied his years.

"No, Ned, remember? Cousin Bess's father became king. His most revered grace King Edward - but your father fought bravely alongside him and helped him to victory." Ned squinted at his cousin thoughtfully, picked up the figure again and examined it closely, his small brow furrowed.

"Didn't my father want to be king after such a valiant battle?" Ned drew himself up from the rug and sat, twisting round as he looked around at his elders in the room expectantly. "And if he did want to be king, why didn't he lead the van? Isn't that the most important part of the battle? Uncle - you held the van and you became king! And my other uncle Edward had already been king!" In a sudden moment of clarity the young boys eyes shone, the bright hazel iris flecked with green. "So, there were three sons of York but only two became king? Will I have to be king now that cousin Ned has gone?"

The room descended into stillness as the wide, innocent gaze sought an answer from the assembled adults. It was Margaret's assured voice that shattered the silence.

"Edward, enough of all this battle talk - it is endlessly tireless!

Alain tells me that one of the stable hounds has whelped. Seven puppies Ned - shall we go see?"

"Can I have one?" Ned asked excitedly, all thoughts of battle and kingship gone, he scrambled up to his feet, scattering figures across the sketched lines and rushed over to his sister, who had risen by this time. She placed a gentle hand on his shoulder. Her eyes held an ancient sadness and met Richard's over the boy's blonde curls and he reached out instinctively, taking her other hand and raising it gently to his lips.

"Fear not for him," he whispered gently, "his care is all my concern."

With Isabel's eyes, she threatened to shed burdening tears but bravely, with a nod of her head, she left the room, the boy pulling eagerly on her arm. As the door closed behind them, Richard looked down at the abandoned battlefield with its scattering of knights and horsemen, some still standing, others scattered across the imagined field.

"Well, " he smiled somewhat ruefully, "Ii did look a bit like that at the end." He raised his face to John's laughter only to see his son's head resting back languidly against the velvet skirts of his niece. From what he could see, although she still appeared totally absorbed in her book, it appeared that her free hand was resting gently on his collar, her fingers enmeshed in his dark silken hair. A strange sensation began to gnaw at his gut.

"Perhaps next time Agincourt? " John grinned winningly. "Ned gets everyone mixed up so it won't matter anyway"

Richard followed the line of his gaze upwards and Bess was now smiling at him demurely. Slightly unnerved, he stepped over the abandoned Tewkesbury plain and sat himself down in the settle beside his daughter, careful to avoid treading on the trailing silks.

"Now - what are you doing here?" he asked lightly, wishing he had found her alone and more than aware that he was the target of Bess's gaze. Kathryn held up the fur trim she held in her hand.

"Papa, I am getting ready for the festivities - this fur is beautiful is it not? Bess let me take it off one of the dresses she no longer wears to adorn my favourite gown!" Richard raised an eyebrow and fingered the miniver pelt gently.

"Don't you have a seamstress to do this for you?" She laughed then, like the clear peal of church bells across rolling hills.

"Of course, Papa! But I do so like to do such things myself. William says we will be going to Raglan after Christmas and I will need to be able to turn my hand to wifely duties." Richard studiously considered her beaming face, looking for any telltale signs of her secret, but seeing nothing.

"I see" he replied, halting for mere seconds before addressing his niece carefully. "That was most kind of you, Bess. What is that you are reading?" The words were merely a distraction as he knew full well what it was she held on her lap, he could see the bright illuminations glowing warmly with jewelled hues and gilt on each page as it turned. The colours lit up as bright as a peacock's plumes, courtesy of the rays of light slanting in from the low winter sun outside.

Bess looked up at his words and stroked the open page with a slender white hand.

"Kathryn allowed me to look at your gift to her, Your Grace," she answered seriously, still casting her eyes over the words on the page before her. "It is beautiful is it not? All the more so for having been cherished so long by the Queen's Grace, God rest her soul." There was a hushed reverence in the chamber where only the muted sounds of some scurrying pages outside the chamber could be heard.

"Turn to the back - read what is says."

Richard spoke gently without looking at her, his attention turned to Kathryn as he put a fatherly arm around his daughter who in turn looked up at him lovingly and rested her head on his damask clad shoulder. Obediently, Bess turned to the very last page and read the words written there. John got up from his position at her feet and kneeled next to her on the window seat the better to see himself, and she shifted to one side slightly to accommodate him.

Bess scanned the writing at the very back of the tome and looked at John uncertainly. He gave her a small affectionate nudge as if to prompt her to read out loud whilst Richard seemed totally preoccupied in Kathryn's handiwork, his head bowed. Bess cleared her throat and read what she saw written there in a neat, cursive hand.

"To the Lady Anne Neville. Richard Gloucester, Middleham Castle, April 1469 - Loyaultie me Lie."

Richard looked up finally, his face appeared to be lost in a memory gone by.

"It was my gift to Anne when I had to leave Middleham, to the cause of my brother's marriage and her father's turn to rebellion. She kept it with her, my raison became hers." There was a brief silence where John and Bess exchanged solemn glances. "Now - Kathryn!" Richard then announced pleasantly, swiftly changing the mood. "I would like to speak to you, alone, if I may."

His daughter's eyes fled across the room in panic towards Bess and she answered quickly, stumbling over her words.

"Papa, please - I am sorry! I was going to tell you but I wanted to wait until the festivities. Please don't be angry with either me or Bess! Please - I couldn't bear it!"

At this point John , who had already risen and made ready to leave, turned and surveyed his half-sister anxiously.

"Is something wrong?" Richard sighed heavily realising that his whole well rehearsed plan for confronting his daughter had been totally ruined by the rest of his family. Despite that, he suppressed a smile.

"I did say "alone" Kate. This is surely a private matter and as your father - and your king..." At that moment the door to the chamber swung open to admit Francis, whose eyes took in the domesticity of the scene, before locating the king.

"Your Grace" he announced with a small bow of deference, which failed to hide a burning urgency in his gaze. "Lord Lincoln has just ridden in."

36. CROSBY PLACE
December 1485

The small but select group of Richard's chosen advisors gathered together in his private apartments in Crosby Place. He had prevaricated only slightly about holding the briefing whilst so many of his council were away from court, attending to their own estates before coming back for the Christmas festivities. It was plain to him that many of the nobler Lords such as Northumberland, Norfolk and Scrope may well feel disgruntled when they discovered what had taken place once they returned - but he could also see a distinct advantage to keeping the meeting as discreet as possible.

Whatever information Lincoln and Catesby had to impart, he wanted it kept from as many ears as possible until he had a mind to know what actions he needed to take. Not one for great formality when he was in his most private of apartments, he had even taken the precaution of posting additional men-at-arms outside and the metallic sound of the halberds slithering together gave him a certain sense of satisfaction, an additional assurance that they would not be disturbed.

The day outside was blisteringly cold and the sky hung low and heavily grey. Most of his guests had arrived on horseback, shunning the additional chill of an icy river breeze on the Thames.   Richard had watched from an upper chamber window as Lincoln and Catesby arrived together, horses hooves clattering on the frosty cobbles noisily announcing their arrival. John was stamping his feet to beat life back into them and clapping his gauntleted hands together as he handed over the reins of his bay. He was a capable lad, Richard mused silently, and adapting well to matters of governing and policy.

Despite his satisfaction with the boy, he did have to acknowledge that his niece had delivered a deadly barb recently. Try as he might, his mind constantly veered off, and he would find himself speculating that if only it could have been his own John, the issue of his body - named as his heir. The two did resemble each other in colouring and build somewhat and he had to admit that this fact contributed to the affection in which he held his sister's boy. But still. Even though he knew it was decided now and the marriage would go ahead, the web Bess had spun in his head still had him in its tendrils, and would not let him go. To have a son of his own blood, his heir... his mind turned back against his will and a pair of clear, innocent, untroubled eyes stared at him across the months long gone. He gripped the cold, stone ledge of the window until his knuckles turned as white as the hoar frost etching the glass, and he waited.

Now they were all gathered together, warmed by the heat of a roaring fire and some generously spiced Hyppocras, which had been well received by all but Catesby, who had graciously declined. Francis sat on Richard's right. He looked particularly nervous and preoccupied as he twirled a small pewter cup round in his hand. Richard wondered if he was thinking of Cecily, knowing as he did that his wife Anna would be making her way to London as she was, for once, attending for the Christmas court, which was not going to be easy for him in many ways.

Next to him, and directly in front of the fire, sat Catesby, looking particularly composed and betraying no ill effect of the journey he had recently undertaken. His face was still and relaxed but Richard could see that legal mind whirring away behind the impassive eyes. Rob was seated between Lincoln and Catesby and Richard had more than a sneaking suspicion that this was deliberately done. He well understood that Catesby would have made for a most staid travelling companion for his energetic nephew, but still, he was convinced he had sent the right people.

Lincoln, also fresh and rested after his journey, had his eyes fixed eagerly on his uncle like a hawk fretting to take flight, anxious to impart his news. Richard knew from the depth of that look that there was both fair and foul tidings to relate. As they all looked at him in anticipation, he leaned back into his chair slowly, his arms stretched before him braced against the table and looked at each man in turn.

"Gentlemen - before we hear the tidings from Burgundy - I

have a few things I wish to say." He paused momentarily to ensure that he had everyone's attention. Catesby was slightly distracted by a sudden spark from the fire which landed perilously close to his cloak, but returned his eyes to the king immediately. "What we are about to hear is for our ears only. The content of our discussion must not be revealed outside of these four walls. If this meeting gives us any hope that we can finally pour daylight on the sinister workings of those who transpired to rent this realm to shreds, then we must closely guard what we discover. On pain of death my friends."

Richard fell silent - the room was quiet as the grave and four pairs of eyes continued to fix on him intently.

"Lord Stanley is currently visiting with his wife in the Wakefield Tower." At this news, Lincoln choked on a mouthful of the spiced wine he had just swallowed, somewhat breaking the tension. "Where," Richard continued ignoring his spluttering nephew, "I had cause to confine her when she disregarded the terms of her house arrest and sought to plead Tudor's case with me in person. She made it clear that she also has information regarding my nephews' fate, and so it will be interesting to hear what she has to say on these events after our discourse today."

A wave of exchanged glances swept around the room. Seeing that his words had been duly absorbed, Richard leaned forward and placed his elbows on the table, his be-jewelled hands resting under his chin as he finally submitted himself to his nephews urgent gaze.

"Now, John, tell me. How did you find your aunt?"

Lincoln looked quickly at Catesby, who merely returned the glance without encouragement or expression, before clearing his throat to speak.

"Sire, I found her to be very well favoured and in fact very much like yourself in truth!" Richard was unable to keep the sardonic smile from playing around his lips.

"Really? How so?"

"A robust sense of humour, Sire, for sure. Although she chose not to on this occasion, I could also imagine her threatening to behead all her closest advisors if they spoke out of turn." He took a quick sip from his cup as Richard's mouth twitched in amusement. "Besides, she also favours you in looks and so I can only believe that we are all blessed by God to be the issue of such an attractive family."

Rob hid a grin behind his hand whereas Catesby sighed, adjusted the cloak on his chair back and looked at John with a somewhat perplexed expression. Francis still seemed to be distracted and was now biting his thumb thoughtfully. If he had been concerned about Richard's warning of the sobriety of this meeting, he was not expressing it. Richard broke into a forbearing smile, shaking his head in disbelief.

"John - you are a true courtier, and I am inordinately pleased to note that you have received my words with such gravity. Every one of you is aware of my intent. Now get on with it, how is my sister?" Lincoln grinned and gestured expansively.

"The duchess is well, my liege, and sends her good wishes and congratulations on your success in battle. She was mightily relieved that Tudor is immured and wishes that you would take the same actions with all members of the legal profession." At Richard's startled expression, John spread his hands in supplication, his dark brows raised archly. "Her words, not mine, Your Grace!"

"My Lord!" Catesby exclaimed loudly at his point shooting Lincoln a pointed glare as Rob let out a snigger. John merely laughed.

"She did tease Will mercilessly, Sire. But he deserved it."

"Nonsense, Your Grace!" Catesby found himself reddening to match the heat of the fire, his mouth gaping in speechless amazement.

"Admit it, man, she found you good sport!"

"John..." Richard employed a fatherly tone with a harder edge, in an effort to end his nephew's enjoyment. "Stop harassing Will and tell us. Did you see the boys?"

The walls of the room seemed to close in as each man waited, breathless, for Lincoln's answer. Somewhere outside, a dog could be heard barking, no doubt one of the king's wolfhounds. If anyone felt the ghosts of the past gathering around the chamber, no one dare mention it.

"One boy - Your Grace. He had the look of Dorset about him."

The words fell into the silence of the room like rocks onto the surface of a still pond, each one making their mark.

"Tom Dorset," Rob whispered incredulously, his cup momentarily halting on it's way to his lips. Catesby eyed him steadily as he now spoke.

"He is the right age and had very good recall of certain recent events."

"What events?" Francis's head jerked up, totally engaged now. Free from whatever had been distracting him, he was now carefully regarding Richard's expression as he took in Catesby's words. Will cleared his throat nervously before continuing, suddenly wishing he had not refused the wine.

"Well, he remembered being in sanctuary. He gave a very good impression of Cardinal Bourchier," he paused as Lincoln let out an amused chuckle, indicating the recall had not been flattering. Will resumed, taking great care over his choice of words. "He also could remember seeing you, Your Grace, but said you were not wearing your boar? He could recall being visited on occasion in the Tower apartments and he also told me he had been married. He said that .."

"Visited?" Richard's voice rang out across the room, stopping the lawyers deliberate recall mid sentence. Catesby shifted in his seat slightly and in the pause, Lincoln leaned forward. Two pairs of dark Plantagenet eyes locked together.

"He said that a gentle, fair lady, who he knew as his aunt, the Lady Anne, did visit them. She took them books and comfits." Richard's lids closed over his eyes slowly, his shoulders raised slightly as he took a long indrawn breath. After what seemed like an age, he opened his eyes once more and continued to look at his nephew.

"Is there more?" His voice cracked slightly on the question.

"What about the elder boy?" Francis interrupted hastily, marking Richard's sudden pallor. Catesby shifted in his seat again and looked decidedly uncomfortable.

"My Lords, I feel we are telling the tale somewhat piecemeal. Perhaps it would be best to tell you all before we discuss each element on its own merit? The tale will be easier in the telling."

There was an eerie calm in the room. Richard pushed himself further back into his chair, leaving his hands spread before him on the table. The jewels on his fingers looked almost pale and dead in the winter's light, not even the fire could bring them to life. He bit his bottom lip, staring down at his own hands.

"I visited the boys the day after they were reunited. Anne advised me not to wear my chain of office, to visit them more as uncle than Lord Protector, she was mindful not to put fear into them, as they hardly knew me. I had no idea she had paid other visits." He halted, feeling the sting of unshed tears prick his eyes. "But you are right Will," he agreed, mastering his emotions and drawing his hands back to fold in his lap. "It would appear that we have found at least one of my brothers sons, and you have a tale to tell so say on."

Catesby again looked at each one of them in turn and Lincoln gave him an encouraging nod, a sanction almost to continue.

"Well, the duchess told us that the boys were smuggled out of the Tower grounds one day after playing at the butts in the garden. Guards of a certain affinity were handsomely paid to walk the boys down to the watergate where they were met by a vintner bringing wine, by river, for the Tower buttery. He had with him two young boys, recently orphaned by the sweating sickness, and to be fair, with not long to survive themselves. They were of similar age and build to the Princes - the Lords Bastard. At the gatehouse the children's clothes were changed. Thus the vintner arrived with two small "prentices" and left with the same. The two orphan children were escorted to the apartment in the Tower - they were not expected to live long due to their condition. One also had an ailment of the jaw which weakened him further but as the Princes were not well known to many, with the elder one living so long at

Ludlow, it was thought the resemblance would be enough to fool anyone who should care to check. The Lords Bastards were smuggled out of port on two ships and crossed to Burgundy." He paused for a second, waiting for questions that didn't come and so continued.

"Two ships, one little Lord in each ship. However, there was a storm and one foundered. Most of the hands were lost. The ship was carrying the elder boy. The younger reached shore safely and was delivered into the care of the duchess."

Richard passed a hand over his eyes. Dear God - he thought - Edward's son dashed upon the rocks in some godforsaken storm! His stomach lurched up towards his chest. Was this also vengeance from the Lord? In the same way his own Edward had been lost to him, was Edwards progeny to be wiped out because of his own lechery?

"The duchess is sure the boy drowned? We don't have a Lord Bastard holed up in France somewhere?" Francis leaned forward to get Catesby's attention but it was Lincoln who answered quietly.

"Margaret is certain. The loss of the craft and its master are on record."

Rob was shaking his head in wonderment.

"But why the involvement of two sick boys? What was the design behind that? And more to the point, where are they?" Richard held up a hand suddenly, silencing further discussion.

"One moment Rob. I think Will is yet to reveal all. This plan has taken some orchestration by persons of both influence and wealth. Tower guards paid handsomely, you say Will? So, come. Reveal who is our Master of the Revels, for this tale surely suits a feast day mystery."

Catesby took an even deeper breath and exhaled on a grim smile.

"Your Grace knows me well as always." Richard nodded as a side of his mouth curled up in an expectant smile. "Tower guards, paid handsomely with court treasure, to act for a person to whom they held an older affinity."

"Jesu!" Francis cursed loudly. "Elizabeth Woodville!"

Richard's face was set in stone, his eyes sparked with the fire of flint against granite and he pushed himself to his feet, leaning on his fisted hands. In his mind he could both hear her voice and picture the demurely inclined head, the lowered eyelids, the falling tear.

"They were in your care…"

Bess whispering, *"she has never accused you of their murder…"*

Lincoln looked up into his uncle's unreadable face and continued Catesby's story.

"Elizabeth feared for her son's safety, but not at your hand, Your Grace. The worst she expected from yourself was that they would be moved north and she would never see them again. However, there were others at court who she did believe were planning to harm the boys. She wrote to the duchess and asked if she would take them into her care, in secret, to remove them from harms way. Margaret, who you should be warned is not at all convinced by the pre-contract issue, agreed to help. It was planned to reveal all this to you at some future time." He faltered, not quite knowing how to proceed, but Francis finished for him.

"Should the king be victorious against Tudor?" He was rewarded by a nod from Lincoln.

"However, Elizabeth has since written to Margaret asking her to remain her confidante on this matter, as Tudor is still living and could yet…" Lincoln's words died on his lips, killed by the look of pure rage descending on his uncle's face like a sudden summer storm. He had raised one hand to his chest and gripped the neck of his doublet tightly. Lincoln looked in alarm to Francis who was already on his feet and at the king's side.

"Your Grace?" Silence descended on all corners of the room as the men waited and watched. "Are you well?"

Richard was rigid with anger and neither moved nor spoke. Francis moved quickly and filled a cup with wine, pushing it towards his friend who eyed it with some suspicion. Something inside him felt as if it was tearing in two. He remembered the familiar feeling from many years ago as he stood in the hall at Middleham and heard the Earl of Warwick turn against the king, his beloved brother. The ground below his feet turning to shifting sand and threatening to wash his certainties away. His certainties were fewer these days, but the effect was just the same.

"Yes," his voice when he found it was low and dangerous. "I can now see why my brother George took so easily to drowning in wine. The air in this place is redolent with greed and treachery. My name has been dragged through the dirt, my reputation destroyed, my wife witness to misery notwithstanding the death of our son. How many treasons have we just been witness to my Lords?" He picked up the cup and drank deeply. "I take it the ships were also provided by the crown, having been stolen by Sir Edward Woodville? No don't answer that, why waste the words! " He tossed the empty cup to one side and it landed on the floor with a resounding ring as metal hit stone.

"Rob was right to ask about the two boys, Your Grace," Lincoln ventured slowly, "but the rest of this story is now only hearsay on the duchess's part. Will, as you are so much more eloquent than I, when you do speak. Would you please continue?"

Catesby gave a small grin and folded his hands together.

"Elizabeth believed the main threat to her boys be from either Lady Stanley or the Duke of Buckingham - separately or together. It is not completely clear, but for either of them to achieve what they had planned the boys had to die. Tudor could not claim the throne after any successful invasion if he still insisted on marrying Princess Elizabeth, so to achieve unity the boys had to be removed. It is believed that the two imposters were killed in their stead by either agents of Lady Stanley..."

"And Buckingham?" Rob asked, looking perplexed by this latest revelation.

"Buckingham felt he could engineer the downfall of both Tudor and - yourself - Your Grace. The rebellion was designed to get Tudor into the country so that both of you could be eliminated in battle - or otherwise - as I said - this is not clear to the duchess. These plans were the work of other conspirators which only forced Elizabeth to take actions regarding the boys."

"Well, I must be truly drunk as a lord because I am not following all this treachery at all." Rob said shaking his head. Richard sat down in his seat again, the anger on his face replaced by a weariness of ages.

"With the death of Edward's boys, myself and Tudor, then my son Edward would have been in his minority. He would have needed a Lord Protector until he came of age."

The words "or died early," hung in the air unspoken.

"Perhaps Buckingham saw what I wrought with my brother's sons and planned to do the same. Why be advisor to the Lord Protector and king, when you can be so yourself."

"Is that why he was so keen to speak to you before he died? " Francis murmured, his voice full of astonishment at the unfurling tale. Richard shook his head - his teeth gnawing at his bottom lip ruminatively.

"So, what we next get to hear from Lady Stanley should complete this tapestry of treachery. The Lady, as I suspected, has much to explain. As has my sister," Richard added as an afterthought.

At those words, Lincoln carefully drew the parchment from inside his doublet and pushed it across the table.

"I think she knew you would require an explanation that she did not see fit to impart to us. She asked that this be handed to you after you had heard all."

Richard reached forward and picked up the letter, frowning. Breaking the seal quickly, he scanned the content written in the familiar flowery hand and a wry smile thinned his lips.

"You are indeed right, John. My sister is seven days behind you - she has invited herself to my Christmas court to explain herself to me in person."

37. THE TOWER OF LONDON
December 1485

"Be seated - both of you."

Margaret and Thomas Stanley did as they were bade by their king and, without looking at each other, surveyed the faces of the assembled courtiers who were ranged on the other side of the large oak table. As Stanley settled himself down, he stroked his beard with his left hand nervously, making small, throat clearing noises

Richard occupied a chair in the centre, looking particularly well rested, his eyes steely-grey and clear. He was flanked on either side by Francis Lovell and William Catesby.   Richard's nephew the Earl of Lincoln sat to Catesby's right as Norfolk did to Lovell. The room was full of candles, fighting away the gloom of the day, providing supplement to the weak, grey light that hung around the windows, with hardly the strength to penetrated the glass. At a small writing desk to one side John Kendall sat, pen poised, patient. A pot of quills sat at his elbow, accompanied by a sheaf of blank parchments, waiting for words.

Stanley moistened his lips anxiously, noting with some concealed anger that Margaret still remained decidedly detached. There was a concerted effort to refrain from displaying any emotions, including fear or shame, and certainly not humility. Their own reunion in the Wakefield Tower had been difficult and nothing at all had been resolved. Stanley knew from the intractable set of her mouth that Margaret would tread her own path in these negotiations, without any regard for her husband, or the impact her revelations could have on him. It seemed to him they had finally reached an impasse, and it could well be that his wife had now decided she had no further advantage to gain by remaining loyal to him.

To be fair, even though they had spoken at length about many things, Stanley was as mystified as the rest of the room about exactly what she was going to reveal. He knew only too well what information she had, as they had shared everything during those difficult and dangerous months. It was that shared ambition which had melded them together, whilst disguising the fact that other than a need to further their own interests, they had little in common. However, how much of that she would now choose to reveal was another matter. Perhaps, he mused silently, it was better that way, yet he remained vigilant, for as soon as she appeared to point the blame his way, he was ready to strike back. This could be a fight to the death, for one of them.

It was William Catesby who spoke first. Standing to address the room, he modulated the voice which could ring out so powerfully as Speaker of the House, his face sanguine but serious.

"Your Grace, my Lords, Lady Stanley, bear witness this 15th day of December, the year of our lord 1485. This is a preliminary hearing to ascertain the extent of Lady Margaret Stanley's knowledge regarding the disappearance of the Lords' Bastard, Edward and Richard Plantagenet - issue of our dearly beloved sovereign King Edward the Fourth. It in no way replaces or eliminates the need for a formal trial, the exact charges for which are to be determined as part of today's due process. I believe everyone in the room is acquainted with one another and no further introductions are necessary?"

Stanley noticed Lincoln, leaning back in his chair with one elbow on its arm casually, as if awaiting an entertainment to begin. The young man was trying to restrain a smirk, but not succeeding. He gritted his teeth tightly, making his jaw ache.

"Thank you, William." Richard nodded his head towards the lawyer, who bowed his head, sitting himself down again, eyes lowered so as not to engage with either Stanley or his wife. Thomas had spent his political career disliking most of these individuals. That emotion was now hardening to hate. There was a short silence in which Richard laced his hands and leaned forwards slightly, looking at Stanley directly.

"Before we proceed to the crux of the matter in hand, I first need to ascertain from Thomas, Lord Stanley, his arrangements with regards to the guardianship of his wife. I am most interested to learn how she was able to ride out from his manor at Bletsoe and arrive, uninvited and unexpected, at Westminster. This upheaval disrupted the proceedings during the entertainment of a Portuguese envoy invited here on state business. So, my Lord," this spoken with cold eyes now pinned on to Margaret's face, silently forbidding her from speaking. "How was this allowed to occur?"

The scratching of Kendall's quill filled the chamber. Stanley knew he looked as uncomfortable as he felt and answered swiftly without a second glance at the wife at his side.

"Your Grace, I remain your loyal servant as you are aware." He paused, thinning his lips as Francis coughed delicately into his hand, but didn't allow his gaze to swerve from the king's face. "I am sore afraid that my wife, after appealing to you personally through the auspices of Sir Robert Percy, was still unhappy with the outcome of her petition. She had hoped that I may be in a position to influence your mind. Being your true servant in all things, I did not deem it appropriate to raise this matter further, knowing what your opinion would be in this. I also tried to explain to her that since our victory against her son, my own influence at court was not what it had once been."

He paused again, his eyes travelling up and down the table at the faces arranged opposite him. The only person without their attention fixed on him was Lincoln, who was showing an uncommon interest in his own fingernails, but he did not let that deter him.

"Believing I could do nothing further to aid his cause with Your Grace, my wife took matters into her own hands. To my shame." Norfolk glared at him from beneath stern, bushy brows, disbelief writ clear on his bluff features.

"My Lord, by the persistent manner in which you profess your loyalty, it is becoming difficult to ascertain exactly whom you are trying to convince. My good Lords here present or yourself."

"I resent that, Jack!" Stanley retorted, his face reddening. "You know full well where my loyalties lie."

"For the nonce..." Francis murmured, brushing the grey velvet of his sleeve with care, as Stanley fumed silently, venting his anger through eyes which Francis did not even seek to meet. Richard held up a calming hand, although he seemed in no way irritated by the interjections of his counsellors.

"Lady Margaret." He turned his attention back to the small, composed figure occupying the other chair. "To escape from such cloistered quarters, all money and possessions being lodged with your husband, was something of a triumph. So tell us, how did you manage this feat? We're you aided and assisted, and if so by whom?"

The thin, pale lips pursed tightly in such a manner that Richard considered he may have to use his dagger to prise the very words from them. Their gazes fenced sharply, almost audibly, as she refrained from answering, which gave her husband the chance to bolster his defences. Savouring the words as one does a tempting morsel of food, he saw the chance for revenge and took it without hesitation.

"A clerk of the household. Reginald Bray, Your Grace."

No sooner had the words left his mouth than Margaret turned her head, visiting on him such a look of burning hatred that he felt obliged to deflect it with a self-satisfied smile. Richard watched the interplay between the married couple with grim amusement.

"Is the said clerk here?" he asked. His tone was casual, and he did not have to wait long before he received an affirmative nod from Stanley.

"He travelled with me Your Grace, and is waiting without."

Long fingers, two of them sporting glittering rings, one emerald, the other ruby, drummed a short stacatto on the table top. The command, when it came, was peremptory.

"Sir Francis, have Reginald Bray detained."

"Your Grace!" Francis was on his feet immediately upon hearing his name and left the chamber in silence, broken only by the slithering metal of halberds at the door. No one spoke further during that time, each man with their own thoughts, only the rustle of fabric to disturb the pensive atmosphere. All could hear the muted voices outside, waited for the door to open again.

"It is done, Your Grace." Francis returned, giving a short bow in obeisance before resuming his seat. Richard did not look at him but nodded in acknowledgement, his full focus was still on Lady Stanley.

"You see now, Madam, how seriously I view these events. What happens next, including the matter of whether you should be allowed to return to your husband's guardianship, rests on what you now have to reveal to me. I would strongly recommend that you are truthful and if so, I can promise you a fair judgement. So, as we discussed briefly some nights ago, you were telling my Lord of Northumberland that you had perfect recall of the events of two years ago. I have all day at leisure now, my Lady, so you may begin."

An expectant hush fell upon the room as all heads turned towards Margaret, that is, all apart from her husbands. The shrill caw of a raven from out on Tower Green raked through the air as if adding witness to the forthcoming testimony. Appearing completely unperturbed, Margaret re-folded her hands in her lap and stared resolutely at Richard alone.

"Before I begin, Your Grace, we did also discuss some terms with regard to my son in exchange for the information I am about to impart. Have you given any consideration to my requests?"

Everyone, to a man, held their breath at the woman's sheer temerity, apart from Stanley who could have predicted every word. Despite offering to think over her requests in council, they all knew that Richard had done no such thing in the end, as what he had said had only been the means to end a meeting after a long and tiring day. The demands had been ridiculous in themselves, anyone could see that. All except for Margaret Stanley, who had spent most of her life scheming and plotting for the ambitions of the man who now lay mere feet away from them in a Tower cell.

Richard leaned further forwards across the table, shortening the distance between them. His lip curled back contemptuously, and his voice was a low snarl.

"If my esteemed counsel's words were not clear enough Madam, let me explain myself. You are here to clarify your comments made seven days past. You have broken the terms of your house arrest and you are perilously close to standing trial for treason. You are, therefore, in no position to broker any arrangement. The outcome of today depends on the events you now relay to me - and if they are favourable, if you were a victim of circumstances outside of your control or manipulated by others to take actions which can be considered questionable - who knows? But until then, no - Madam, no promises, not from me!"

Both Francis and Lincoln had shrunk back in their seats at his tone, unaccustomed to hearing him speak so harshly, and particularly to a woman. There was an undercurrent of sheer malevolence there which had taken the room completely by surprise. Catesby remained as impassive as ever his downcast eyes fixed on the table before him, whilst Norfolk, inwardly pleased that Richard was now showing this woman his true mettle, nodded sagely in agreement with his words.

"Margaret..." Stanley whispered a warning, his voice somewhat fearful. Knowing Richard well and sensing the danger, he gave her a sidelong glance, which she deliberately ignored. Unblinking, she continued to hold Richard's intense gaze, ignoring everyone else around the table and if she was shocked or frightened by his outburst, her emotions were well hidden. She appeared to consider his words for a long moment, and then, with a small re-adjustment of her posture, she raised her chin a little, whether in either defiance or anger, it was not clear.

"Very well. If that is the case, we shall see indeed. Perhaps I should begin by telling you that I was visited by the Duke of Buckingham in August , two years ago." Norfolk and Lincoln exchanged glances but it was Francis who spoke.

"Who unfortunately is unable to bear witness to any of what you are about to say," he murmured quietly, cupping his fist with his hand as she watched her face for a reaction. Richard flicked a quick glance towards him and so did Margaret who, unperturbed, continued speaking.

"He informed me that he was uneasy with Your Grace's future plans - of what you proposed to do once you had taken the throne.

He was unhappy that your loyalties all lie northwards and that your ties there continued, as did your control. He had been hoping that you would grant the authority of the Council of the North to him, I believe, and was sorely disappointed that you chose to give this to your son, even as a nominal appointment. But of course.." her eyes swivelled to Lincoln, full of condescension, "we can see that is an appointment that you grant only to your heir." Lincoln shook his head slowly, smiling, as she took up her story once again.

" As you would not relinquish your grip, he believed that in short order, all of the south would be consumed by a tide of northerners sweeping away all those in their path, even those who had aided you in your accession to the throne. It was his opinion that, if he had been able to take control of the council, he could rule the north in much the way it had been during the late king's reign." She inclined her head thoughtfully, appearing totally unperturbed by the effect of anything she was saying. Particularly on Richard.

"I did tactfully point out to him that our friend Northumberland may have had something to say about that, but he appears to have had little regard for him either. His argument was that you had made it alarmingly clear you trusted no-one who had previously been aligned to your brother the king, and that all others would gradually go the way of Hastings, Rivers and Grey. Only those who had shown support to you whilst you lived in the north would prosper. All else would be done away with."

Norfolk was pulling on his ear as he listened, his face screwed up, as if he had difficulty concentrating.

"But, he wasn't close to Edward. Yes, he served at court, but he was more of a Woodville lackey, wasn't he? Because of his wife?" Jack looked towards Catesby for affirmation and received a curt nod. Lincoln had sat back in his chair at the mention of his northern council, and folded his arms across his chest. Margaret spread her hands before her, once again resting them on her skirts.

"Well, all I can say is that he perceived an imminent threat to himself, to his position and power. It seemed to me that he believed the only way he could secure his own position was to become Your

Graces deputy in the north, thereby ruling half the country in your stead. But he knew that there was about to be an appointment there which would cut his ambitions in this respect dead." Margaret let out a heavy sigh and rolled her eyes dramatically. "Although, he was obviously a fool. Who on earth would voluntarily immure themselves for years on end in a cold, unforgiving fortress to be daily harrassed by the savages from the other side of the border?"

She cast her gaze around the table, Richard merely smiled sardonically at her casual slander of his previous tenure, and began twisting his ruby set thumb ring.

"Did he say how he had become privy to this information? In particular with regard to changes in the north?" The question came from Norfolk, as Richard just continued to keep careful watch on her. Lincoln cast a covert glance over to his uncle's face, but could read nothing from the set expression. He appeared completely at ease, apart from the motion of his fingers.

"I understood it to be from the king himself." Margaret halted for a second, knowing how closely she was being scrutinised, and she fixed Norfolk with an accusatory stare. "One has to acknowledge that this did, in some respects, come to pass, with northern men marching south and taking over many of the offices which had been held by loyal Yorkist lords for years."

Francis laughed out loud then.

"Of course it did! The man caused the very need for it by raising southern lords in rebellion! Are you telling us that this is how he managed to get them to commit treason?" She blinked slowly, raising an eyebrow, but returned her gaze to Richard's face.

"Possibly, I only know what he said to me, so that is all I can bear witness to. He also informed me that there was was an immediate danger to the boys in the Tower, with them remaining a focus for rebellion and discontent. They were to be removed for the "security and peace of the realm", was how I believe he phrased it. He told me that the boys were to be moved in secret so that they could not be used against the king. It was to be done with the assistance of the aforesaid northern lords, and their whereabouts, nor the method of their removal, would ever be disclosed. Not even to him. In fact, to all intents and purposes, they would be as good as dead, vanished, with no one knowing where it was they went or how it was done." Richard's jaw tightened and a muscle flexed in his cheek but he did not respond. His continual turning of his jewelled ring stalled for a second, but then resumed in the opposite direction as he waited for her to continue.

"He was most anxious of the fact that they were both, still, close to the throne and that if allowed to slip out of the country, they would always be a threat to whoever..." her words trailed off suddenly as she saw Richard smile. Cold-eyed.

"Overthrew me? Murdered me?" he offered, inclining his head. "Come Madam! Now is not the time to become shy with words. I am sure you have not been reluctant to use such terms whilst huddling in shadowed corners late at night with your conspirator friends. You may speak just as freely here. In fact, I demand it." Margaret licked her lips, and gave a rueful smile in answer, the firelight caught her eyes making them glint like the jet rosary beads that lie pooled in her lap.

"He said he had offered all good counsel to the king who had turned away from him in favour of advice from his northern lords. Feeling he was losing his influence and in fear that what you had so readily given could as easily be taken away, he offered his allegiance to my son who was then in exile in Brittany. As you are aware, he asked that I informed Henry that he was ready and willing to provide armed men to support an invasion to remove the threat of the boy's - disposal. This had to happen quickly, he said, as the plans were well advanced. I wrote to Henry and told him of Buckingham's offer, " she continued, watching as Catesby made some notes of his own on a parchment - and knew that scratching scribe Kendall would also be setting this down, hence the need to tread very carefully.

"I believe I need go into no great detail about the uprising itself as you have already judged me guilty of that involvement, hence my current situation. Buckingham also corresponded with Henry on his own accord, the records of this will evidence what was said between them. Henry's intent you are already aware of, but the correspondence, held safe in France, will substantiate Buckingham's role and the things he had said to me."

Lincoln barked a short sharp laugh.

"Yes, I am sure those around the new French King will be only too happy to hand that over!" Norfolk shifted in his seat, his face crumpled in thought.

"So, your son accepted Buckingham's offer?" he prompted, ignoring Lincoln's comment, with which he did, silently, agree wholeheartedly. Louis was dead now, and the country was in the hands of its own struggle around a minority rule. In supporting Tudor, the country had shown itself hostile to Richard's reign, and those advisors would now be the men ruling in the young king's stead. There was no guarantee that their allegiance would change, despite Tudor's defeat and the death of their wily old spider king. This was were the alliances with Portugal would be advantageous. Margaret nodded towards Norfolk.

"Indeed he did, and the invasion plans which you are already aware of were drawn up." She paused momentarily - knowing she was now entering the most delicate, and dangerous, part of this meeting.

"He must have wanted something in return," said Lincoln, looking to either side of him to gain agreement, and gratified to see nods of acquiescence. "Buckingham never made a move without a motive." Francis nodded vigorously in agreement, casting a quick look at Richard before speaking himself, his voice betraying his barely controlled anger.

"I am having a great deal of difficulty believing that Harry Stafford was going to change his allegiance when it profited him very little. I just don't see what he had to gain! He already had the Bohun lands he craved so long, he had been generously rewarded for his support and affinity, he had the king's ear. Good God, he acted like a king himself half the time! He cared nothing for those boys, I would lay one of my manor houses on it! They were Woodvilles to him, and his hatred of the Woodvilles is well documented. Ask anyone in this room who has heard him venting his resentment late at night over a flagon or two. It didn't take much for him to give chapter and verse." He leaned forward onto his elbows. "So - what was his prize?"

Margaret carried on as if she had not heard him, studiously avoiding his direct stare, ignoring his low gasp of exasperation.

"He offered to support my son if he could be named his heir until he married and produced a son of his own.   He also wished for any of his issue to be betrothed at the earliest stage to any children Henry may beget.   At that time he was alluding, I believe, to his young son - but made it clear that he had a young and fertile wife who he expected to provide him with more children. Whilst this took effect, he wanted total control of the north. The estates, the council, everything." She allowed the occupants of the room some seconds to think about what she was saying.   "He wanted all of the Neville lands, as well as the Percy estates.   He said he knew Northumberland would never engage in battle, on either side, so Henry could imprison him and strip him of his titles." Once again, she appeared in full control.   "It would appear he didn't care much for Wales.   He was more than happy to relinquish his original estates for those in the north." Her lips pursed in grudging amusement as she looked at Richard. "You should be flattered, Your Grace! He seemed to want to emulate you in all ways!"

Francis opened his mouth to speak but Richard forestalled him with a gesture.

"At this point in your treasonous activities, who was the anticipated bride for your son?   The intention, certainly after the uprising, was his betrothal to my niece was it not?   Only, there would surely be no point in prevailing with such a union whilst the progeny of Dame Grey were declared illegitimate. Had your son abandoned hope of such a match?"

"There were other suitable brides, Your Grace" Margaret snapped haughtily.

"But none as attractive surely?" Richard smiled without pleasure "How did he intend to unite York and Lancaster without a

York bride?”

"It was not necessary to unite the houses by marriage, there are other ways..." Margaret stopped speaking suddenly as she realised where her words were leading her. Her mind worked frantically behind the calm exterior ensuring her small dark eyes were giving nothing away in advance of her carefully rehearsed words. She was up to her slim, white neck in treasonous activity. She knew it, Richard knew it, everyone in the room knew it and she had walked right into this particular trap herself. Her gut instinct doubted that Richard would have her head, he was too concerned for his mortal sins, but he could imprison her for life, immure her in an abbey or worse - leave her at Stanley's will.

She had to step carefully. It didn't matter where she ended up as long as she kept her head and Henry's. There were still those who would fight for him when the time was right. The main purpose of today was to impart what she knew whilst ensuring Henry kept his life. If she had to endanger her own to achieve this, she would, without hesitation. With some disdain, she noticed her husband was remaining silent, even though he had witnessed every conversation that had taken place. Always playing the main chance, she wondered exactly when he would chose to enter the fray this time... and on whose side.

"Your Grace?” one slim hand raised to cover her neck with affected fragility. “Would it be possible to take some refreshment? All this talking, my throat is quite dry..." Richard looked over his shoulder towards Kendall, there being no cupbearer or servant in the room due to the nature of the meeting. John put down his pen and pushing himself from his chair, moved towards a flagon which was sitting on the sideboard. He began to pour, the only sound in the room being the gurgle of the liquid as it filled the cup.

"Continue...” Richard commanded curtly as John placed the cup on the broad table and pushed it towards Margaret.

"Thank you, Your Grace." She smiled, appearing almost humble and picking up the cup, sipped delicately. It was a Vernage, which she didn't care for normally, but she hid this and appeared grateful for the consideration.   All the time her mind whirred ceaselessly.   She would need to give Richard a sacrificial lamb if she was going to save her son. But who? Whilst sitting in her Tower cell these past days she had given that her constant consideration. She gave a sidelong glance at her husband's profile - he was sitting with his head down, eyes lowered, chin resting on his hands, his expression hidden from her.

"Whatever the true nature of the correspondence between Henry and Buckingham, I cannot fully attest to. Care was taken in all communications, as you can imagine. Buckingham had fully supported your claim to the throne, but now it was openly acknowledged that to get support for Henry to invade, Edward's sons would need to be acknowledged as the rightful heirs. Those rightful heirs who were in the process of being secreted away by yourself. Buckingham didn't agree, as far as he was concerned they were illegitimate, but they still had their uses.   Yet, why should my son risk his life and the lives of his men," she ignored a snort of laughter from Lovell at this point, "to re-install Edward's sons when he had a claim of his own? A rightful claim descended down the Lancastrian line."

"A bastard Lancastrian line.." Lincoln interrupted tersely. Margaret turned and looked at him without emotion, carrying on as if he had not spoken.

"We met with Buckingham one night to discuss the pre-contract issue, to determine his concerns with regard to the princes. Many believed, and still do, that this was a story concocted to allow you to take the throne, but Buckingham was not one of them.   It took a while to convince him that it was merely a construct, a tool with which you had built the ladder to your kingship. But, with the help of others more knowledgeable in this area than I, it was accomplished." Margaret remembered the meeting well, her memories taking her back to a smoky, dank room in a Soutwark Inn. Buckingham, voicing his resentment of Richard's northern loyalties, his refusal to grant him more lands and estates, to wed his son Edward to his own young daughter.

The drink he poured constantly down his throat as he raved, she could still see him. Swallowing great gulps of wine, sweat beading his upper lip as he talked incessantly and his tongue grew looser. The sudden gape of his slack jaw as he realised that he could only attain his true desires if Henry became king - and to do that - the boys had to be disposed of. Not moved, not hidden, but killed. Disposed of - whilst Richard could be held culpable, and the word spread abroad of his violence to his brother's sons. Turning the country against him.

They would attack him in secret, revive all the old stories. He would suffer death by the quill, purgatory of a thousand words. It would be put abroad how he benefited from his brother's death. How, in fact, it was Clarence who lied about killing Margaret of Anjou's son.... when it was Richard who did the deed, violently and without mercy. How he personally took charge of the order to dispose of mad King Henry, the convenient death of his wife, just as his niece Elizabeth was out of sanctuary. How the Scots had let him walk straight into their capital, how they saw him as one of their own, as fearsome and warlike as they.

There were stories they could frame and embellish to a frightened southern audience who already believed he was half-savage anyway. By the end of it, Henry would not have needed to marry a York princess. The populace would be so grateful for the overthrow of this murdering tyrant that they would welcome Henry with open arms, no matter who he married.

Buckingham had shown a sudden reticence, his protestations that he knew the pre-contract to be valid so there was no need to worry about the princes, as long as they kept them close so no one else could use them. Then, the voice from the shadowy corner of the room, the heavily hooded eyes , the calm, insinuating tones, the dark glimmer of the crucifix as the robed chest rose and fell...

"But, surely, are they not just two bastard boys my lord...?"

Lost in her thoughts, the silence had made her spectators uneasy and the men before her were exchanging concerned glances. Catesby in particular was regarding her with great interest. He rolled his eyes upwards for a second, examining the ceiling of the chamber. Margaret watched him warily, full of the knowledge that he knew more about the circumstances of the pre-contract than anyone else in that room, having family connections to the Butler's themselves, his own father having provided them with legal representation.

She swallowed, taking another quick sip of her wine, deciding to keep this on one track. The track that an already executed man had trod.

"Buckingham saw himself as a Kingmaker, and once he had achieved that, it was a short step to a powerful affinity and an attempt at the throne himself," she continued cautiously. "He had begun to achieve that easily with your help, but his ambition and greed knew no bounds. He sought to be the most influential noble in the county - to be seen as more powerful than the king himself. Whatever you could have offered him, Your Grace, it would never have been enough. Had you granted him the whole of the north as well as the West Marches and East Anglia, he would still have used it against you. He hated the fact that you had so many men, "men of low blood" I think he called them, and that they swore an undying loyalty to you, looking down their northern noses at him. He resented the fact that he had achieved so much, yet that he still had to bend the knee to you, it was a resentment that began to grow in him like a canker. He turned against you, he would have turned against my son. It was not difficult to turn him against those boys."

Richard sat back in his chair once more - his lowered lids suddenly hiding his eyes. Memories of old conversations, words long since spoken and forgotten were coming back to haunt him. He avoided looking at Francis, who he knew would be recalling those same words. In the far reaches of his memory he could hear Francis's pleading voice... *"Don't trust him Dickon ..I know he has shown his support - but...there is something..."*

Then his brother, Edward, long dead. Golden tones whispering in Richard's ear, making the hair on the back of his neck stand up, he seemed so alive. *"Stafford.....he has an air of George about him.."*

Buckingham's unfailing support, nay, at times pure eagerness.

He could see now, when it was all too late.

Hastings, Rivers...Buckingham's words, his guiding hand on his arm, whispering of enemies and conspiracy everywhere, making full sense at the time. Even, on one afternoon, casting doubts about Francis. He gave the man a quick sideways glance, only he was too deep in thought himself at the words being spoken to notice. But now..? Richard inhaled deeply and leaned back, wanting to increase the distance between them so he could breathe.

"So - you said with the assistance of others? Of whom do you speak? You would not have mentioned them if you were not prepared to give up their names." Stanley shuffled in his seat causing Richard to swivel his tempered gaze away from the man's wife.

"Uncomfortable my Lord?" he almost sneered. "You should try sitting in this chair!" Stanley had the good grace to look embarrassed but kept quiet, preferring to see how much his wife was going to reveal. He had no doubt she was about to send someone to the block - but who?

38. THE TOWER OF LONDON
December 1485

No one was speaking. The room was airless and it was so quiet even the flames made not a sound as everyone waited for Margaret to continue her story.

Francis was becoming impatient, and tapped on his thigh with his thumb, silently, wondering exactly where this cold, heartless woman was about to lay the blame. Her eyes looked at each one of them in turn before she began speaking once more.

"Dame Grey tried to convince Buckingham that the pre-contract was a lie, but to be fair, by that time, he was well set upon another course and cared not for the facts of the situation. The plans, the intentions with regards to the boys were drawn up by Bishop Morton and executed, to use a turn of phrase, by Buckingham himself. Morton made it clear that the only way Buckingham could achieve his full potential was at Henry's side - and the only way Henry would risk his life were if he were to become king and unite the houses as he planned. I believe the correspondence in France confirms this and Buckingham, well, like the vane weathercock he was, turned direction with the prevailing wind."

Richard made to speak but was interrupted by Catesby, who touched the king's sleeve and leaned closer to his side. Richard inclined his head, eyes lowered whilst the lawyer spoke softly into his ear. They parted and Richard returned his eyes to Margaret, enquiring.

"So, my nephews were killed by Buckingham's actions? How was this effected in a building so secure as the Tower?" Margaret coughed delicately into her hand.

"Many men saw how powerful Buckingham had become. All watched as he became your foremost supporter, supplanting existing favourites, " she shot a sly, smiling glance across to Lovell whose clenched jaw and narrowed eyes showed a barely suppressed anger, simmering dangerously close to the surface. "Some believed that an order from him was an order which in actual fact came directly from yourself. One such person was Sir Robert Brackenbury, Constable of the Tower."

"Foul slander!" Francis shouted as his fury burst forwards across the table with the force of a physical object being thrown. Margaret's satisfied smile crept slowly across her face in response to his outburst. He would have risen, but it was Richard's turn to place a hand,across that of his friend.

"Soft..." he murmured, keeping his eyes on Margaret. Francis remained in his seat, but the tension in his limbs could be felt under the king's hand. "Sir Robert was one of my most trusted men, Lady Stanley, who died a brave death on Redemore Plain. Do not expect me to take a blackening of his name lightly." At this point Stanley finally joined the conversation, somewhat relieved to be able to do so.

"Your Grace, my Lords - I also knew Sir Robert well. I truly believe he thought he was carrying out a direct order from yourself when he gave Buckingham's men access to the Tower." Richard turned and looked at Francis who was now settled back in his seat but far from happy. They exchanged a glance, no words were spoken but the younger man appeared to relax, and a strange composure fell upon his features.

Margaret watched this unfold before her eyes, her former triumph draining away, frustrated at these northern raised Lords who seemed to act and think as one, and could understand each others whims without words being spoken. Only, she also had to acknowledge that it was what she was witnessing now that had allowed them to use Brackenbury as they had.

"How?" asked Lincoln suddenly across the silence.

"How?" Echoed Stanley, bemused by the sudden question.

"How were they killed?" A tense silence developed over the next few seconds as Margaret considered her words and the men facing her waited to hear them. It was an atmosphere that was raw with emotion.

"Smothered I believe," she said somewhat matter of factly. "It had to be bloodless."

Someone was breathing deeply, it could be heard clearly in the expectant hush.

"You believe? Do you not know? How, then, do you know the deed was done at all?"   Richard's voice was cold as death itself, but Margaret seemed not to notice and merely inclined her head as she answered.

"The deed was witnessed by my clerk Reginald Bray. He reported back to me. He was outside the chamber, but he saw the ..." she trailed off at Richard's burgeoning expression, the sudden set of his shoulders, the hard line of his lips as he placed his hands, palms down, on the table before him.

"Say it Madam! Don't pretend to play the faint heart now! Tell us that he saw the bodies of my murdered nephews." The words were forced through gritted teeth but the rage in them was audible to all. Not one person in the room who was aware of the revelations from Burgundy would have known that Richard knew his nephews had escaped, had they not been party to that information.

His rage, at the outright betrayal and treason he was listening to in every sentence, allowed him to vent his anger as if every word he was hearing was true. Which from her perspective, it was.

"Yes, Your Grace, that he did," she replied almost demurely, and without a flicker of fear on her face. "Reginald Bray saw the bodies of the murdered boys. He bore witness to the murder." Somewhere a bell chimed the hour. It was the only sound in the room. To Richard it was the only sound on earth at that moment.

"Where are their bodies now?" Norfolk asked, more gently, his tone almost reverential. Margaret sighed and sagged back a little in her chair, finally betraying the effects of the tensions of the day. Her voice became somewhat weary.

"I know not my Lord. Buckingham said Brackenbury was told to dispose of them within the precincts of the Tower. They could be buried somewhere or maybe - it could be they were disposed of in the river. That, to me, seems the easiest option for them to remain undiscovered." She paused only momentarily to clasp her hands together in her lap once more. "What is, of course, obvious to you now, is that whoever these "boys" are abroad, they are impostors and no doubt to be used in some way to incite further unrest and rebellion. You should take care, Your Grace, in believing what you are told - a matter which will be easier for you now that we have spoken."

Richard carefully pushed himself up from his chair and walked around the table slowly, coming to stand closer to the seated couple. He looked deliberately from one to the other, searching for the slightest hint of shame or regret, some shred of emotion, bearing in mind the tale they had just been relating.

"Lady Margaret," he began, as calmly and courteously as he could, although to the Lords around the table the danger signs were there. Richard was standing stock still, with his restless nature this happened only when he was determined to keep his emotions in check. His hands were still busy, the ring on his thumb being twisted, removed, replaced, twisted again, over and over. "You, I know, are a God fearing and devout woman. Your reputation in this is matched by none other, not even the Archbishops themselves. So explain to me, in the simplest of terms. How you are able to sit in my presence and talk so dispassionately about the disposal of two small boys, whose only sins were committed by their parents, and who were related to me by blood?"

His voice began to get lower- the pitch more sinister. It was a characteristic of Richard that his voice did not rise in anger, but took on a much lower timbre, at times could lower into a growl of anger.

"Bastard boys they may have been, but I have bastard children of my own and they receive as much affection from me as I afforded my own dear son, God assoil him, whilst he was alive. My bastard children are not responsible for their station is life - that is my sin. Listening to you today, Madam, I find it difficult to believe that you possess a single grain of compassion for your fellow man. Has all of your energy and emotion been charged towards placing your own son upon a throne to the absolute exclusion of everything else? And now that has failed, what next?"

He paused, still remaining in place, mere feet before them, the room soundless apart from the scratching of quill on parchment, Stanley's heavy breathing, obviously uncomfortable that Richard was standing so close.

"Do you sleep well of a night?" he continued, addressing each one of them in turn with a penetrating stare. "Dear God, I have lost count of the sleepless nights I have had since the crown was placed upon my head, yet I would imagine the both of you slept soundly in your beds, exhausted no doubt by hours of plotting and scheming - treason by any other name. The murder of innocents? And yet, it was my sleepless state which was put abroad to evidence my guilt, my name which was put to the foul murder of children, and I would imagine that if I ask you to name the perpetrator of these slanders, the purveyor of lies and untruths, I will hear the name Morton - will I not? And all the while, all the time the country was ready to turn their backs upon me, call me tyrant and murderer, my nephews lie under cold-clay soil or resting in sodden silt and you slept soundly in comfort on estates, some of which were granted by my hand. But all the time, I had one advantage over all of you, I knew the truth. I knew my soul was free of that sin, even though you had even robbed me of the ability to prove my innocence. May you never spend a good nights rest again, you will only experience a fraction of the despair you have visited upon my reign."

Both of them looked back at him, neither moving a muscle, except to breathe.

"Exactly where did the slander of murdering innocents come from may I ask."

Stanley looked at his wife quickly before speaking.

"The duke, Your Grace. He talked about murderous hordes of northmen and Scots, sweeping down the country, *"raping women and murdering innocents in their sleep,"* to quote, I believe. Morton was quite taken by the imagery..."

Richard swallowed hard, then turned to his friends, his first physical movement since speaking.

"My Lords, I think I have heard enough. We need to consider these events, distasteful as it may be." Turning back, he looked directly at Stanley for a few seconds, biting his bottom lip. "Sir Thomas - I believe that since Redemore you have been anxious to prove yourself of use to me. To prove you are indeed a loyal subject?" Stanley sat up suddenly alert, a look - a mixture of surprise and astonishment spread across his face.

"Your Grace, this is true. I admit that my actions on the field may have appeared somewhat confusing but I have tried to account for this in truth."

"Indeed," Richard smiled grimly. "Well, you have one final opportunity to prove your affinity. Lady Stanley, you will return to the Wakefield Tower whilst the facts of the matter are discussed and a decision with regard to your future is decided. Thomas, you will stay in London. Do you have men here?" Thomas Stanley nodded, slightly perplexed.

"Yes, Your Grace!"

"Good. You will remain in the capital and you will set your men to watching every move our friend Morton makes. The man is newly pardoned, but I had no doubt it would not be long before his true affinities came to light. You will report daily to Master Kendall here," at this point Richard gestured over to his Secretary, who raised his head in acknowledgement. "Every morning, after Matins, you will report back what your men report to you. If he discovers he is being watched, and readies to leave the county, I want Kendall to know before he is able to pack a chest. If he is at any time acquainted with what Lady Stanley has told me today, if he is warned or alerted in any way, your wife will have a companion in the Tower. For as long as it takes me to arrange removal of your head. Do you accept the terms of this "opportunity" my Lord?"

Stanley smiled slowly, a ghastly smile that spoke of revenge and retribution, hoping his wife would turn to see it. She, however, sat silent and immobile beside him, her thoughts and feelings known only to herself.

"Yes, Your Grace. I accept."

39. THE TOWER OF LONDON
December 1485

After a pause in proceedings where Lady Stanley was escorted back to the Tower and Stanley made his leave, the five occupants of the room assembled once more.

Servants had hurried in at Francis's request, refilling wine goblets and laying out cold capon, cheese, fruit and bread. No-one appeared to have much of an appetite but the Rhenish was welcome, cups were refilled and emptied - each man lost in their own thoughts. Only Richard and Kendall busied themselves, talking quietly in a corner of the chamber, discussing other business of the day and the arrangements for Stanley's daily attendances.

This done, Richard walked swiftly back into the centre of the room and seated himself once more. Kendall gave quick nod to the assembled group and departed, his arms full of the tools of his trade as usual. Francis pushed a cup towards Richard, which he accepted by pulling it closer to him, but leaving it on the table.

"Well, gentleman," he reached forward to pick an orange from a bowl instead, weighing it in his hand for a second. "You are all no doubt anxious to discuss what we have just witnessed. Who would like to begin?"

A thoughtful smile played around his mouth and Francis noticed that there was a gleam, a small glimmer of the Richard who he had not seen since Middleham some many months past. Something indefinable was burning in his eyes, even the ever preent tension across his shoulders seemed to have relaxed slightly.

"I will, lad." Norfolk's fatherly tone was heard first, but he waited to swallow the capon he had just consumed, wiping his mouth with a napkin. "After the lessons we learned at Redemore, why in all that is holy have you allowed Stanley and Morton to walk free - again?"

Catesby coughed, trying to catch his eye. As a relatively recent addition to Richard's court, he was still greatly in awe of this gentleman of the old nobility.

"I must bear some responsibility for that my Lord," he explained. "I asked his Grace to refrain from apprehending Morton at this particular moment - as we may only alert any others who are still playing a waiting game. At least until the identity of the boy in Burgundy is verified to all our and brought home. I believe the duchess's upcoming visit to be a vital step in finalising events. Her appearance at court itself will be unremarkable, coming as she does to congratulate the king on his victory this year. After that, we can move on tackle Morton, and anyone else who we find to be implicated in his actions. Setting Stanley to spy on him, however, sheer brilliance Your Grace! He will have to comply to save his own skin."

Richard smiled again, and this time raised his cup to Catesby, although once more he did not drink.

"If you can trust him..." Lincoln said quietly, using a small, jewelled dagger to slice himself a piece of cheese. Francis nodded silently in agreement, contemplating the untouched food on his own trencher.

"Well," Richard answered with a small, unconcerned shrug, "he will find himself in the Tower if he tries anything. And of course, Kendall is just about to set Dick Ratcliffe to following Stanley, who will also be reporting on his movements to him every evening. So, we shall very soon find out his true intentions." The room was silent again as each one of them considered his words. Francis took a large draught of wine from his own cup, and swallowed with difficulty.

"Brackenbury.." his voice was choked with emotion as he mentioned his friends name. "Richard, you surely can't believe he would betray you in this way?" They had all been together at Middleham and it was difficult for Francis to reconcile the story he heard the Stanley woman re-tell so calmly with the man of honour he knew so well. "He wouldn't be party to such a thing, not without your express instruction, either in word or by hand. That damn woman is very adept at placing the blame on men who can no longer speak for themselves - apart from handing us Morton's head on a platter. I notice she didn't implicate her husband at all, but he must have known what was happening. She would have confided in him, planned some of it with him? Surely that makes him as guilty of treason as she is? Her, her godforsaken son and her husband! Why don't we just put them all on trial and be done with it?"

In the silence which followed, Lincoln pushed his chair back so he could stand. He moved over to the front of the table, leaning over the back of the chair which had previously been occupied by Lady Stanley.

"I have been thinking about this," he said quietly, "and when she was talking about the access to the Tower, something crossed my mind." Richard's lips were curved in an expression of approval as he swirled the wine in his cup slowly.

"Go on..."

"Well, it's this Tower guard's business. Alright so a couple of men sympathetic to the boys plight took a bribe to help them escape. But - the Tower is a fortress as well as a royal residence, it would need more than that to take those boys out and smuggle two more in without anyone noticing. It would take someone with an intimate knowledge of the timings of different activities, movements, routes of access and so forth for any such plan have a chance of success."

"Indeed, it would," Richard was still looking at his cup, with much more interest than it merited. Francis shot from his seat.

"Good God! Robert helped the boys escape? Is that where this is going?"

Richard sat back in his chair and regarded his friend placidly - his face seemed to have lost years in one afternoon.

"It is one explanation."

"But why would he not tell you?" Lincoln had joined in now, puzzled. "This version of events had him allowing access to the boys for them to be murdered in their beds, believing this to be a direct order from yourself. Now, that seemed odd to me, I just couldn't see him taking such a command from Harry Stafford. He would have wanted a signed warrant. He didn't like Harry any more than most of us did." The realisation of his words dawned on him as he air in the room chilled slightly. No one had trusted Buckingham, aside from Richard. Everyone was avoiding eye contact - they all knew it to be true. Richard himself kept his eyes lowered and bit his bottom lip. Lincoln moved round and sat himself in the chair he had been leaning on, opposite his uncle.

"But if Robert knew those boys were not truly Edward's sons... if he had already ensured their safety...." Francis remained standing, but his colour had lessened now, beginning to form the picture of events in his mind. He turned to Richard. "But when the rumours started, the lies... wouldn't he have told you...?" He sat down again slowly, his face betraying the conflict in his mind. "He surely could not have listened to all of those lies, known them to be false and said nothing?"

"What could he have said or done that would have made any difference to what people believed?" Richard's words were reflective, tinged with more than a hint of sadness. "Yes - he could have told me they were alive and let me know where they were. Perhaps he feared I would react badly - things were particularly fluid then if you recall. Some of my decisions... well, there is at least one I heartily regret." His voice tailed off, his mind taken back to a June afternoon in the very chamber where they all sat.

"It would appear that our erstwhile friend Buckingham played you more falsely than we knew," grumbled Norfolk, resting his chin on his hands. "I always felt he was much too quick to rush to judgement, begging your pardon Your Grace." Richard nodded silently in acknowledgement. "Full of the wrong type of energy, like he was burning up inside. "

"Like George, "mused Richard, finally taking a sip of wine. "Edward knew it - you.." he cut his eyes across to Francis, "tried to warn me, but I was so overwhelmed by his immediate support, by the strength of his conviction, I didn't listen to any of you. My Lords, that was wrong of me and I beg your pardons."

"So," Norfolk spoke up briskly, changing the subject. "Robert knew that Buckingham ordered the murder of two poor sickly orphans. And that creature Reginald Bray didn't know the boys any better than most of the realm. He just saw the sad corpses of two children and considered the deed done. Neither Lord or Lady Stanley, even Morton come to that, appear to be aware that they participated in the killing of two unknown orphans. They really think it was Edward's sons who were put to death that night. Thanks to the ignorance of that simpering dolt Bray!"

"Now there's one who can be punished, at present if only for allowing Lady Stanley to break the terms of her house arrest." Richard went quiet and then thoughtful. "I wonder what Robert did with the bodies of those pour souls." Once again silence fell around the room as the significance of what they had heard sank in. It was Lincoln who spoke up next, hoping to clear some of the disbelief he himself was feeling.

"What about all that business over the council? Did Buckingham truly seek control over the whole of the north? He made no outward display of it. He was exceedingly ingratiating to me most of the time. Irritatingly so in fact." Richard nodded.

"Thinking about it, there were a few signs. He did mention the Warwick lands on occasion and it's true he didn't care for Henry Percy."

"He's not alone there," mumbled Francis under his breath. Richard gave a grudging grin.

"He mentioned the council a few times, now that I come to think of it, but I paid it no mind. There was never an occasion where he asked outright that I can recall....although I do remember the night he suggested that Edward could be betrothed to his daughter. I have a feeling that is what began the whole change in his loyalties. With his daughter married to the heir to the throne, and if I had granted him control of the north... I can see how he would have been attracted to that prospect. As you all know, life in the north can be isolating, but it does mean that you very much rule somewhat remotely from Westminster. It is not a role I would ever have deemed suitable for Harry."

Lincoln sat forward, leaning towards his uncle.

"Yet... he believed you were about to make a change in the council?" Richard nodded sagely.

"Yes, I told him that. It was not completely true, however. I just wanted the subject closed." Finally, he took a deep draught from his cup. The room descended once more into quiet as everyone considered the picture which had just been painted for them with the recent revelations. Richard heaved a sigh to break their reverie. "It goes without saying that none of this goes outside this chamber."

"On pain of death!" Lincoln whispered and Francis gave a chuckle. Richard allowed them a smile.

"We wait now, until my sister arrives from Burgundy, but all please expect to be called to similar meetings over the festivities. We must then arrange for the boy - for Richard," he halted momentarily on speaking of his own namesake, "to be brought home. Once that is done , we can make public all that we know. We can begin to inform the opinions of those who blacken my name and believe me guilty of these heinous crimes. Hopefully, it will be enough." Catesby made a small dissenting noise.

"Will, "Lincoln grinned jovially, "speak up man! Just think, you have more meetings with the duchess to look forward to! What a Christmas you will have in truth!" Catesby looked up with a small smile.

"I was just thinking Your Grace, we should consider if bringing the boy home is the wisest move? I understand your eagerness to let the people see he is alive, and well, in your hands. Tudor is immured in the Tower, but the boy could still be a focus for those who may have old loyalties, Woodville loyalties."

Richard pushed his chair back and stood up slowly.

"You are right of course Will, as ever. But at least allow me my dream for a few nights. We can discuss the boy's final settlement when my sister is here. Until then, and whilst only us few know the truth, I can sleep easier knowing exactly what became of my brother's sons." He moved around the table and walked to the

355

door, but halted before he reached for the latch and turned to give them one final look. "Do you know, my Lords, if I could place the crown upon that table, walk away and return to the north to live the rest of my live in peace - I would. In a heartbeat, gentlemen. The weight of the crown is a pressure you should all think yourselves truly fortunate not to bear."

He left the room then, leaving his closest friends experiencing a range of emotions including a mixture of relief and concern.

40. BAYNARD'S CASTLE
December 1485

Margaret, Duchess of Burgundy raised her skirts to ascend the stone steps, moving sure-footedly from her barge up towards the entrance to Baynard's Castle, whose tall walls towered over the river imposingly, providing a reflection of its fortified glory.

A small, select family group were gathered above in the icy breeze, laden with the foretaste of snow. Awaiting her arrival she could see Richard, her mother Cecily, and John, Earl of Lincoln. It was Richard who moved down the stairs swiftly to take her hand thereby assisting her up to the top of the embankment, before swiftly grasping her by the upper arms, forestalling her curtsey. He pressed his lips to her chilled cheek and as they drew apart Margaret looked deep into his blue-grey eyes with an expression of real affection.

"Dearest brother," she murmured quietly, secretly reflecting how much he seemed to have aged in the five long years since she had last seen him. But with good reason, she had to admit.

"Margaret - sister, thank you for coming," Richard replied, a warm smile wreathing his face with pleasure. Margaret looked over to where the duchess stood, displaying her usual regal elegance. Heavily cloaked in furs against the cold, she was studiously surveying her daughter from a distance. The two hadn't seen each other since Margaret left for her marriage some years ago, but their relationship had always been more cordial than comfortable. Once again she reflected that Yorks appeared to wear time uncomfortably.

"Mother continues to thrive I see," she whispered quietly. Her lips hardly moved but her eyes sparkled with humour as she moved away from to him submit to her mother's more formal embrace.

"Daughter, you look well," Cecily commented as if she had seen her only last week. "Now come inside, this weather is set to turn for the worse." Eyeing the heavy sky with a swift critical appraisal, she turned on her heel and went inside, skirts trailing against the damp stone.

"It wouldn't dare!" Margaret gave yet another murmured aside to her youngest brother, who in return delivered a most unroyal nudge in the ribs with his elbow.

The group passed into Cecily's private chamber where a roaring fire blasted out enough heat to dispel the December chill. Margaret crossed immediately to the hearth and stripping off her fine leather gloves, spread out her sturdy white fingers to the welcome warmth.

"Ye Gods, Mama, I think you may be right!" Cecily frowned at the curse but Margaret either ignored it or did not see it. "I think snow is on the way as you predict. What a journey! I am so glad to be here, finally."

She quickly dispensed with her own furred cloak and threw it across the back of the nearest chair, addressing Lincoln whilst she did so.

"Now then, nephew, is there any drink to be had? If not - I have brought a fine Burgundy with me. You are welcome to some barrels, I would think you could do with some decent wine and it doesn't come any finer than from our vines. The last lot from France went bad I believe." Cecily and Richard both exchanged glances at the reference to the bounty brought back to England as part of the last French campaign by their brother Edward.

"Malmsey was ever George's vice," Cecily countered smoothly, but added a reproving riposte. "And you should be more respectful to your brother's memory."

The earl turned his head curiously as he crossed to the sideboard and filled a cup with Vernage. He could see that Margaret had no intention of treating either her mother or brother with anything other than the normal camaraderie to be expected between any close family members. It reminded him of some particular afternoons spent with Edward, who could in turns be regal, amusing, ironic and endlessly entertaining. He smiled to himself at the memory and took the cup over to Margaret with a deferential nod, which she accepted, only to examine the wine it contained closely, wrinkling her nose in distaste.

"Dearest Mama, perhaps you should enter the order if this is the only wine to your taste." Lincoln bit the inside of his tongue to stop himself from laughing outright and stole a quick glance at Duchess Cecily's resigned shake of the head but Margaret had now turned her attention to her brother.

"As for you, Dickon, you have not worn at all well since we last met. You bear too passing a resemblance to our father for my liking, only with a more," she struggled for words, raising her eyes to the ceiling as if the words she needed were written there and which were obediently revealed, "tragic- air about you."

Not knowing whether to be shocked or amused, Lincoln in the end managed a mixture of both when he witnessed the forbearance on both Cecily and Richard's faces. They appeared well used to Margaret's manner and were showing neither displeasure or amusement. It seemed they accepted her manner as completely normal, for her.

"And you have not changed in the slightest my daughter. Life with the duke obviously suited you." Cecily remarked drily. "You were ever the irreverent. I thought Charles would calm that in you." Margaret laughed shortly and loudly.

"He tried Mama, I can assure you, but he did need a bride who could bite back. It tempered him slightly, in the end." She paused, turning to Lincoln suddenly, her brow creased beneath her headdress. "Where is that close mouthed lawyer friend of yours? I was looking forward to seeing his discomforted face again. I am bereft!" Lincoln adopted his best mocking air and putting his hand over his heart, executed a reverent bow, grinning all the while.

"William is in his chambers, my Lady. My uncle thought it best that only family be here at present. I am sure he will be delighted to see you again this evening when we sup." Margaret returned Lincoln a sidelong grin before turning a more direct look on Richard.

"I love baiting learned men. They have such wit - most of them. Your lawyer friend was extremely entertaining when he could finally bring himself to speak." She looked round the room at the assembled company. "I take it, by this small select gathering that we are straight to business then?"

"Unless you prefer to rest first? Your journey has been long - but as you instigated the visit I thought you may be eager to discuss recent events. It can, however, wait until the morrow if you prefer?" Margaret once again looked around and gave a deliberately exaggerated shrug, to signal her disinterest one way of the other.

Richard nodded, then gestured for everyone to sit down, and the small group seated themselves around the fire. His tone was conversational and reserved but both Lincoln and Cecily had spied the relief in his face as they knew how anxious he was to hear his sister's full version of events. He would, they knew, spend an anxious night if she should play the innocent and prefer to retire to her chambers. Although her journey may have been long, she was not travelling without the comforts of a royal progress.

Margaret settled back comfortably in the chair, turning her feet towards the warming flames, their glow caught in her dark eyes.

"What you really mean is, to explain myself." Her tone turned suddenly sombre as she regarded her brother carefully. "I am more than happy to do so, on the condition that you also explain your actions to me. Tell me, brother, how come it is that you, my youngest sibling, are sitting on the throne of England and not my nephew?"

Richard deflected her attack demurely by ignoring most of it, but examined his hands momentarily before looking back at her.

"You did not see fit to bring the boy to meet me?" The sinister undercurrents of their exchange were totally at odds to their friendly expressions and the familiarity of their earlier greeting. The flames guttered as if disturbed by a draught.

"Not until I am sure he is safe back in this country, and in your care," the duchess countered without hesitation. She held her hands out to the fire briefly before folding them across the front of her richly brocaded gown. "Explain, if you would, the basis behind the act of Titulus Regis. For I admit, I find it truly a work of artistry."

To all in the room it seemed as if the cold Thames mist had risen and crept over the sills of the windows to pervade the room.

"I need explain nothing to you!" Richard's reply was cloaked in a sudden anger and he turned his head towards his mother as she rose from her seat and moved back to the mantel. Standing by his chair, she rested one hand on the stone lintel and looked at her youngest son briefly before she spoke, taking in the thin, tense line of his lips.

"The pre-contract with Eleanor Butler, although seen as a pure invention in order for Richard to seize the throne, is fact. Do you think I would stand aside and let my grandchildren be disinherited by a lie? You should know me much better than that Margaret. I knew of it when it happened, Edward told me some of it himself and the rest I wrung out of that idiot Stillington. Unfortunately, after Edward played the same hand and secretly married, again.." her voice halted for a second and she studied the carved symbol of the falcon and fetterlock on the wall above her head as she recalled difficult events not spoken of for many years.

"I kept his secret for as long as I was able, but when Warwick turned against Edward, and then was killed at Barnet - well, he was my kinsman. It was difficult for me, my allegiance to my son, my nephew, all that your father fought for. What he lost his life for." No one moved or spoke and Lincoln would later relate that he believed no - one even dared to draw breath as they awaited her next words. "I watched my family torn apart because of that foolish marriage. Although I have real affection for my grandchildren, my fear is for the blood that runs through their veins. That woman seeped her poison into the very fabric of our royal house turning brother against brother. No marriage was beyond consideration until she had all her siblings and kinsmen entwined around the old noble houses of this land like bindweed. Babe married dowager, commoner wed nobility. Please forgive me Richard," she shot a pleading glance to her sombre-faced son, "but even though the Neville girls were vastly endowed, and suitable matches for my sons, it was just as well they were. All other options were gone, absorbed into the Woodville family."

She stopped and drew a heavy reluctant sigh, her advancing years all too visible in the harsh winter light, lines of grief etched dark against her pale skin.

"I regret to this day my rage after Barnet. I was indiscreet. I was so upset by the deaths of Warwick and Montagu that I raged fully for an hour, my senses lost. Mea culpa." Her voice had fallen quieter and she moved over to the window, fondling the reliquary at her breast as if in absent prayer. Her eyes scanned the winding river outside. "I told George what I knew and in doing so - sealed his fate with my own words. Can you imagine how difficult that has been to live with all these years?"

Both of Cecily's children looked at each other with uncertain expressions. Richard had known some of this, but never had heard it relayed to him with the passion and despair as had just coloured his mother's words. She spoke infrequently of their father, although Richard knew that it hurt her to look at him sometimes, the resemblance was so true. Cecily of York, who stood fast whilst Ludlow was sacked, sent her youngest children abroad for their safety and then suffered the loss of kinsmen, husband and son in one day - bodies mutilated and mocked by the enemy. Proud Cis she had been called, and she had worn that mantle defiantly down the years. Her hatred for Elizabeth Woodville, although never directly expressed, oozed out of every one of her words like blood from a deep seated wound.

"Of course," she continued, turning to her rapt audience with a wry smile, "I should have realised George would be his own undoing. He was ever unhappy with his lot, something which grew stronger with the passing of time. When Edward refused him the hand of your step- daughter," she glanced quickly to Margaret, "he was wroth. Angrier than I have ever seen him, and then for Edward to offer the hand of Anthony Rivers! It was a poor jest! Edward was cruel there - in a way I didn't know he was capable of. Something in George turned, with the loss of his wife as well. He employed astronomers, soothsayers, that poor Twynyhoe woman..!"

She stopped speaking and signed her breast with the cross as she thought of the servant woman whom George had executed, accusing her of the murder of his wife Isabel by poisoning. Margaret's brow settled in a deep frown.

"Didn't one of George's astrologers predict that the name of the next king would begin with a G?" She looked at Richard, the former Duke of Gloucester and felt slightly guilty as his face, normally deathly pale, suffused with colour. Cecily crossed herself quickly once again.

"Shame on you, daughter! What George dabbled in was ungodly, and contributed to his end."

"I did write to Edward," Margaret replied, somewhat chastened. "He would not listen. His mind was set on George paying the price for his treason."

"Set by whom?" Lincoln pondered aloud, and was rewarded by a tight, but warm smile from Cecily in thanks that she had not had to say those words. "I take it Edward found out that George knew about the pre-contract?"

"The Bishop and George were incarcerated at the same time in the Tower." Richard's voice was just above a whisper. "When Stillington told me what he knew it explained a lot about Elizabeth's actions after Edward died. She needed her son crowned before her secret was revealed, with Stillington still walking abroad. Quite how he escaped his fate I do not to this day know. He is a very fortunate fellow - though I must admit I often wish I had just thrown him back in the Tower when he came to Crosby Place that day." Richard had lowered his lids, so his eyes appeared closed and Margaret watched as he drew a hand across his brow tiredly. "You should also speak to Will Catesby on the matter, he has information on this that will more than satisfy you I think." Margaret threw Lincoln a swift questioning look, but his eyes were on Richard as he continued wearily.

"I would that things had been different. I did not seek to be king." For one moment, it looked as if Margaret was about to rise from her seat, but she settled back once more. Reaching for her cup, she took another sip, her attention fixed on her brother.

"Do you know," he continued, his voice edged in bitterness, the words spoken directly to Margaret, "not one member of that family, my family, wrote to tell me my brother was dead. Not even Bess!"

"Ahh, we shall come to her," murmured Margaret, almost as an aside. If Richard heard the remark, he ignored it and talked as the festering rage consumed him afresh, his hands curled into fists as he rested them on the arms of his chair.

"Elizabeth plotted to have me killed on the way to meet with her son at Northampton. Those accursed brothers of hers planned to thwart my power as Lord Protector and rush the young king to his coronation. Why? Well, we know why, because she should never have been queen in the first place and knew that she would be found out. She would know that if George knew the truth - my mother also knew the truth, but she could hardly hurl her into the Tower, although I have no doubt she may have tried! Whispering in Edward's ear, plotting and planning and scheming, he was bewitched by her right up until his death!"

The laugh that crossed the chamber was heavy with irony and Richard shot his sister a look of pure anger a the sound of it.

"That old tale! Some water witch isn't it?" Again Margaret looked at her mother who merely turned her cheek to the window.

"She didn't need that type of sorcery." Cecily's words were spoken so quietly they had to strain to hear her. "For some reason, the power to make my son do what she wanted lay in her very being... she needed nothing more."

Margaret frowned again, thinking hard. Whilst doing so, she waggled her cup in Lincoln's direction and he took the welcome distraction of refilling it. He was becoming increasingly astounded by the conversation, finding himself very much a silent observer. It amused him to think that the Christmas mummers would really need to earn their angels from him this year to rival this entertainment. Margaret accepted the cup from his hand gracefully, appraising him with a glint in her dark eye and now happily drinking the Vernage which was so unspeakable earlier.

"That's still no excuse to kill off half her family," she retorted after taking a small sip. Richard sighed loudly at this, and began to twist the ring on his smallest finger.

"There was reason, but also.... I received poor counsel.." Margaret nearly spat out the wine she had just drunk.

"Buckingham - of all men! You did ever trust too easily Dickon, and I had hoped you had learned that not every man can hold to the standards of loyalty and chivalry you expect. It's just not possible! Edward wrote me why he never gave our cousin his rightful place at court. He didn't trust him. He saw him as vainglorious and only interested in how much he could amass for himself. He likened him to George and refused to open himself up to another such individual for as much as we loved George we all knew his faults. It is surely no co-incidence that they both shared the same fate!"

"I know that now as I knew it then." Richard's tone was terse. "But at the time he offered his loyal support, when there were very few who I felt I could trust. You were not here, you have not had to bear witness to the treachery I was subject to. He gave me advice I now know was false. I have only very recently come to find out how false."

"Hastings was innocent?" Lincoln asked speculatively.

"Guilty only of probably being a fool, and easily led by a wanton," Richard gave a desperate gesture of acknowledgement with his left hand as his voice cracked. "But he betrayed me. The man I believed to be the one loyal man who respected my brother's memory. The man who let me know he was dead. I was beyond anger at his involvement with the queen's kin, his entanglement with Edward's whore, I believed - I was told, my very life was in danger and if I was in danger, so was Anne and my son. How was I supposed to react to such a threat?"

Margaret's eyebrows were raised skywards as she answered this and her tone had become truly scathing.

"Buckingham, on the contrary, seemed very keen to support your claim as it was told to me. But it was not just the pre-contract was it? Blayborne? Really? And a true English prince? God's Blood Dickon, why did you allow it?"

Cecily turned slowly from the window, her face bearing witness to the toll these old memories were taking. She took two paces towards where her daughter sat.

"That was my doing." she admitted quietly. "I allowed it. There were mutterings that the pre-contract was all invention, so convenient did the timing of its revelation seem. Some did not want to acknowledge what common sense told them was true. I allowed those things to be said to keep that Woodville woman from placing her bastard stock on the throne and ruling in their stead. A throne won by my blood with power and sacrifice. It was not her place to rule!"

The two women looked at each other fixedly, and it was the younger who looked away first.

"Still," she mused, unfailingly resilient. "A few rash actions which have caused untold discord and could plague you for years to come. Summary execution will tend to turn the populace against you - in fear. I hope you now have better judgement of the people who counsel you ?"

"Indeed." Richard's answer was filled with resentment. "I thought Harry was my true kinsman. Even now, knowing what he said to me and what some of his actions were, I still find it hard to comprehend he could be so false. It would appear the rewards I gave him were not enough, he even wanted to marry his daughter to my son. I believe that may have been a refusal too far for him."

Margaret was listening carefully as she tapped the stem of her wine cup noisily with finger bearing an emerald the size of a quail's egg.

"Hmmn. As we are on the subject of marriage, my niece's fair face comes to mind. Is this more gossip and rumour? For I must admit Dickon, you seem to have a plethora of stories raging around your kingship. If I were to believe them all, I would have to wonder at your ability to achieve so much in such a short space of time."

At this admonishment, Richard leant forward in his chair and to all intents and purposes looked like he was about to leap out of it and hurl himself towards his sister. With sheer force of will he managed to remain in his seat but could not keep the acidity out of his voice.

"Much as I resent the whiff of an inquisition here, I can assure you my intentions with regard to Bess have always been honourable. The unfortunate girl has feelings for me. She has been at great pains to make me aware of them and although I once felt her mother to be the architect of these designs, I do now believe them to be genuine. But..." he moved to the edge of his seat in order to further emphasise his point, eyes the colour of granite pinning her to her chair as the tension in the room increased unbearably, "although we have always been close, there has never - I am repeating this for you, sister, in case your journey has made you hard of hearing, never, acted inappropriately with her. Contrary to all popular rumour of course. Jesu! I even made a public declaration - just about tore open my shirt and beat my breast in public! How much else am I supposed to endure?"

The room thrummed with tension, like a recently plucked harp string. Cecily and Lincoln watched brother and sister fence both glances and words, both aiming true. Margaret's response to this tirade was delivered demurely - but their locked gazes spoke a language of their own.

"Delivered under duress, I believe. Not an action you took willingly."

This time Richard did rise out of his seat, his chair scudding backwards over the tiled floor making both Cecily and Lincoln start.

"Of course it was under duress! I didn't want to embarrass the girl! She had already exposed herself enough by telling me of her feelings, and I had only just laid my wife to rest! Dear God, sister, whatever you now think of me, I am not made of stone! She is a young girl, subject to a young girl's whims and fancies. This will pass. I didn't want to publicly humiliate her but I was advised that it had to be done! To protect myself!"

These last three words were spat out slowly and with utter distaste. The whole affair sickened him to his stomach and he turned away from the faces of his assembled family to replenish his cup with more wine. Cecily watched her son wordlessly and marked with concern that his hands were shaking.

Margaret, however, was in no mood to show mercy.

"Talking of advice, there is one face missing from this chamber. One whose advice has been constant through the years but I believe was somewhat left in the shadows as Buckingham's star ascended the heavens?" Richard's head turned slightly so his profile could be seen, but his back remained turned to the room.

"Francis?" His question was also a sigh.

"Where is he today?"

Cecily answered her daughter firmly.

"This is a family matter. We agreed it was advisable to keep it so." She moved towards her son who had still not turned fully turned around. He was leaning against the sideboard, cup in hand, but his eyes had closed and she shot a worried glance to Lincoln, who was also watching his uncle's reaction.

"Francis and I have discussed this," Richard's voice was tired, constrained, but he turned back to face his tormentor. "Times were difficult, he understands." Margaret shook her head in exasperation.

"I have no objection to Francis being in attendance here! I know he is one of your oldest friends, indeed he is more like family along with others like Rob Percy and your impenetrable lawyer. After all - you do have Brackenbury to thank for saving the boys."

Those words did nothing to lighten the atmosphere within the room and Richard fixed her with a pointed stare.

"Go on..." he said quietly and although he knew that Lincoln was desperate to catch his eye, he avoided the contact and looked instead at his sister.

"He wrote to me," Margaret said through pursed lips. "He feared for their lives, not at your hand," she added hastily aware of the impact of her words. "He, wisely, didn't trust Buckingham and knew you were being blinded by his overwhelming display of loyalty and support. He was worried about the amount of responsibility he had and of his free range of access to the Tower. Brackenbury's tone was guarded, he was worried his letter may be intercepted, but he worked with Elizabeth to ensure a safe passage for the boys. I do have a letter which he sent to me whilst you were mustering to meet Tudor. He asked that the letter be given to you personally in the event of his death in battle. It is in a safe place with my belongings. I think he wished to explain his reasons, that you may have seen what he did as a betrayal once the truth be known."

As the room descended into silence once more, she stood up and smoothed down the skirts of her gown, all the time paying close attention to Richard's face. She thought she could see the gleam of a tear in his eye and suddenly she felt a lump rise in her throat. He was her younger brother and although she had only seen him periodically over the years, she could still remember him as the shy, quiet boy who loved and trusted completely, with his whole heart and soul. He appeared to have carried those traits with him into manhood and they had been his undoing.

"I think I shall retire now...this must be very difficult for you."

At this point Lincoln also stood up, more hastily than he intended, but a sardonic smile curved his lips as he studied Margaret's face.

"I think we can stand a few more arrows from your van, Your Grace. Uncle, I think our adversary is just about to flee the field and I for one don't think she deserves to fight another day." Margaret's dark eyes, so like Richard's, registered a grudging admiration in response to Lincoln's inclined head.

"Oh nicely done, you've been spending far too much time with that lawyer!"

Richard appeared distracted. He was very pale and still looking down at his cup. Lincoln watched as Cecily moved a step closer to him, saw him shake his head dismissively. There was an exchange of words, spoken too low for anyone else to hear and Richard moved back to his seat. Lincoln's face registered a grim amusement as he turned back to his aunt.

"Thanks to our recent visit to yourself, my Lady, I have spent more time with lawyers than I ever had a desire to. Which would not have been necessary if you had not hidden the presence of your nephew from the king. So the question to be answered has to be - why? Why did you not let us know your involvement in this matter. You were very well informed of events here, you knew what was being said abroad, knew the aspersions this was casting on your own brothers character, the dangers to his sovereignty." He stopped speaking as he saw her nodding in agreement as he spoke. "Yet you did, and said, nothing."

The duchess bridled a little, but she found it hard to be angry with this handsome lad.

"It was by my auspices that you heard that there was a boy in Burgundy. I allowed that rumour to surface to ensure his presence to be discovered."

"Rather late in the day." Cecily's intervention was delivered with scorn. She was now standing behind Richard's chair, her hand gripping the carved back. In direct contrast to her children, her hands were always devoid of jewels, save a plain gold wedding band.

"It was too precarious to declare earlier, what with Tudor set to invade," her daughter responded. "Elizabeth feared for their lives, from any quarter. She wanted them kept safe and she was happy to encourage the rumour that they were dead. It prevented anyone seeking their whereabouts. Buckingham played into her hands perfectly without even realising it. She hated Dickon for taking the crown, hated Buckingham for assisting him and then held him in contempt for his betrayal. And she feared Tudor. She knew that Tudor would want the boys dead as he was set on marrying Bess and could not do so if the boys were alive." At this Richard revelation suddenly raised his hands in dismay.

"So why in all the heavens above would she agree to the betrothal? She knew that to marry Bess he would have to legitimise the boys. That itself put them at risk from him!"

"Not if he believed them dead, one of the main reasons she was happy to participate in the lies. With the Stanley's backing, and Morton's confidences, Elizabeth was certain you would be killed in battle. It was almost as if she had been assured of it - that she knew who planned to show false colours. She then believed that when the boys were revealed to be alive, those supporters who turned against you for Tudor would turn against him." She stopped speaking only to heave a deep sigh. "And on that note, may I ask why your erstwhile friend Morton is still attached to his head. The man is a veritable plague. Worse than all of them put together." The sound of soft laughter turned all eyes towards Lincoln.

"What are you laughing at?" For the first time Margaret had a note of frustration in her voice.

"I was thinking earlier that the mummers this year will be sore pressed to match this for entertainment. Uncle - you could have saved yourself the expense." He was rewarded by a quick grin before Richard returned his focus to Margaret.

"So - you waited until recently to let me know he was alive. And still not directly, by yet another rumour set running." His voice betrayed the weariness he felt at the sheer scale of the underhanded plotting, scheming and treachery which had been flowing beneath his court like a river of sewage.

"You would have heard from me directly if you had dealt with Tudor in August. Pray tell me, why is that man also still breathing? How did you deal with Hastings so adroitly but fail to dispatch a proven traitor?" Richard ignored her.

"You sat back and listened as calumny and lies ranged free across my kingdom, casting me as tyrant and despot. Murderer! Of my own blood! How could you do that?" Margaret pouted like a sulky child caught out in a misdemeanour. Her response was both trite and inadequate.

"Justice will out."

"Will it?" Richard snarled sarcastically. "Then, madam, what if I had been killed in battle? What would have been said of me then? Would my hell be to watch men slander my name down the ages and be able to do nothing to stop it?"

Margaret studied his face for a few seconds and then crossed the room to stand before him. Reaching over, she placed a hand gently against his pale cheek. Her formerly strident tones softened and she spoke with real affection as some of the ice in the room began to commence a welcome thaw.

"Dearest Richard, you did not die. You have time now, time for things to be corrected. I will help you, we can do this together." Her thumb stroked his cheek as she went on. "I was deeply saddened to hear of the loss of your son, and dear Anne. A tragedy in truth." Richard swallowed with difficulty, the two of them standing very close, their voices low.

"Even in that, men say..."

"Ssh!" Margaret moved her hand to place a finger of his lips. "Give them no credence. The truth is known. You need no common mans affirmation but you do need a change of scenery. I recall you always hated the capital. It ages you for one thing." He managed a smile as he took her hand away from his lips and held it.

"After Christmas maybe. The Portuguese alliances are finalised, there are a few outstanding matters, but then I will try to go north. Make sure Northumberland is behaving, visit York and Middleham. Perhaps attend the Council." Margaret smiled broadly and they clasped hands as she leant towards him reassuringly.

"Good. After that, Richard shall come home. We will announce the good news and show him to the people. Then we will decide where he should reside. It may then be better for him to return to Burgundy with me. Unless you plan to marry him off, of course!" She fair chortled with laughter. "I would imagine Elizabeth may have compiled a list! I hope you are ready for this Dickon, for she will have ambitions for him, despite his bastard status."

Cecily had been watching her two children finally make their peace and although she displayed no outward sign, she was relieved. At one point during the afternoon she had been certain that Richard was in some pain, whether mental or physical she was not sure, but she had seen how his body had appeared to tighten, his face had blanched and Margaret could have been announcing the Second Coming of Christ and he would not have known it.

He had brushed away her solicitous enquiry, and appeared to have recovered shortly afterwards and certainly at the moment there was no sign that anything had been amiss. His expression was now one of pleasure and gratitude as he had finally discovered the truth. She offered up a silent prayer that her youngest son could now experience some small period of peace, but with Dame Grey still to account for her action and with two Tudors in the Tower, her hopes were not high. Cecily was a devout woman, but she would pronounce a death sentence herself if she had the power. They had all committed treason but even so she knew Richard would be loathe to shed more blood; a life spent in the Tower may be the only way to resolve this. She moved forward silently to stand beside Margaret and caught her sons eye.

"This is all very well, but you have a traitor and his mother in the Tower, and one of their acolytes out at Grafton. It is most gratifying that one grandchild - bastard tho' he be - is alive and well, and I greatly grieve the loss of Edward. However, the fact that either one of them is alive will revive old alliances. You will have to act decisively, Richard. The jest about marriage may not be as amusing as it appears. A foreign marriage perhaps, similar to that arranged for Bess." Richard and Margaret exchanged glances before meeting their mother's gaze.

"The fact that he will have to be securely settled is not in doubt, but a foreign marriage..?" Richard hesitated before continuing to explain. "Bess is but a girl, and the Portuguese are keen to make an alliance. Even if things were to change, they would never be a major threat to England as would France or Spain. The boy is another matter. A foreign marriage, for a bastard prince, even if we could get someone to accept him, is a different matter.

As head of his own court, who knows what could happen in years to come? No - it may be much better to keep the boy close."

"Which worked so well last time," Lincoln drawled sarcastically over the rim of his cup. Richard shot him an angry glare, but Margaret allowed herself a small smile in his direction.

"Well it's true!' he declared in his defence. "You can't put him in the Tower, you can't put him with his mother, and you surely don't want him wandering around at court talking to Stanleys, and Morton and anyone who has a lingering affinity for King Edward. The boy, though as my Grandmama says, God bless he is still breathing - is a problem. Always was a problem."

Richard cursed silently and moved away from his sister. Lincoln pressed his point further home.

"You cannot rely on him remaining loyal, no matter how well you treat him. He will still view you as the thief of his birthright, and possibly as contributor to the death of his brother." Margaret was shaking her head, she turned and re-traced her footsteps back to her seat.

"You have no worry in that concern." She seated herself once more, and leaned back against the chair. "He appears to have no enmity, in fact, remembers his uncle quite fondly. His disposition is much lighter than Edward's ever was, I believe, after all, he was never raised to be king. He is a cheerful soul. Treated well..."

Lincoln put down his cup noisily and leaned forwards so he could meet his aunts eyes.

"Treating someone well is no guarantee of fidelity. Buckingham? Stanley? George, for Jesu sake! They had favours and privilege both, but when a crown is dangled on a thread of power, it means nothing to such men. How do we know he will not grow to be such a man? How?" Cecily's icy tone cut across the air.

"You speak almost as if you regret he has been found alive." She was rewarded with a casual shrug.

"In one sense, that is correct. But he is living and is a threat - still. Whatever is done with him, we have to ensure there are no further opportunities for him to be used against the king, either spiritually or physically. Once we announce to the world he is alive, all those who deny the Titulus Regis will have been given a raison de terre - and believe me, there are such people still abroad. Even those who have sworn loyalty to the crown."

During this exchange, Richard had been quietly contemplating one of the tapestries which hung against the wall, a depiction of the Passion of our Lord, with the disciples ranged around the foot of the cross. He reached out and traced the face of one of the faithful followers with his ring finger, slowly considering all that had been said. No-one had been paying him any attention, too absorbed in the conversation around the boy, which was beginning to raise dissention in the room. He had missed some of the words, but his mother was now arguing with Lincoln about immuring the boy in a northern stronghold. Barnard Castle, was mentioned.

"No." he interrupted so suddenly that all eyes swivelled to rest on his back as his hand fell back to his side. He turned slowly, his eyes contemplative in a look his mother knew all too well and she gave a small sigh. "You were right sister,' he continued, his own lips sketching a smile. "There is someone missing from this conversation. John," he turned towards his nephew. "Have someone request Francis to join us."

41. GREENWICH
December 1485

Francis squinted up at the leaden sky, looking left and right as his falcon looped and soared above him. The day was exceptionally cold, with a stiff breeze, but he had been feeling restless for the past few days and had felt the need to escape the confines of the court.

Knowing he would not be required by Richard for most of the day, the spell of free time was just too good to be wasted, and he had persuaded Rob to ride out with him for a morning's sport. Only things had not quite gone to plan as Ralph Scrope, Cecily's husband, now recently returned from his northern estates, had invited himself along.

It had cast a slight pall over the morning but Francis was still glad of the respite after the intensity of the past few days. Listening to Margaret Stanley had turned his stomach, and he found he had little appetite for either food or sleep at present. It was like a surgeon lancing a festering wound. It needed to be done, but the process was painful, and not at all pleasant. He just hoped everything would get back to normal once the healing process had begun.

He held up his gauntleted hand and his sakker circled once more, swooping down to land on his wrist, balancing delicately on sharply clawed feet. Francis wound the trailing leather cords around his little finger to anchor him safely to his down and smiling, he gently stroked the birds breast, smoothing the tawny feathers below the fierce beak and beady watchful eyes. A fleeting memory crossed his mind of Rob likening his old hawk to Duchess Cecily when they were back at Middleham.

Rob had even wanted to name the bird Cis - but dare not for fear of Richard's reaction. His smile broadened at the memory, as the resemblance had been remarkable to the young boys they were then. Although Richard wasn't aware, they had referred to the bird as Cis in private anyway once the jest had been made, even though he had almost caught them out one day. Quick thinking Rob had saved the day, announcing the birds name was actually Cicero - but which was later considered just too grand and so it was shortened. They had got away with it - just!

Walking back to Fides who was waiting patiently, he handed the bird over to his squire, before mounting swiftly. It had been a welcome distraction for a few hours, but he was ready to return to Westminster himself. He was more than aware of the Scrope's presence and was growing increasingly uncomfortable, more than he liked to admit. It was obvious that the marriage was not working out, and Francis was debating whether to approach Richard about it now that Cecily's brother had been found and was in all likelihood returning to England.

If the wishes of his heart could be realised, he would divorce Anna and gain his freedom. From what Cecily had been telling him of her own marriage, it could easily be annulled. It would appear that Scrope felt he was worth much more than a tainted Woodville bride - only dare not voice that to Richard who had arranged the marriage. There was no happiness to be found on all sides, but Francis's kinship with the Fitzhugh's made a resolution exceeding difficult, if not unlikely.

As if he knew he was being considered, Scrope's northern burr boomed across the meadow.

"Lovell, you not putting that bird up again?" Francis fixed an amiable, if false, grin on his face and turned in his saddle to answer, the leather creaking under his weight, when his eyes caught three riders cantering towards them up the hill. He thought he recognised Lincoln, but not the men with him; then, he wasn't familiar with all of the earl's retainers.

Scrope readied to loose his own bird once more, but Francis shouted,

"Wait!"

Ralph, following the direction of his gaze, also caught sight of their approaching visitors. By this time Rob had also wheeled his horse around and was at Francis's side.

"Lincoln." he observed flatly. "What's he doing here?" Francis shook his head in answer.

"It won't be good or else he would have waited for our return. Personally, I was just readying to ride back anyway. Not such a good days sport today, but the fresh air has been welcome." He looked at his companion's innocent expression pointedly. Rob raised his gloved hands helplessly from his reins and looked back at Scrope to make sure they would not be overheard.

"He invited himself. What was I to do? Tell him to stay at home with his wife?" He watched Francis's face tighten furiously, and his grin grew wider. "See? At least there is some advantage to him being here?"

By this time, the riders were only yards away. Lincoln hauled his bay mount to a standstill so rapidly that his front legs reared up, causing his blue cloak to billow around him like a sail. The outriders slowed to a halt further away, leaving space for their master to speak to his quarry.

"Lincoln." Rob's voice was perfunctory in greeting, and he nodded as the rider slewed his horse round to line up with them. John caught his breath and dipped his head in acknowledgement of the greeting.

"Francis, Richard requests your presence at Baynard's. He sent me to bring you back." His mount danced sidewards after its sudden stop, the dagged harness swaying, caught by the breeze and the animals constant motion.

"Now?" Rob questioned, turning to look at his friend who appeared to be absently examining his horses ears as if he had not heard Lincoln's words. "I thought he was in audience with the Duchess of Burgundy today? That's why we rode out." Lincoln did not reply but flicked his eyes back to Francis.

"Lovell?" At the surname, Francis raised his eyes.

"Yes, we were returning anyway. Rob, will you see to the rest of the men, get them all gathered up and the birds back to the mews? I will return with John directly."

"Certainly." He saw the consternation in his friend's face and wondered what he was thinking. Although they were all close friends, Francis had the measure on all of them where it came to Richard's confidences. There had been a distance in that relationship whilst Buckingham was around, but since his demise, it appeared to Rob that the bond between Richard and Francis had only grown stronger. There was both privilege and responsibility in that, and though Rob could somewhat envy the former, he was happy that the latter did not affect him as much. He was a close confidant of Richard, yes; close enough to brave the odd jest and be involved in certain matters. However, there were some discussions he was more than grateful not to be included in and he felt this may be such an occasion.

With a backward look over his shoulder, Francis spurred his horse forwards and Lincoln joined him as they headed back towards the river and Baynard's Castle. Francis was uncertain what awaited him, and Lincoln wasn't offering any conversation to assure him, his eyes fixed firmly forwards in the direction of the journey. He was keenly aware that Richard wanted to resolve the matter of the Lord Bastard with his sister as quickly as possible having waited so long to get to the truth of the matter, but his uneasiness refused to be quelled.

Tudor was still in the Tower, as was his mother. Stanley was at liberty and although being trailed, was untrustworthy. The Earl of Oxford was still at large and no-one had heard a word of him since Redemore. More and more loose ends. He didn't like it at all.

And then there was the ever present influence of Elizabeth Woodville. No longer at court, yet her presence could be felt like ethereal tendrils which curled through windows, down chimneys and permeated the very air. They needed the Portuguese Queen in place to begin to make her own impression on the court. And soon.

It was almost as if Anne had never existed, he thought sadly. Her quiet, gentle presence seemed to have soaked away into the stone walls like a summer rain. But the presence of Elizabeth was much harder to eliminate. Even as he ruminated, his conscience weighed heavy as he thought of Cecily. She was so gentle, so totally trusting and pure of nature, totally unlike either her mother or elder sister. Bess - another trailing lace - but hopefully one soon tied to Portuguese boots.

Which brought his thoughts back to the impending marriage and the sudden realisation that as Chamberlain and Chief Butler, he could well end up with the responsibility of arranging the festivities. He groaned inwardly against the pounding beat of hooves beneath him. That was a pass he would make if he could. Organising an arranged marriage for a foreign bride and a reluctant groom, a poisoned chalice for sure. His face broke out into an evil grin of its own accord. Rob liked a good banquet. He was Richard's Comptroller of the Household, so maybe...

Lincoln saw his change of expression and gave him a sideways frown in question, but Francis just grinned, and touched his heels to Fides flanks, who responded with a burst of speed as they headed back to the city and before too much longer they were entering the bailey of the castle.

Margaret's lushly appointed barge was still tied up at the steps, and the sun had begun its fast descent through the lower quarter of the sky. The two men dismounted and made their way through the Great Hall where preparations for the evening meal were being laid out. Servants ran to and fro and the central fire burned brightly warding off the chill which increased with the setting sun. The high table up on the dais was being prepared to receive their esteemed guest and it had all the trappings of a veritable feast being readied in the duchess's honour.

Francis followed Lincoln through the torch-lit passages to Duchess Cecily's chamber and he paused outside the door, as the waiting guards stood to attention, parting their halberds to allow them access to their king.

The room was thankfully warm, and the first figure Francis saw was Richard, sitting by the fire with his legs stretched out to the hearth. He looked around expecting to see others, but as far as he could see he appeared to be the only other occupant.

"Your Grace," he bowed quickly, his chin grazing his velvet

doublet, his face beginning to tingle as his chilled skin began to thaw. Richard's face broke out into a welcoming, but weary smile.

"Francis! Take a seat, John, pour the man a drink. He has just spent the afternoon with our friend Scrope and I perceive that it will be most welcome!" He paused, a twinkle in his eyes. "Good hunting, Francis?"

"No." Francis replied curtly, but with a grin. "Both myself and my falcon were somewhat distracted today. Our quarry remained elusive." Removing his cloak, he swung it over the back of the chair, before accepting the cup from Lincoln. He drank thirstily as Richard watched him in undisguised amusement. The warmth against his calves and in his belly were welcome after the ride from Greenwich and his eyes swept the room once more. Richard's watchful gaze caught the gesture.

"My mother sends her apologies, as does Margaret, who looks forward to the pleasure of your company this evening. They have both retired to prepare for the feast, as we must also do shortly. So, we must be about our business with little pre-amble."

"Your Grace, I am at your disposal."

Lincoln leaned on the sideboard and watched the two friends with interest. Having been dispatched by Richard to bring Francis here, he had no idea what had been discussed during his absence, and what Richard's intentions were. That irked him slightly, if he admitted the truth, but as his uncle had not dismissed him from his presence, he was about to be a first hand witness to events anyway. He took a deep draught from his cup and remained quiet in case his presence should be remembered and his uncle ask him to leave.

Richard re-crossed his ankles in the hearth and folded his hands in front of him, appearing totally relaxed and at ease. Francis, having spent many hours in his company knew that something was about to be asked of him. There was a familiar expression on his friend's face. He had seen the same thing many times, most particularly some months ago, when Richard had decided to take the throne and was seeking for Francis to reaffirm his loyalty in approval of his actions. His throat began to dry and he took another swallow of wine. This was bigger than arranging a royal wedding, he was sure of it.

"My sister and I have had a long, difficult, and in turns entertaining, conversation regarding the Lord Bastard. Margaret is happy for him to return home, and we will be able to finally dispel the slanders that have been attached to my name."

"Amen to that!" Francis responded, then pursed his lips thoughtfully. "Are you thinking a proclamation, followed by some sort of pageant showing..?" He stopped as Richard shook his head and waved his hand in dismissal.

"Yes, there will be all that to arrange, but that is not what I want to talk about. Revealing the boy to the population is the easy part of this process, what we actually do with him once he is here is more problematical."

"Do with him?"

Richard regarded Francis in silence despite the question. His eyes had an intensity about them that made Francis slightly nervous. He reached over and put his cup on a small side table.

"Dickon, please, what are you thinking?" His friend gave a small, quiet laugh that made his shoulders rise. Steepling his fingers under his chin, elbows on the arms of his chair as he continued to keep his gaze firmly fixed on him.

"The boy needs a secure place, a home if you will. I do not feel inclined to let him stay with his mother now that I am fully aware of her duplicity in this matter. I would not be averse to her visiting him, wherever he may be settled in due course, but I cannot allow her to be his guardian. It is the place of safety which is causing me concern, and all options discussed so far - court, foreign marriage and such, do not appeal to me. I need to ensure that he is kept well, safe and happy somewhere in this country, with someone who I can trust completely." The pause was heavy with intimation. "Someone who has shown me nothing other than complete, if not always unquestioning, loyalty."

"Brilliant!" Lincoln whispered in awe from his resting place at the back of the room. Richard turned his head, a slight smile on his lips, acknowledging his nephew's approval. Francis sat up in surprise, his eyes widening in shock.

"Me?" He looked backwards and forwards between the two smiling men. "You want me to take him into my care?" Francis stopped speaking, confused. "How... my position... Dickon, you have me at a disadvantage here! What are you plotting?" At this Richard clapped his hands together and laughed out loud, throwing his head back.

"At last!" His tone was almost joyful. "I find myself involved in a plot concerning one of my brother's son's! You have to appreciate the irony, taking into account the past two years. Yes, I am plotting my dear friend, plotting to ensure a satisfactory end to a situation which almost destroyed my reign, and with your help, I can be successful." At this point Lincoln picked up the flagon and made his way over to Francis's side where he refilled his cup with a sardonic grin. He placed a comforting hand on his shoulder, and gave it a comradely squeeze as he moved away.

Francis felt his heart begin to accelerate, and he breathed deeply to try to restore its normal rhythm. For some reason, he was suspecting more in this than was immediately apparent, certain that Richard had some master stroke up his sleeve. And once he had, well, if Francis didn't approve, what next? He shook his head exasperated. These two were having far too much fun at his expense and for a moment he was glad Rob wasn't here.

"Cease, Uncle, put the man out of his misery!" chuckled Lincoln, gesturing towards Francis with his cup. "He's fit to have an apoplexy - besides, I am also curious as you sent me out on your errand. I have dutifully returned with my quarry, so now, the reward. What is it you want Francis to do?"

Richard stretched back in his chair, his face a mask of mingled satisfaction and pleasure. For some seconds he only looked at Francis from beneath dark brows drawn together in inquisition.

"What would you say, Francis, if I were to ask you to completely change your life for me?"

"I'm not rising to the bait, Dickon." Francis was smiling himself now, but more as a counter to the nervousness he was experiencing. A soft chuckle preceded his next words.

"Fair play. I have teased you enough so I will show you my hand. Francis Lovell, I intend to grant you the ownership of Middleham Castle and attendant estates. I would then wish you to install your household there to act for me as I see fit in affairs convening the west marches and Scotland, including a place on the Council of the North. I would then ask that you," for the first time he hesitated as if uncertain how Francis would respond, "make it your main residence and undertake the ward-ship of Richard Plantagenet, Lord Bastard. Under your tutelage and supervision, he will learn the skills of a knight and true loyalty to the realm. With the presence of your wife, he will have a ready made family who, I know, will nurture and regard him as if their very own." Francis leaned forward at that last sentence, his brow furrowed.

"My wife?" Richard nodded, but his eyes began to cast about the room, reluctant to meet his questioning gaze, yet he continued nevertheless.

"Anna will make a fine job of managing the household there. You would of course retain Minster Lovell and your other holdings. I would just ask that you make Middleham your main residence in order to fulfil all that I ask of you." Francis looked at Lincoln quickly - who looked somewhat dumbstruck himself.

"Dickon, did you just offer me the lands you inherited upon your marriage to Anne?"

"I did." His eyes finally returned from their journey around the chamber walls and now roved over his friends face, looking for some sign of his reaction. "Well, some of them. With the attached conditions of course."

"Dickon," Francis's voice cracked, "I don't know what to say."

"Yes?" offered Lincoln, by way of amused assistance, which was met only with silence. Richard locked eyes with his friend across the fireplace, and saw the mute appeal there. Without breaking his gaze he spoke to Lincoln quietly.

"John, would you make sure Margaret has everything she needs? You know how demanding she can be. "

Lincoln noticed the sudden strain between the two men at the fireside, and although disappointed, he took the hint and placed his cup down. He had heard rumours regarding Francis's relationship with his wife and he wondered if that was going to be a sticking point. At least he now knew what Richard had discussed with the others. This next conversation would either seal the matter or prevent its fruition. He didn't envy Francis if he had to sacrifice his marriage for his loyalty. Unless of course.....

"John?" Richard was now looking at him sternly as he had been lost in thoughts and not yet departed. He blushed slightly, and rising from his chair moved quickly out of the chamber.

"Thank you," said Francis quietly, breathing deeply to release some tension once the door had closed. Richard shrugged easily.

"John is still my heir, I need to include him as much as possible, but I sense there is much you now need to say to me which he has no part in, am I correct?" He needed no verbal affirmation, just the expression of relief that flooded his friends face was enough. "Will Anna not like the prospect of making her home at Middleham, do you think? Or is this hesitancy around another lady in question?"

"It is." Francis's cheek flexed as he intoned his answer through a clamped jaw, suddenly reluctant to make the admission. Richard sighed unhappily.

"This is difficult in truth, although I do know something of it. I am afraid she gives herself away, but, she is young." He broke off, the consternation in Francis's face was all too clear. "The lady is already married. I arranged it myself."

"Unhappily married," Francis countered miserably.

"A fate shared by many," Richard retorted, but not sharply, his tone tinged with amusement. "How are matters between you and Anna?" Francis closed his eyes and exhaled.

"She is happy at Minster Lovell. Prefers it there to court, although she will attend whenever I ask. I feel sure she would be both honoured and excited to move to Middleham, it being the former home to yourself and... Anne."

"But?"

"And I myself, of course," Francis continued heatedly, ignoring the interjection. "You do me great honour Dickon, and Middleham holds such happy memories for me. You overwhelm me with your generosity!"

"You are making me repeat myself Francis. But?"

Francis finally met Richard's gaze to find he was looking at him with all the sage amusement of an elder brother or father figure, considering there were few years between them this made him smile.

"Cecily."

"Ah!" he nodded, again like an elderly uncle. Francis had a sudden urge to thump him in the arm but resorted to setting his mouth in a grim line of frustration.

"Don't "ah" me like that, Dickon! You know full well what the problem is so don't pretend you have to drag it out of me. Cecily is unhappily married to Scrope, and by all accounts, he is not happy with her. If things were different..."

"If things were different, Scrope would give up his Woodville prize and you would divorce Anna and the two of you could make your home at Middleham." Richard was shaking his head sadly. "And in my dreams, Anne is currently at her embroidery frame in the solar and Ned is with John at the butts. I can almost convince myself of it if I try." His tone became wistful, his eyes misted over as if watching a scene played out inwardly, and he looked away, over towards the closed chamber door. "That she will walk in here at any moment, worrying at me that Ned is playing too hard..." The sentence dissolved into the silence between them, neither of them finding the right words to say for a while, leaving the crackling of the fire to fill the silence caused by their memories.

"I am sorry Dickon." Francis sighed quietly after a short while, and remonstrating himself on his selfishness. "Compared to that, my wishes seem trivial." Richard shook his head vehemently, but Francis could see his eyes were still brimming with pain.

"They are not. I was in love once too, remember, and I had George to fight, and had to make sacrifices to get what I wanted. There is a double edged sword here. Even if - if all the pieces fell into place, if I could make this happen for my dearest friend - there is another side to it. Cecily is young and this is her brother we are talking about. Her age I could overlook, because of the blood bond - she would no doubt care for her brother and want to keep him safe. But her affinity to her mother, that link to the Woodville affinity is a risk. I could not allow it Francis. Much as it grieves me to tell you this."

Richard surveyed him closely, recognising the inner struggle which he was having difficulty in masking, he had to force himself to press on, knowing despite himself the hurt he was about to cause.

"There is also the Fitzhugh connection. Divorce from Anna would be difficult I think. I need no more enemies Francis, as you are aware, and giving you a northern domain and a Woodville wife is precisely the sort of action that caused chaos within Edward's reign." Francis didn't trust himself to answer. Richard saw this and continued talking softly.

"You are long overdue a true reward for your services to me, and it pains me to see that this gives you such trouble. It is not a command Francis, think on it more of a request. If you are unhappy, if you feel you cannot fulfil this duty for me, I do understand. You were my first thought when I realised that I could only place the boy with someone who has my ultimate trust. Who would die rather than break that bond. I looked to the heavens for an answer to my problem and found your name writ large."

Francis closed his eyes, felt the hard chair back against his head. He knew the truth of it, he knew that Richard would deny him nothing if it were possible. How could he refuse such an honour, such an acknowledgement of his service from his king? It would not only bestow great power and responsibility on him, but give him the opportunity to keep the realm secure for his friend.

It was all Buckingham had coveted and more. Richard was raising him up to become the most powerful noble in the country without royal blood. What was more, he missed the north. The way the sun raced its shadows over the green rolling hills, the sound of the wind in the trees and as it snapped at the banners on the battlements. The clear crystal waters of the River Cover, sparkling like a jewelled ribbon as the sun rose over the hills. His vision of Middleham was replaced by Cecily's dark eyes, pleading, hurt....

He shook his head quickly to clear his thoughts. There was a deep longing in his gut and he knew what he had to do. There was really no decision to make, his duty was clear. And maybe, once he had done this, sometime in the future... he raised his eyes.

"When will the boy arrive?" Richard's lips curved in a cautious smile.

"A lot depends on you. However, I have discussed with my sister that we should have him secure by mid-February, he needs to be here before..." There was a brief pause then which revealed so much without words, "my marriage ceremony. That will also allow Bess to meet with him before she is also wed. I owe her that kindness. We need time to make the necessary arrangements on how we present him to court and the wider population. I am also planning to go north myself after Ephipany. I want to see how the plans for my chantry chapel in the Minster are progressing. So my plans now also involve a visit to York and Middleham. It would please me if you would meet me there." He did not ask if he was going to accept the plans laid out for him, but it was there, all too clearly in his eyes.

"Chantry chapel?" Francis queried, hoping to gain more time to think.

"Don't you remember? I commissioned the work some time ago and would like to see it complete. Originally, it was to provide a final resting place for Ned, but now Anne will join him there as well, in time. In fact, it will be my wish that both myself and Anne be buried there in a ceremony similar to that which we carried out in Fotheringhay for my father and Edmund." He laughed abruptly. "Jesu! I better get Kendall to get this all down! I can arrange the ceremony for Ned, but I would rather that Anne and I are interred together at the same time. Fitting, I think."

He looked down at his hands, downcast lids veiling any emotion that may be showing in his eyes. The jewel in the ring that Anne presented him with winked approval in the firelight.

"Morbid - I think." Francis snorted grudgingly, hoping to lift the mood a little.

"Our mortal remains all have to rest somewhere my friend," he responded in a matter of fact tone. "I would rather I had a say in that than not and I feel Anne would want it that way. The ceremony for our Ned was not as we had wanted."

The former joy had fled from his face. Francis was one of the few who knew Richard's son's current resting place. Such had been the fear of unrest and rebellion, that the grieving parents had taken an unprecedented decision, and laid him in a temporary, discreet tomb. Once again, Francis weighed his own troubles against those of his friend and found the scales tipped in his favour. He still had a living wife, he could yet have an heir - if he stayed at home long enough to try. Perhaps the north would provide that solution.

He would not be in daily attendance on the king, but he would be in regular contact, and would still have duties at court. It was a good place to bring up a young boy. And Richard loved Middleham. They could hunt, hawk, ride whenever he visited and he had a feeling that may be often. Without further deliberation, he picked up the cup at his elbow and raised it in Richard's directions.

"Middleham it is then!"

The smile which crossed Richards face was broader than he had seen for some years.

42. THE TOWER OF LONDON
January 1486

Bess stood alone on the embankment, watching the murky grey waters of the river lap against the walls below her and pulled the fur collar tightly around her neck, battling to keep the cold wind blowing across the Thames from penetrating any further through her clothing. The air was frosty, the lowering sky threatening to release a further burden of snow at any moment and she watched her own warm breath materialise in front of her as she waited impatiently. Her foot tapped restlessly against the ground, both in frustration and in an attempt to restore some feeling to her chilled toes. The sound of the crunching snow beneath her feet made her feel even colder.

From somewhere behind her, across the crisp, cruel air, bells chimed for Sext, sounding sharper and more musical than usual. He was late, damn him! Her lips curved slightly at the irony of her thought. Of course he was late - she was waiting for a Stanley! She pulled her chin further into the solace of the fur. Her mood had not been good for some time now, and the Christmas court had certainly done nothing to improve it. She was now cursing herself inwardly for agreeing to meet with a man she had no reason to trust or even wish to be associated with.

Back when they were all closeted in Westminster sanctuary, her own mother had believed that by courting the Stanleys, she would regain her former status and power and have everything returned to her. She had forgotten one vital fact, and that was that the Stanleys looked out only for themselves. If they could have gained any profit from her brother Edward being on the throne, he would be there now and her life would be taking a different path.

They had been certain that Stanley was intent on turning against Richard in the middle of the battle, but he had surprised them all, unusual in one such as he. What exactly had made him turn against his own wife's son was a mystery, but one which had flooded her body with relief. Her limbs shivered involuntarily, and with more than the cold. Now she had seen Tudor, she knew there is no way she would have been happy wed to such a man.

Admittedly, Manuel was also not her choice, but he was handsome, polite and charming, an ideal match - if she could cast aside her feelings for Richard. She gave a quick glance up the river, watching random flakes of snow begin to speckle the wind as she stepped back into the shelter of an archway.

Her thoughts wandered back to the recent festivities. She had found the whole season thoroughly depressing, attending each meal and entertainment with a heavy heart, not even taking any pleasure in dressing for the occasion. All the usual gaiety and entertainment had been there to see and with even more splendour due to the presence of Duchess Margaret and her small contingent.

There had been lavish banquets, the tables groaning with the burden of the food served, rich and fantastic dishes laid out on blindingly white cloths trimmed with greenery. The thrum of the tabor, accompanied by rebec and flute had been a constant backdrop to the feasting and had echoed throughout every hall and chamber of the palace. Parti-coloured fools and gaudily dressed mummers plied their art every day to wildly appreciative audiences. Each marchpane subtlety served was bigger and more intricate than the last, as the bakers in the kitchen strove to outdo each other for their king's pleasure, hoping to be rewarded for their efforts.

There had been a touching tribute to Queen Anne, played out before the covered dais where Richard sat with his sister at his side in place of his wife. A slim young girl attired in gold gauze, had depicted the dead queen as Arthur's Guenivere. Bess had been close enough at that point to see the torches lining the brightly lit hall betray him by reflecting the film of tears in his eyes.

Moved beyond words, she had taken a hesitant step forward. She had almost been rash enough to move closer to the dais to comfort him, longing to show him how she understood his pain. Margaret, seated at his side, had turned to offer her brother a kind smile and lay a comforting hand over his, and his face had turned to her instead, in grateful thanks. Bess had halted at that act of sibling kindness and remained still, watching them, her heart heavy with longing. As she had paused there, out of the corner of her eye, she had seen Francis draw Cecily quietly out of the hall, and Bess had turned away, her isolation threatening to engulf her.

That evening had been a form of torture for her; too proud to approach the dais and beg for leave to retire, yet too miserable to join in any of the dancing or revelry, despite young John's many repeated attempts. She had feigned a headache, and was grateful when the king rose and left the hall and she could finally retire to the cool darkness of her chamber. Slipping under the coverlets that night, her loneliness had finally overwhelmed her, and she had sobbed, muffling the sounds of her distress with her pillow, until her chest and throat were raw.

As they reached Ephipany, the final play performed in the hall was a re-enactment of the battle of Redemore, depicting the king on a huge silver boar defeating and slaying the dragon, to huge cheers and applause from the assembled guests. Richard himself had stood up and clapped in genuine appreciation, before stepping down from the dais to reward the beaming Master of Revels with an additional purse of coin. As the dragon lay on the tiled floor, prostrate in defeat and groaning dramatically, Bess's only wish had been that Margaret Stanley had been let out of her Tower lodgings to see her son's defeat so thunderously accepted by a merry court.

That evening, as had been the pattern of the previous days, the king himself had been constantly surrounded by his family. Duchess Cecily, Kathryn and her husband William, Lincoln - even his mother, had attended court to be reunited with her sister. Bess had watched them all smiling, exchanging gifts, talking animatedly, and she remained on the outskirts of his life, as if watching through a window outside in the cold, the vision distorted by the glass of tears in her eyes.

Her own mother had remained firmly rooted at Grafton, even though Richard had invited her to attend court, which was somewhat generous on his part, she thought at the time, considering they had never seen eye to eye on anything. Even the release from sanctuary and the restitution of some of her wealth, had not improved her demeanour. That polite refusal had puzzled Bess as she had never known her mother turn down an opportunity to flaunt herself at court, especially as the Burgundians had been in attendance. They were related after all, which is why Margaret had ended up married to Charles, her late husband, in the first place.

Bess had delivered the invitation herself, and had an uneasy feeling that it was the Duchess of Burgundy's very presence that had been the reason for her mothers change of heart. She was as certain as she could be that her mother had been relishing the thought of a visit to Westminster since the end of summer, had even been planning the gowns she would wear, so her sudden reversal was a surprise, and one that had left her bemused.

Elizabeth had flatly refused to discuss the matter, just indicating that she was disinclined to travel in the cold weather as she was beginning to feel a stiffness in her joints which pained her at times. Watching her move gracefully around the rooms at Grafton, with all the elegance she had shown as queen, Bess found this difficult to believe, but she did not gainsay her, and let her keep her reasons to herself. She was even wishing she had stayed with her at the manor house now, but the feeling was fleeting.

Even with the sensation she had of total detachment from everyone, she could not stay away. She was a singular, fluttering moth, attracted to the brightly burning flame that was the presence of Richard at the centre of his glittering court, and even with the danger that the attraction could cause her real pain, she could no more turn away from him than she could deny breath from her body.

Some of her other younger sisters had been there. Cecily had been forced to spend time in the company of her husband, and with Francis in almost constant attendance on his wife, neither of them appeared to have been enjoying the festivities very much at all. The only time Cecily became animated was when she was sneaking off to a secret assignation, after letting her husband think she was spending time with her family. She would return just after Compline, breathless, glowing and full of secrets, which just infuriated Bess even more.

How she envied her sister those exciting, secret assignations; the thrill of watching the man she loved across the hall and wondering if he would get the opportunity to share a brief kiss or caress in some shadowy corner during the evening.

She imagined what it would be like if she had been able to think such of Richard and she had lain in her bed night after night, tossing restlessly. In her dreams she imagined Richard sending for her after supper, receiving his short , urgently penned note, making a hurried walk through the darkened corridors - cloaked in secrecy. Her visions were so clear, they were as real. She saw herself reaching his chamber, Lovell's discreet exit, smiling, the heat of the room as she entered from the cold outside, the warmth of his embrace as he stood to greet her, his hands unfastening her cloak, his dark eyes intense with passion, his body...

Those nights ended with her pounding her pillows in frustration, the dreams being almost as much a torture as the reality of her situation. Her own marriage was fast approaching, being set for March and try as she might, she could not think of any way of avoiding her fate. Until now.

It had happened at that last banquet. As Bess had been watching the travelling players retrieve the debris of their battle scene, she had become aware of someone standing slightly too close to her for comfort. She turned, to find Thomas Stanley at her side, also surveying the scene before the dais. The young boy who was swathed in red as Henry Tudor's dragon had hit his head as he fell to his death and was sitting dazed and bemused amid the carnage strewn around him. Feeling sorry for him, she had been considering if she should move forward and assist him, when Stanley moved a step closer to her.

"It lacks something in the telling, don't you think?" His urbane voice had whispered into her ear. Bess had cast a downward smile as she recalled the descending angel figure who had handed the king his crown, as God's approval of his victory.

"Oh I don't know" she had replied, raising her eyes to the dais where Richard sat smiling at some tale Lincoln had been re-telling, his arms animatedly embellishing his story to Richard's obvious amusement. "I wasn't there, but God was obviously with the king from the very start - not just at the turn of the tide."

She had been rewarded by the sight of two flags of colour flying across his cheeks, reminded of his late entry into the battle to the king's cause. That was the only flaw she could see in his smoothly polished surface, the man who played both sides of the board at once, giving nothing away.

"And now he has a new marriage to look forward to, which will further endow his reign and with the blessing God has undoubtedly bestowed on him, produce a healthy son and heir with the beauteous Joanna," Stanley said silkily, his eyes fixed on the figure on the dais. Now he had the advantage as it was her turn to flush pink. His smile was filled with barely concealed malice but she had smiled back at him, if somewhat tightly.

"It will be a joyous time for England, my Lord. The resurgence of the Yorkist dynasty. My uncle Richard is still a young man, and with the princess could father many children."

How she had managed to keep her voice steady whilst speaking words which ripped her heart apart anew was a mystery to her. She also kept her attention fixed on Richard, watching his eyes, his hands, noting that he seemed much more relaxed and finding it difficult to believe that it was the thought of the impending marriage that had cheered his spirits. Something significant had changed, and it only made her desire him more, something she had not considered possible. Turning away, she faced the man at her side who was also still looking at the king, but with an expression akin to distaste.

"Indeed," he had agreed thoughtfully, nodding his head at her litany of hope, "but in my experience, it is always a good strategy to be cognisant of all possible outcomes - not just the most obvious ." Bess had glowered at him, her fair brows meeting together in frustration, but he caught the quizzical glint in her eye that she had been unable to hide. Cupping her elbow gently, he led her into a deep window embrasure away from the main revels, and out of sight of hungry, inquisitive eyes.

"To illustrate my point, I offer you an example. If I had said to you - even five years hence, that your own dynasty would be at an end and the Duke of Gloucester king of the realm instead of your father, you would not have believed me. Your mother would have laughed outright in my face. King Edward - tall, strong, golden. His male heirs, two of them, thriving well." He licked his lips in a repulsively lizard like gesture and she had suppressed a shudder. "Who ever would have dreamed that each of them would meet their end, and your uncle, the last Son of York, would be sitting so comfortably on the throne of England?"

Bess had tried to keep her face blank to hide the furious workings of her mind. What he was saying was undoubtedly true. No-one could have anticipated the loss of the king and two male heirs. Or indeed, the loss of Richard's own wife and son. She had inclined her head in acknowledgement.

"I think my uncle himself would agree - he has lost brother, nephews, son and wife."

"And gained a throne," Stanley whispered back, his lips almost brushing her ear. She was unable to repress a shiver that time.

"A poor bargain - and one I am certain he would wish he had never had to make."

At that, Stanley had stepped back slightly and barked a sharp laugh.

"Had to make? Chose to make, surely! No one forced the crown down onto his head, my dear I can assure you. Despite any tale you may have heard to the contrary." Infuriated beyond measure, Bess had then summoned all of the imperious Woodville veneer she could muster.

"Really? You surprise me my Lord. You were closely involved in events as I recall, and in particular were present at the Council Meeting at The White Tower? In fact," she paused, letting her lips form a smile, "yes, I believe you spent time in the Tower itself. Suspected treason, wasn't it? " Bess had taken great pleasure from the sight of a sudden tightening of his features. "I may have been in sanctuary my Lord, but I was made very much aware of everything that occurred outside of its confining walls. I could give you chapter and verse on the conversations I heard over those interminable months. Conversations, I may add, which may still turn the king to imprison those implicated should I ever choose to reveal what I heard. So do not," she had paused again, her eyes narrowing, her tone emphasising her words, unaware that she sounded now much more akin to her father than she knew, "do not, try to pretend to me that my uncle had a free hand in his fate. He is lucky not to be cold in the ground himself after - how many plots? It was be king or be killed as I recall."

Stanley had opened his mouth to reply, his jaw working in preparation, but she took a step towards him, closing the space he had created, her eyes dark with anger.

"And yes, I count my own mother amongst those who sealed his fate, do not think I do not understand that." To her astonishment, Stanleys face had creased into the broadest of grins and he had raised a gnarled hand to stroke his beard as he looked on her in undisguised admiration.

"My, my, Henry Tudor would have been well outmatched I feel. My Lady wife, for one, has certainly underestimated your abilities. Perhaps it is as well that you will marry the Portuguese Princeling." His grin had increased as he watched her face register displeasure. "Unless, of course, I can tempt you also to see the other side of the board?"

"What are you talking about?" She had snapped back at him irritably, all composure fled at one mention of her unwanted forthcoming marriage. Stanley spread his hands then in innocent supplication at her words.

"Only that there are usually other options available to win any game. Should you be willing to spare the time to explore them." By this time, Bess was annoyed and had become very weary of his games, the evening had been long and as tortuous as any of its forebears.

"You talk in riddles my lord. It is tiresome, please speak plainly."

She had then cast her glance back towards the centre of the room and saw Richard raise her sister Cecily's hand to his lips as they finished a courtly dance. Lovell watched from the sidelines, his mousy wife at his side. She had watched Richard turn and walk away from the dance, and for a moment he was alone. Believing himself to be unobserved, his eyes had swept the room searchingly. He was seeking someone. Someone he could not find and his brows formed a dark line of concern under the glimmering circlet of his crown.

Bess's heart had begun to beat louder in her chest. He is looking for me - she had realised. Her throat went dry and she had tried hard to swallow. Everyone else was still in the room, he had to be looking for her. There was a strange buzzing sound in her head. Stanley's breath was warm in her ear.

"Meet me at the Tower embankment, two days hence. We will talk on how to change the play of the board, should you wish to do so." Turning away on a bow, he had departed swiftly, leaving her alone in the embrasure.

As she had slowly moved back out of the shadows, Bess fixed her eyes on her uncle who was now seated, a cup in his hand, listening, straight-faced, to Rob Percy, who leant casually on the side of the throne with an easy familiarity. Bess had closed her eyes and taken a deep breath, silently willing him to notice her. Her teeth nipped the inside of her bottom lip and she had opened her eyes only to find her wish granted. To find her own eyes directly connecting with his intense stare.

Rob was still talking, but she knew that at that point Richard was no longer listening. He was looking at her, not smiling, not frowning, just fixing her with his contemplative gaze and what she saw there had kept her rooted to the spot.

43. TOWER OF LONDON
January 1486

Now as she waited past the appointed hour, the stupidity of her actions were beginning to dawn and she started to wonder what on earth she was doing here, and considered going back to the Palace.

As if summoned by these wavering thoughts, she saw Stanley's barge round the bend of the river and steer purposefully towards the steps. With increasing frustration she watched its progress, quickly looking around to make sure no-one was observing her, wondering what King Edward's daughter was doing loitering around outside the Tower like some kitchen scullion. After what seemed like an eternity the barge drew up to the steps, and Stanley, also heavily cloaked and furred against the elements, leapt up the stairs, taking them two at a time, surprisingly light-footed for his build.

As he reached the top, Bess stood back a pace or two, only to be surprised by his sudden action as he caught her immediately by the arm, and looking cautiously up and down the embankment, he drew her under the arched gate and into the Tower grounds. Wordlessly, a dark figure emerged from the shadows. Bess squinted, still uncomfortable at the pressure on her arm, and could make out one of the Tower guards wearing the king's livery. He was tall, but his face was in shadow as Stanley turned towards him, by necessity now releasing her from his guiding grip. This action also had the effect of obscuring Bess from getting a clear look at the man, which she took to be deliberate, and which now increased her general unease to something more specific and worrying.

What on earth had she got herself into?

Casting her eyes about frantically, she tried to think of how she could extricate herself from the situation she had so willingly sleepwalked towards, but the only way back was to push past the collaborating figures before her, so she settled for just wrapping her arms tightly around her body. Stanley was talking to the guard quietly, even straining her ears as hard as she could did not help her determine what was said, but what was clear was the chink of coin, exchanged before Stanley turned quickly back to face her.

Once again, and without word or explanation, he took her arm and drew her into the room at the side of the gate. By this time too frightened to speak, her silence was mirrored by her escort as he hurried her up a flight of stone stairs and along a dimly lit corridor, eventually coming to a halt before an oaken door. Things had happened so quickly that her eyes had not even had time to adjust to the gloom surrounding them. Bess could hear hushed voices at the other end of the corridor, they echoed off the old stone walls, but she was unable to make out from whom they came.

Even with that lack of perception, her heart was firmly lodged in her mouth for more than one reason. In a few swift steps they appeared to have penetrated the fortified walls of the Tower with as much ease as walking from one chamber to another at Grafton. Admittedly it had been rushed, and Stanley was obviously concerned that they may be discovered, but the sheer ease in which they had got this far left her astounded. She was not familiar with this area of the Tower and could only assume they were still on the very outskirts of the walls, and therefore not about to commit any great act for which she may have to confess later.

A fact that was somewhat disabused as Stanley produced a key from his doublet, and swiftly inserted it into the lock in the door before them. Glancing quickly to his left, he swung open the door and pushed Bess inside unceremoniously, his hand placed, with brazen familiarity, in the small of her back. She was about to protest indignantly as she stumbled headlong into the inner chamber, when the sight that greeted her eyes choked any words of reproach way back down into her throat.

This room was well lit with a large window and supplemented by the light of many wall sconces. A large bed canopied with dark damask curtaining sat back against the far wall, the light from the window picking out the fine embroidery on the rich fabrics. A pre-dieu, furnished with a rich velvet cushion, stood in the corner before a burning candle and a picture of the Virgin Mary, its gold leaf embellishment illuminated in the gently dancing flame.

There, seated in front of her at a small table stacked neatly with paper rolls and books, was a diminutive female figure dressed in black. The bowed head raised at the sound of her ungainly entrance and Margaret Stanley looked up, swathed in a blindingly white wimple. As her dark, fathomless gaze fell on her face, Bess gave an involuntary shudder, which she knew would not go unnoticed. Above the frantic beating of her heart, she heard the door close behind her followed by the finality of the key turning in the lock and her heart plummeted into her stomach.

At that sound, Bess whipped her head round to find Stanley, his features illuminated now and wreathed in a satisfied smile as he stood, somewhat triumphantly, with his back to the door. Bess swallowed hard, licking her lips anxiously, and as she did, her fear began to dissipate to be replaced by a rising tide of anger. She had been duped, she was certain of that, and was now unable to extract herself from a situation that was completely inexcusable in anyone's eyes.

The fury she felt removed any thoughts she had of flight. Not that she could have escaped anyway, it being obvious that now they had trapped their prize, they fully intended to keep her here until they had played their game. At the realisation that they could not keep her there long for fear of discovery, her pulse began to slow and her thoughts clear. She took a deep steadying breath, her mind racing, consciously aware that now, more than ever, she needed to keep her composure and be careful, not make one slip or false step. Her own stupidity had brought her to this place and if her uncle had any inkling of what was happening here... her mind stopped its continual whirl.

But what was happening?

Her natural curiosity calmed her racing heart even further, even though she remained cautious. Margaret had turned slightly in her chair, her hand poised, holding the quill pen with which she had been writing something on a parchment before her. She seemed in no hurry to speak herself, to offer either excuse of question. Bess stuck her chin out in defiance, and broke the silence.

"Lady Stanley," she announced, allowing a measure of sarcasm to colour her tone. "This is an unexpected - turn of events."

Margaret remained seated but placed her pen on the table with deliberate care. Turning further in her chair, she gave her full attention to the young girl standing before her, eyes travelling up and down the young girl's form in the manner of a merchant assessing his wares. Bess's skin began to crawl, hairs prickling at the back of her neck despite the warmth of the fur collar.

"Have you given yourself to him yet?"

The sharp but quiet voice cut the air in the room, underlining the distaste Bess could see blazing from the eyes below the creased brow. The question hit her like a blow to the body and Bess stifled a gasp of breath, both at the surprise and the sheer audacity of the question. Her cheeks burned, despite her best attempts to keep her temper, and she swallowed hard so that she could speak without faltering.

"That is a strange greeting, my Lady, but I will allow it as you have been spending much of your time deprived of civilised company." She folded her gloved hands before her, to disguise any trembling in them and to hopefully appear confidently relaxed. As if by thinking it, she felt her body loosen significantly, her tension melting away. Having escaped marriage to this woman's son, who himself currently resided somewhere close by, she was not about to be intimidated and made to feel like some truculent child. Margaret was a prisoner of the king, Bess was about to marry a prince. A small pang pierced her heart through her as the thought hit home, along with the fact that she had so easily brought it to mind as a weapon to wield in this battle. It spoke of an acceptance that she was not willing to admit to.

Margaret rose slowly, her skirts rustling in the quiet as she walked over to stand before Bess, who towered over the much smaller woman. Instead of giving her a sense of power, her height only served to make her feel large and gawky in comparison, and she had to look down to meet Margaret's shrewdly indeterminate eyes. They were scheming something, the pair of them, and she wondered how her uncle would react when he not only found out about what they were up to, but also how easily his fortress could be invaded. He was a man who placed such a high price on loyalty, what would be the punishment for so blatant a betrayal? Particularly now?

There was something else about that which bothered her greatly, only it would not present itself whilst this infuriating woman stood before her like some accusatory persecutor. Margaret tipped up her chin in an effort to make up a portion of the difference in height.

"I will ask you again, as this meeting will go no further unless you can give me a fair and honest answer, girl, and be sure God will know the truth of it should you try to lie. Have you, or have you not, given yourself to him? To the king. To your murdering, usurping uncle?" Her voice was drenched with disgust, each word formed with venom.

Across the small silence between them, Bess appeared to consider the question for a time. Slowly, she drew her shoulders up, making herself even taller against the slight figure in black.

"You do know I am betrothed to a prince of Portugal, a prince of royal blood?" A marriage she didn't want she reflected inwardly, but now grateful for the ability to use the bare fact itself as a defence against this deviously scheming woman. To flaunt before her a match so much more suitable than her cowardly dullard of a son. She smiled to herself at the comparison. "A match more fitting for the daughter of an anointed king than that of a Welsh pretender." The rejoinder was quick, but not unexpected.

"A bastard daughter." Margaret snapped, her lips curling into a sneer.

"A bastard you thought a fit enough match for your son, no less." Bess countered quickly, impressed somewhat by her own courage, but fueled by the indignation that was once again threatening to rise inside her. How dare this woman talk to her in this way? Had her incarceration, no matter how comfortable, deranged her? She was no longer a mere pawn to be dangled in front of the Tudor succession, she was still a royal princess, still close to the king and she was somewhat independent, as far as she could be. Until March.

She noticed Margaret's hand flex and felt sure that in different circumstances she would have felt the sting of her palm against her cheek. Lady Stanley was a woman used to getting her own way, and this period of captivity, particularly at Richard's hands, would be festering inside her, eating her up, consuming her along with the knowledge that her own son suffered the same fate. Bess felt a surge of confidence return and continued to speak, enunciating each work carefully.

"You should have a care on how you speak of my uncle the king. He will also not take kindly to hearing of any insult given to me at your hands. He has taken great pains to allow me to live the life my father intended for me. This..." she stopped speaking and emphasised her words by looking around the room disparagingly, "assignation may make him remember you are still here, for I feel he may have forgotten you. Who knows what action he will take if I have to recount this meeting to him?" Margaret laughed sharply then, her head thrown back revealing small sharp teeth, like those of a fox, Bess thought idly. Her reply had an annoying arrogance to it.

"Oh I assure you he has not forgotten me, far from it. I am relying on it in fact. If he had any intention of taking drastic action against either myself or my son, he would have done so by now. The man is plagued by an obsession to restore his reputation which will lead him down a path as destructive as the one he took to carry out his brother's wishes. He is a pious man, your uncle, when he chooses to be, and so my head is safe I can assure you of that."

Struggling not to react, Bess fumed inwardly at the woman's insufferable self confidence, made more unbearable by the fact that there was a lot of truth in what she said. She was well aware that Richard would never give the order to strike this irritating head from its shoulders, he would never take such an action against a woman. The fact that he had made such short work of Hastings, along with her own uncle and half-brother was only remarkable in the fact that he had not shown any indication of such ruthless tendencies whilst ruling the north.

Lady Anne had tried to explain it to her last year, trying valiantly to justify the execution of her own kin once Bess became a lady of her chamber so that no bad blood flowed between them. How the one thing that could make Richard's blood run cold was betrayal of trust.   All throughout his life, he had strived to cleave to the standards of chivalry and honour, passed down from his father, qualities honed during the wars of the last fifty years. Richard expected and demanded loyalty - and when he was let down - he could be intractable.

"That may be so," she countered coolly, desperate to keep Margaret from goading her into blurting out any rash declarations, "but your son is a different matter is he not?   He is a traitor, and there is only one end for such, that being execution.   The block... or worse."   The hush in the room was noticeable only for the slight cough which Stanley gave, still playing the sentinel by the chamber door.

Margaret's smile remained fixed in place, although Bess thought she saw a flicker of anger in the reptilian eyes.   The two of them had never been friendly, despite several meetings before King Edward's death and during the interminable days in sanctuary.   The relationship between Margaret and Bess's mother could only ever have been described as a matter of convenience, and even that had its flaws.   Elizabeth wanted her son restored to the throne. Margaret wanted her son on it despite that, and their one common cause had been their hatred of current occupant. Richard.

Bess knew that they must need her for something, and that it could only be for some futile wish for the resurgence of the Tudor threat to the throne. But how?   The man's army had been defeated. He was a prisoner - yet - he was still alive.   As she was thinking, Margaret began to speak again, her attention still firmly fixed on Bess's face.   Searching for a reaction, a weakness, a chink in the armour she was cloaking herself with to get through this afternoon.

"Your king is weak, he has always been weak, and this weakness will lead to his undoing, as will his obsession to be seen innocent of the crimes lauded against him. We do not have much time now and this idle exchange of insults will further us nothing. I am well aware of your fascination with your uncle, so before we talk further I need to know if you have given yourself to him. For if you have, we can end this meeting now and be done with each other."

Bess half turned, checking to see if Stanley still blocked the door, which he did, but was leaning back, examining his fingernails absently, as if the scene being played had nothing at all to do with him. But she knew the old fox's ears would be keenly absorbing every word, this meeting would have been discussed, rehearsed, she was certain.

"As far as I am concerned, this meeting can end now. I have nothing to say to you and find your comments insulting if not verging on treason and putting each one of us in peril." Her voice had a confidence she did not feel as she looked about uncertainly. How foolish had she been agreeing to meet Stanley today. Richard would be furious if he found out, and after the way he had looked at her that night...

"I am sorry!" A falsely apologetic tone rang out from behind her, as Stanley raised eyes which were crinkled in amusement. "I was under the impression that you did not wish to marry Manuel of Portugal. I appear to have been mistaken." A slight pause made Bess turn back in Margaret's direction. Her eyes appeared narrower and darker.

"Stanley, our business is done." As if he was an obedient servant awaiting command from his master, Lord Stanley sighed and finally heaved his back away from the door.

"Margaret," he sighed placatingly, "you are getting this all wrong. You have insulted the girl, our royal princess. Just wait a moment. Let her think on things a little."

Bess looked from one to the other of them in frustration, feeling somewhat like a trapped animal in a snare of her own making, which doubled her fear and anxiety. Stanley continued, stroking his beard thoughtfully, turning his mild brown gaze in her direction.

"I know you do not favour the Portuguese match Richard has arranged, as much as I suspect he does not favour his own. Alliances, affinities, marriages of convenience, they are by nature only made to secure power or wealth. There is no "love" there and you waste your energies by fighting against the tide. You may wish and dream for more, but I can assure you, there is greater satisfaction to be had out of a match based on mutual agreement, rather than fleeting passion. The former has a much longer lifespan. Passion dies, it withers on the vine of wedlock and age. And what then? What is left?"

Bess now berated herself inwardly for showing her emotions so publicly during the Portuguese visit for all to see. How could she have been so stupid! Her head felt light and there was a strange sensation in her chest. Although Stanley was not present during the royal visit, he would have had ears and eyes at court. She thought she had been so careful but she only had to think about it. Her sister knew, Lovell knew, Richard knew. Her heart sank at the thought of him. What was she doing here?

"There are other options." Stanley was saying through the sound of her own thoughts. She looked up, too suddenly to veil her thoughts and she saw his eyes flicker.

"Options? Other options than marriage?" she said quietly, in her mind seeing only Richard's face, seeing Richard's face at the Epiphany feast.

"An eventual marriage certainly!" Margaret's voice broke into her reverie, her eyes shooting a warning to her husband that Bess did not catch, "but not yet. But before we can discuss any of that, we need to ascertain two things. The first, whether you have already surrendered to your incestuous passion, the second depends on your answer to the first." Bess's face flushed hotly, but she did not say a word. Margaret snorted in derision and swirled around to face her husband whom she addressed with all the scorn she could muster.

"Get her out of my sight! It is obvious she has become a Woodville whore! Like mother, like daughter and in heaven's eyes like the Father as well. I am surprised you had not seen it yourself,

410

which would have eliminated the need for this waste of hours. Only I constantly forget that you are not as favoured in Richard's court as you once were!" Stanley was goaded into replying, but his voice remained calm and urbanely low.

"A situation I am working hard to address."

"Not fast enough, not by far!" his wife spat disagreeably.

Bess's heart was pounding in her ears, blood rushing hotly to her face despite all her efforts, Margaret's parting shot had hit true and all her hard won restraint had broken at the mention of her father.

"I am not! I am not a whore! I am a king's daughter, and you disgrace me Madam!"

The two Stanley's - Lady and Lord, looked at each other across the chamber with slowly growing smiles. Stanley moved away from his post at the door, and went over to the fireplace, leaning against the mantel. Margaret, clasped her hands together in a satisfactory gesture and walked back to her chair, where, turning, she sat down with an air of deliberation and purpose

"Finally! Now we can begin."

44. THE PALACE OF WESTMINSTER
January 1486

There was the usual general commotion filling the courtyard which preceded any period of travel by the king. As well as his chosen companions for the journey, there was to be the usual procession of baggage trains, weaponry and supplies, accompanied by the melee of servants, squires and scribes who made up the whole royal retinue. Bess had been pleased to leave the noise behind and disappear into the quiet calmness of the chapel just off the royal apartments. Richard was travelling north and Bess was screaming inwardly because of the timing.

It had been three days since her meeting with the Stanleys and she was both shocked and disturbed by what she had been confronted with. Their sheer audacity took the very breath from her body, and left her wracked with confusion and guilt. She had spent the last few nights tossing and turning in between bouts of restless sleep as her mind refused to give her peace.

Any sleep she did get was filled with vivid and nightmarish dreams involving Henry Tudor. Henry Tudor standing at the bottom of her marriage bed. Henry Tudor, locking her in a tall, dark tower. Henry Tudor, grinning, with blood on his hands. Richards blood. Her fervent wish was that she had never seen the man in the flesh as his thin, mean face was now haunting her in a way that she found terrifying. She had little appetite, and as time passed, needed even less sleep. Even Cecily had commented on the change in her, but then she had her own problems to deal with.

What was she to do?

As she knelt at her devotions, Bess reflected to her shame that it was the king's progress she was thinking of and not her own mortal soul. She had only just found out today that Richard was leaving for the north, having enquired of his squire who she saw in the courtyard below. This was confirmed by John who she had come across in the chapel, fully attired for travelling, doublet, heavy, furred cloak and high boots, his sword securely fastened onto his belt, his hands gloved.

Bess had a soft spot in her heart for John, and she believed that he also felt the same for her. It wasn't love, just a true fondness, but one she felt could have blossomed in the fullness of time if it had been nurtured, especially when she considered how like his father he was in appearance. The suggestion she had made to Richard regarding John had been completely serious, and for her a much better proposition than the Portuguese match. In fact, if she was to be truly honest with herself, she would rather have married John anyway, even if Richard declined to naturalise him and he remained a bastard. They were equal, they could grow to love each other and they could remain at court. Close to the king, where else would his son be? Crossing herself quickly, she rose and stood for a moment in thought, before turning on her heel and leaving the chapel to its ethereal silence.

To her surprise, John was waiting for her by the entrance, leaning casually against the wall, sliding his sword in and out of its gilded sheath absently. He looked up from beneath his shock of dark hair as she halted beside him and smiled.

"So, you're leaving today." It was a statement of fact rather than a question and she was slightly surprised to see the young boy's face tinge with pink. He nodded in agreement, but seemed troubled as if he had something on his mind. "John?" it was a gentle nudge, and she lowered her head to try to catch his eyes which were studiously avoiding her face. His lips twisted in an awkward half smile.

"I just wanted to say… I… my father the king is taking me north with him and I think I may not be back for some time." He was still fiddling anxiously with the hilt of his sword. "I just wondered if you would be gone by the time I get back, because if you are… will be…"

Bess raised her head up and moved forwards without answering immediately, pulling on her gloves against the chill. John fell into step alongside her without a word. She stole a quick glance at his profile before beginning to speak, taking in the confusion. The mixture of excitement at the prospect of the journey with his father, and sadness... but at what?"

"I don't know John,'" she replied, trying to be as casual as possible. " I hope I will still be here. The wedding is set for March. Has the king not said when he will be returning?"

"Not until after the month end, and then I believe I may be staying behind. He has expressed a wish that I become more involved in the council. It could be some time..." his words trailed off again and they walked some steps in silence, all the time the noise in the bailey growing louder.

"Kathryn is going back to Raglan Castle, she will have her child there," he said quietly. "Ned has to stay here, but he will have Margaret with him, you and Cecily are staying here." His words faded into a miserable silence but his head jerked up suddenly, his eyes anxious. "Please don't misunderstand me! I am honoured to be accompanying my father north, but, well, we are all moving away and who knows when we will see each other again? We have been so happy here, the past few months."

They had reached the entrance to the courtyard now and the din was almost deafening. Horses stamped on the the ground impatiently as they were saddled and caparisoned, metallic clangs rang across the yard as the men-at-arms organised their weaponry, wagons were piled high with supplies and clothing, everything to meet a king's needs and more. Richard's hounds paced up and down beside the horses, patiently, waiting to be gone.

Out of the corner of her eye, Bess spotted Francis walking amongst the chaotic scene, pointing, talking to men and issuing orders. He was attired in his usual day clothes, a sure sign he was not travelling with the king's party.

"Bess?"

She turned her face back towards John and bestowed on him her most radiant smile, making her appeared much more assured than she felt.

"Don't fret so John. We will see each other again soon, I will make sure of it. I am sure your father, the king, will not make me leave without a proper goodbye to those I hold dear." She was rewarded, and amused, by the hot red flush that now swept across his features, which she spotted even though he dipped his head quickly to try and hide it. Overcome by a wave of emotion, Bess moved forwards and enveloped the boy in her embrace, and felt his arms return the gesture. She pressed her lips against the silky dark hair covering his ears and whispered.

"Dearest John. May God keep you safe in his care until we see each other again." She stepped back and held him at arms length, surveying a face which was both beaming and embarrassed at the same time. "Soon!" she finished, squeezing his arms.

Impulsively, and before she could react, John stepped forward again and gave her a further embrace, but this time they were both laughing together and Bess hoped that he could not see her holding back the tears that threatened to fall. They parted again, and Bess looked away from his face and over his shoulder, only for her eyes to be filled by the silently regarding figure of her uncle, the King, fully cloaked for his journey, one gauntleted hand resting on the hilt of his sword.

Now it was Bess's turn to feel the heat of her blood suffuse her face. John stiffened at her sudden reaction and twisted round himself.

"Father!" John's voice was joyful, and Richard turned his attention to his son, who was moving into the courtyard towards him in greeting whilst Bess stayed rooted to the spot. Richard's expression changed as John bowed before him. "Are we ready to go?"

"Not yet," he replied somewhat gravely. "Go find Kathryn and Will, would you? Ask them to meet me in the solar before we leave. Also gather up your cousin on the way, if you can." John grinned amiably at the acknowledgement that Ned was not always the easiest of the children to track down. "I wish to see everyone before we leave."

John nodded, bowed again, and ran off in the direction of the stables, his green cloak billowing out behind him in the breeze.

Bess watched him go and for some unexplained reason felt a sharp pang of regret. Although her outburst last year when she had suggested that she could be his bride had been borne of desperation, she had found herself paying more and more attention to him and this had left her feeling slightly bereft at the thought of his absence if Richard commanded that he stay in the north.

She shook herself mentally - what was she thinking? She would be permanently separated from him when she married Manuel. Richard had also watched his son depart and Bess found that they both turned back to look at each other at exactly the same moment.

She tried not to let him notice how thoroughly she was examining him, as if to burn his memory into her mind like a brand. He looked every inch the king as he stood before her, his attire of deepest burgundy topped by a long cloak of midnight blue, one side of which was tossed casually over his shoulder leaving a glimpse of his belt, supporting a fine dagger with a jewelled hilt. She stood, frozen in time, unable to stop looking at every part of him from the caps of his soft spanish leather boots, to the dark crown of his hair, as if she feared she would never see him again. A lump rose in her throat as he broke away from the courtyard and began to walk towards her.

Richard stopped within inches of her and Bess was pleased that she had picked one of her finest day dresses in pale green, a colour she knew set off the burnished gold of her hair. If he was going to leave, for however long, she wanted to give him a memory to match the one she had from that Christmas afternoon. Her heart began to beat harder and faster as she saw his face break into a warm smile.

"Bess, I am so happy to see you here. Would you accompany me to the solar where I am hoping there will be a bit of a gathering? I want to see everyone before we all go separate ways."

"All?" She answered, aware her voice sounded feeble, struggling as she was with the nearness of him, not having been this close for some weeks. Beneath the suppressed emotions she was also now feeling an overwhelming guilt about her meeting with the Stanleys. Should he find out, he would surely consider it an ultimate betrayal, even if she had no intention of going along with any of their plans. She needed to tell him what they had said to her, but how? How, when he was leaving today, and she herself had not worked out how to explain it to him without appearing disloyal herself?

If only she had gone to him that same night! Now, it was too late.

"Bess?" His voice was both encouraging and questioning. His eyes, when she raised her head to look at him, were burning into her and she felt her knees weaken at the intensity of his attention, was sure that he could see inside her very soul and that with very little resistance from her, he would clearly see into every part of her being. Know her every thought and desire. She couldn't wait any longer. She had waited too long.

"Richard, I...I need to speak to you alone. Could we go into the chapel for a moment?" Seizing the opportunity, she made her decision. She would tell him everything and take the consequences. But as she continued to watch him closely, she saw the weariness flood across his face.

"Bess, not this again, please!" His jaw was tight, the words uttered through gritted teeth. "We have discussed this. Arrangements are well advanced..."

Whatever he said next, she could not be entirely sure, as over his shoulder she spotted Lincoln and Francis in deep conversation. Lincoln was standing very close to speak directly into his ear, so that his words could not be overheard. As he whispered, Francis's face settled into a mask of stone, his eyes glittering with mounting fury and those eyes were looking directly at her.

She felt her heart missed several beats. Tears began to well in her eyes and she felt her hands begin to shake so that she had to clasp them together to keep Richard from noticing. Her stomach was cold with fear. They knew, she didn't know how but she was sure that they knew about her meeting at the Tower. It was too late.

The eyes she turned back to Richard were full of desperation, but still he misunderstood. He was speaking but her heart was pounding, the blood roaring in her ears, and she found she was shaking her head slowly, yet not in answer to whatever it was he was saying to her. Tears began to fall as Francis moved towards them, his figure growing larger as he came closer with Lincoln trailing behind, casually turning an apple in his hand, as if he was without a care in the world. How she envied him! It was a long time since she had felt so free of worldly cares.

"Bess?" Richard had finally realised that he no longer had his niece's attention and he turned to see Francis just a few paces away from him.

"Your Grace, everyone is assembled in the solar and everything is in readiness for your departure." Without a single glance in her direction, Bess still knew without a doubt that she was undone. She had, in one foolish moment, confirmed his fears about her, and she knew she would never be able to turn back that tide.

"Good!" Richard said firmly and turning his attention back to Bess, he held out his gloved hand, taking it for granted that she had been mollified by his words and would accompany him as he requested. Meekly, she placed her hand on his, and the small party progressed through the bailey, past the horses and litters, stable-hands and lackeys. Without really knowing how they got there, she found herself standing in the solar, where Richard released her hand with a courtly bow and smile, and moved to the fireplace at the end of the room. Once there, he turned to survey his assembled family. Bess looked about her, desolate.

Kathryn, glowing and growing rounder by the day, was leaning on the arm of her surlier husband Will. They were travelling to Wales, and would remain there until after the birth of the baby, and if she was unhappy about this, it didn't show. She looked at her father with a radiant expression, and her hand was curled round her husband's forearm affectionately.

Margaret, Ned's sister, was also there. Ned was clutching a small tabby kitten as if his life would end if he let it go. The poor animal was being held too tightly and began to struggle, but to no avail, until it made high-pitched mewling sounds of protest. Margaret, drawn by the cries, turned to Ned and made him loosen his grip.

John had been seated on a settle by the wall, but stood as his father entered and was now moving closer to where Bess stood. She managed to give him an empty smile, which he returned, but with real warmth. Cecily was also there, but standing with her husband, Ralph Scrope. Bess noticed with sadness that although they were standing together, there could have been a thousand leagues between them. Cecily looked as if she had been weeping herself, her eyes appeared strained, and Bess furrowed her brow as she looked at her, but Cecily merely dipped her chin to the floor disconsolately.

Francis and Lincoln both came to a halt before the king, where Rob Percy and Jack Howard already stood patiently waiting at his pleasure. Richard swept the room with one majestic gaze. He appeared anxious to be on his way, longing to head north and be as far as he could from the stink of the London alleyways. She had to admit that he looked well, had more colour in his face than he usually carried and that his whole air was much more open. Much the same as he had appeared at the Christmas pageant.

Was it the forthcoming marriage? Had he finally reconciled himself to his plan? Her heart sank a little further at the thought. There was a sudden feeling of time slowing down. The palace already felt large, cold and empty and she looked around desperately at all the anticipating, smiling faces. She was losing him! How could they smile when her heart was breaking? Couldn't they hear it? Her breath began to come in short gasps. She knew she couldn't bear it!

The room settled as Richard began to speak and Bess watched him, dumbstruck.

"My family, it gives me great heart to see you here. I asked you all to attend so that you could all say your farewells to each other as we will all be going our separate ways for the immediate future. Sir Robert and Lincoln here will be accompanying me to York and Middleham, as will my son John. John will then remain at Sherriff Hutton when I return so that he can gain experience with the Council of the North. Ned.." he smiled down at the young boy who was stroking the now sleeping kitten's head, "and Meg will also go to Sherriff Hutton for a while." Margaret looked up unconcerned. If she was surprised this announcement, she didn't show it.

"My daughter Kathryn and her husband will return to their seat at Raglan Castle, where they will prepare for the arrival of a child, my first grand child." Richard was almost beaming, an expression not usually associated with him at all. Bess's stomach just tightened further with every word, like a pulled lace. "Lord Howard will remain here to carry on the business of state as will Lord Lovell, who will follow me to Middleham in the next two weeks."

Richard paused, his benign gaze swept the room.

"I should at this point let you know that it has given me great pleasure to appoint Lord Lovell as my Lieutenant of the North, with all the attendant lands and manors, including the castle of Middleham. This appointment is in reward for his affinity and loyalty to his king and to the House of York."

All eyes swivelled to look at Francis who remained impassive, his eyes fixed on the king. It would appear that word of this had reached most ears in advance of the announcement and Bess looked over at Cecily, who had finally raised her head and was struggling bravely to fight back her tears. So that was it then, thought Bess, and the reality of the situation rang hollowly through her head like shouts in an empty chamber.

You are both to lose the men we love, a small voice inside her whispered plaintively. But Richard was still talking.

"Francis will remain in the north and establish a household there. I cannot think of a better custodian of my childhood home, and the place where I spent many years in the service of my king." Richard paused and took a deep breath, and looked directly at Bess, taking her aback. "Lady Elizabeth will remain here to enjoy the preparations for her own marriage. Dame Grey has been invited to come and stay during these arrangements, which I am sure she will wish to be party to." Bess opened her mouth in astonishment as if to speak, but his eyes moved away quickly, before she could try to respond either in word or gesture. He smiled broadly then and clapped his gloved hands together.

"We will all be together soon, in celebration of the joining of the House of York with the House of Aviz. Until then, safe journey for those who are about to leave, and may the good lord keep all of us in his watchful care."

Thus dismissed, the room began to empty with a rumble of quiet conversation. Kathryn crossed to her father where they exchanged words, and Bess watched as he kissed her on both cheeks. The couple moved away and as they passed Bess, Kathryn stopped and flung her arms around her cousin excitedly, whilst her husband moved on, paying her no attention at all. Almost as if she was invisible.

"Please say you will come and visit?" The young girl's face was flushed, her eyes bright and pleading, full of excitement. "I will grow huge and will not be able to walk, never mind mount a horse! Please Bess, say you will come!"

Bess nodded, smiling, but was unable to speak, frightened that one word would cause the burgeoning tears to fall. She kissed the girl's cheek and squeezed her hand reassuringly. As they left the room, she turned back and saw Richard call Francis over to him and her heart lurched for a moment, threatening to jump from her chest.

Her attention was then taken by Ned and Margaret and she distractedly wished them goodbye, stroking the young kitten on its soft, furry head with one finger. Looking into Ned's innocent eyes she felt her heart would break. How many times would she have to be separated from those she cared for? Margaret was saying her goodbyes, wishing her well, but Bess kept one wary eye on the conversation taking place by the hearth.

As they moved away, she was then confronted by John. So many farewells! She didn't know how she could stand it.

"Goodbye, Cousin Bess," he said very seriously. "I hope to see you soon, may God keep you."

"And you John," she managed to smile, her throat constricting and threatening to reveal her distress. They hugged once again briefly before he all but ran out of the room, excited to be on his way, hurtling towards his new future. Her constant memory of John would be of him running, she thought in despair, from one place to the next, always in a hurry to be gone somewhere else.

Bess looked back at Richard and Francis, who was now holding a parchment in his hand. As she watched, he bent the knee to his king, and Richard, smiling, raised him back up, throwing a companionable am around his shoulder for a few moments. Francis was smiling, turning the parchment in his hand, and as he retreated back to join Lincoln and Howard, Richard crossed the room to stand in front of Bess. They looked at each other levelly. She was so close she could smell the costmary on his clothes and she took a deep breath.

"Goodbye Bess. God keep you." His face was completely closed to her, but the look in his eyes was soft and kind. Bess dipped down deep in a curtsey, hiding all her conflicting emotions.

"And you, Your Grace," she murmured, almost holding her breath. Had Francis told him? Surely not. Surely he would say something? Be angry, issue a command, something?

Rising up to meet his eyes again, unbelievably, in those few seconds, his expression had changed. She saw the same unfathomable look in his eyes that she recognised from Epiphany. A searching, questioning look that also seemed to require no answer. He said nothing else, but raised her hands to his lips, leaving a burning imprint on her fingers. Calling over his shoulder, he left the room and was gone, the sound of his footsteps echoing around the walls of the chamber, and the chambers of her heart.

Lincoln, responding, clapped Francis on the arm and followed Richard out, giving Bess a dark glance and a nod of the head in a silence that spoke much, his expression full of restrained resentment. Bess breathed deeply, pulling large lungfuls of air into her body and closed her eyes. She felt suddenly faint. It was over - he was gone!

But when she opened her eyes, Francis was standing in front of her and the fury in his dark brown eyes was unmistakable.

45. THE PALACE OF WESTMINSTER
January 1486

Francis could hear Scrope and Howard talking quietly to one another in the background now that Richard had departed.

He was still smarting from his meeting with Cecily earlier that day and had been planning on finding some time to consider how he could repair the damage, if that was even humanly possible. The fact of the matter was that his future was now with Anna in the north, a future which had led him to accept certain compromises in order to serve the king whom was like a brother to him. The grant of lands which he had been bestowed was beyond his expectations, which he had to admit to himself had always been on the small side.

Having found a place at Middleham by Richard's side whilst just a young boy, he had been more than happy to hitch his horse to that litter, without thought of power or reward. Richard was his family, he would do whatever was asked of him without expecting favour. Deep down inside, he was very excited about the position he had been placed in. Now it was settled, he couldn't wait to get up to Middleham and walk those familiar passages once more with Richard at his side. He knew it would be a bittersweet experience, for the last time they had all been there, so had Anne and young Edward, but those ghosts needed to be exorcised.

The one jarring element in the whole affair was Cecily. Her small face had registered shock, before crumpling into despair, despite his best efforts, when he slowly explained what the future now meant for him. He had even tried, naively, to suggest that this may not be the end for their relationship, that things changed, that the unexpected could happen.

"Look where we all are now," he remembered saying with amazement in his voice. "Who knows what will happen over the coming months?"

Those words, spoken with affection and intended to comfort, had little effect. Secretly he was hoping that a forthcoming campaign to France, once the marriages were settled, would keep

Scrope more than busy. Who knew, with Francis as guardian of the Lord Bastard, Cecily's brother, a visit would be expected. A long visit. His mouth twisted involuntarily as a pang of guilt hit his gut.

Anna.

She had attended the Christmas court, but the distance between them had been as wide as ever. Yet, she had been surprisingly accepting of their new responsibilities and very pleased with the grants which now were appointed to them. Pleased, he knew, not to have to attend court and seeing Middleham as an even better position from which to distance herself from that necessity. With that, and the fact that she would have Francis exactly where she wanted him, she could do nothing else but express her gratitude.

But his private arrangements needed to be forgotten at present as he had more urgent matters to attend to which had made his blood run cold. Lincoln had sought him out that morning as he supervised the baggage train for the journey and he had listened incredulously to what the earl had to say. As the anger rose in him, his eyes fell on Bess, the very subject of Lincoln's confidence, standing with Richard in close conversation.

Now he stood in front of her himself, having said her goodbyes to her uncle, he cupped her elbow with his hand and guided her from the room, none too gently.

"We need to talk, and we need to talk now, my Lady," he whispered into her ear as she showed some slight resistance to his intention. At his words, she grudgingly allowed herself to be led from the hall to an outer chamber. Francis opened the door and then ignored all pretence of chivalry as he pushed her inside the room, following her in and almost slamming the door behind him.

Bess stumbled into the centre of the chamber, and regaining her footing, looked around, recalling with ire that this was the second time in only a few days that she had been manhandled by one of her uncle's servants. Setting her lips together firmly, she wondered what he would have to say about it if he knew, then she recalled why he could not know. She noticed that they were in the same chamber where she had spoken to Richard about her marriage some weeks ago, and she smiled at the irony. The hearth was empty, the room cold as she remembered it, why did no-one ever lay a fire in this chamber, she thought absently.

It was a chamber of cold words.

"Well?" The one word cut across the room like a sword in play, and hit her almost as sharply. Francis strode away from the door and moved towards her, his arms folded across his chest, waiting for an answer. Every inch of him betrayed his anger, his feet planted wide apart as he waited.

"This is hardly courtly behaviour, my Lord," Bess countered recovering some of her composure. "It does you no credit at all, Sir Francis."

He snorted in disgust at her response.

"I need no credit with you my Lady! You know full well why you are here and you will tell me exactly what I want to hear, or you will regret it for the rest of your days. Gods blood - I knew you would do something like this! Knew it! We discussed it on the road from Grafton. Bess.." he was beginning to ramble in his anger. "Bess - what are you doing? I expected you try to talk Richard out of his marriage, but treason Bess? From you?"

Bess's own fury began to rise. Who did he think he was? She had been a royal princess and he was just a jumped up lackey, fortunate enough to find a best friend in a king.

"I have committed no treason my Lord, and have a care how you speak to me! I am sure the king would not approve of you addressing me as you would a servant, no matter what he has seen to fit to reward you with!" Francis moved even closer, his breath hot on her face.

"So you deny it?"

"Deny what?"

"That you have indulged in treasonous activity. Against your own uncle."

"I can assure you," Bess retorted with an indignance she was using like a shield to hide her guilt, "I have committed no treason. At the worst I have...' she struggled to explain herself, her mind working furiously, "listened to treason." He laughed again in derision at the naivety of her statement, the sound harsh on her ears.

"My God, you really are your mother's daughter!"

Bess winced at what she knew was intended to be an insult and tugged at the points of her sleeves nervously.

"Lord Stanley asked to meet with me. I had no idea what his intentions were, he had merely expressed an interest in hearing about my forthcoming marriage." Francis clenched his fists in exasperation, his arms now by his sides, taking a step closer to her.

"Do not play the coquette with me, Bess. To listen to treason and not report it is to indulge in treasonous activity. Why did you not come to me? To Rob? For Heaven's Sake, to Richard himself?"

Bess felt an overwhelming flood of guilt and regret. She knew that is exactly what she should have done and had held back. Why?

Was it anger at Richard for her marriage, his marriage, his rejection of her? Or temptation? A promise of another way out? A way to involve herself with these despicable people, who she would then use to her own ends? She had been upset, isolated, somewhat jealous, and Stanley had seen it. She had been a fool and he had taken advantage of it. What had she been thinking? Did she really believe she would have been able to manipulate people such as the Stanleys, when even her mother had failed? She bit her bottom lip carefully, aware of the steady brown gaze watching every inch of her face.

"Are you ready to tell me what happened?" Francis's voice had both softened and lost its force, much to her relief. Bess sighed in final resignation. What else could she do?

"Lord Stanley offered me the opportunity to consider other options than my arranged marriage," she began, carefully considering every word she said, knowing full well how dreadful this was going to sound.

"That is treason, right there!" Francis could not resist pointing it out, emphasising it with a jab of his finger towards her and her tears welled up once again.

"I did not know what he meant, but he asked me to meet him

at the Tower watergate, which I did. Please believe me Francis, I really don't know why I did, but... I was so unhappy! I had been so lonely over the festivities." She pleaded with him, her voice full of helplessness, but he stood before her unmoved. Like a statue. "Once there, he bribed a guard, some guards - I don't know - and before I knew where I was, he had taken me to Lady Stanley's apartment."

"Prison cell." Francis corrected her, flatly.

"A bit too comfortable for a cell," she remarked archly and Francis grinned wryly in response.

"Your uncle is far too generous a gaoler. There are those being treated well who deserve no more than the darkest dungeon. If it were down to me..."

"Treason my lord?" She sniffed back her tears and looked at him, watched the muscle in his cheek flex. Even in anger, he was a handsome man, and she could fully understand how Cecily could feel so bereft at losing him.

"Truth - and he knows it," he snapped forcefully. "Continue." Bess sighed, and moved over to seat herself in a chair. She felt a certain relief now that she was to unburden herself, at least it was to Francis, and not Richard himself. Francis already disliked her. She would not have been able to bear to see disappointment and betrayal in Richard's eyes.

"They, Lady Stanley. She wanted to know if... if..." she hesitated and felt her face begin to burn but pressed on, now almost desperate to talk, "if I had given myself to the king." She watched his shoulders rise as he inhaled deeply, his eyes flashing with anger. "She said if I had, the meeting could go no further. She needed to be assured that I had no personal attachment to him, and also that I wanted an alternative to the Portuguese marriage. An alternative that did not involve marriage to my uncle."

"And?"

Bess bit her lip and sighed heavily.

"The Earl of Oxford is in France. He has others with him who fled the field at Redemore. Lady Stanley has people who are receiving correspondence from him - I know not who!" she said hastily seeing the question in his eyes. "She told me that these imposter boys in Burgundy were not my brothers, she confirmed that she knew for a fact they were dead, and that Richard had given Sir Robert Brackenbury the order. She said my only option to get out of the Portuguese marriage was to align myself with their new campaign, to put her son back on the throne."

"Jesu! Richard should give the order to take off his head, should have done it weeks ago." Francis spoke almost to himself, in a voice filled with anger and regret. He looked at her intently. "You do realise what position this puts you in, Bess? Whatever you thought you were doing, this was treason, pure and simple. The are plotting to depose a king, your uncle. Again! God Forfend! Do they never learn? They are taking full advantage of the current disarray in France, although I must admit I am surprised they are willing to finance Tudor again so soon. There must be something else..." He began to pace the room slowly, his hand fondling the hilt of his dagger as his thoughts ran their course.

"How could they not know you would run straight to Richard with what they had said? Your feelings for him are strong, by your own admission. I don't understand. There is something here that doesn't make sense."

"Francis..." Bess had waited, but her voice cut across his musings. "These boys in Burgundy? What did she mean?" Francis stopped in his tracks, his mind so engaged on trying to unravel what the Stanleys were up to that he dropped his guard.

"Ha! She still believes the boys to be dead. Not so clever, Lady Stanley, not so clever at all."

"My brothers? They are not dead?"

Francis closed his eyes on an agonising realisation of what he had just said as Bess stared at him in complete disbelief.

"Francis?" The young voice was pleading, trembling. "Please?"

He instinctively put his hand on his chest. There, inside his doublet, he had placed the parchment that Richard had given him.

It was a letter from Brackenbury, written to Richard, which he had read and passed on to Francis, who had as yet not had chance to read his friends words. To read the reasons he had acted as he did.

In halting tones, he told Bess what he knew of the fate of her brothers, and watched her face fill with sadness, joy, and at times fury when she began to understand how much her mother knew, how much she had known all along. Tears brimmed along her lashes, but they did not fall, and the smile on her face when she heard the real reason behind Francis's move to Middleham transformed her beauty into a radiance that was almost painful to behold. She rose quickly and crossed the distance between them, laying a hand on Francis's sleeve. The gesture made him soften towards her, just a little.

"When you ride to Middleham, I am coming with you."

"Bess..." his voice was bleak, his whole demeanour had changed, knowing he had said far too much. "I shouldn't have told you. I was taken aback by events today. That you should consort with traitors..."

"And that you should betray your kings secrets!" He flinched and coloured hotly at her words, resenting her for finding an advantage over him. "We are both in trouble Francis. I think it is only right that we both ride north and explain ourselves to the king."

46. MIDDLEHAM CASTLE
January 1486

The small party of riders entered the eastern gatehouse as the wind whipped and howled around the-rain lashed walls of Middleham like an anguished beast. The castle's grey aspect was painted darker by the heavy skies lowering above, but even that could not dampen the pleasure Francis felt upon seeing it's stark outline etched against the clouds. It had been a foul journey, cold enough for snow. Yet as they traversed further north, what had fallen was almost worse. An icy rain thrown towards them on winds that stripped through to the bone. Francis was relieved more than he could express to be finally riding over the drawbridge of the place he once called home, and where he knew Richard would be waiting for them. During the last two days of the journey he had thought of nothing but the warming fires in the Great Hall, plates of roasted venison, a brimming flask of Rhenish and the opportunity to roam the halls of his youth. It seemed so much longer than the two years and some months that had passed since they rode south to meet their new king, and mourn the death of the old. How naive they had all been then.

Once he had confronted Bess and been delivered of the full extent of the Stanley's intentions, he had dispatched a messenger to the Earl of Lincoln, which had reached the king's party at Coventry. Lincoln had then informed Richard of Bess's confession and he had acted without hesitation. Lincoln was sent straight back to Westminster to detain Lord Stanley and then to arrange trials for the scheming Lord, his duplicitous wife and Henry Tudor, arraigning them all for high treason. The earl had ridden hard in order to get back to the city and carry out Richard's wishes, but by the time he had, Stanley himself was nowhere to be found.

Richard had issued proclamations declaring him a traitor, and put a price on his head. His properties where all guarded lest he should return and they remained hopeful that someone would be overcome by greed turn him in before too much longer. After all, that ploy had worked for Buckingham who had been handed over by his own men.

Preparation for the trials was underway as Francis and Bess departed London, and were to be presided over by Lincoln, with assistance from Norfolk. With this in their capable hands, Richard would remain on his sojourn north intending to return in time to be present for the sentencing, which was expected to take place early February.

Francis therefore left London wearing a veneer of grim satisfaction that finally, the main faction of traitorous Lancastrian stalwarts were to receive their just end. He trusted they would all be explaining their actions to a greater power by Candlemas, although he still doubted that Richard would allow the passing of a death sentence on a woman. As long as she was safely locked up somewhere, out of reach, it should be enough. If her support was eliminated she would have nothing but her faith to last her the rest of her days. A fate that had seen the end of another Lancastrian Margaret. That thought, along with the prospective demise of her errant husband, warmed his frozen bones no end.

His other primary concern during the ride had been for Bess. The conditions on their journey had been hard but he found himself smiling in grudging admiration that she neither complained, nor uttered a single gripe - meeting each stop on the way with a grateful smile, and becoming the most charming guest that any Innkeeper could wish to house. When word got about, which it inevitably did to ascertain the best rooms, the welcome afforded to the eldest daughter of King Edward was enough to make Francis a touch uneasy. With her wit, charm, and unquestionable lineage, she beguiled everyone she came upon. A dark cloud drifted across his mind as he reflected that had Richard been slain at Redemore, she would have been a queen greatly loved by her people, and for one moment sharp teeth of fear ripped at his gut.

And what if she had married her uncle, as she admittedly wanted to do?

Would the resplendent glory of the Sunne in Splendour that

remained in Edward's daughter have shone brightly enough to warm the reputation that Richard's enemies had mired him with? Richard was confident that the actions he was planning to take regarding her brother would be certain to restore his good name and settle the realm, but would that really be enough?

He couldn't believe he was even letting himself consider the thoughts that now flitted furiously across his mind no matter how he tried to stop them, even disturbing his sleep as they drew further north, causing him to toss and turn on his hard, stuffed mattress as the relentless hail hammered at the window. Would marriage to his niece be better than marriage to a Portuguese bride, bearing in mind the way people seemed to love her? It occurred to him that this was the one thing that Tudor had got right. Thankfully, and much to his relief, his mind felt a lot clearer as they entered the bailey of the castle. The long, soulless journey on the road had left far too much time for his thoughts to wander, to turn innocent musings into the stuff of nightmares. Now there would be other things to occupy him and Bess, as they both had their king to answer to.

As the weary train clattered through the gatehouse, Francis was assailed by memories and suddenly, with a regretful pang, aware that there would be no mistress of the household, no reassuring presence of Anne and her ladies to meet them. As the squires hurried out, heads bowed against the wind to meet the oncoming horses, Francis hauled his mount to a halt and saw John striding towards them, having emerged from the Steward's lodging's by the north gatehouse. Even in the short time they had been apart he seemed to have grown even older.

As he dismounted and handed his reins over, he readied to greet Richard's son, only to find John had moved right past him and was helping Bess down from her palfrey, smiling broadly. Francis stopped in his tracks, his hand in mid-air, no longer holding the reins, to the amusement of the damp, tow-headed squire. He watched the two embrace and heard John speak with obvious pleasure in every word.

"Cousin, we did truly not expect to see each other so soon did we? Father has rooms readied for your comfort and I am to show you there. We will then all sup together in the Great Hall after Vespers."

Bess smiled back and held John at arms length.

"Thank you, John. Could I ask that you show me to the chapel first? I would like to light a candle for Queen Anne."

John looked at Francis uncertainly for a moment, and he shrugged, taken slightly aback. As he watched the two depart in the direction of the keep stairs which led directly to both the chapel and the Great Hall, Francis turned to John Conyers, the Steward who had now appeared in John's wake.

"I would like to see the king. Now - if at all possible?"

"He awaits you my Lord, in his Privy Chamber. I believe you know the way?"

Francis thanked the Steward and made his own way up the stairs to the Great Hall, where servants bustled around setting up the trestles, then crossed the covered bridge over to the private apartments. It felt both strange and familiar at the same time, and he was having great difficulty imagining himself as the owner of this proud edifice. This was the domain of Warwick, of the Duke of Gloucester, not of the son of a sometime Lancastrian lord. It was strange, exciting and humbling all at the same time.

He had to remind himself that he would have Anna here to run the household, but instead of seeing her, a small, heart- shaped face began to form in his mind, which he just as quickly pushed away. It would be Anna who would be poring over accounts previously handled by Anne, just as his lordship would be compared to others who went before him. It was a daunting prospect, even without taking into account the wardship of the bastard son of his former king. His future held so much hope, mixed with a measure of uncertainty and responsibility. It was an honour that would be heavy to bear.

Having reached Richard's chamber, he smiled as he saw the door ajar, unguarded. It was a clear signal that he was truly at home here and had even dispensed with his personal guards, something else that would help Richard relax and regain some normality. As he thought this, Lance, one of Richard's Middleham hounds, sensed his presence. The brindled, whiskered muzzle nosed the door open and loped up in greeting, his wet nose pushing into Francis's palm with a welcoming nudge. The door swung open further as Richard was rising from his writing table, laughing.

"Lance, you disobedient hound! Desist!"

Francis walked into the room and the alaunt followed him faithfully, its tail lowered but still wagging in welcome. Richard continued to grin as Francis bowed to his king in deference.

"Disloyal?" Richard spoke to the hound in an admonishing tone. "Do you desert your old master for your new with such abandon? You would do well at court, you cur!"

The dog took no notice, regarding Francis with bright eyes, his tail now performing a lazy circling motion. Richard snapped his ringed fingers and the animal moved back to his spot before the fire as Richard surveyed his friend's travel stained cloak, and unshaven appearance. Francis inhaled the welcome fragrance of the pine cones burning away in the flames, bringing back a myriad of memories.

"Good journey?" Richard's smile was both sardonic and appraising.

"I have had better," Francis grumbled, removing his remaining glove, "and am in sore need of a good drink to soothe my road weary bones."

A cupbearer moved out of the shadows by the fireplace and placed a cup in his hand without further ado, departing the chamber after a curt nod, and a sideways glance at the man he obviously knew was to be his new master. The door closed behind him, offering the privacy Francis knew they would need.

"Bess?" Richards brows quirked in question.

"Gone to the chapel. John is with her." He saw Richard's face darken slightly. "He's growing fast." Francis commented simply, sipping his drink with deliberation, although he would have dearly loved to have quaffed the whole flagon in one.

"Yes," Richard agreed thoughtfully, his eyes now on the roaring flames in the hearth. "They seem to have formed a close bond, which in itself is not a problem." He stopped to reconsider, his eyes distant, filled with flame. "What does it matter? She will be in Portugal by Lent and he will soon forget her." The inference took Francis by surprise.

"There is affection between them? Has it gone far?"

He watched as Richard shrugged his shoulders and moved back to seat himself again, gesturing Francis to do the same. He did, but only after moving the chair nearer to the fire.

"I think a burgeoning one. Fostered by Bess. I feel she is desperate to find a way out of her marriage and I think she believes I would relent if it meant disappointing my own blood. She forgets that dynastic marriage takes no account of emotions." A portentous silence filled the room and Francis wondered if Richard was also thinking about his own marriage, and his own emotions. "Are there any more developments in Westminster?" The sharp question snapped him out of his reverie with a jolt.

"Not really - Stanley is still abroad and will possibly try to join up with Oxford. We did hear his brother may be with him. Lincoln is relishing his task, if I do say so myself and Jack is aching to get to Tudor. He's like a rabid dog straining to be let off the leash." He gave him a few seconds to absorb his words. "You have done the right thing Richard. You gave them every chance and they threw it in your face. Trying to get Bess to involve herself in their schemes was just plain lunacy. Did they not consider she would tell you what they were doing?" Richard inclined his head thoughtfully

"She didn't though did she? Lincoln only found out because we were having Stanley followed. I now know that we can trust nothing that Stanley was reporting about Morton, although I did suspect that. If you go by his accounts , Morton is a paragon of churchly virtue. I should have realised, Stanley has his wife's fortune now, so has no care what happens to her. Hopefully, he did not carry off too much of it with him, the rest will be forfeit to the crown."

The silent spectre of Margaret Stanley almost appeared in the shadows as they both considered what these latest treasons meant for her.

"Speaking of Bess," Francis swallowed hard before biting the inside of his cheek nervously, "I am sorry that I let it slip about her brother..." He was halted by a dismissive wave of Richard's hand.

"No matter, she had a right to know. With all that has happened, I will ensure she is moved to Sheriff Hutton when she leaves here, to keep her away from what is happening at court." He looked at Francis quickly, eyes narrowed in humour. "If you can avoid letting her provoke you into revealing that particular plan it would be very much appreciated." Francis pursed his lips, restraining a smile.

"She's a clever girl that one. Not in the same way as her mother, not quite as devious I think, but clever, and determined. She charmed her way north, Dickon, everyone loved her." Richard's face softened.

"Like her father. Ned could charm the birds out of the trees and the fish from the streams. It's a gift that played him both fair and foul. I am truly sorry she is not happy about her marriage, I was hoping the opportunity it afforded her would overrule all other feelings she may have. She may be a queen one day, how could that not appeal to her? Her mother has wanted it for her from her very birth!"

"She desires it also." Francis held his hands out to the fire so that he could avoid eye contact with Richard as he uttered his next words. "Only she wants to be an English Queen, and no other."

"You think she was tempted by the Stanley's offer?" The words fell like frozen stones in the quiet of the warm chamber. Francis was so surprised by his tone that his head snapped round. Richard had picked up a quill and was twirling it round between his fingers absently, his eyes shielded by lowered lids.

"I wasn't thinking of Tudor. I was thinking of you." Francis hesitated a little before continuing, apologetically. "I didn't want to bring her here Dickon. I didn't want to collect her from Grafton and I didn't want to bring her here. I..." he stopped. He was in danger of saying far too much as he was still somewhat unsettled from his thoughts on the road. Richard threw the pen down and sat back, fixing him with a resigned gaze.

"Spit it out. We're back at Middleham, where we belong. This is my home, and is going to be your home, so – let's have no artifice. Speak as you would to a brother, for you are surely the only one I have left."

At those words, Francis felt a tightening in his chest. He loved this man with a ferocity he didn't understand, but knew he would do so until he could no longer breathe.

"She is in love with you. That much is clear. She admitted it to me, on the road from Grafton last year. " Richard still kept his eyes on Francis but picked up the pen again and began stroking the feather quill with his left hand.

"Really? You did not see fit to tell me?"

"No. I made her pledge to remain at a distance from you. Which she agreed to. It was Cecily who pointed out to me that I may have been making the bargain with the wrong person." In the distance, the sound of the Vespers bell could be heard, pealing out from the tower at St Akelda's church. Richard raised his head at the sound.

"You should go and change, we shall sup in an hour or so."

"Dickon..?" Francis was desperate not to leave their conversation on an unresolved note but Richard only sighed and gave his friend a look that was almost unfathomable.

"She's my niece, Francis."

"But, are your feelings for the niece or for the woman?" There was a strained silence which could have lasted hours but was only seconds in duration. When Richard replied there was a certain hesitancy to his voice.

"Sometimes... I have to admit, I feel confused. It is difficult to remain detached from such - adoration. Her passion humbles me, I am not worthy of such." Francis shifted uncomfortably in his seat, looking into his empty flagon.

"I shouldn't have brought her here, " he murmured, but

Richard shook his head and rose from his chair.

"No, my friend. You did right, as always. I owe her the truth about her brothers and she shall hear it from me and no other. I thank you for your care and concern, for I know you always have my best interests at heart. You are my one true rock Francis, on which the waves of my sovereignty break, so don't let it concern you. She has the wiles of the Woodvilles, and many have fallen foul of their manipulations." He gave his friend a consoling grin. "Now, we must both change for supper. You must be starving after such a journey, even taking to account the exceptional hospitality of the northern hostelries. And, the people of Middleham must meet their new Lord."

47. MIDDLEHAM CASTLE
January 1486

The following day was as bright and clear as the preceding days had been foul and rain sodden. Frost rimed the valleys and hills of Wensleydale, and a cool, crisp breeze swept around the battlements as Richard stood and surveyed the view with Francis at his side.

At supper last night he had announced that Francis would be the new lord of Middleham, to the grinning embarrassment of his friend as men stood to applaud and cheer. Francis was well known to all who lived and worked in the castle and indeed the village beyond, having spent his formative years there and served Richard as Duke of Gloucester. There had been a fine banquet, attended by some of the aldermen of York who had been invited at the visit to the city a week before. The relationship between the Lords of Middleham and the city had always been strong, and that would need to continue, so Richard had felt it important that this should be built on as early as possible.

Again, these were all people Francis was familiar with, but they needed to be aware that his rank and position were about to change. Indeed, Francis also needed to understand this, and Richard knew he would react quickly, aware that in a few weeks he would undertake his most important role, when Edward's son came to make his home at the castle.

Amongst the celebrations, however, there had been two spectres at the feast. The scowling presence of Northumberland who was in no way pleased to hear who had been granted the former Warwick lands... and Bess. Although Northumberland had expressed no verbal dissatisfaction, it was obvious to Richard how he felt, having spent far too much time sparring with Percy over the past few years. To a certain extent they had shared power whilst Edward was alive, but with Richard being a royal duke, and with both men approaching the same problems with a different viewpoint, there had been times when issues had been difficult to resolve.

Northumberland had attended the castle for the feast as

summoned, but Richard watched as his retinue rode out at the earliest possible opportunity, heading back to Topcliffe. With the uncovering of Stanleys actions, they would have to ensure that Francis kept a keen eye on his neighbour. Northumberland may not be happy with Francis as Lord of Middleham, but the matter was settled. He could either accept it, or Richard would take actions to resolve the conflict himself.

Which left Bess.

Bess was another matter entirely. She had spent the entire evening in John's company, and they had been very close, smiling and laughing all the time. Richard had to admit that he felt a stab of pride as his bastard son paid courtly attention to his cousin, behaviour fitting a prince of royal blood. Bess had lapped up the attention, casting the occasional glance over to Richard up on the dais, where he had sat with Francis, Northumberland, John Sherwood, the Bishop of Durham and Thomas Wrangwysh, Richard's good friend and Mayor of York.

His reverie was broken by Francis's voice.

"This is truly the Godliest place in the world, Dickon. So far removed from the stifling atmosphere in the south, the smell of the river... I wish we had never had to leave here."

He watched Richard's profile, which remained still, outlined against the frost-etched landscape, only a slight flex of the jaw giving away any emotion. A sudden gust of wind caught the royal standard and it snapped loudly as it unfurled in the breeze.

"Anne said the same thing to me after our son died. It is easy to think that we could have carried on our lives here untroubled and untouched by the political machinations in the south. But I know in the deepest recesses of my heart that I would still have lost my son and Anne would still have died, although, she may have lasted some weeks longer had she been here... and certainly happier. I often wonder myself what Elizabeth, as Queen Regent, would have persuaded my nephew to sign if things had turned out differently. If we had just stayed here and let the court destroy itself... and the country. If only Edward had taken more care, or had lived to a better age." He shook his head to dispel his unquiet thoughts. "No matter. Here we are, and now you have this castle in your care. When does Anna arrive?"

"Not quite yet. She is still fussing over arrangements at Minster Lovell but she will be here and settled ready for the boy, I assure you of that, Dickon. In truth, I think she is quite relishing it, us not having been blessed ourselves." Richard turned his face to regard his friend seriously.

"How did Cecily take the news?" Francis pulled a face and Richard's lips curved in a contemplative smile.

"Ah." He turned back to survey the vista that lie before them. "Who knows what the future will bring. God does not always make our paths clear. Speaking of which, I have arranged for Sherwood to carry out a service of blessing for the new lord of Middleham, and his lady, at the Church of St Akelda. Of course," he said giving Francis a sidelong amused glance, "it can't take place without the new Lady of Middleham."

Francis ignored this and leaned on the parapet, looking down the grey walls at the drop below. He could see the thin silver line of the River Cover in the distance, and he longed to get on his horse and ride out, ride until he was breathless over the hills and dales, as he did when he was a boy.

"Speaking of ladies."

"Bess." Richard's voice was drenched in resignation.

"Indeed. I was watching her last night. Is she as fond of John as she seems to be, or is she just trying to provoke a reaction from you?" Richard's shoulders heaved in a huge, somewhat weary sigh.

"I think she is fond of him, but I worry he is far fonder of her. He is more than aware she is bound for Portugal. I fear for him, Francis. Perhaps Anne and I shielded him too well, he is not that cognisant of politics, although I am making every effort to change that. He is interested, mildly, but I do not think he will ever be as," he hesitated, struggling for the right words to express himself, "astute as he needs to be. He could be so easily led, I feel. He can be a trifle hotheaded."

445

"Ha!" Francis barked. "From the boy who stood up to the Earl of Warwick! Lesser mortals would have been headless by Compline!"

"Still," Richard mused, unsmiling, his eyes roving the hills. "Look out for him would you? I will feel so much more at peace if I know he has you to turn to, should he find the need."

"Of course, Dickon. Whilst he remains in the north, you can count on me to watch out for him. You had no need to ask." He finally turned his back on the view.

"Good. Thank you again, my friend, I am constantly in your debt. As for Bess, I have asked her to attend me later today. I will let her know about her brother and after that, we must leave for the south." There was such sadness in his voice as he cast a final glance over the battlements that Francis narrowed his eyes in scrutiny, trying to work out what he was thinking, but the face was impenetrable. "Come' he said, laying his hand on Francis's shoulder. "It grows colder."

As he moved off towards the staircase in the corner which led back down to the south range, Francis watched the bright orb of the sun beating down and making the icy rime glitter as it began to succumb to its power. He could feel the heat on his back as he turned to follow down the stairs.

48. MIDDLEHAM CASTLE
January 1486

Bess wandered away from the Great Hall having eaten very little, desperate to have the meal over and done with in as short a time as possible. John had been chattering away in her ear incessantly throughout the ordeal and although she had spent a pleasant afternoon with him hawking on the moors, she was anxious to be gone from the hall. Richard had left the dais some time ago, and she had spent the whole of the evening with a continual nervous fluttering in her stomach at the thought of her forthcoming meeting with him.

It was some time since they had been alone together and she had a suspicion that Francis had more of a hand in that than he would ever admit to. Tonight, though, she knew all his efforts would be in vain, as her instincts told her that whatever she was about to discover, however good or bad the news he had to impart was, he would do so in private.

As John had continued to regale her with his hawk's unrivalled abilities, her eyes had drifted across the smoky hall where Francis was engrossed in conversation with the Steward and John Kendall. For some reason that she could not fathom, she was genuinely pleased that he was now lord of this castle which had once been his childhood home. Why she should feel so quite so pleased for the man who had tried to thwart her passions at every turn, she knew not, but she could not deny was how close his friendship with Richard was. The gesture was a more than fitting reward for his loyalty and she had no doubt that he would serve his king well here.

Francis had looked across at her a few times during the evening, and even smiled at one point, which she had been mildly surprised at. Knowing his opinion of her, she was taken aback that he should actually show any public display of approval, or affection, to her at all. Watching him stand there, elegantly attired in murrey damask, she had to admit he made a handsome figure. He was not a man who wore many jewels on his hands, but he wore his collar of office and a small dagger gleamed at his hip. Her thoughts drifted to Cecily as she watched him talking, smiling, listening - noted how he often bit the inside of his cheek, noticed how when he inclined his head, he had a tendency to look upwards, making his eyes appear large and lustrous. She could entirely see why her sister had fallen for his undoubted charms. He was a confident man, totally at ease with himself, which made Cecily's attraction to him very understandable.

From household gossip, Bess had heard that Anna Lovell was on her way, ready and willing to take up her role as chatelain of this massive castle. If Francis thought at all of Cecily, if he felt any sadness at parting from her, he was hiding it well. She knew she could not be so sanguine when she would be finally forced to part from Richard. Her despair would scream out from every part of her body, be visible to all. There was no way she would be able to hide it, of that she was certain, and how her new husband would accept that, she had no idea. She couldn't even think of it, not now, not here.

She was turning these thoughts over and over in her head as she crossed the covered bridge over the bailey towards the privy apartments, when one of Richard's hounds came padding towards her. Hesitantly, she held out her hand, which it sniffed obligingly, before carrying on in a gentle lope across the bridge, obviously making its way to the hall for a share of uneaten supper scraps. As Bess turned the corner she saw a chamber with a door ajar, noticed the flickering of candles within and so could only assume that was where the errant visitor had emerged from.

Slowly, she approached the room and pushed the door open wider, taking two steps in. There was a fire burning in the hearth, a book lie open on a table before it and a cloak was draped carelessly over the back of a carved chair. A sudden feeling of familiarity dawned on her, and she turned to see that, on the sideboard, the night livery of bread and wine had already been laid out even though Compline was still an hour or so away. She was in the ante-room to Richard's bedchamber.

Suddenly, her senses were assailed by a familiar scent. Jasmine. She turned her head to follow the heady fragrance. Hesitating only momentarily, she moved further inside. Thankfully, the inner room appeared to be empty, no page or squire in sight, and she walked across to the far side of the room where the fragrance was strongest. There was a table against the wall, and a looking glass. Bess checked her own reflection, noting how the soft candlelight made her hair appear to have a halo of gold, noted her flushed cheeks and bright, blue eyes. She looked down, where laid in front of the mirror was a hairbrush, and some small vials, one with a ornately carved silver stopper.

Swallowing hard, her heart beating erratically, she realised these were Anne's things, laid out, waiting for their owner as if she were expected to walk into the room at any moment and prepare for the night. Bess could almost hear her light laughter, but shook away the memory guiltily. Carefully, she lowered herself onto the stool by the glass and examined her own image again, now framed within the mirror which for many years would have reflected Anne of Gloucester's face shining back out of it and sadness overwhelmed her.

Reaching out her hand, she turned over the hairbrush in which she saw strands of brown hair still entwined in the bristles and she withdrew her hand quickly as if scalded. Bess felt as though time had frozen and her heart began to beat more rapidly in her chest, making her feel dizzily short of breath. She raised her eyes back to regard her own reflection.

What would it have been like?

She tried to imagine Anne sitting here after disrobing for the night, laughing and chattering to her ladies of the bedchamber about the events of the day. Would Richard have then come behind her, dismissing her ladies, who would have scurried away with fond, knowing glances as he picked up that very brush, caressing Anne's shoulders affectionately as he did? Would they have exchanged gentle, loving smiles in this very glass, as the brush ran through his wife's tresses with long, practised strokes, the jewels on his ringed hands catching the light from the candles and the mirror?

Her mouth was dry but she couldn't stop herself, even though she knew this is the last place she should be, it was also the only place she really wanted to be. She picked up the small vial with the silver stopper and lifted the lid, recognising it immediately as Anne's favourite perfume. Light and floral but at the same time having a sensual fragrance that the flower itself exuded after a long hot day in the height of summer, the delicious perfume that the small star-like flowers released as the sun set, having been warmed by the day. Suddenly, jolting her out of her reverie, she heard voices in the passage and at once recognised Richard's deep tones. He was no doubt making his way to the privy chamber where they were supposed to meet.

Reacting impulsively, without even really thinking, she slipped the small vial into her sleeve and rose quickly from the stool, ready to leave and follow the voices down the passage. The footsteps came to a halt outside the door and she stopped, her breath caught in her throat. It was quiet, so quiet she dare not move or breathe out, only to turn her head to assess if there was any other means of escape should someone enter the room. She was sure Richard would be infuriated to find her in here with Anne's things, and as she strained to hear in the sudden quiet, she thought she heard Richard himself speak, but as if in a whisper and then she heard footsteps retreating.

After a few silent seconds, she exhaled in relief and sat back down in a nearby chair to stop her legs shaking, only to hear the door move on its hinges and she watched in mounting terror as Richard entered the chamber. He stopped, his hand still resting on the latch as he saw her sitting there and appeared hesitant. His face registered shock, surprise even, but no anger, at least not yet. She turned her best beseeching look on him, desperate not to incur his rage but fully understanding that she may deserve it.

Finally, after an unbearably long silence, he turned his head and spoke to someone outside in the passage in a voice too low to hear. Then, without a word, only fixing her with his dark eyes which gave away no hint of emotion, he closed the door behind him and crossed the room to stand before her. His expression was still unreadable, his skin was warmed by the candlelight, but still pale against the dark purple of his doublet. Still without any word of either greeting or rebuke, he crossed to the sideboard and filled two cups, bringing them over to the fireside and pressing one into her hand, he took the seat opposite and regarded her over the rim of his own cup as he took a small sip of wine.

Unable to bear the tension any longer, Bess lost any composure she had retained and tried to fill the unforgiving silence with words. Knowing that nothing she could say could excuse her presence here.

"Forgive me, Your Grace," she began, her face beginning to flush hotly as she tried to explain herself. But, what was she doing there? How did she intend to explain it? She stopped. There was no excuse she could give and she knew it.

"Hush Bess, don't trouble yourself." Her breathing began to return to normal as he spoke, his face relaxing and the firelight creating candles in his eyes. He was not angry, if anything, his expression was one of mixed amusement and resignation. "One of the servants must have left the chamber door open, although that damned hound Gideon appears to have treacherously abandoned his post." He smiled ruefully, referring to the wandering hound she had encountered on the walkway. "We can talk here, as well as any other place, if you are quite comfortable?"

Bess took a grateful sip of the wine and nodded, pleased to notice that her hands were no longer shaking as her legs had been earlier. Her heartbeat slowed, but she still felt slightly nervous being alone in his presence. His whole demeanour seemed different here, she had noticed it from the very first sight of him when she arrived. He was so much more at ease, his manner not so sober and tightly drawn. His face even appeared to have some high colour, which could have been the warmth of the fire or the candlelight, but in general he just seemed much less troubled.

At Westminster he held himself like a coiled spring, almost

wary, as if waiting to react to the next trouble to reach his ears. This man sitting before the fire was a Richard she had not seen since she was a much younger girl, the fond uncle of her earlier memories, who would ride in from the wild north, ruffle her hair and cup her chin, telling her with a broad smile how fair she had grown. She smiled back at him, artlessly.

"I am most comfortable, your Grace, but I..." He shook his head, dismissing any further words and turned the cup in his hand, running his thumb over its embossed surface, watching her still.

"I won't keep you in suspense Bess, I know you had a hard journey here and that Francis would remain tight lipped, once he had let slip our little secret. That can't have been easy." His smile remained gentle, but his eyes were more coolly appraising. "However, it would be remiss of me if I did not address the not inconsequential matter of your clandestine meeting with the Stanleys. It is only your relationship to me that prevents you from occupying the cell next to Lady Stanley, anyone else would have been there before Lincoln could snap his fingers. You do realise how dangerous that meeting was? Not to mention disloyal.....to me."

The more words he spoke, the more intensity deepened his gaze, and Bess felt her face continue to heat up under the constant scrutiny. How stupid she had been? Was she a child to be running here and there to get her own way? What in heaven's name did she ever think to gain from a Stanley? She only had to look what had happened to her mother to learn that lesson.

Knowing she had no defence other than her own passionate stupidity, she exhaled deeply and sat back in her chair. In order to pluck up the courage she felt she would need to admit to her folly, she drank deeply from her cup, throwing her head back slightly, only to hear Richard laugh out loud.

"Careful Bess, you drink as deeply as Rob! Surely 'tis not that bad?" She managed a rueful grin over the top of the cup.

"Not to you, uncle, perhaps. You have not been seen to be the fool here."

"Oh?" the dark head was inclined to one side, his eyes dancing with an unexpected amusement.

"I was foolish. Am foolish. This marriage - you know how difficult I am finding it. You recall..." She looked at him quickly, thinking of that night at Westminster when she had tried so hard to make him change his mind about her betrothal, then thought better of it. "Perhaps then, at the Christmas feast, I drank too much wine, listened to a friendly voice and took their intentions to be other than they were. I thought he wanted to help me, not help himself. There was no one more surprised than I to find myself spirited inside the Tower. Inside her room!" Her urgency spent for the moment, she leaned forward in her chair. "Stanley bribed the guards, Richard. Tower guards!"

The room was exceptionally hot, and Richard drained his own cup without speaking. The silence remained as he rose and retrieved a flagon, refilling both their cups once more without a question. Bess had to admit she was grateful for it.

"And what was the purpose of this meeting?" His voice was almost seductively soft as he handed back her brimming vessel. "What did my Lord and Lady Stanley wish you to do?"

Without daring to look at his face, she took another drink, hoping to steady her voice, the memories of that night flooding back. Her fear, anger, helplessness. She swallowed, then took another sip of wine.

"At first her main concern was if... if... I was still a maid."

Her face coloured crimson at the reference and it was a few seconds before she could raise her eyes in his direction. He rewarded her with a puzzled look, but then some comprehension began to spread over his features. It was clear he understood, but once again his expression gave hint of neither distaste, anger or amusement, his face was as if carved in granite.

"Go on."

"She said that I should keep myself pure. That the dragon had only been chained, not defeated. She said that the Earl of Oxford was gaining allies abroad, and that I should do everything in my power to prevent this Portuguese marriage ceremony from going ahead."

Richard's eyes were shielded, he was looking down at his hands which were curled around the jewelled cup, his thumb stroked an oval garnet absently.

"And why would she trust you with this information, do you think? Did she not expect, you being so close to me, that you would immediately run to my side and avail me of all of her plans? What did they say - Bess - that made them trust you so?"

At this last, his eyes rose and what she saw in them made her stomach lurch. The anger was there, no doubt, deep down and well hidden, but what did show was something worse. His sense of betrayal. Bess cleared her throat awkwardly and placed a hand around her neck as if to aid herself. She knew her voice would tremble and let her down.

"Lady Stanley said her clerk - Reginald Bray? - had witnessed the murder of my brothers in the Tower. That he had also seen the written order from yourself to Sir Robert Brackenbury, and had seen the evil carried out. She told me that was why Bray is currently in the Tower, awaiting trial on a lesser charge, so that you can be rid of his testimony in this matter. That you had them killed precisely because it transpired that they were not in fact bastards, that the truth was about to come out and you only still had the claim to the throne if they were dead."

A log broke noisily in the hearth and the flames crackled loudly as it was consumed into ashes and dust. It was the only sound, until he spoke in a tone tinged with sadness.

"And you believed her? You believed that of me?"

Bess was quick to jump to her own defence.

"I didn't know what to believe! She was very convincing. You know the woman, she can be quite compelling. She could not see how I could continue to have affection for... an uncle who was guilty of such a feat of cruelty." Tears began to well in her blue eyes, taking his face out of focus. "I remonstrated with her, argued in fact, said that if you were truly a tyrant as they said, how come she, her son and others were still alive to this day, despite their treason?

That you had more cause to see them gone than my two young brothers, who where no threat to you." Richard rewarded her with a small grin in admiration of his advocate.

"And what did she say to that?"

Bess didn't return his smile, only looked at him carefully, and took the deepest of breaths.

"That you were a fool. A fool who already feared he had lost the favour of God, and was now afeared for his mortal soul. That it would be a long time before you would make such judgements to send any more men to their deaths. And as for punishing a woman… she judged herself safe." Bess took another sip of wine, relishing in the feeling it had on her whole body. She began to feel more relaxed, she knew she could tell him anything. "I told her I didn't intend to marry her lily-livered son, particularly now that I had seen him, and she said I would change my mind once he was sitting on the throne of England, and I had the chance to be queen in my own country and not some foreign land. She said if it came to a choice between two men I didn't want to marry, her son was the better choice of the two. The longer I stalled on the Portuguese marriage, the better." Bess rolled her eyes upwards. "She even suggested I take myself into sanctuary again if necessary."

She paused, looking at his downcast eyes, seeing the shadow of his lashes against his skin.

"She said I had nothing to lose. By avoiding the marriage and biding my time, I could be Queen of England one way or the other. Her son would defeat you the next time you met, as they had all learned their lessons well, and if he didn't…" she broke off, taking yet another sip, even though she could feel the dizzying effect on her senses.

"If he didn't?"

Bess placed her cup down carefully before replying.

"She said that if their attempt failed, there was always you. By that time, you would probably succumb to the inevitable. She seemed to intimate that if I managed to forestall my own marriage, the duke would not allow the marriage of his kinswoman to go ahead. That he would suffer a political loss of face to do so."

Her voice trailed off. She could still hear Lady Stanley's scathing tones in her ears, seeping into her consciousness, making her think that she may be right. That if her marriage could be delayed, and Richard's plans foiled, it might be possible. Of course, he would have to meet Tudor again in battle, but he would win again. In that she had no doubt. Tudor was not a warrior - that much was clear.

Richard was silently drumming his jewelled fingers on the carved chair arm. Grim amusement played around his lips as Bess watched him anxiously and tried to work out if she had gone too far by relating what that odious woman had spat at her on that January evening, even if she felt completely cleansed by unburdening her conscience.

"I do have a question," he said quietly, finally, still avoiding her eyes, his fingers moving incessantly on the arm rest. "Why did you not immediately seek me out once you had heard what they had to say? No doubt you knew it was treason. You certainly knew you should not have been in her apartment in the Tower. You knew guards had been bribed." His fingers stilled, two of them still in mid air as if pointing in accusation. "So why did you not come to me?"

He raised his eyes slowly and fixed her with a burning, questioning stare which had the effect of scorching her skin. She bit her bottom lip, carefully weighing her next words.

"Once I realised what I had become involved in, I was frightened. Don't forget Richard, I had heard my mother plotting for months, years - if I am honest, and witnessed the outcome of some of her actions. I felt small, alone and very scared. What future had I to look forward to? A marriage with a foreign prince, life in a foreign land or the wife of a scrawny Lancastrian rebel."

At these last words Richard burst out laughing unexpectedly, and she joined him with a grateful but tentative smile.

"An apt description of your prospective husband of last year." He chuckled, and took another long drink from his cup. But the laughter did not linger long in his eyes. "And what of the story of the murder of your brothers? Did that not even tempt you to come and confront me? If I recall, you sought me out some months ago at Westminster specifically to make it clear that you did not believe I was responsible for their deaths." If she had not known him better, she would have judged his pause to be mischievous. "You must remember that night." Bess nodded and lowered her head.

How many more times would he see her blush this evening? She could not bring herself to answer, remembering herself how she had prostrated herself at his feet, declaring her love for the first time whilst he was still married to Anne.   She was, however, somewhat taken aback that he mentioned it himself, and at the same time secretly pleased.   The scene in the dusky, fragrant gardens at Greenwich had obviously stayed with him. Richard gestured towards the flagon again, and Bess shook her head. His lips twisted in a sardonic smile.

"Well, then, you will not be surprised to find out that your brothers were not murdered, not by my order or my hand." He took a further drink, watching closely now as she paid rapt attention to his words. He relayed the whole story to Bess and watched her eyes narrow and widen in turn, then eventually fill with tears as he outlined his own plans for the future security of her remaining brother.

As he finished speaking, she rose from her chair and walked over to a window, looking out into the winter darkness that covered the rolling dales. This was to be her brother's home? He had been safe all this time, and her mother knew of it? She bit back her anger quickly. She did not want to think about that now, but she would have many words to say when she saw her again. How could she? How could she have known, have had a hand in arranging it and allowed things to happen as they did? Her hatred for Richard, her voicing of the loss of her sons!

Bess lowered her head, thinking. Loss. She remembered, she had only ever blamed Richard for their loss.

"Bess?" His voice was gentle now, caring. He was uncle Richard, or Richard, but not the king. She folded her arms around herself protectively, feeling a sudden chill, and suddenly remembered he small vial she had been hiding in her sleeve. She felt guilty and was glad he could not see her face.

Turning back to look at him, she was gratified to find he was regarding her with a benevolent expression. Now she understood why he seemed so different here. It was not so much being at Middleham, it was the combination of what he now knew to be true. Being back here, at his home, at the place where he had been most content, just made that so much more complete. He could vindicate himself in the eyes of all those who had silently - and not so silently - judged him, and found him guilty. The relief was so overwhelming, it had changed him physically.

"Thank you," she whispered, the tears she was holding back choking her voice, making it hushed and quiet as she became engulfed in a storm of emotions. They welled in her eyes and made it difficult for her to see, but she didn't to want them to fall. She was sad for her brother Edward, to have died a dreadful death by drowning. That must have been truly awful and she tried not to think about the fair young boy who had resembled her uncle Anthony so much.

Then there was a rush of joy and she silently thanked God that her younger brother, who she had been much closer to, and who was the king's namesake, was alive, and coming home. She was distressed that her mother had known, known everything all along. That she had instigated the whole charade, had cried and beat her breast about the loss of her sons and had let Richard's name become tarnished with lies. Her heart was also saddened for the lives of two small, impoverished, orphan boys, who now lie in the cold ground, God knows where.

"Thank you," she said again, much firmer this time, lifting her head, feeling a touch more in control of her feelings. "What you are doing is very kind. Francis and Anna will be suitable guardians for my brother, I am sure my mother will approve." Richard pushed himself up from his chair and crossed the floor to stand before her. He cupped her elbows and looked into her face with the gentlest of expressions, his own eyes appeared to be slightly moist.

"Oh, I don't for one minute think she will approve, Bess, but it is generous of you to think so. She will want the boy at her side, but he seems by all accounts to be a lively lad, who finds much amusement in life. I think Francis can mould him into a fine knight, much like himself. Middleham has a tradition for it."

She looked into the chasm of his dark eyes, trying to find what she was looking for, it was there somewhere, she knew it was, she had seen it before.

"My father said it was Warwick's lasting legacy."

Richard's brows furrowed in question, but his smile remained.

"The Duke of Gloucester." She said quietly. "Warwick's finest work. My father considered your training to be of greater significance than his king-making." Richard laughed softly, but coloured slightly at the compliment.

"Yes, that sounds like my brother. He wouldn't want Warwick to be remembered too kindly as a king-maker. Edward would have become king anyway, it was his destiny. Although, Warwick was a crucial part of his success. My brother liked to bask in glory, in all his golden splendour. Jesu, I miss him so!"

The joy disappeared as the large, golden figure of Edward Plantagenet strode into the room like a splendid colossus, and left again as swiftly, disappearing like the morning mist, leaving only a huge void where his radiating presence had been. Richard and Bess stood together, looking into each other's faces in silence and time stood still.

There it was!

She saw it and her heart stopped.

That look she had seen when Richard scanned the hall at Epiphany and could not find her there. A look that spoke of love and loss, of sadness - and desire. It was as if he reached down into her very soul and caressed it, cherishing the very essence of her. His dark gaze, turned liquid in the gently gathering shadows, and she submerged herself in the depths, happy never to emerge again. Without speaking, he told her everything she had ever dreamed he would say, yet she didn't hear his voice.

Almost trance-like, she moved forwards. They were of similar height and she had no need to do more than that. She reached her slender neck forwards and gently, hesitantly, pressed her lips onto his, closing her burning blue eyes at the last moment, watching the comprehension dawn deep in his gaze, waiting for him to draw back. He didn't.

His lips accepted hers with a compliant sweetness, confirming everything she had suspected for so long. She feared her heart would burst out from her chest and was sure he must be able to hear the sound it was making, must feel the drumming of her desire against his chest. This couldn't be happening!

Richard moved a step forwards himself, slipping his arm around her waist as he did so. His lips moved under hers, increasing the delightful pressure and they remained joined together as the world stopped around them. Bess was too frightened to breathe, not wanting to draw away in case it broke the spell she felt was weaving its magic around them. Not wanting to stop the moment, wanting it to go on forever, wanting to end her life right here if this was to be the only moment they would ever have together.

The effects of the wine began to tell and she began to feel dizzy, almost to the point of faintness. As she began to fall, to collapse against him, she felt his arm tighten around her waist, sensing her weakness, clasping her closer against his finely muscled body. Her heart soared and a single tear escaped from below her closed lid, began to track slowly down her cheek.

He was hers!

The Compline bell chimed across the cool night air and suddenly he drew back his head and parted from her. The burning intensity was still there in his eyes and he seemed to want to say something, but the words didn't come.

Slowly, almost agonizingly so, he slipped his arms from around her, turning away as a man dragging himself from a temptation which he knows will leave him damned. He moved back to the hearth to study the flames, his head bowed, his hair hiding his expression.

"Forgive me Bess, I..." The words were muffled, but choked with emotion. "I should not... I am sorry."

Bess crossed the room quickly to be back at his side and laid a hand on his shoulder, trying to see into his face, but he resisted her attempts and would not turn. Her voice betrayed her sudden desperation.

"Please, Richard, don't be sorry - you know this is what I have wanted for us. Please! You know how I feel about you, you always have done! I knew you felt something for me, I just did, which is why I have been unable to settle for anyone else. Please, Richard, please! Look at me!"

He shook his head, avoiding her eyes as if frightened to even look at her.

"No, Bess, please. You must go. You must go, now."

Bess was beside herself. The burning rapture she had felt but moments ago was turning to ice in her veins.

"But Richard, why? Why?" She was pleading, scalding tears of disappointment filling her eyes. Her hand gripped the soft velvet of his sleeve tightly, as if she knew that when she released her grip, she would never get him back. She could not do that, she could never let him go. This was right, she knew it was! She had felt it in every fibre of her being, and she knew he had too.

At this, he did finally turn around and look at her, but his face was wretched, fear was written large in every careworn line.

"Because I don't trust myself Bess, and you are betrothed to another. Please, go now. Go."

49. MIDDLEHAM CASTLE
January 1486

Once he was sure he was alone, Richard walked to the window, and threw open the casement. A blast of cold, fresh wind assailed his being and he breathed in the sharp winter air deeply, hoping to clear his mind. What had he done?

How had he let himself dishonour both his own position, and his niece? He turned and cast his eyes about desperately. Finally, he had achieved what he had set out to do, able to prove to a doubting world that he had been much maligned, that the slurs on his good name and character were all a cruel slander and he was to ruin it all now?

"Dear God, forgive me!" he whispered under his breath casting the words out to the stark night sky, but there was no answer there for him. Sighing wearily, he ran a hand over his face, suddenly feeling immensely tired and he pulled the window closed, trying to calm the turmoil in his mind.

No. It was only a kiss. Only a shared second of emotion evoked by memories gone by. She had plucked at his loss like lute strings under the hands of the most practised of minstrels and the music he heard had been so pleasureable as to transport him back in time. He could not deny the depth of his feelings, although he dearly wanted to.

Bess was a beautiful young girl, his blood relation, but he knew that in recent months his feelings, hard though he may try to deny them, had been sorely tested by her continual presence. When not within the sight of her beseeching blue gaze, he had begun to wonder where she would be, when he may next cross her path. Whilst he had other matters to occupy him, he had been able to push these fancies away, but here, back in his home, back where he felt most comfortable and away from the sheer pestilence of the court atmosphere, he had relaxed too much.

Now he had raised a hope and expectation in her where there could be none. At night, alone in his chamber, his mind had begun to travel down dangerous paths, trying to find a road in which they could be together. But it was impossible. God had spared him on the battle field, and given him the opportunity to clear his name. He now needed to pursue his chosen path and would have to move her far away, for her sake and for his. If he didn't - he wasn't sure how strong he could be. Or for how long. The taste of her lips had stirred feelings in him that he thought long dead, and once roused he feared for the outcome.

Feeling totally disgusted with himself, he moved over and refilled his wine cup, knowing he had eaten little and feeling the familiar burning in his stomach that told him he should really refrain from any more. He had never been a great drinker, no match for his two brothers, but tonight he knew he would need to sleep. He needed to forget, to dam the well of emotion which was in danger of breaking and washing away all he was working towards. Throwing his head back, he drained his cup in one swift gulp and then threw it at the wall in frustration, his ears ringing with the resounding clang of metal on stone. Such was his anger at himself that he didn't hear Francis enter the room.

"Dickon?" Richard turned with a start to see Francis with his hand on the door. "Is aught wrong? Pardon me for saying but you look dreadful! Did it not go well with Bess?"

Richard turned back to the sideboard and refilled a further cup, ignoring the spinning receptacle on the floor. He drank deeply, more than aware that he should stop but feeling the need to try and blank out the thoughts that were filling his head. He waved a flagon at Francis who shook his head, although he walked into the room and picked up the errant cup from the rushes - placing it back on the sideboard.

Francis waited for Richard to speak, fearing what he would hear when he did, his own anger rising again in a furious tide. Why on earth had he allowed Bess to persuade him to bring her here? What evil demon had sat on his shoulder that day, striving so long as he had to keep them apart? She was nothing but a burr under the saddle and the sooner she was wedded off the better. Only, he had an uneasy feeling there was something else here, something rooted in the conversation they had when he first arrived a few days ago. His thoughts were broken by Richard's voice, which was unusually unsteady.

"Francis, I wonder, could I ask you to escort Bess to Sherriff Hutton immediately, as we discussed?" Francis's heart sank into his boots. He knew it! Something had happened, something he had feared for some time and this was Richard's attempt to nip it in in the bud. He bit his bottom lip anxiously.

"She will then not be at court for her brother's homecoming," he said choosing his words carefully. "Will that not look strange?"

Richard raised his shoulders up stiffly, his back was paining him and he tried to stretch out the sensation of having a cord drawn tight down his spine. It had been a long week, his arm had become troublesome again not long before he left London, but it had been calmed whilst he had been here. As he thought about it, he felt a familiar ache begin again as if the mere remembrance woke the beast.

"She can visit him once he is safely housed here, after all he will not be in London for overlong. With Stanley on the loose and the trials about to take place, we need to move him north as soon as possible after he has been presented to the Lords and Commons. John will be at Sherriff Hutton, he can keep Bess company." Richard was aware he sounded more than a little irritable, but it was himself he was angry with. Angry and ashamed. By this time, Francis was at his side, full of concern.

"What happened, Dickon?"

His brown eyes were expectant but Richard could see that he already suspected what he himself had not yet confirmed.

"Nothing," he sighed, breathing deeply, although he felt his chest was somehow restricted. Too much wine, he reflected sourly and pushed the cup away. "Nothing much, I should say. Only far too much from my point of view and I need to remove the temptation to act in a similarly foolhardy way again. By God, if only she didn't remind me so much of my brothers, if only she was more

Woodville!" Francis finally met his friend's eyes and shot him an inquisitive glance. Richard bit his lip in a mirror of his friend's recent action, looking slightly embarrassed.

"An embrace only, but not a fatherly one I admit. So easily it..." A faint colour painted his usually pale cheeks and he said no more. Francis gave short laugh in response, which made Richard start.

"God's Blood Richard, give yourself a measure of credit! The girl has been throwing herself at you for months. If you have finally, finally been worn down, it is nothing to berate yourself for! You hardly threw her on the settle and ravished her, did you?"

Richard knew that Francis was hoping to raise a smile, but the look he gave him was serious.

"I could have, quite easily. And she would have been all too willing. If Compline hadn't sounded..." He shook his head to clear his thoughts. "No matter. We need to make an end of this. I can no longer trust myself in her company so she must go and await her wedding where there can be no chance that we meet alone again. I cannot be trusted." He turned suddenly, and crossed to the fireplace, leaning heavily on the mantel. "Did you read Brackenbury's letter?" Francis raised his brows at the sudden change of subject, but was inwardly glad to return to safer ground.

"Yes. Yes, I did."

He paused, thinking back over the words, the slanting black scrawl tumbling over the parchment which he had been handed before he left London.

"It confirms everything that we have been told, as you are aware. I have to admit I still don't completely understand how he could achieve so much without any of us suspecting anything. But then we had no reason to suppose he would throw his lot in with the Woodvilles. He took a great risk, but in doing so, has done you a great service, with no thought of reward or favour."

Richard was immobile, made neither sound nor movement to acknowledge what had been said so Francis continued.

"If something had gone wrong, and you had discovered what

he was doing, would you really have been able to believe that he was acting in your interests? I think it would have been difficult. He would probably have lost his head."

Richard didn't argue, just pushed at a fallen log in the hearth with the toe of his boot, which dissolved into fragments and ashes at the pressure, dust rising into the room and coating the black leather.

"And the other matter. Has that been attended to?" Francis tried to see his face, but the angle of his neck was causing his hair to fall forwards and obscure enough of his face to make this difficult.

"Yes, I have it here, secure as you requested. Kendall has his copy to take back to Westminster. Everything is in order." He hesitated, thinking over the contents of the document which he knew he could not divulge to anyone. "All this talk of your nephew.... it cannot fail to make you think of Ned, I am sure. " Francis hesitated, not sure if this was the right time to divulge something he had been thinking on recently. "I would be honoured to help arrange for his reburial, Richard. As I will be on hand, so to speak."

There was no immediate answer, but Richard finally pushed himself away from the mantel and returned Francis's anxious gaze. He wore his sadness like a sodden, woollen cloak. It weighed him down so.

"Thank you, my friend. Once the chapel in the Minster is ready, I will call in that favour. Hopefully, it will progress well and my son can be laid to rest in peace at last."

Silence fell across the room. It was late, and Richard felt exhaustion seeping through his limbs, as if he had donned the heaviest suit of armour and it wanted to drag him down onto the floor. Francis's voice was quiet, but still cut across the room like a sudden crack of thunder.

"Do you love her, Dickon?"

"I still love Anne, " he replied simply, without pause, and managed a small, wistful smile.

"Anne's gone. 'Tis no sin to love again."

Richard winced as his arm began it's familiar reminder, not a pain, just a gnawing ache.

"It is a sin to love Bess, Francis. She is my niece and I stood in front of an assembled crowd and denied I had any intentions towards her. So I prove I am not a murderer, but replace that reputation with one of a fornicator and dissembler? Will I ever truly purge these stains from my name if I give in to my carnal desires?" Francis took a step forward, but Richard waved him away and slumped down into the chair. "Forgive me, I am not myself at present. A good nights sleep will clear these thoughts, and we can get on with the business we had planned. Once these marriages are done, it will settle much. Would you send in that wandering page on your way out, I have no doubt he is loitering out there somewhere."

Francis hesitated, not sure that he wanted to leave. He almost felt he should offer his own services as body servant tonight, but he could trust Tom. He smiled to himself, it was a familiar name for the king's squires. He had lost two former Tom's at Barnet, it appeared to be a name which instilled loyalty, when not given to a Stanley. He turned to go, but was stopped as he heard Richard's voice once more.

"Francis?" The two friends eyes met across the room and years of unspoken understanding passed between them. "Thank you." Richard said simply. "There would be no-one else I could bare my soul to in this way save a priest. You are truly a brother to me, in all things, since we first met within these walls." Francis dipped his head in silence. There was nothing he could say, other than bid him to his rest.

"Good night Dickon. Sleep well. I'll arrange the escort to Sheriff Hutton in the morning."

"Good." said Richard smiling, and Francis left the chamber in search of Tom.

50. MIDDLEHAM CASTLE
January 1486

Bess lay abed in the dark, listening to the sounds of the castle closing down for the night. Being in one of the private apartments not far from Richard's own, she had heard footsteps earlier, and a low conversation between two men. She thought that she recognised one voice as belonging to Francis, but not that of his companion.

Her mind was whirling, reliving every moment of Richard's kiss. Her kiss? No matter - he had not flung her away from him, even though she had seen the conflict in his eyes as they parted. Conflict it was for sure, he wanted her, she had felt the unmistakable evidence in his body. He didn't want to desire her as he did - that much was plain - but despite that, he did. It was enough. It was a beacon of hope where she had almost given up looking, had lost belief in finding even the smallest flame.

Inwardly, she berated herself for thinking more about their embrace than the revelation that one of her brothers was indeed dead, and that her youngest brother had been found alive and was coming home. Poor Edward! To die at sea by drowning. She couldn't imagine how that would have felt, but as for Edward himself, she hardly knew him. He was a small, vague shadow. He had been sent to Ludlow so early in his life and she had been in sanctuary when he had finally arrived in London accompanied by Richard and Buckingham. Should she feel more grief at his passing, for a boy she hardly knew? Strangely, she felt more compassion for the two orphan boys who had been murdered in their place.

Despite herself, a devilish grin began to creep over her lips in the darkness. If only she could tell Margaret Stanley what she knew! Watch that supercilious, righteous expression shatter into a million pieces when she found out which boys she had actually disposed of. What satisfaction she would gain from that! She also hoped to be back in London for her trial so she could revel in the woman's long awaited downfall and wondered idly if her mother would extract herself from Grafton to see Margaret stand and answer for her treacheries - but then... Bess stopped her thoughts and pulled the linen sheets up to her chin.

Her mother was also implicated. Bribing Tower guards, corresponding behind Richard's back and with his own sister! Continuing to perpetuate the monstrous lie that the king was responsible for their deaths, no matter how subtly she had executed it, when all the time she knew what had really happened to them. Exasperated, Bess tossed onto her left side, her eyes straining in the dimness.

No. She wouldn't think about that, not when there was Richard to think about and a way out of this unwanted marriage to plan. For, how could she marry that Portuguese peacock now? If her uncle wanted her as much as he had displayed tonight, how could he let her go? How could the passion she had felt in that wondrously slow kiss be denied?

She slipped her hand under her pillow to make herself more comfortable and touched something cold and metallic. Closing her fingers round it, she extracted Anne's perfume vial. She sat up quickly then, leaning back on her pillows, turning the small vial round and round in her fingers. Removing the carved silver lid, she inhaled deeply, the familiar scent filling the room. Instantly, Anne's face came to mind, brought back to life by the power of her fragrance. Bess smiled, then threw back the counterpane.

The moon was full, filling the passage with an ethereal light as she walked barefoot, clad only in her linen shift, towards Richard's chamber. She hoped - almost knew for a certainty - that there would be no guards there, for he was more at home here than anywhere and tried to live without the ceremony he needed back at Westminster. Approaching the door, she smiled at the confirmation of her desires. There was only the brindled wolfhound she had met earlier on the covered bridge, who was curled up outside the chamber door.

He raised an inquisitive head as she approached, and bending down, she ruffled his head and ears and he closed his eyes again in appreciative contentment. Stepping over him carefully, she raised the latch with care and entered the chamber. It was hot in the room. It was no wonder the hound had taken to sleeping outside where it was much cooler. The only light came from the hearth where the fire had been stoked up for the night and was burning fiercely.

Every part of the chamber was bathed in a golden glow, which made the scene more like something from her imagination rather than the reality which she now faced. She could see Anne's table, and she crossed silently, placing the vial back in its rightful place. Her hand reached out and stroked the fur collar of Richard's discarded robe, carelessly placed across the back of a chair. The night livery was so far untouched, apart from one of the cups being on its side and the book still lay open on the table before the roaring fire. Picking up her shift as if it skirting the floor would make too much noise, she went to look. It was his Book of Hours, beautifully illustrated, the gold leaf illuminated hauntingly in the firelight, the brightly coloured figures leaping out of the page.

She turned and padded through the open doors to face the curtained bed, moving slowly forwards, her heart beginning to pound in her chest. She could hear his regular breathing and as she moved closer, could see his dark hair spread out on the pillow. He was lying on his side, one arm, his left, lay on top of the counterpane. The sleeve of his nightshirt had ridden up, showing the clearly defined muscle of his upper bicep. The arm of a soldier. She swallowed with difficulty. Was she really going to do this? Should she not run - now - whilst she still could?

What if his squire came in? What if the dog suddenly raised an alarm? What if..?

It all came to naught now. With memories of his embrace burning on her skin, she stepped up on to the dais and climbed onto the bed.

51. MIDDLEHAM CASTLE
January 1486

Richard was dreaming.

It was summer. He and Anne were riding through the fields down to the lush green banks of the River Cover, to one of their favourite haunts. They rode out through the east gatehouse, hearing the banners bearing the White Boar snapping overhead against a brilliant blue sky dotted with white, scudding clouds. The warm summer breeze covered them in the scents and sounds of the north that they loved. Larks sang, swallows swooped and dived overhead, he could smell the meadowsweet, and the grass, and the damp tang of the riverbank as they approached their destination.

White Surrey's coat was blindingly bright in the sunshine - so white it hurt his eyes! A reflection came off him like the burst of sun against polished armour, which for some reason gave him a brief pang of unease, of a long dead memory which was then gone. Chased away by the beauty of the day.

Dismounting easily, he turned, his hair lifting in the breeze and reaching up, swung Anne down from her palfrey. Light as a feather, she was smiling, her face glowing from the ride. Her hair was worn loose like a veil and her dove grey eyes sparkling, bright and full of love for him.

"Oh I so love this place Richard." Anne breathed as she looked up into his face. "Let us hope we never have to leave. That we stay here until we are both too old to ride, and too toothless to eat anything but broth. Too haggard to be of consequence to anyone but each other!"

She laughed gaily as he smiled back and folded her in his arms, inhaling the jasmine fragrance she liked to wear in the hollows of her neck, her elbows, between her breasts. Soft, secret places where it would drive him mad with desire.

"My darling Anne, my wife, my love," he murmured, burying his face into her hair, drowning in the scent of her. "I had a bad dream, I dreamed you had gone from me. My life was a torture from which I could never wake."

Her small hand lifted his chin, as she was won't to do when she wanted to be listened to.

"Never!" Her small delicate face was serious. "Never. Even death could not part us, it wouldn't dare to try! We are each a part of the other, and would not exist long without the whole." He crushed her lips with his own impetuously, so suddenly that she let out a small laugh from beneath the pressure, which soon turned to sighs of pleasure at his touch. His hands roamed her body, and they were on the ground in a heartbeat, lying in the long meadow grass, the sun beating down with a ferocious heat to match their desire as it grew.

She was so precious and beautiful, and it seemed so long since they had been together. The cloak of her hair entangled him as he moved upon her, her body so rounded, so fair, her eyes entreated him to take her with the passion that rose in a surging tide throughout their bodies. Her hands were guiding him, caressing him, taking him further into an ecstasy which he had not felt for so long. She lie back in the grass, smiling at him enigmatically, her hair spread out around her like a silken veil as her body arched and welcomed him home.

"My love! Anne..!" he sobbed, choked full of desire as he reached the peak of his ecstasy, the scent of jasmine and the heat of the sun making him dizzy with the joy of release.

"Dickon..!" Her eyes widened as she cried out. They were blue. Bluer than he had ever seen them, reflecting the summer skies above. He couldn't remember them ever being so blue!

"Richard! Oh God, Richard!"

Suddenly he couldn't see Anne at all. The fields around him began to shrink, the bright colours of the day receded into the smallest pinprick of light, which became a flame, the flame contained in the blazing blue eyes staring up at him rapt with joy and moist with tears.

Jasmine was all that was left of Anne. As his body shuddered, he tried to focus, tried to get back the riverbank, the larks, the rush of the water over stone… but all around was flickering firelight, and beneath him, the warmth of skin and spent passion.

He looked down, confused, into Bess's adoring eyes and knew the truth.

"Oh Jesu!" he whispered under his breath, and began to roll away from her, but she caught his arms quickly, holding him in place, their bodies still joined together as one.

"No, Richard, please my love, forgive me. Forgive me, but…"

With difficulty, he disengaged from her, only to lie at her side, staring up in horror at the canopy above the bed. Confused, he made no other effort to move, feeling only exhaustion mixed with an overwhelming sadness and remorse. Bess propped herself up on one elbow beside him, and laid her arm across his chest, reaching up to caress his face.

"I love you, Richard. I always knew how it would be and I was not wrong. You are so kind, so gentle, even when…"

"Bess, please!" He closed his eyes and placed his hand over them, pressing on his temples with his forefinger and thumb, forcing himself to think. Why couldn't he think? "This is wrong."

"How can it be?" she asked innocently, her touch as tempting as the devil himself, her voice silky in the darkness. A hand strayed, feather light across his bare chest, moving down across his abdomen. He swallowed hard, listening to her speak while he tried to make sense of the situation. "If we love each other. People will understand. Everyone understands what it is like to fall in love - don't they?" Her fingers roamed his body, softly, agonising in their tenderness.

Despite himself, he felt a stirring of desire as she played her game delicately across his skin, and he roused, quickly enough to drop his hand and catch her wrist, turning to look at her. Her eyes were large and lustrous and devouring him with such a burning devotion that he felt both humbled and embarrassed at he same time.

"Bess…" he started to speak, but she leaned over impetuously and pressed her lips against his. It was an action so reminiscent of

Anne that he was taken aback and words failed him. Instead, he pushed himself up against the pillows, feeling the old familiar twinge in his arm. He felt helpless, lost. Torn between a wondrous dream and this reality. His mind groped for the receding memory, wishing that this present were his imagination and that he would awaken and find himself back on that riverbank, cloaked in Anne's hair.

With a lingering caress across his cheek, Bess slipped from the bed and across to the sideboard. He watched her, his mute admiration tinged with despair, her naked body a white flame burning in the moonlit chamber. He heard the wine pour, and watched the silver beams caress the curves of her body as she walked back to the dais and climbed back beside him.

His body felt leaden, tied down by weights, his mind shrouded in mist, winding tendrils invading his every thought. He wanted to get up, to move, to do something that would stop what was happening, but he seemed unable to react to his inner instincts. Unable - or unwilling? Bess, was back beside him, glorious in her nakedness, her hair loose around her shoulders, almost gilt in the silver light. Gilt. The colour of a Woodville. Suddenly his stomach turned and he sagged further back against the pillows and closed his eyes.

"Richard?"

There was alarm in Bess's voice. He felt her warm skin and the curve of her breasts against him as she leaned over, pressing the wine cup to his lips. He swallowed, opening his eyes once more to find her face close to his. Her eyes were wide and alarmed, but softened as he looked back into her anxious gaze. Slowly, he lifted a hand up and cupped her cheek. She leaned her head further into his hand and smiled at him. Edward's smile? Edmund's smile?

"You need to leave Bess," he said in a voice that belonged to someone else. "You cannot be found here." He watched her brows furrow, saw the anxious glance she cast him and his heart ached.

"What will happen now? You love me, it is clear that you love me, you have proved that. You don't realise how happy that has made me, how wonderful tonight has been! My mother told me not to expect... that the first time... but it wasn't. Not at all."

His hand fell back at the realisation of her words, but she seized possession of it and held it to her lips, lying back down at his side, her head upon his bare chest. She was examining his hand intently, caressing each finger in turn as she spoke again, more hesitantly this time.

"Richard, I didn't realise. Your back, it... does it pain you?"

Her words seemed to reach him from afar, he clasped his fingers round her hand. What did it matter? The deed was done now. There was nothing he could do to take it back. Tomorrow, she would go. Tomorrow he could put it out of his mind and carry on. He answered her absently.

"No, not so much these days. Only when I am tired."

She shifted her body to turn her blue eyes up towards him in the moonlight, the fire almost out now. He groaned inwardly at his body's response to her movement.

"It matters not, not to me," she said simply. He gave her a weak smile and lifted a hand to stroke the bright hair on her head whilst he tried in vain to gather his thoughts.

"I know," was all he could manage. "Bess, you still have to leave. It is not seemly that you should be found here." Reaching up to touch his face gently, she reluctantly peeled herself away from his side. Richard watched her moving languidly, picking up her linen shift and slipping it over her head to cover her nakedness . The smell of Jasmine wafted over him once again and it was then he realised. It was in her clothes, on her skin, not the heady fragrance of rose which he usually associated with his niece when she had embraced him in the past. All trace of that was gone.

All he could smell was Jasmine. All he could smell was Anne.

His dream was making a traitor of his body, once again he felt the unmistakable ache of wanting. It was not unnatural, he had known no woman since her death - until tonight. Now she had to go before he succumbed again. She was too beautiful and too clever for him to think that he could resist in his current state and he cursed the excess of wine he had taken earlier that evening. Is this what it had been like for Edward? Did one lose oneself in drink and flesh to forget what you decided you no longer wanted to remember?

He managed another small smile, aware she was still watching his every move, every nuance.

"We will talk tomorrow Bess, there is much we must now discuss." He saw the curve of her cheeks as she smiled, even though her face was in shadow.

"The marriage. Portugal..."

"Tomorrow, Bess. Now hurry. Thomas could come at any moment, he worries that I do not keep guards at my door, even though this is the safest of places for me."

"Gideon was on guard," she laughed gently. "But I think he recognised me." Recognised your fragrance more likely, thought Richard silently, but only smiled again. His face felt numb from smiling against his despair. She leaned over him once again and pressed a kiss on his lips, he responded, despite himself he revelled in the bittersweet taste of her. Better to let this night end easily and sort it out on the morrow, he decided. He lifted his hand once more to stroke her hair.

"Jesu, but you are fair Bess. You would truly drive a man to madness should you wish to wield that power." Like your mother, he again thought to himself, his mind saying more than his lips would let him form. She lowered her eyelids, and looked back up at him from beneath silvered lashes.

"Richard... I know at the last, you called out... I know it was not my name, but that will change. Once we can proclaim our love, and everything is settled, we can make our own memories, have our own children. Anne - she would not deny you happiness if you should find it."

His rational mind continued an internal discourse as she chattered on eagerly, carried away by her own plans. But others may not feel the same, he thought. Once again he managed a reluctant smile.

"I know. As you say, all will be well. Now, you must go." He brushed his thumb across her lips, then raised her hand to his.

Mollified, she once again pressed her mouth against his lips, and slipped from the bed, running across to the door, where she turned, her every curve outlined in silver. She threw him a look of longing and left the chamber.

She was gone.

Richard heaved a heavy sigh.

He was tired, more tired than he had ever felt in his life. His body had finally betrayed him. Inwardly cursing himself for not seeking to slake his lusts before this night, he slipped further down into the bed. It was only as he drifted back into sleep that his mind answered him.

But you didn't have any lust to slake! You had no urge or desire for anyone but Anne. Even tonight, there was a strange satisfaction deep down, an indescribable feeling - even though he knew it not to be true - that it was Anne he had made love to. He had no recollection of Bess. That would make tomorrow so much easier....for him at least.

With this thought, he drifted back into a deep sleep. Found himself walking back to the river bank, his feet bare and damp with dew, moving closer to where Anne sat picking daisies and hearing her light joyous laughter as he approached.

"Dickon, where have you been? Look, Ned is here. He rode his horse down from the castle, all on his own! What a brave boy he is!" Richard walked faster, saw his son standing in front of Anne, watched as she linked hands with him. They both turned to look at him with smiles that were brighter than the morning sun. He walked closer towards them, his heart soared, everything would be fine now that they were here.

Ned picked up a sword from the blanket.

"Father, I challenge you to a duel!" All of a sudden Ned was older, splendidly attired in gleaming armour and Richard was looking at himself as a young duke and found a sword in his own hand. He arced the blade forwards and the swords clashed, sparking shafts of rainbow sunlight off the blades. Ned smiled and danced in front of him, ably parrying every thrust, his dark hair lit from behind with an auburn halo.

Above the swordplay Richard heard his brother Edward's laugh, the sound of his mother's voice intoning prayers, George arguing with someone in the background. His sword arm began to tire, began to ache with a tightening constriction. He couldn't catch his breath, his son was growing into a true warrior.

"Enough Ned! Enough - I yield!"

He laughed, surrendering his weapon at Ned's feet. How strange dreams were, he thought distractedly as Ned was now ten years old again and whooping as he swung his wooden sword above his head.

"You are bested, Dickon," Anne laughed. "It is time for a rest now, we've been waiting for you." Richard grinned in agreement and fell down on the damp grass before his wife and son and was overcome with the smell of Jasmine.

52. MIDDLEHAM CASTLE
January 1486

The scream was that of a tortured animal, howling out loud at the pain it was enduring, crying out for it to stop. It bounced off the walls of the passages and echoed across the bailey with an unearthly resonance. It was followed by another, as tortuous and bloodcurdling as the last. Francis was in the Great Hall, talking to Kendall, his first step in arranging Bess's removal to Sherriff Hutton. Kendall was to write the missive to the Steward for Richard's signet. His head turned sharply at the noise, only to be met by a sight which brought back too many memories, which made his breath stop.

No... was his first instinctive thought.

Thomas stood in the doorway, pale, his face streaked with tears but unable to speak. Francis was across the hall in three strides and pushed past him, breaking into a run across the covered bridge, turning into the passage leading to Richard's room. He was dimly aware that Kendall would follow him, but unable to wait, he crashed into Richards' chamber.

Inside the room, his eyes first fell on Bess, kneeling by Richard's bed. She was still in her nightshift, sobbing with a strangulated, thick sound which was almost inhuman. He felt the small breakfast he had consumed earlier rise up in his throat as he walked towards the bed and he swallowed it back down hard. He tasted acid, felt his hands beginning to shake.

Bess, her hair totally dishevelled as if she had only just arisen, had hold of Richard's hand, feverishly stroking the arm that was extended outside the counterpane. It looked deathly pale, which meant nothing itself when taking into account Richard's pallor on occasion. With difficulty, knowing deep in his gut what he was about to see, Francis dragged his gaze upwards from her hands to look at his friend.

The ghastly pallor of his arm extended to his face, dark hair spread out on his pillow, grey eyes half open - staring lifelessly at the window. He looked again, it appeared as if there was a slight smile on his lips, impossible surely? Francis thought it was more probably down to the angle in which his face was rested on the pillow.

He reached out, stepping around Bess who was still sobbing inconsolably, and laid a hand on Richard's face, trying not to look at those eyes which would never again meet his in humour and friendship. It was cool, but not cold. Whatever had happened, it had not been too long ago and was so sudden that he had been unable to summon help. He heard another noise above the sobbing and turned his head away from the sight that was tearing his heart in two, Gideon sat in a corner of the room, shaking and whining, the only witness to what had taken place? From the corner of his eye he saw that Thomas and Kendall were both in the chamber now.

"Hobbes..." Francis choked, but Thomas had already done his duty and the royal physician moved around from behind them and walked swiftly over to the bed, turning back the sleeves on his furred robes. Francis gathered Bess up bodily and moved her away. At first she resisted, turning wild eyes up to him in which he was not sure he was recognised. Stalling only momentarily, she gave in and let him move her away to the hearth and its dying embers. He beckoned Thomas over as Hobbes bent over the bed.

"What happened here?" He struggled to keep the tremor out of his voice and to keep his eyes away from where Hobbes was leaning over the bed.

Thomas looked at Bess fearfully.

"His Grace dismissed me after Compline my Lord. Said he wished to be alone. I carried out my duties and left him for the night, he had the hound with him. I did not... should I have returned in the night? I did not as he had commanded me to go. I came this morning to wake him and prepare his bath..." Again his gaze moved fitfully to the young girl, his eyes full of anxiety and grief. Bess took a deep breath, her eyes closed slowly to help her gain some composure.

"I was already here. I came to see if... I found him here. I could not wake him."

A wave of anger surfaced - the like of which Francis had rarely experienced. He grabbed the girl by her shoulder and pulled her away from the squire and into a corner of the room. Gideon began to whine more plaintively as they approached him, his dark eyes rolling from one to the other, almost imploring, seeming to convey his loss and seeking consolation. Thomas called the hound's name, and it slunk across the room, leaving Francis and Bess face to face.

"What in God's name were you doing here at this hour? Have you no morals?" Francis felt his colour drain at the look he suddenly saw in her eyes, in the burning flush that scorched her paled face. "What have you done?" he spat through gritted teeth.

Her eyes widened in fear, the blue almost drowned in black as she took a step backwards.

"My Lord." Hobbes voice cut across the room from his place by the bed. Bess went to move but was frozen on the spot by the look on Francis's face. He turned and moved across to the dais.

"William?"

"My lord, I am sorely afraid the king is dead. It is difficult to say, there is a slight tinge around his lips which I believe may indicate his heart may have failed. Of course, this could be..."

"Ssh!" Francis warned sharply, looking across the room urgently. He wanted no reference to Richard's condition until he had time to think. He desperately needed time to think. Hobbes reached forwards again but Francis stopped him.

"Thank you William, there is no more you can do. Can I ask you to keep your counsel on this until we can convene some sense of what to do next. We are far from court, and many of the nobles are dispersed. There are people who need to be summoned." His mind reeled, trying to frame thoughts he didn't want to think. He wanted it all to go away, to be sat breaking fast, waiting to have Richard sign the order for Bess to go to Sheriff Hutton.

Lincoln, Howard....Northumberland... Acid rose in his throat.

"Of course, my Lord." Hobbes was mumbling reverently. "Such a great shock, totally unexpected, the king has always been in such good health. I await your summons but His Grace will of course need be embalmed, to return him.."

Francis shook his head, tears beginning to form in his eyes at the realities of what would need to happen next.

"As you say. Await my summons. Thank you."

Hobbes moved away from him with a backward glance. Francis slowly dropped to his knees at the side of the bed and looked for the last time into the dark grey eyes of his childhood friend. He reached forward and slowly drew the open lids down over his sightless gaze.   He had died, alone and unshriven, and now...why now?

As the physician moved away, the remaining occupants of the chamber fell to their knees in prayer, taking in the confirmation of what they had feared to be true.   The only person left standing was Bess, who hung on to the mantel as if she would fall should she let go.   The sound of her continual weeping filled the room as the grey dawn lightened the sky beyond the window. Francis thought he could smell flowers.

"Ahh Dickon...I loved you so much!"

Francis bowed his head and unable to control himself any longer he began to weep uncontrollably, not caring who saw or who heard.

53. MIDDLEHAM CASTLE
January 1486

Recovering himself with great effort , Francis tried to turn his attention to the things he needed to do.

He was aware of Bess's presence and the fact that John and Rob were still unaware of what had happened.   He pushed himself up from the steps of the dais, trying not to look at Richard's face, but at the same time, wanting to, for fear he would never see it again. He wanted him to sit up, to laugh, to burst out in anger that they were all in his room, and as he fumbled with his thoughts he heard running footfall outside and was aware news was spreading.   At least within the castle precincts.

What should he do?   Thomas and Kendall rose to their feet, tears were still streaming down Tom's face. Francis put a hand on his shoulder.

"Tom..." The words were no sooner out of his mouth when a white faced John appeared at the door, and as he took a step forward Francis saw Rob immediately behind him, disbelief writ large on his face.   On catching his friend's expression, he placed a restraining arm round the boy's shoulder.

"Father... Papa!" Johns plaintive cry turned from his adult greeting back to the name he used in childhood, and he strained against Rob's grip. "No! No! Let me see!"

Galvanised into action Francis moved towards them and as he did was cut off by Bess who looked like she was walking in her sleep as she moved over to John.   She locked eyes with the boy and then glanced at Rob, who seemed to understand the unspoken request, releasing his grip.   John flung himself at Bess and sobbed onto her shoulder as she folded her arms around him, her eyes fixed on Francis.

Turning, she led him out into the passage, suddenly displaying a depth of composure which Francis would never have imagined. That left Rob free to move forwards and he walked over to stand at the foot of the bed whilst Francis continued his conversation with

Thomas.

"Tom. Is the Bishop still here?" Tom nodded dumbly. "Then I need to ask you to find Father Doget and..."

Tom looked quickly over his shoulder to the bed. Rob was standing motionless, his hand gripping one of the bedposts, shoulders sagging. His face turned towards the body on the bed.

"I know what to do my Lord," the squire said softly. Francis nodded and squeezed the boy's shoulder gratefully.

"I don't want anyone else..."

"Neither do I my Lord." The young man stopped him. "It has been my privilege to serve him in life, it will be an honour to do so in death."

Death. Richard dead. The hairs rose on the back of his neck as Francis leaned closer to speak in his ear.

"If you see anything, find anything..." A quick nod confirmed the unspoken agreement, and Tom left the room. Francis knew he could trust him to lay out Richard's body as required, only then would Francis let John see him. He didn't want him to remember him like this. There as also the matter of Richard's condition, which very few knew of. He intended to keep that knowledge restricted as much as he was able. If only they had been at Westminster - he almost bit off his tongue as he had the thought.

No.

If Richard had to die, better that he passed from this world having had the chance to breathe the clean, fresh air in the dales of his youth. Was it only this time yesterday that they stood on the battlements talking? His throat constricted as fingers gripped his arm. Rob was at his side.

"Dear God Francis, what happened? He was fine, he hadn't been ill?" His words were laden with shock.

"Hobbes thinks it may have been his heart. A sudden failure." He paused and turned to look at his friend, two pairs of disbelieving grief stricken eyes locked onto each other. "Bess was here," he whispered. Rob's eyebrows arched in silent question and Francis shrugged. "We need to get everyone away from here. Tom has gone for the Bishop and will attend to..." He couldn't say it. He couldn't refer to Richard as just a body, no longer a living breathing person. "Let's get Kendall and John to the Privy Chamber. We need to get a message to Lincoln and Howard. Jesus! Tudor's still in the Tower!" Rob gave a gasp.

"Surely - you don't think?"

Francis looked around, keeping his voice low, each word soaked in urgency.

"We have Stanley on the loose and Oxford God knows where! When this news gets out..."

Both men turned to look at the bed each lost in their own private thoughts, echoed by soft sobs from outside in the passageway. The sun began to rise and its weakened rays filtered through the window onto the dead king's face, bathing him in an etheral light.

54. MIDDLEHAM CASTLE
January 1486

Having left Richards body in the care of Thomas and Hobbes, Francis assembled all those he could in the Great Chamber. He knew he could entrust those two faithful servants, along with Sherwood and John Doget, Richard's personal chaplain, to do everything that needed to be done for Richard now. His duties lay elsewhere.

He looked round the room taking into account the dispositions of all those present. Kendall sat at a table with parchment and quills ready to record whatever events would unfold, ready to scribe missives for distribution around the realm. His jowled face was as solemn and sober as always, but a certain light appeared to have diminshed in his eyes.

Francis had been relieved to see that some of the northern lords had arrived that very morning answering a previous summons from Richard to travel back south with him. He was therefore relieved to see Metcalf, and the Harrington brothers amongst the assembled throng and he had greeted each one personally, briefing them on the events of the past few hours. Although the sheer range of shock, concern and grief had been difficult to handle, on the whole it made him feel the burden of the next few days was not just his alone to bear. It was some comfort - but not much.

Bess sat silent and white-faced on a window seat, her arm around John's shoulders. John was slumped forwards, disconsolate, his arms hanging down between his knees, his head lowered. Francis's heart went out to the boy who looked so much like his father that it forced him to swallow hard to ensure he did not fail in his continuing service to his friend.

Rob was leaning against the mantel, his usually pleasant and amiable countenance transfixed into stone. It was an unreadable mask which Francis knew he had donned to hide his grief. The heavy silence was suddenly broken by the tolling of a bell, deep and sonorous and caused everyone to look around the room. Some of the exchanged glances were full of grief, others with a sense of unease. With the arrival of local priests from St Akelda's, the news was now beginning to seep abroad and the solemn peal from the church Richard had visited so often now confirmed what had happened to all around.

There was no further time to prevaricate.

"Kendall, send missives to the Earl of Lincoln, Northumberland and the Mayor and Archbishop of York. Lincoln is Richard's heir…'

"God save King John," murmured Rob, crossing himself more out of habit than any other duty, and the cry, although somewhat muted, was echoed by the other lords assembled in the hall. At these words, young John's head shot up, and his red-rimmed eyes glared at Rob with an accusatory stare. Bess laid a hand on his arm, and he turned to look at her with desperation covering his face.

"The king's will, be it at Westminster? " This came from Metcalf who looked just as stunned as everyone else. "Alcock…"

"The Lord Chancellor does not have the will."

The voice Francis used to respond across the hall was not his, but was newly forged, hard and cold. "I have it here under safe guard. Richard entrusted me with it. For some reason which he didn't go into, he wanted it kept here, at Middleham." Rob's brows furrowed.

"Did you know about this?" Metcalf's question was addressed to Kendall, who nodded sagely in accession.

"His Grace drew up the will in Westminster. It is duly witnessed, and he declared his desire to bring it north with him and entrust it to the new Lord of Middleham. However, he did take the unusual step of providing a copy to Sir William Catesby. It would appear that he wished to cover for any situation in the event of his untimely death, be that in the north… or south."

The men in the hall all looked at each other uncertainly, whilst Francis studied his feet.

"Francis, is there something you are not telling us?" James Harrington had taken a step forward, his face a mixture of concern and confusion. Francis struggled with his demons. Did he tell those who didn't know about the Prince now? Or was that Lincoln's decision? The first act of his new king? To provide redemption to the old?

He inhaled deeply to try to get some clarity into his fuddled brain. He didn't dislike Lincoln, he was a good man, but he was young, relatively inexperienced, and not Richard.

Not for the first time, he reflected how comforting it must have been for the young King Edward to have the strong hand of the then Earl of Warwick behind him. He wished that Norfolk had come north with them, even Lincoln to be fair, as two heads this day were surely better than one. He found his heart beginning to pound again.

A bastard prince, just about to set sail for England. Another nephew the declared heir. A Tudor pretender in the Tower, about to stand trial. He shook his head, secretly hoping that Lincoln had the fortitude to stand up to the challenges ahead. It was hardly likely to be a easy transference of power, he was sure of that. Hopefully the Lord's would comply, Richards will was quite clear. He chose to ignore the question posed by James and carried on.

"We also need to notify the duchess's at Berkhamstead, and in Burgundy. This can wait a day or so," this was an aside to Kendall. "Richard laid out in his will that he wished to be laid to rest in the chapel he is building in York Minster. We need to get this underway as quickly as possible and make our way back to Westminster. Sherwood is arranging for a mass in St Akeldas before we leave. From York, Bess and John will leave for Sheriff Hutton."

"No!" Bess declared loudly, her voice strident across the quiet atmosphere of the room. Putting John's arm aside and standing up, she folded her hands together before her defiantly. All eyes in the room moved to look at the young girl standing by the window and Francis wondered how many of them were thinking of her father. Francis raised his hand and shot her a warning glance.

"Robert," he turned to another of the Harrington brothers, "if you would be the escort? It was one of Richard's last wishes. This may change the political situation in Portugal, the marriage pact was based on Richard's joining with Joanna. They will also need to be informed, but we will leave that to Lincoln to negotiate. In the meantime, until Lincoln..."

"Don't you mean His Grace King John?"

Bess's voice was laced with venom, directed at Francis, who raised his eyes to the ceiling, but refused to look at her. He couldn't trust himself to look at her.

"Beg pardon my lords, of course," Francis corrected himself with difficulty. "His Grace, the king, will need to negotiate new terms, if he deems it necessary."

Jesu! He swore inwardly, if only Bess hadn't had that confounded meeting with Stanley, Lincoln would be here! It would all be much more straightforward than having a dead king at one end of the country and his heir at the other. Bess's caustic tone cut across the room once more.

"I don't understand why my uncle wouldn't wish to be interred with his wife at the Abbey. Isn't that the more usual practice with Kings and Queens?"

It was Rob who replied to Bess, acknowledging by one glance at his friend's face that he had no intention of answering her.

"Dickon long expressed his wish that he, Anne and Edward be interred together in the chantry in York Minster. It was never his intention for Anne to be in London, only a necessity due to the events of the past two years. His home was, is, in the north." This was followed by a general rumble of assent around the hall, and Bess's eyes swept their faces as she stood silent, rigid and defiant.

"Thank you Rob." Francis said quickly. "Now I need to make arrangements with the Steward, if we are all happy with the ...' He paused as the door opened and Tom appeared, a guarded look on his face. "One moment."

No one spoke as Francis crossed to the door and inclined his head for the squire to speak urgently into his ear. If it was possible for his face to harden any more, it did at that moment, and his eyes moved to Bess, almost imperceptibly, then back down again to fix on the floor. This passed unnoticed by anyone, besides Rob. Everyone else appeared absorbed in their own thoughts. Francis dismissed the squire with a nod and turned back to the room.

"John?" The boy looked up at Francis with eyes full of hurt and despair. "You may go and say goodbye to your father now. Gentleman, John will show you the way."

John rose uncertainly, as all eyes rested on him and he looked around helplessly, his gaze finally resting on Bess, who in turn was watching Francis.

"Come on lad, we'll go in together," Metcalf called to him kindly and took his shoulder under his arm as they left the room. Bess turned and began to follow them, but Francis laid a hand on her arm.

"I need a moment, Bess."

She halted, but looked determinedly forwards, leaving him faced with her fixed profile as she watched the others leave. Rob was by this time in the doorway at the tail end of the procession and turned, his hand gripping the edge of the oaken door. His dark eyes moved from one to the other with a appraising gaze.

"Do you wish me to stay?" Francis shook his head.

"I'll join you presently."

With a final glance, Rob closed the door and Francis drew himself up to his full height, taking a few steps to place himself in front of Bess, forcing her to look at him.

"Harlot!" he spat ferociously, the venom in his voice echoing through the now emptied chamber.

Bess recoiled, visibly stung, but her face coloured as she realised he now knew what had happened last night. How, she wasn't sure, but she resented both his tone and his manner. She was not at all happy at being held here when she wanted to be with Richard, wanted to comfort John, needed to comfort herself.

"You don't understand," she began hesitantly, battling to stop her feelings from showing. "Richard..."

Francis took two steps forwards so that he stood almost toe to toe with her. His brown eyes - usually so mild and friendly - now empty and hard as sun baked clay.

"Luckily, Thomas is a faithful servant and has been able to hide the evidence of what took place last night. What I cannot understand is how you came to be there, bearing in mind I left Richard as he retired. You, my Lady, were nowhere in sight and not mentioned."

This last was a direct lie and he knew it, but in the context of Richard awaiting a bedmate, it was certainly the truth. Bess bristled, partly in shame and humiliation that she had been found out, and by Francis, but mostly as her royal blood objected to the manner in which she was being spoken to.

"I need not defend my actions to you!" She retorted imperiously. "Who are you now, after all? What position will you keep now that your best friend is dead? Will the new king require such a willing lapdog?" The words came out before she knew what she was saying, only knowing she would wound and wanting to draw blood.

There was an urgent need to make sure he was feeling as much pain as she was. For one terrifying moment she feared she may have said too much. Dark colour suffused his fair complexion and she saw his hand ball into a fist. He took one hesitant step backwards, but then stopped. She held her breath as she waited for the hand to raise, but the words came instead.

"Bitch!' he swore. "Woodville bitch! Did you use one of your mother's rumoured charms to overcome him as your mother did your father? Look where that left the country! Look what you have done!"

Bess herself took a step back, faltered, stumbling against a chair.

"Done?" The shock of his words and the intimation hit her like a blow to the stomach, where she had been expecting a slap to her cheek. The ferocity forced her down into the seat of the chair, where she clung onto the carved wooden arm. "Are you saying…? Do you think he died because of me?" Her tone was horrified, her face crumpling in distress. "He was well when I left him, we drank together… we talked…he was well, Francis, I swear! I love him, God help me, I would never seek to harm him! It has taken me months, years to get him to acknowledge his feelings for me!"

She dissolved into sobs, no longer capable of coherent speech. Francis watched her, totally unmoved by the sight of her heaving shoulders, and the hands twisting the folds of her dress in unspoken agony. He knew she was hurting and was pleased by it.

They were two wounded animals, each determined to inflict more damage on each other, each ravaged by the pain of love and loss, neither to be satisfied until their souls were laid bare in all their despair.

"Yes, you were right." Francis spoke with a voice that froze the air in the room. "He did have feelings for you. Are you content now? He was sending you to the safety of Sheriff Hutton for his peace and yours. He didn't want to dishonour you. He wanted you to see your brother return to England, and then send you off to be a royal princess, perhaps even a queen. To love you was to destroy himself, and your own kin have done a pretty good job of that over the past few years without any help from you. It would appear his heart failed, mayhap helped by the strain you placed upon it. Your love may have killed him Bess. Your love, or the guilt it placed on him, think on that! "

As her stunned, white face stared up at him, blue eyes liquid with tears, he turned on his heel and heaved open the door.

"Get out of here! You will leave for Sheriff Hutton in the morning."

Slowly, Bess rose and wiping her eyes on her sleeve, she walked slowly towards the door, only to receive a final barb as she passed close to her tormentor.

"You should rejoice, Bess. You wanted a way out of your marriage and you have found one. Richard has finally complied to your demands. Well done."

She walked through the arched doorway with as much dignity as she could muster, tears streaming down her cheeks and heard the door slam closed behind her. For a second not knowing what to do, she stood frozen in her agony, when she heard a further dull thud behind her.

Inside the chamber, Francis slumped against the other side of the door, his head pounded against the timbers. Clinging desperately onto the latch to keep himself upright, he began to sob.

Outside, Bess closed her eyes momentarily, and then she walked away.

55. MIDDLEHAM CASTLE
January 1486

Much later, after the service in the main chapel where masses had been sung for Richard's soul, Francis returned to the smaller, family chapel by the east wall where his body had been laid out on a bier. Vespers had rung, fighting to be heard against the continual tolling of the bell mourning a king's passing. Villagers had flocked to the local church and filled it to the doors, all giving up fervent prayer for their dearly loved lord. Servants and henchmen walked around with their heads bowed, supper had been laid in the Great Hall, but those who did stop to eat did so in silence and with very little appetite. Even the fire seemed to be fighting a battle to warm the room.

He entered the chapel and immediately saw the figure of John, on his knees in prayer by his father's feet. Richard lay, lapped in the soft, golden light of four thick pillared candles, one at each corner. He was covered up to his hips in cloth of gold. The familiar profile was turned heavenward towards the timbered roof, the dark hair smoothed out onto the white pillow where his head rested, at peace. Francis moved towards the kneeling figure and laid a hand on his shoulder, gently. John raised his head and crossing himself, rose to his feet. Together, they both looked down at the body laid out before them.

Clad in a fresh linen nightshirt, his hands were crossed over his chest, now bare of the coronation ring which had been removed ready for its journey back down to London. He thanked God hourly for Tom, who had been so discreet regarding the blood he had found on the sheets, evidence of Bess's visit and Richard's final act of indiscretion, or madness. He had also cleverly been able to hide the spinal deformity which had been such a closely guarded secret, and which now, God willing, would remain so.

He thought it odd that Bess had not mentioned it and wondered why, but then thought that as Richard himself had said, so many months ago, "in the throes of passion..."

She may not have even noticed it. He was sure she would have said something, either that, or in her own blind passion she was unable to see anything other than the Richard she loved and desired, free of all mortal faults. Sighing, he turned his thoughts to Richard's son and squeezed John's shoulder.

"Come. You haven't eaten. You need to keep up your strength, we have a difficult few days ahead." The silence in the chapel was filled with unspoken pain, and the boy's next words did nothing to dispel that.

"What will happen to me now?" The voice was full of fear and somewhat tremulous. "What will happen to me without my father, the king? I am a bastard. I was the king's bastard, but he is gone now." He sniffed loudly. "He cared for me. I was safe where I could have been discarded. My mother didn't want me. My father took me in when he didn't need to. Kathryn has a husband." He halted, a choked sob catching in his throat. "I'm sorry, it's just... I can't bear it Sir Francis!"

Francis smiled sadly, looking at Richard's pale face and fighting down his own emotions once more. He could feel the boy's agony which had an equal in his own. The man laid out before him had been as flesh and blood to him, for as long as he could remember and he couldn't begin to imagine how he would go on now. He knew he would, but he was just unable to think any further ahead than the next task in hand.

"Your father was an honourable man. You are his son, made of the same blood, and he loved you John. Never doubt that. I am sure he has made provision for you, I am sure you need not worry."

John sniffed again, dabbed at his face with a linen kerchief, unable to tear his eyes away from the pallid face on the bier.

"What about Bess? Will she still have to leave? She doesn't want to marry, Sir Francis, not someone from a foreign country. She wants to stay here."

One of the candles guttered in some unseen draught, but then steadied. Francis himself continued to look at Richard's face. He didn't feel comfortable talking about Bess, not here.

"That's up to the king now, it will be for him to decide."

Once again at the mention of the new king, John choked back a sob. Then suddenly he turned desperate eyes up to Francis's face.

"Kathryn! We have to let Kathryn know! The baby!"

He stopped, wild eyed in despair.

"We will, John," Francis soothed, as much as he was able. "Messengers are on their way, Lin... His Grace will know what to do. Try not to worry." The boy was full of endless questions. Questions Francis didn't have the will or strength to answer. But John was innocently merciless.

"With John now king, who will preside over the Council of the North? Father wanted me to learn from him. I thought I..." his voice trailed off miserably.

"What is it?" The elder man's brows furrowed in concern. He wanted to provide the boy with comfort, but was struggling to know what to say.

"Bess said, she thought, if Father was getting me involved in the Council, he may have plans to..." again he seemed unable to finish what he wanted to say, but Francis had guessed, and his anger once again began to rise to the surface. Damn that girl! "Did he mention it to you Francis? You were his good friend. Was he going to do that, for me? Was he going to name me his heir?"

Francis gave a heavy sigh, his blood was pounding painfully at his temples. Yesterday felt a hundred years away and now this boy was looking up at him expectantly, so reminiscent of his father at the same age that his heart ached.

"I don't know, John. He didn't confide in me if he was. Which doesn't mean it wasn't his intention, but, it would not have been easy for him to do. He would not have wanted to jeopardies your cousin's claim, or any future son he could have had with the princess." The same invisible hand rippled the cloth of gold pall, making it shimmer as if molten.

"None of which will happen now," the boy replied sadly, his eyes returning to the still form before them.

"No. It was not to be." Francis paused. "Come now,

tomorrow will be a long day, you need to rest." John heaved a sigh of his own.

"I have all the remainder of my life to rest, Sir Francis. I would rather stay here in vigil, and pray for my father's soul, if that is possible." He hesitated, looked away towards the chapel window so that his expression was hidden. "People have said some terrible things about him Sir Francis, I have heard them. Some awful things! How can people believe it? Why don't they know what a good man he truly was? I don't want to go back to Westminster if that is what they will say of him now he is dead. I will be much happier to stay here in the north, bastard or no."

Francis could think of nothing else to say. He would also be pleased to remain here and he could only assume that he would. He hoped that the new king would be happy to continue with the arrangement Richard had set in motion. He couldn't see why not, could think of no good reason why Lincoln would change things, after all, it was a problem solved. It crossed his mind that he could mentor John as well as Edward's returning son. Surely there would be no opposition to that? Francis didn't know Lincoln all that well, but enough to know he had more than his share of common sense. He looked back at the young boy's tear stained face.

"Can I stay with you on your vigil, John? Would you mind?"

"I would like that very much, and so would Papa!" the boy replied, his eyes once again brimming with tears.

Francis looked at the face of his friend, already struggling to recall what his voice had sounded like, and sank down to his knees.

56. MIDDLEHAM CASTLE
January 1486

Two days later the funeral procession was assembling in the bailey of the castle. The horses were caparisoned in black, Richard's rider-less charger was harnessed up to the hastily obtained hearse, which was more serviceable than grand, but this would be redeemed once they reached the outskirts of York, where the true pomp and ceremony would take place, courtesy of the arrangements made by the Mayor, Thomas Wrangwysh. There was an air of sombre tension and sadness pervading the castle from the lowest servants quarters, through the buttery and armoury and up to the Great Hall itself.

Many of the servants had been at Middleham throughout Richard's time as duke and his marriage to Anne and the sorrow lie heavy all around like the darkly oppressing clouds. The full range of servants, from John Conyers the Steward, the Comptroller, Masters of Henchmen and Horse, pages, squires, kitchen maids - everyone had stopped work. White, silent faces lined the walls and looked down from the covered walkway, regarding the waiting funeral procession without a word spoken. At the turn of the hour, the bell of St Akelda's began to toll again.

Francis ran down the steps of the keep and cast a quick glance around the assembled mourners. John and Bess stood together, exchanging quiet conversation. Bess cast him a cold glance from above her furs and then continued talking to John as if she hadn't even seen him.

Rob stood by Richard's horse, checking its funeral trappings with a grim expression on his face. Kendall, Metcalf, Scrope of Masham, everyone was looking at him and he almost bowed under the weight of the pressure of their expectations. He could feel hundred's of pairs of eyes on him as he walked slowly towards the hearse. Pausing, he crossed himself and gave a bow of his head.

Due to the well established courier system in place for riders to reach London using two hour journeys, he knew that Lincoln would be aware of the situation by now and he could only hope that he was acting in a way which his new king would approve of. One thing he could be certain of, is that he was acting in accordance with Richard's will, and that would have to be enough should he be challenged later. By anyone.

With only a days travelling between Middleham and York, he had that morning received a letter from the Mayor expressing the condolences of the city and letting him know that preparations were being made for their arrival. Even had his death occurred in London, Richard had dictated that the procession to York should be dignified, solemn but small. Not until he reached his beloved city of York would the true ceremonies begin. After that, there were further instructions for Francis to attend to, concerning Anne and Edward, but that was in the weeks to come.

The reverent hush continued, the sound of the bell the only voice as Francis walked away from the hearse containing the body of his king and moved towards his own mount, trusty Fides, looking all the more magnificent for being cloaked in black. He cast a quick glance back to the hearse before nodding to Rob and Metcalf, and as if rehearsed, everyone moved to their respective horses to mount for the journey. There was a sudden flurry, the jingling of harness, the creak of saddle leather, boots scuffing the ground and the restless pawing and snorting of impatient horses, waiting to receive the signal to move. The tense silence was suddenly shattered by a shout from the north gatehouse.

"Rider!"

Francis stopped with one foot in his stirrup and his left hand on the pommel of his saddle, but everyone else continued to ready themselves for the journey. There was something in the guard's voice which made Francis halt and as he turned towards the gatehouse he saw he was right. The rider clattering across the drawbridge at speed wore Lincoln's livery.

The horse was well lathered and the rider was remarkably travel stained for a two hour ride. Everyone waited with patient interest as the rider threw himself from the saddle and then looked round in confusion, not quite sure who to give his message to.

Seeing his quandry, Francis disengaged his foot and strode up to the rider who sank on his knees and held out a letter. His face was grim, too grim. These hands held bad tidings, Francis was sure of it.

"My Lord Lovell, The Earl of Lincoln...." he began. Francis held out a hand. "Surely you mean His Grace, King John? The messenger thrust out the letter, not deterred.

"The Earl of Lincoln has sent this message. London is in disarray, Henry Tudor...."

The words formed a death knell of their own and Francis blanched, holding up a gloved hand to cut off his words. He glanced up to the waiting funeral party, looking for Rob, catching his eyes as he spoke.

Rob, Kendall, Metcalf, Scrope, all of you, attend me!" He took the missive in a hand he tried to stop from trembling. "Follow me," he said curtly to the rider and turned on his heel, striding back to the steps of the keep, taking them two at a time, leaving behind the stunned faces of the assembled household. Only Tom stayed behind, and crossed back to stand by the hearse, stroking the silvered neck of Argentum slowly.

As everyone assembled in the deserted Great Hall, Francis had seconds to read the missive written in Lincoln's hasty hand. Two days old! He shook his head, tried to think clearly but the clouds of despair built like thunderheads.

Richard, oh God, Richard, your chivalry has undone us! We have run out of time... and what now?

The hall filled quickly, a mass of shuffling of boots and murmuring, unquiet voices, everyone looking at Francis with questioning eyes, but anticipating bad news, most of them hardly daring to wonder what could be worse than that which had already happened. The travel-stained rider stood by uncertainly, panting slightly from his exertions, eyeing the company around him with a troubled expression.

"Francis. What is it man?" It was Rob, striding across the hall, his riding cloak billowing out behind him. Francis held up the letter and cleared his throat nervously.

"London is taken. Jasper Tudor, Oxford, Fogge and others have released Henry Tudor who is claiming the throne on the basis of direct descent and on the ..." he hesitated, his voice drying, his lips twisting into a snarl, 'the death of a usurper. He has revived his original claim from before his defeat at Redemore."

A wave of shock rippled around the assembled group as they looked at each other with consternation and disbelief.

"The king?" Kendall asked, his face white with shock.

"Lincoln has fled, is heading to the coast and Burgundy. Catesby is captured. Norfolk was killed in the attack on the Tower. The Stanleys are marching north with an army. Oxford is not far behind."

"We are not prepared for a fight!" Metcalf said shocked, moving forwards from the back of the group. "We have no time to muster men! How did this happen? How could it happen? What the hell was Lincoln doing down there?"

The incredulity in his voice was not lost on the room. Metcalf was northern through and through and said exactly what he thought. It was a characteristic Richard had valued, he preferred – had preferred to treat with those who pulled no punches.

It was Bess's voice that cut across the tension in the room.

"Tower guards. Stanley had some Tower guards in his pocket." She had been trying to help, but Metcalf turned on her instantly.

"How in the name of all that is most holy do you know that? And if we knew, what was done about it? Nothing it would appear! Jesu! We are done for! Oxford! Jesus Christ!" The curses began to run thick and fast, James Harrington moved forward also, shaking his head.

"Christ, Francis, the country is split in two! Where is Northumberland in all this?"

"Sitting on his fat arse at Topcliffe I shouldn't wonder," remarked Rob drily. "Do we summon him?" Francis gave a desperate laugh that was underlined with faint panic.

"The only man who stood a chance of summoning him is laid out on a bier. We need to adjust our plans. We can't fight, not in the next two days. I suggest we secure the kings body and then regroup. The situation needs to settle. We can call on Burgundy and Ireland, but that will take time. We have to take evasive action... today!"

"What do you suggest?"

Scrope surveyed him from beneath his bushy brows, his hand anxiously fiddling with his dagger. Francis looked around. He had to think quickly. They couldn't flee with the body of a dead king hampering their progress. The very thought made him feel nauseous.

"We get Richard to York, as quickly as possible. We could claim sanctuary there, get a message to Margaret." He stopped suddenly, thinking of the young boy across the water. If Lincoln was captured, his days would be surely numbered. There was a bastard prince in waiting, surely better him than a Tudor? The Titulus Regis....

"Francis?' Rob was looking at him with worried anticipation. It seemed odd. It seemed years since he had seen him laugh, yet it was only a few days. His features did not suit a serious demeanour, it made him appear much older. He looked around the room again – but then they all did!

"Kendall, take Bess to Sherriff Hutton. The rest of the children are there. John, you will come with us to York."

"No!" John shook his head vehemently. "I will go with Bess. Ned and Margaret are there. They will be frightened when they hear what has happened. I will not linger in sanctuary whist they fear for their lives."

Francis stepped towards him in exasperation. He didn't want to frighten the boy, but he had to make his situation plain.

"John - you are Richard's blood. If you are captured, Stanley wouldn't hesitate to kill you, neither would Oxford. They are your father's enemies." Francis knew his voice was tight with tension but he had no time to reason with the boy. Minutes, vital minutes were slipping away.

"I will go to Sheriff Hutton," John replied assuredly. "We will gather everyone together, then can we then not get to the coast? As father did, when Warwick rebelled?"

It was possible. Francis tried to think quickly. Kendall was no soldier.

"Metcalf, Scrope, you go with them. Secure the children and then head for the coast. Look for a passage to Burgundy. Margaret will hopefully be expecting something to happen." He cast about desperately. "Jesu! I feel so helpless!"

At this point the watching rider turned to Francis.

"Should you wish, my Lord, I can take a message to Burgundy. If I cannot be of service to the earl, I will help his relatives find safe passage to the duchess."

Francis placed a hand on the man's shoulder thankfully.

"I will write a note, quickly, we have a slight advantage in time. We need to make the most of it. We all need to move with the greatest of speed and the greatest of care. I wish you all Godspeed, and trust in the Lord that we will meet again."

Kendall had produced a parchment and quill from nowhere and Francis began to scrawl hastily whilst the room emptied, leaving them all in a grey silence. It seemed to take an age, with the nib scratching endlessly against the paper, but once the letter was sealed, he turned.

Bess stood in the centre of the hall looking at him with empty eyes.

"Tudor will want me. Henry Tudor will want me for his bride, he needs me to cement his claim to the throne. I am frightened Francis."

Francis ignored her and handed the missive to the rider as Kendall handed him a purse of coin. The man nodded and ran from the room, followed closely by Kendall at a more sedate pace, his expression a closed book. Francis and Bess stood looking at each other with faces etched in grief and eyes full of fear.

"I can't save you Bess. But if I can and if I need to, I will see your brother on the throne rather than Tudor. If anything happens to Lincoln..."

"But Richard is..?"

Francis snorted.

"Tudor is from a bastard descent. So is your brother, but his claim is still better than Tudor's, whose descent bars him from taking the throne. Besides which, people loved your father. They will love his son better than a bastard Welshman who is surely now more French than English. I swear to you now, in this castle which Richard loved, my loyalty remains with his bloodline, and I will restore Plantagenet blood to the throne, no matter how dilute, or die in the attempt. I have no wish to live in a Tudor reign."

Bess wrapped her arms around herself disconsolately. Her usually fair skin was pale. She looked extremely young and vulnerable, but Francis found his heart far too empty to spare her any sympathy. His emotional well had run dry.

"And me?" It was a plaintive plea but all he saw were Woodville eyes, beseeching him. He felt sick to his stomach. Grief, fear and anger swirled around inside him making him feel dizzy. He ran his hand through his hair, distractedly.

"You need to go and pray that you can get across to Burgundy before Stanley and his men arrive north. And Bess..." She raised her head slightly at her name. "Take care of John for me. I can't forgive you for what you did, not now, but if you could take care of John, maybe one day, things will be different." She smiled wanly.

"He reminds me of his father. How could I not have a care for him. I will redeem myself in your eyes my lord. I am determined to do so, you will see."

Francis inclined his head, his lips pressed firmly together. He wondered idly exactly how she thought she would ever achieve that aim after what she had wrought, but he merely sighed.

"Then, I look forward to the day Bess. Now, we must both go."

Epilogue I.
Sheriff Hutton

August 1485

Bess opened her eyes, squinting against the strong sunlight which pushed its way through the casement windows, washing the chamber in early morning light. She knew it was early, yet she felt as if she had slept for a year and that all her limbs had grown stiff and heavy over time. Trying to push herself up, she moved only slightly, there being no strength in her arms at all. Defeated, she collapsed back with a sigh.

Suddenly, her heart began to race, remembering all that had taken place. She needed to get up, to find out if Francis had reached York. If Richard...

Her throat prickled and tears sprung to her eyes. Waves of grief mingled with guilt, one subsuming the other at a turn and she rolled over into her pillow with effort, trying to remember, trying to forget. She knew she should get up, for soon they would be making for the coast. There was no time to delay, or to linger abed feeling sorry for herself. Nothing was certain any more. All the plans Richard had laid were all cast to the winds, but there was one shred of hope. Her brother, still alive and well in the Low Countries.

She heard the door open, but still couldn't bring herself to stir, exhaustion deadening every limb.

"Bess! The Lord be praised! You are awake!" Her cousin Margaret moved around the bed and knelt down beside it, peering up into her face with some relief. "I thought you would never wake!"

Elizabeth looked into her innocent hazel eyes, so like Margaret's father's, and she tried to speak, but no words came out. Her throat was dry, completely parched. Margaret leapt up and hurried to the sideboard, pouring wine and adding a measure of water to temper it.

"I should bring the physician," she remarked, returning to the bed with an assured competence which Bess had never noticed in the young girl before. "Can you sit up?"

Elizabeth swallowed furiously, trying to make the words come. "H... Hobbes is here?"

Margaret frowned uncertainly, cradling the bowl of the cup in her hands.

"Hobbes? Why would Hobbes be here?"

Bess closed her eyes again, images spinning around in her head. The great hall at Middleham, the panic and confusion. Francis glaring at her with accusatory eyes. Hobbes, his lined face creased even deeper with sadness, bending over a supine figure. A pale arm stretched out helplessly.

With a strength she dredged up from her very soul, she hauled herself up against the pillows and dropped back, exhausted. Why did she feel so strange, almost as if she had been drugged? Was it just her grief which tied her down with lead? Her head felt heavy, like her neck could no longer bear its weight, but she kept Margaret pinned in her gaze.

"What day is it? Did we get word? Have they reached York?"

Margaret looked even more confused and held out the cup again, which Bess took, her arm responding slowly to her command.

"Who? The king?"

Elizabeth sipped the cool, watered wine, feeling it soothe her rough throat, trickling slowly down to pool in the pit of her stomach which felt strangely hollow.

"The king is dead. Richard is dead."

Margaret sat down on the bed beside her, looking at Bess with solemn eyes.

"I know Bess. I know. But he is at rest now."

She closed her eyes with some relief. So, they made it then. They evaded Stanley's men. She breathed in deeply.

"What of the others? Is there news of when we leave for Burgundy?"

The young girl sitting on the bed leaned forwards then, placing a cool hand over the pale, slim fingers which lay on the linen sheets.

"The fever has left you confused. No one is going to Burgundy, Bess. We are for London, as soon as you are well. King... Henry, he..."

"King Henry?" It was a whisper, the wine now boiling in her gut. "No."

Suddenly, by sheer force of will, some of the fog cleared and she looked around. She was in her chamber at Sheriff Hutton. Her mind reached for something she could no longer grasp. She couldn't remember when she had gone to bed. What day had it been? She had been at Middleham, bound for Sheriff Hutton and then the Low Countries. But, she could not remember getting here. All she could see was that last, desperate gathering in the great hall. The plans being formed quickly and decisively. The anxiety on faces already waxen with sadness.

"Where is everyone?"

Margaret was shaking her head, her fingers curled around Bess's reassuringly.

"Bess, you are worrying me now! Don't you remember? Cousin Lincoln, Ned and John have all been taken to London. After the battle..."

Bess looked at her in confusion. Battle?

An image began to form in her mind. A silver armoured figure, sword in hand. A vambrace spattered in blood, a golden crown surmounting a helm which glinted in the morning light as the mists rolled away. Where had that been? When had she seen that? She had been sent here when Richard marched into battle to meet the Tudor pretender. How could she know what Richard had looked like on the battlefield? Margaret was still talking.

"King Henry sent his men here and you fell into a dead faint when they told us what had happened. How Uncle Richard was defeated, how they carried him into Leicester on the back of a horse, leaving him naked and despoiled for all to see in the market place." Her own eyes were bright with tears now. She had also been fond of Richard who had cared not only for her, but also her brother, despite their father's attainder. "You took it very badly. You have been ill for almost a week."

Slowly, Bess tried to make sense of what her head told her was the truth, despite Margaret's awful words.

"But Richard won! Henry Tudor was placed in the Tower. What..?" A single tear tracked down her cheek. "My brother is alive in Burgundy. He is coming home! He is coming home to live at Middleham!"

Even as she formed the words before Margaret's increasingly distressed face, she began to remember something else. She had been standing with John, looking down into the bailey. They were holding hands. There had been riders, banners. A red dragon straddling a green and white field. John had screamed. Young Ned had been sitting on the floor, confused. He had asked one of the men where his uncle was. Margaret was still talking, telling her everything that had happened and she tried to reach back in her mind – fearing she was somehow going mad.

Then – how had she seen Richard distraught by Anne's tomb? How could he have been consoling her after her first sight of Henry Tudor? When did they hold each other in a warm embrace? She could still feel her hot fury as he arranged her marriage to a prince of Portugal. Surely that must have been real? There had been the smooth metal of the ornate boar badge as she turned it around in her hand. The wink of the diamond in its eye.

That last night. The smell of jasmine.

Richard, lying sightless in his bed. Francis infused with despair and anger. As she searched those memories, each one began to fade and crumble, like illuminated pages exposed too long to the light. Bright colours, bittersweet emotions, melting in the climbing sunlight. Becoming shadows, no longer holding shape or form. It had all seemed so real. Her anger, her despair, her love.

"But... I thought..." A cold chill descended rapidly down her spine as a frozen reality set in. She had dreamed it all. Everything. Vivid scenes, hot words. Passion, despair and hope. All conjured up by the heat of her fever? How could that be? But then...

There were things she could not have known, words she would

never have heard, events she could not have seen, but which had been played out with a crystal clear reality which only now was beginning to blur, fading back into the shadows of the past. Was it possible?

"Margaret, where is Lord Lovell?"

Margaret shook her head slowly.

"No one knows. He may be among the dead, with Sir Robert, Sir Richard. Poor John Kendall... he was no soldier, but he was devoted to his king."

Bess sipped her wine, carefully, still struggling to shake off the memories which seemed so real. So, it was not just her grief that made her feel so completely ravaged. Fever had coursed through her body, giving heat to the visions which breathed life into the dead. Months of life with the man she loved, played out over a few, fever induced days. The dawning of this realisation brought with it mixed emotions, brought with it fear.

"What now?" she asked tremulously, reluctant to explain much more to Margaret for fear she would seem addled.

"We are expected in London. As soon as you are declared fit by King Henry's physician."

Of course. She was to be his bride. The man she loved was dead, the prince she was promised to was now a memory, an ambition of his never to be achieved. She was to be wed to a stranger, the intention to unite their houses after the divisions caused by Richard's assumption of the throne.

But he didn't know. Henry Tudor did not know her brother was alive. She shook her head. No. Was that just a dream? Tears filmed her eyes. Her heart was full of them.

"Margaret, I'm scared."

Margaret gripped her fingers even tighter.

"Me too. But we will be there for each other. We will help each other Bess."

"But... I don't want to be queen. Not his queen." She tightened her own grip. "I can't be queen. Not if my brother is to come home."

Margaret looked towards the door anxiously.

"Hush, Bess. Stop this talk! You are still distressed, and not yet fully recovered. Have a care what you say now, we know not who we can trust."

Bess turned her face towards the sunlit window, her lips curving in a tremulous smile.

"I do know who I can trust, Margaret. The only man I can trust lies cold in Leicester."

Tower of London
September 1485

Bess folded her hands together in her lap conscious that her fingers were trembling.

The journey down from the north had been bearable only because she had her cousin Margaret for company, but that companionship had come to and end as soon as they had reached the royal palace. Despite her protestations, Bess was escorted into the palace whilst Margaret waited forlornly beside her horse, surrounded by men-at-arms. That had been yesterday, and since then she had seen no one but servants of whom she could ask nothing, and so had not.

The door to the chamber swung open and she rose hastily, only to gasp in relief as her mother entered the room, stoically elegant as ever, dressed in storm grey silk. Jewels still winked around her slender white throat, jewels her daughter recognised well. Her face was a mask of stillness, from which pale blue eyes shone like polished gems as she walked over to Bess and held out her hands, which joined with hers tightly. Too tightly.

"My blessed daughter, God be praised you are safe! How I have feared for you immured in that northern wilderness."

The words were silkily smooth but Bess heard the rancour in them, the subtle insult towards her former king, even though he was now no more. She swallowed hard, wondering if her mother's face would crack when they found out that her son was still alive.

"*But that was a dream...*" a small voice in her head reminded her, "*nothing but a dream...*"

She had examined every scene she could recall on the long journey from Yorkshire, and found small relief only in the fact that she had played no part in Richard's death. That privilege was all to be laid at the feet of her betrothed. Before she could respond, two other figures entered the room, one familiar, the other strange.

Margaret Stanley stalked into the chamber with a staccato

step. She held a book and a small casket in her hand which she placed on a sideboard before turning to look at Bess with a sanguine expression. It was only as her mother sank in a curtsey that Bess realised her other visitor must be Henry Tudor and she sank down herself without even marking his appearance.

"You may rise."

It was the first time she heard him speak and by the time she had risen up, Henry had seated himself in a chair by the window and motioned them both to sit, whereas his mother moved over to stand by the arm of his chair, like a sentinel.

Bess tried to remember what Henry had looked like in her dream, but he was now only a shadow. Yet, here he was in the flesh, and totally different from Richard. His hair was long, brushing his shoulders, and unremarkable in colour. He was not handsome, yet not disfigured in any way. She knew he was younger than Richard had been, yet he looked years older and she was unable to determine the shade of his eyes, but he looked about him in a way that made her think he was every bit as nervous as she was. His skin was pale, and somewhat weathered, a sign that perhaps his life had not been so easy in exile as it could have been, but she felt no empathy for that. He wore a long, crimson robe, furred at the edges, and his hands were bare, bereft of any sign of his assumed kingship

Bess swallowed hard. One day, one day very soon, he would wear the ring that so recently had adorned Richard's finger. The coronation ring. It did not cross her mind, not then, that the ring she would wear had last been worn by Anne.

"My lady, I trust you have been treated well?"

He had a strange burr to his voice, something unfamiliar. He was a stranger to her, yet would be her husband.

"Yes, Your Grace. Although..." she saw Margaret Stanley flinch as she carried on speaking, " I would know that my cousin Margaret is well. I had hoped we would remain together."

"You are a royal princess, my dear," Margaret replied without even waiting for Henry to respond. "She is the daughter of a traitor."

"Do not fear," Henry interjected succinctly, tilting his head slightly to one side, the side his mother stood at. "She will be well cared for." Bess bit her lip.

"I was hoping she could become one of my ladies?"

"Forgive my daughter, Your Grace," the dowager queen said smoothly. "She has been schooled in the ways of the usurper's court. Please do not blame her for her impetuosity."

Bess whipped her head around and shot her mother a steely glance. She well knew that she had little experience of life at Richard's court, for certain, she had not been welcome there. Her mother had been housed very comfortably since their emergence from sanctuary, and given an income which was more than generous, considering how she had plotted against Richard for most of her time at the abbey lodgings. There was no one person present who was less qualified to impart what her life had been like over these last few months.

"The Clarence girl is not suitable for a place in the queen's household," Margaret Stanley interjected coldly. "Her father was an acknowledged traitor!"

"Yet she was welcome in King Richard's household despite that," Bess replied hotly, turning a fierce gaze on the diminutive figure who remained at her son's side.

"Which tells us all we need to know about him! That man was no king!"

"That 'man' was my uncle!"

"The uncle who murdered your brothers and stole their inheritance," Margaret sneered, her lips twisting, contorting her face into an ugly mask. "The sooner you begin to remember that, the easier your life will become."

Her cheeks burning, Bess stepped forwards. In her dream, she remembered that this vile woman had been locked away in the Tower for her plots and schemes. The memory made her smile, but suddenly Henry stood up.

"Enough!" He snapped, visibly irritated either at this heated display or the fact that Richard's name had been brought into the conversation. "I wish to visit with my betrothed alone, ladies, if you would be so kind?"

Bess's mother rose instantly, but Margaret was not so easily dismissed and turned around to look at her son pointedly.

"But, Henry, I hardly think it is appropriate for you to be alone with this… girl!"

Henry tapped a finger on his chair arm impatiently.

"This – girl – is my betrothed. I am hardly going to ravish her within the walls of my own palace am I?"

An expression was exchanged between them which Bess could not clearly see, but whatever it was, it had the desired effect. Margaret followed her former queen from the chamber, but not without throwing a departing glare at the young girl as she closed the door behind them.

Henry pursed his lips thoughtfully as the two of them sat in silence. Elizabeth began to feel weary, bone tired. She felt as if the walls were pressing in on her and found it hard to breathe. It was a few moments more before Henry looked back at her.

"Your mother tells me you had no feelings for your – uncle, yet there are many who inform me otherwise. Whatever the truth be, I would know it before our wedding day moves any closer."

Bess pressed her nails into her palms as his grey-green eyes dared her to look away. There was an inner core of steel there, although one would not expect it from such a man as he appeared. Richard had been assured, his ability to command woven through every fibre. This man looked more cautious, almost hesitant. Careful.

"He was my uncle. What more could there be? My feelings for him were as a niece for her uncle. I was fond of him. He was fond of me." She struggled to prevent her cheeks from flushing as a vision from her dream returned to haunt her. "I grieve his loss."

"So you did not share his bed?"

The bedchamber at Middleham. The roaring of the fire. The heady smell of perfume…

Bess gave a heavy sigh and lifted her gaze to his.

"No."

"But, he wished it?" The eyes were sharp and piercing.

"No. I did, but he refused me." She swallowed hard over the knot in her throat. Still, she could not bring herself to believe that she would never see him again. Henry pushed himself to his feet and walked over to the hearth slowly, his face taut with thoughts.

"You are, at least, bluntly honest."

"And he was a more honourable man than you are being led to believe."

His lips lifted in a rueful smile. There were no redeeming features that she could determine, but at least, she thought, he did not appear to be a monster. He was just not who she would have chosen. Henry cleared his throat, making her jump.

"I would be more inclined to believe that if your two brothers were still residing in the Tower."

It was her turn to smile.

"But if they were, where would that leave you, Your Grace?" His face darkened as she looked up at him guilelessly. "It would not be our marriage and coronation that you would be arranging."

Henry rubbed his fingertips together as if his hands were grimy and he sought to remove the stain. He took a couple of steps away from her before turning, his face a mask of pleasantry which did not suit his lean features.

"My coronation. Then our marriage." He replied smoothly. "The House of York is dead. They placed too much power in the hands of women. Gave them too much power and privilege." He looked away as her cheeks coloured once more, she knew he was talking about her mother. About her own family. But it was Richard and Anne who had held a joint coronation, not her father and mother, and Anne was as different to her mother as the sun was from the moon. She smoothed a hand down her skirts slowly.

"Some would call it love, Your Grace."

A small grunt of derision escaped his lips.

"Mayhap they would, but time and tides change. I have waited and watched from afar and seen how lesser men have gambled with Fortune and paid its price. I do not intend to repeat their folly."

He moved to the door then, reaching his hand for the latch, the audience now appearing to be at an end.

"You will lodge with my lady mother at Coldharbour until after my coronation. She will take good care of you and see you have all you require." Tears pricked Elizabeth's eyes but she blinked them back. She had at least hoped to be reunited with her mother and her sisters. "We will see each other again, my lady. And then, if you would be so kind, you should address me as Your Majesty. At least until our vows have been exchanged."

He was gone in an instant, leaving her alone and crushed with sadness. Somehow, it reminded her of the dream she had, how heavy her heart had been, how desperate she had felt. Why had that been? Then she remembered and one silver tear rolled down her cheek. How she wished it could all have been true, even if in the end she had been sent to Portugal, to marry as Richard had designed. Her brother would have been alive and who knew what other twists and turns Fortune would have had in store for her.

Slowly, she rose and walked over to the table where Margaret had earlier placed the things she had carried into the chamber with her and her chest tightened. It was her copy of "Prose Tristan" and she opened the cover slowly, the dark, lovingly formed letters blurring before her eyes as she ran her fingers over his name where he had written it in the book that had been his gift. She could almost imagine the warmth of his skin.

Next to the book was her own small jewellery casket. The last time she could remember it, it had been in her bedchamber. There were so many memories, and she was having difficulty sifting the fact from her dreams. In one way, Henry had been right. All her life, Fortune had smiled on her, had spun the wheel which would one day make her queen. Richard, Manuel, Henry. Each one of them had the power to grant what had never been more than a dream. To be a queen. It was indeed time to pay.

Carefully, she lifted the lid on her small, ornately carved casket and her breath caught in her throat.

Nestling inside the velvet covering which enveloped the few precious gems she owned, was a small glass vial, topped in silver. Suddenly, the world was full of Jasmine.

Epilogue II – Alternate Ending
The Palace of Westminster

February 1486

"Well?"

That one word delivered with such cold expectancy rolled around the Painted Chamber, across the heads of the few who had assembled at the king's command.

"The Princess is secured, Your Majesty. She resides in Greenwich awaiting your pleasure."

Thomas Stanley flicked a glance over to his wife, who stood at the foot of the dais, eyes of black jet glittering almost wildly. In response, he bowed deeply from the waist towards the man dominating the attention of the room. Henry Tudor held a rolled parchment in his right hand, tapping it thoughtfully against his left palm, watching the red wax seal swing to and fro.

"And the rest? How many do we have?"

"We have Lincoln, Warwick and the usurper's bastard son. They are all under guard in the Tower awaiting your pleasure. Everyone else of any note is dead, the rest have bent the knee. Northumberland is acquiescent, but we have imprisoned him also, for now, until your wishes are known. Lovell has fled as have the Stafford brothers and a few others, but we will find them."

"The lawyer. Catesby?"

There was a shuffling of feet which made Henry raise his heavily hooded eyes from the document in his hand.

"Executed in Leicester, Your Majesty. He knew far too much to let him live." Stanley's voice held a note of obeisance that matched his bending posture.

"How do you know what he knew? Was he tortured?" Henry

continued to look at the roll in his hand. His question received only a discreet cough before the answer.

"We bought his confession, Your Majesty."

The tapping stopped abruptly and pale, brown eyes harnessed his step-father's gaze, preventing him from saying more as he rose up.

"Did he beg for mercy, Stanley?" The thin lips curved in a thin, sarcastic arc. "Did he beg for mercy from you?"

Stanley's face reddened as he caught his wife's demure smile, giving every indication she was enjoying his humiliation. Bile began to rise in his throat. If it wasn't for his family...! His thoughts skidded to a halt as he realised the whole chamber was focused on him, waiting for his answer. There were smiles there, smiles that hid secrets.

"He hoped I would intercede for him, Your Majesty. As Lord High Constable."

"As the usurper's Lord High Constable! I think he had other relationships in mind. You were a kinsman, were you not?"

Stanley bowed again, more to hide his embarrassment than for any further sense of obligation. But it would not do him any harm. An uneasy silence drifted through the hall.

"And the usurper himself?" John de Vere, Earl of Oxford folded his arms across his chest, watching his king with guarded eyes.

"Buried in the Abbey of the Greyfriars, Leicester, will all due haste and little ceremony. The friars were glad to see the back of their burden."

Henry's brows pulled together suddenly and Oxford leaned forward, lowering his voice.

"Are you vexed that his soul may dwell in purgatory for eternity? You shouldn't be. There will have been prayers. Some. Enough." He leaned back, looking around the room again, assessing faces, judging moods. "We took everyone by such surprise they are only too willing to change their allegiance. It is only those who were in the north we need to concern ourselves with." He paused, thinking for a second. "A visit to York would be recommended as soon as is possible, I think. If there is any rebellion in this land, it will spark there. Lovell is still at large and we can be assured he will be raising men as we speak."

No one heard John Morton enter the room, but all of a sudden he was there, standing at Margaret's side, the funereal colour of his robes showing his skin to be uniformly sallow. He rubbed his hands together, as if cleansing them from whatever he had recently been dabbling in.

"Not at all. He is in Colchester. In sanctuary, with the Staffords. We can leash the dog with no real difficulty. Without his master, he is toothless."

Sir Giles Daubney stood behind Morton, carrying a small chest and Henry looked at Morton quizzically. His urbane expression did not change.

"That will be all!" Oxford's voice carried across the hall and the assembled men began to leave, some of them almost perspiring with relief. "Not you Thomas!"

Stanley had no intention of going anywhere, but he resented the implied command anyway and clamped his lips together. The small group waited patiently for the chamber to empty and heard the comforting slither of the halberds outside the door.

Daubney walked forwards and placed the small chest on a nearby table, next to Margaret, before bowing to Henry and leaving the room himself.

"What's this?" Henry peered over suspiciously at the oaken chest.

"From Middleham, Your Majesty."

Margaret released the rosary beads which she had been unconsciously telling throughout the last few minutes, and lifted the lid. The box was full of parchments, letters, unfinished documents, a journal. There was a calfskin bound book resting on the papers, decorated and edged in gold. Margaret gave a small appreciative sigh and picked it up, opening the gold clasps.

"His Book of Hours. I have seen this many times, when I was

in Anne Neville's household.   It is a worthy tome.   Beautifully illustrated."   She turned the pages one by one, smoothing her hand across the vellum.

Henry looked down into the contents of the chest.   There were other books, what looked like a mirror. Henry thought he could smell perfume.

"Have you read it all?"   The shrewd eyes met Morton's placid ones.

"Of course, Your Majesty."

Henry held the parchment roll up like a torch, brandishing it for all to see.

"Is there another one of these? A copy?"

Morton shook his head. Appearing appeased, Henry fingered the parchment for a few moments more before cracking the seal and unrolling the copy of Richard's will which had been handed to him earlier that day. His eyes scanned the neat, dark hand, further and further down the page. Past the provisions for burial at a chantry chapel at York Minster, the instructions to reinter the remains of his wife and his son there in due course.   A generous grant to Clarence's son, to his own bastard son and daughter, to…

The blood drained from Henry's face and his eyes skipped to the elaborate signature at the bottom of the page.

Ricardus Rex.

To the date.

His stomach began to somersault, the nervous energy that fueled his every day and troubled his nights began to turn his meagre breakfast to acid.   He took a step forward and tossed the document into the box.

"Burn them all.   Burn anything you find that is not part of the rolls or statues.   This man was an evil tyrant and as such his memory should be expunged to the Glory of God."

Margaret clasped the Book of Hours to her chest possessively and no one dare ask her to place it back in the chest. Oxford stepped forwards, somewhat alarmed by the supercilious smile on Morton's face.

"There will be problems, will there not? If we destroy records which should be noted in the rolls or elsewhere. Replies to correspondence. Hasty entries written in local annals?"

He stopped as Henry's eyes fixed on him, felt himself go cold at Morton's smile.

"I thank you for your concern, but you need no worry. My learned friend Morton and I can ably assist any of the officers of the household or chancery with the information they need. We can carry out a search of all shire records, we have plenty of time."

Stepping down off the dais, he walked over to the oaken chest and closed the lid without looking inside. The sun broke from behind a cloud, heralding a crimson sunset to end the day. A few rays caught the pane of a stained glass window, highlighting a white rose sitting under a crown, suffusing it with colour.

Henry looked at it for a while thoughtfully, before lowering his eyes once again.

"I am the king. What happened in the usurper's reign will be well documented. By me. The minds of men are as fickle as their hearts. In a few years, no one will even remember his name, without reproaching him for the tyranny of his rule. People will be all too happy to forget what he did, not waste time searching in the annals for scant declarations of his wisdom and good lordship. I have waited a long time for my destiny to be fulfilled and I will not waste this opportunity God has given me! History is mine to write now, and write it I will."

The sun fell further in the sky, seeking its rest, filling the clear, white rose in the window with a blood-red stain.

Author's Notes

Well, I assume you will either have loved this story or hated it. At least that was the reaction from those who have read it in advance of publication. The main cry of woe has been 'why the hell did you kill off Richard?' That's a hard one, because I don't know! All I can tell you is that a story which began with wanting to see a different ending to the Battle of Bosworth, then seemed to write itself.

For the past four years, this manuscript has lingered around under the working title of 'Corrigenda' (Things to be corrected). The vision being that Richard would survive, find out what really happened to his nephews - based on the theory that they just disappeared and he didn't know what had happened to them. But what then? A happy marriage to Joanna of Portugal, more children, war with France, crusades...?

Somehow, that just didn't form in my head. Probably because I am in no way clever enough to predict what may or may not have happened politically if Richard had lived to a ripe old age. However, there is something which tells me, and I have no idea why, that even if Richard had survived Bosworth, he was not destined for a long life. With this acknowledged, it gave an opportunity – albeit somewhat unrealistically – to show exactly how much fiction Tudor propaganda could invent. But I can still hear the questions at every turn.

Why didn't Richard immediately execute Henry Tudor? Well, like many others I still don't see Richard as a ruthless man. Besides which, if he had no hand in the 'murder' of his nephews, and Tudor had already declared his intention to marry Elizabeth of York to bolster up his weak claim to the throne, exactly what did he know about their fate? He must have been the ultimate chancer if he didn't know their true fate, unless there was no 'fate' to know and he had a different plan. And wouldn't Richard have wanted the opportunity to find that out? So while we would all more than like Henry to get his just deserts, much of that is based on the outcome of Bosworth. Without that outcome, his treatment should be viewed in light of him being in the hands of a man with a more merciful nature. As we Ricardians know, the trouble with Richard is that he wasn't ruthless enough!

The same goes for those shifty Stanleys. If William and Thomas didn't betray him on the field, even if they were tardy in their response, Richard would probably have viewed them differently. So many opinions are formed because of the actions many took at Bosworth – where those outcomes to change, who can predict what Richard would have thought, or would have done?

As for Elizabeth Woodville and her daughter, I place the older at a distance, exactly where I think Richard would have placed her. And with Bess, to remain a beautiful young girl in a glittering court. Fatherless, friendless. Her future blasted apart by a long ago infidelity. Do I believe there was a relationship between herself and her uncle? No, I don't. I believe there was gossip and rumour. I believe there was a man, struggling with grief and the shifting sands of court affinity which were his brother's legacy. I believe that Bess was attractive, well-loved and a flame that would have drawn many moths – all to suffer different fates. The rest is dramatic licence.

Francis and Cecily. Bit of a stretch maybe, as she would have been fourteen in 1485. However, as most girls were considered sexually mature at the age of thirteen, and Francis of course much older, I didn't see the harm in a gentle, romantic relationship. Which leads on to the Lovell marriage. Depending on when you believe Francis was born – and although I pitch him at being born in 1454 – there is much evidence to show it was more likely to have been 1456 as he was finally granted his inheritance in 1477 which would then have made him twenty one. His wife was younger than he was, being born in 1460 – and their marriage took place when she was only six years old. Francis would then have been either twelve or ten. Again, marriages between young children were not unusual, as were the marriages between young girls and much older men. Francis's sister-in-law Elizabeth Fitzhugh was herself married to Sir William Parr when she was around sixteen and he was around twenty eight years her senior. Of course, then there was the marriage of John Woodville to the Dowager Duchess of Norfolk. Described as "maritagium diabolicum" at the time, John was only nineteen to Catherine Neville's estimated age of sixty five. You can see why John was a target for the Earl of Warwick during the rebellions of 1469. Catherine was his aunt, and the marriage was seen, by the earl and his partner in crime, George, Duke of Clarence, as just another example of the grasping greed of the Woodville family.

The fate of the Princes. There is much conjecture that if they did make it away from England, only one of them survived. This seems to have arisen from the belief that the elder Edward was suffering from some form of illness. Even whilst in the Tower it is known that he was visited regularly by one Dr Argentine. A lot had been made of this, and the fact that Edward supposedly felt every day that he was about to die. This, again, has been used to prove that Richard did intend to get rid of his pesky nephews for once and for all. Like the fact that Edward's servants, including Dr Argentine, were dismissed. Of course, the boys wouldn't need servants if they were dead. They also wouldn't need servants if they were about to be moved to a safer location – especially servants who may have other loyalties.

One also has to consider the behavior of Bishop John Alcock, who was Edward's tutor, had previously served as King Edward's Master of the Rolls, and who was with the young boy when Richard intercepted the party at Stoney Stratford. Although temporarily removed from office, he later rejoined Richard's council, was with him when he entered York in 1483 on his royal progress an met with the Scots ambassadors in Nottingham in 1484. Would he really have countenanced such service to Richard if he believed that he had murdered his former student? Although he does not feature in this story, it is certainly food for thought.

Finally, why two endings? Hard to answer. The second ending was the first, if you follow, but I was never really happy with it. It shows the beginning of major Tudor propaganda to the tune that they would have to falsify a whole battle where the ruling king was slain. But in relation to many other lies perpetrated by this dynasty, I felt them capable of anything. Then, when I came to dust off the file that had been lingering around for so long, I was reading it through, and wondered if it would work as Elizabeth's fevered dream. Or as my trusty proof reader helpfully pointed out Dallas's 'Bobby in the shower' moment.

I read them both again and again and couldn't decide which worked best, so – you choose! If you like the book rather than loathe it (and berate me for still not giving Richard a long, happy life) decide which end you prefer. For me, both apply. It would be a dream come true to see Richard triumph at Bosworth (surely we can arrange that at the Bosworth Battlefield Centre one day) and we all surely know that the scale of Tudor lies was on a scale so unprecedented, that they ruined a man's good reputation for over 500 years. That was my dilemma. The dream and the reality. Truth has slept for too long, but since 2012, I think it has at least opened one sleepy eye…

A further note – when I decided to go back to this story and ready it for publication – I did a lot of editing work in my garden. Behind me, somewhat forgotten, was a small shrub which had thrived, but not flowered since I moved to my home seventeen years before. As I polished the words and phrases, one day, as I set up in the garden to begin my work, I noticed it was covered in small white buds. My Jasmine shrub, long dormant, had begun to bloom.

27085507R00300

Printed in Poland
by Amazon Fulfillment
Poland Sp. z o.o., Wrocław